The House with the Green Shutters

GEORGE DOUGLAS BROWN

Edited with an Introduction, Notes and Glossary

by

J. T. Low

Holmes McDougall

ACKNOWLEDGMENTS

WHILE I was preparing this edition, I had the good fortune to make contact with certain people in Ochiltree and Coylton who had connections with or a deep interest in George Douglas Brown and his work. To Mrs J. M. Roney of Coylton, Mrs Robina Nicol of Coylton, Miss Smith of Kelburn, Ochiltree, and Mr and Mrs John Dalrymple of the Noble House, Ochiltree, I am greatly indebted for information and suggestions about aspects of the life of the author and the location of places mentioned in the novel. I am particularly grateful to Mrs Nicol for letting me have for a time George Douglas Brown's letters to Tom Smith. Works and memoirs on the author which I have consulted are indicated in the select bibliography; but I should like to make special mention of James Veitch's biography which remains a very rich and reliable source of information on the author's life.

I should like also to thank Mr R. E. Rogerson of Milngavie for much valuable information, and Mr David Murison of the Scottish National Dictionary for advice on certain Scots words and allusions. My thanks are also due to members of the editorial staff of Holmes McDougall for their assistance and co-operation, and for the stimulating discussions we have had in the course of the preparation of the volume.

J.T.L.

Printed by Sun Print, Perth
Published by Holmes McDougall Ltd.,
137-141 Leith Walk Edinburgh EH6 8NS   SBN 7157 1295-0

PREFACE

In the seventy-odd years that have elapsed since the publication of George Douglas Brown's novel interest in the work has hardly flagged. Its power has always been recognised amongst those who care for serious literature. Now that we are experiencing a revival of interest in Scottish writing, the time seems ripe for a critical reappraisal of *The House with the Green Shutters*. A renewal of interest in Scottish novels of importance can only be to the benefit of literature study generally, whether here in Scotland or elsewhere.

In editing the work I have been impressed afresh by the author's skill in handling language. Those who are a little apprehensive about Scots may be comforted to know that here is a Scottish work in which a variety of English styles is used – English styles that are the more effective for being thrown against Scots in dialogue and narration. The Scots used is greatly varied in texture but is not particularly difficult to understand. It proves to be a means of enriching the story in tone and colour rather than of adding linguistic complications.

This is a novel about Scottish small-town life. One critic – Andrew Lang – actually described it as "urban". If it does not exactly reflect the human comedy, neither is it, despite its reputation, all stark tragedy – except in the last four highly concentrated chapters. It has a domineering brooding brute of a man as hero or anti-hero, a gallery of peripheral characters including a chorus of gossips and busy-bodies, and at its heart a character study of a youth in his most formative years on the way to decadence and destruction. It may be regarded as a psychological novel or as a social novel or as an experiment in tragic form. It certainly has not dated. If anything, despite its late nineteenth-century setting, it has become more relevant with the years. We feel it is worthy of a revival and a presentation in a critical edition with introduction, notes and glossary.

J.T.L.

NOTE ON THE TEXT AND GLOSSARY

IN working out a text for this edition, I have consulted a number of earlier editions but have followed for the most part the text of the first of 1901 and the Memorial of 1923, the first because, apart from an occasional weakness, it brings us closest to the original, and the Memorial because of its prestige and the care taken by Andrew Melrose in its preparation. The few divergencies from the original versions have been indicated in notes.

There are few real textual problems about the novel: most inconsistencies arise in the punctuation and spelling. The spelling has been regularised; but the punctuation remains substantially that of the earliest editions. Two defective sentences that can be traced back to the first edition have been corrected, but the original versions have been indicated in footnotes. The first is on page 222 – "What's this 'expelled' is, now?", and the second on page 251 – the phrase beginning "as (one) who should . . ." The author's own footnotes are indicated by asterisk or dagger (* †).

As a rule explanations of Scottish idioms and proverbs appear in the notes; meanings of Scots words are given in the glossary. In compiling the glossary however I have not been concerned wholly with definitions: the intention has also been to show the Scottish forms or versions of words known to us in standard English.

J.T.L.

CONTENTS

CONTENTS

INTRODUCTION

The Author: Biographical Note

GEORGE DOUGLAS BROWN was born in Ochiltree, Ayrshire, on 26th January, 1869, the illegitimate son of Sarah Gemmell and George Douglas Brown, farmer of Drumsmudden (three to four miles south-west of Ochiltree). It seems that there was a tradition of intelligence and education in the family of Brown senior – one brother John became a professor of English at Paris and another Francis became a French master at George Watson's College, Edinburgh; but there was also a streak of snobbery: Helen, his sister, and her husband, who had enabled Brown to take the farm, objected to his becoming involved with "an Irish servant"; and Sarah Gemmell herself refused to be patronised and walked out of Drumsmudden to have her baby on her own.

For a time young George Douglas Brown attended the village school at Ochiltree; but when his mother became "bower" or "boo'er" (dairymaid) to a Coylton farmer James Dickson of Duchray, he transferred to Coylton school. Here he came under the influence of one of the best-loved dominies of the time – John Smith, father of the Tom Smith who became his life-long friend. Although he distinguished himself as a pupil at Coylton and was happy in the environment of books and country scenes, George Douglas Brown felt he had to leave school at twelve to earn money and help his mother. He found work at the pithead at Trabboch, four miles north of Coylton, where his job was "craw-picking" – separating dirt and stones from coal. But he continued to read and study; so that it was easy for him to go back to school again when he and his mother moved first of all back to Ochiltree and then to Cronberry on the edge of Aird's Moss. All these experiences were a preparation for his period at Ayr Academy which he was able to attend because of the interest taken in him by John Smith of Coylton and William Maybin, rector of the Academy. By this time he and his mother had settled down in a cottage at Crofthead near Ayr. As a

pupil at the Academy, George Douglas Brown revealed
his talents for literary studies; he impressed Maybin by
his wide and deep reading, by his skill in writing, and by
his outstanding work in classics. The essays he wrote for
Maybin revealed not only a skill in the art of writing but
also an appreciation of the works of Burns, Milton and
Shakespeare.

At Glasgow University, George Douglas Brown worked
sporadically at his studies: Professor Gilbert Murray, who
had the highest regard for him, was inclined to believe he
was not cut out to be purely a scholar. Yet he was capable
of tremendous bursts of intellectual energy and had the
ability to absorb books and learning quickly. During
vacation he taught Greek at Ayr Academy: Tom Smith
was one of his pupils. After winning the Cowan Gold Medal
in Greek, Brown graduated M.A. in 1890 with first-class
honours in classics and was awarded the Eglinton Classical
Fellowship. At the end of his post-graduate year at Glasgow
he was awarded the Snell Exhibition Scholarship entitling
him to £130 for three years at Balliol College, Oxford.

At Oxford he formed friendships with Montague
Emmanuel, David Maughan, William Menzies and Ernest
Barker; but he reacted against the cloistered life and spent
more time reading English literature than preparing for
examinations in classics. By dint of a furious spurt of work,
he took a first in Moderations in 1893; but just when he
should have been making a similar last-minute effort to
prepare for Greats in 1895 his mother became seriously ill
and he returned to Ayrshire to look after her. After her
death he returned to Oxford and attempted the final
examination. He finished by taking a third. It was clear
that his mind had not always been on his studies: he did
not believe wholly in the academic life and was highly
critical of his courses. Contacts in Ochiltree emphasised
to me recently that he was not happy at Oxford.

In 1895 George Douglas Brown went to live in London,
and became involved in free-lance journalism. He contributed
an article on Burns to *Blackwood's Magazine,* a short story
"John Rockingham's Wife" to *Chapman's Magazine,* and

various other pieces, sketches and stories to *The Illustrated London News*, *Success*, and *Sandow's Magazine*. He turned to writing popular fiction in order to eke out a living: his pot-boiler *Love and a Sword* was published by Macqueen in 1899 under the pseudonym Kennedy King. More important for his development as a Scottish writer was the short story "How Janet Goudie Came Home" which was published by *The Speaker* in 1899.

A story in an Ayrshire setting had been germinating in his mind for some time; and in June 1900 he finished the first draft of his study of Gourlay – as a short story of about 20,000 words. Andrew Melrose tells how Brown read the story in this version one afternoon to friends in a cottage down in Surrey, and summarises the reaction: "When it was finished, the cumulative effect was tremendous". By those friends who had been so impressed he was advised and encouraged to expand the work into a novel; and he settled down in the winter of 1900 at Briar Cottage, Haslemere, Surrey, to write the full version of *The House with the Green Shutters*. ("I lived alone in a cottage at Haslemere and wrote that book", he said in a letter to Tom Smith.) The novel was published by John Macqueen in 1901.

At first reviewers recognised the importance of the novel without fully realising its qualities. *The Scotsman* devoted a long notice to it, criticising its "coarse bitterness" and its literary workmanship. *The Glasgow Herald* put it first in their list of fiction and described it as being "disagreeably powerful" but also as having "brilliant vigour and undeniable power". *The Pall Mall Gazette* praised the work as "one of the most penetrating studies of human nature", and *The Manchester Guardian* recommended it as "a thoroughly surprising book which breaks with every sentimental tradition of the British novel". More important than any of these reviews however was the verdict of Andrew Lang, the leading critic of the day. Not only did he send a letter of praise to the author; he wrote a long review in *Longman's Magazine* in which he extolled the work as being "the kind of novel which Balzac or Flaubert might have written, had either been a Scot, with a bitter sense of humour". Lang also claimed that Gourlay himself was "worthy of the hand that drew Weir of Hermiston". This great boost from Lang meant that every other journalist in the country came out in a chorus of acclaim for the book; and the *New York Evening Sun* led the praise in America by proclaiming that "*The House with the Green Shutters* is like the tragedy of the Greeks, human woe in every accent and the heavens lowering back".

Despite the critical note in the reviews by Scottish newspapers, George Douglas Brown seems to have been rather better received by his ain folk after the publication of *The House* than was Lewis Grassic Gibbon after the publication of *Sunset Song*. Although there were local objections, he was acclaimed in some Ayrshire circles, and invited to become guest of honour and chairman at the annual reunion of Ochiltree Schoolfellows. He appears to have felt very much at home on this occasion and at other times when he returned to Scotland from London: he was particularly friendly with David Wilson of Auchencloigh, the Maybins, and the Smiths of Coylton. Some years previously at the Smiths' he had met and fallen in love with Isabella McLennan, a cousin of Tom Smith's; and he had hoped to become engaged to her when they met on holiday in Paris. Instead, the meeting brought to an end all Brown's hopes for his future with Isabella: she had decided to marry a man with a much more secure future – J. A. Russell. Now, quite soon after the success of his novel, he became engaged to Lizzie McLennan, a sister of Isabella.

In the last year of his life he was immersed in a number of literary activities. He began work on a second novel – "a love story, a romance of Cromwell's time", according to Andrew Melrose; and he made plans for a third novel that promised to be more of a follow-up to *The House* – *The Incompatibles*. He also worked hard over a period on a study of *Hamlet* which he hoped to publish in a volume of essays. At the beginning of August 1902, he paid a visit to the McLennans in Glasgow: by this time arrangements were being made for the wedding; but by the time he was on his way south he began to feel unwell. For the next two weeks he struggled against his illness alone, but finally he decided to seek help from his friends the Emmanuels in Queensborough Terrace, London. They, however, had gone on holiday, so he turned to his friend Andrew Melrose in Highgate. It was at Highgate that George Douglas Brown died on 28th August, 1902. The cause of death was given officially as pneumonia; but Cuthbert Lennox in his memoir says that the medical theory was that "a clot of blood had travelled towards the heart".

There is no doubt that George Douglas Brown was at times a lonely man; in fact he seemed positively to need isolation at times. On the other hand, those letters he wrote to Tom Smith reveal a friendly, cheerful person, ready to relax and enjoy a joke or chat. The letters reveal also that he suffered from sleeplessness and indigestion which induced depression. On one occasion he wrote to Tom Smith:

> I am suffering from dyspepsia, insomnia, hypochondria and all the horrors of hell.

In his earlier years he brooded over his illegitimacy; and at Oxford, despite his close friendship with Montague Emmanuel and David Maughan, he was frequently unhappy and at times questioned the value of his studies. Although in later years he might have given the impression of being a difficult person to get on with, he was basically of an affectionate disposition: this is clearly proved by the great love he bore his mother and by his life-long friendship with Tom Smith. He had a lively mind that could absorb the classics and appreciate the power behind great works of literature, but for him scholarship was not enough. He had a deeply rooted love for the Scottish scene and for Scottish ways that is illustrated, strange though it may seem, in *The House*. From a cursory reading of his one great work, one might expect George Douglas Brown to be a morose satirical person; but there are other sides to the personality of the author – and the novel. In fact George Douglas Brown frequently gave the impression, particularly when he was in Scotland, of being brisk, hearty and even jovial. His friendly lively personality emerges best in that letter he wrote in Scots to Tom Smith which begins:

> We are a' sittin thegither cheek by jowl bletherin awa like Biddy McAnally when the soo piggit. Bella's on my richt, Mary's on ma left an the snores o' Maggie Steen are sughin oot through the kitchen door. I hae been stravaigin aboot the kintraside an' as Hugh McMillan wad say "have taken up my domicile for the night at the Schoolhouse".

Did the Oxford experience unsettle him too much? It may well be that his uneasiness and lack of balance may have been due to a conflict between the intellectual and the emotional, between the English or cosmopolitan culture and the Scots upbringing; and it may well be that this conflict is behind the achievement of *The House with the Green Shutters*.

The Setting

IT is generally agreed that Barbie is based or modelled on George Douglas Brown's birthplace Ochiltree, an Ayrshire village situated between Coylton and Cumnock on the road that runs east from Ayr to Lanark. The opening paragraphs of the novel describe the view down towards the inn – the Red Lion – from John Gourlay's new house at the head of the brae. Although there is no square there as described, the scene in Ochiltree today on a fine summer morning might not be so different from that described by George Douglas Brown at the beginning of the work. Certainly the freshness and the peace of such a little country town as Barbie-Ochiltree are caught and presented to us in the most vivid terms in those opening passages:

> The freshness of the air, the smoke rising thin and far above the red chimneys, the sunshine glistering on the roofs and gables, the rosy clearness of everything beneath the dawn, above all the quietness and peace, made Barbie, usually so poor to see, a very pleasant place to look down at on a summer

morning. At this hour there was an unfamiliar delicacy in the familiar scene, a freshness and purity of aspect – almost an unearthliness – as though you viewed it through a crystal dream.

But it is not only the natural surroundings of the setting that are evoked: the human scene is also painted for us – and with a Hogarthian or Brueghelian wealth of detail. This is how the stirring into life of the village is suggested:

> The smith came out in his leather apron, shoving back, as he gazed, the grimy cap from his white-sweating brow; bowed old men stood in front of their doorways, leaning with one hand on short trembling staffs, while the slaver slid unheeded along the cutties which the left hand held to their toothless mouths; white-mutched grannies were keeking past the jambs; an early urchin, standing wide-legged to stare, waved his cap and shouted, "Hooray!" – and all because John Gourlay's carts were setting off upon their morning rounds, a brave procession for a single town!

The country-town flavour is there in such flicks of the brush as "the smith . . . in his leather apron", "bowed old men . . . on short trembling staffs", . . . the slaver sliding "unheeded along the cutties", "white-mutched grannies . . . keeking past the jambs", and later in the reference to the "white peep of the landlord's waistcoat".

An important aspect of the setting is viewed in George Douglas Brown's handling of his chorus – the bodies. They are pictured as "standing at the Cross, to enjoy their Saturday at e'en", or "dandering slowly or gossiping at ease". Later, in Chapter 5, we are told the "Bend o' the Brae" was their favourite stance. This had certain advantages: it was within easy range of the Red Lion; you could look down from there to the Cross and "streets that guttered away from it"; and you could look up Main Street to the House with the Green Shutters. The description does not fit Ochiltree exactly; but there are enough resemblances to assure us that here is the kind of thing you might see in an Ayrshire village – the brae, the roads going left and right, the Inn, the Cross at the bottom, a kenspeckle house near the top.

The setting tends to concentrate not on the Brae or even the Cross but rather on the House. It is mentioned frequently in the course of the novel; and its situation and appearance are carefully described in Chapter 3. This description brings out its spaciousness, its firm-set quality, its conspicuousness and commanding site:

> Both in appearance and position the house was a worthy counterpart of its owner. It was a substantial two-story dwelling, planted firm and gawcey on a little natural terrace that projected a considerable distance into the Square. At the foot of the steep little bank shelving to the terrace ran a stone wall, of no great height, and the iron railings it uplifted were no higher than the sward within. Thus the whole house was bare to the view from the ground up, nothing in front to screen its admirable qualities. From each corner, behind, flanking walls went out to the right and left, and hid the yard and the granaries. In front of these walls the dwelling seemed to thrust itself out for notice.

But again it is not only the physical appearance that is dealt with: the effect it has on others is carefully noted and elaborated, so that this aspect of the setting too is animated and built into the study of the life of the people:

> And its position, "cockit up there on the brae", made it the theme of constant remark, to men because of the tyrant who owned it, and to women because of the poor woman who mismanaged its affairs . . . In short, the House with the Green Shutters was on every tongue – and with a scoff in the voice if possible.

There seems to be good reason to believe that Kelburn, a house standing by itself on a commanding site half-way down the brae at Ochiltree, may have been a model for George Douglas Brown's House with the Green Shutters. Miss Smith, the present occupier, drew our attention to the relatively high ceilings, the yard at the back, and the dominating position – all necessary features of the Gourlay domain. It seems too that Kelburn is situated at the edge of – or just above – what used to be a Square: we are told in the novel that the Gourlay house "projected a considerable distance into the Square". One final point about Kelburn is that from it one can see the Cross, the Inn, and the bottom of the brae as it bends right.

The natural setting is used most dramatically in the flash-back scene of Gourlay's mad drive to Skeighan to fetch a young doctor for his wife just before the birth of young John. The story told by Johnny Coe describes the collapse of the bridge on the Fleckie road, the great roaring of the Barbie Water in spate, and the flooding of the roads:

"He was born the day the brig on the Fleckie Road gaed down, in the year of the great flood; and since the great flood it's twelve year come Lammas. Rab Tosh o' Fleckie's wife was heavy-footed at the time, and Doctor Munn had been a' nicht wi' her, and when he cam to Barbie Water in the morning it was roaring wide frae bank to brae; where the brig should have been there was naething but the swashing of the yellow waves. Munn had to drive a' the way round to the Fechars Brig, and in parts o' the road the water was so deep that it lapped his horse's bellyband . . . ."

At the bottom of the brae in Ochiltree you come upon the junction of the Burnock Water with the Lugar, and there you can visualise the kind of scene described by Johnny Coe. On the right from the present-day bridge you can see the remains of an old bridge, just such a bridge, on the Fleckie Road, as – "gaed down, in the year o' the great flood".

Identification of the region of Barbie with that of Ochiltree is not to be pushed too closely. Neither the features nor the geographical positions correspond exactly. On the other hand, if Ochiltree is Barbie, it does seem that Coylton corresponds to Fleckie and Cumnock to Skeighan; and as I have mentioned in the notes (p. 258) the association of the groset-fair with Fechars means we are on firm ground in identifying Fechars with Kilmarnock. Elsewhere in the novel there are references to real places in the area such as the Nith and Corsoncon Hill. We should realise however that it is no part of George Douglas Brown's scheme to give exact physical descriptions of his setting. The Ayrshire setting is implicit rather than explicit, implicit in the atmosphere and general features, the speech and characteristics of the area; but the Ayrshire colouring is less important in the end than the main motif of the setting – a House set apart but dominating the brae of a village. This emphasises less the local than the universal aspect of the novel.

Structure: Main Lines of Development

THE novel appears to me to be structured in two parts. The First Part, up to the end of Chapter 23, seems to fall into three movements – the prosperity of John Gourlay, the Gourlay-Wilson *agon*, the rise and fall of young Gourlay. The Second Part concentrates on the Fall of the House of Gourlay, and takes the form of a five-act tragedy with prelude leading to dramatic confrontation, first tragedy, bridging section depicting young John's break-down, final triple tragedy with epilogue.

The novel begins on a deceptively sunny and prosperous note: the description of the early summer morning in Barbie, although it throws into dark silhouette the figure of Gourlay as he surveys the scene, matches the mood of complacency and optimism built up within Gourlay's mind. The first movement of the novel takes us up to the end of Chapter 9 and gives a picture of Gourlay at the height of his prosperity, proud of his power and proud of his house. It is in fact the House that becomes the symbol of his *hubris*, the House set apart at the top of the brae overlooking the village and its activities.

This first movement is interesting too for the way the bodies are used as a Greek chorus commenting on Gourlay, but also ready to take action to bring down his pride. Other members of the Gourlay family are shadowy figures at this point; more important are the props or symbols introduced – the new kitchen range with the massive fender and the magnificent poker. There is obvious tragic irony in Gourlay's warning to his son playing with the poker:

> "Put it down, sir," said his father with a grim smile at Loranogie. "You'll be killing folk next."

Two highly important confrontations give dramatic shape to this first movement. The first is between the bodies and Gourlay on the subject of the water supply. Gourlay is asked if he will allow water to be led from beyond his garden into the main part of the town to supply "the high side of Main Street" and the pump at the Cross as well. An uneasy conversation marked by Gourlay's sarcasm and sneers leads to a contemptuous refusal:

"You'll surely accommodate the town," asked Allardyce, the Deacon.

"I'll see the town damned first," said Gourlay, and passed on his steady way.

The second confrontation is perhaps structurally more important, linking as it does the business theme with the university theme; but it also, like the first confrontation, strengthens the impression of a deliberate build-up of Gourlay's *hubris*. James Wilson, returning to Barbie after five years, plans to build up a business for himself and is prepared to be friends with Gourlay. But again Gourlay is unyielding: the confrontation ends in insults – Gourlay has nothing but contempt for the mole-catcher's son. Wilson is dismissed fuming with anger and ready to wage war on Gourlay:

Wilson was as furious at himself as at Gourlay . . . he had gone forward to pass pleasant remarks about the weather . . . And here Gourlay had treated him like a doag! Ah, well, he would be upsides with Gourlay yet, so he might!

This first movement of the novel ends with the *agon* between Gourlay and Wilson clearly adumbrated.

The second movement seems to me to run from Chapter 10 to Chapter 15. Here we read of Wilson's counter-attack on Gourlay – his setting up in business as a tea and tobacco merchant and carrier, and his gradual ousting of Gourlay through an alliance with Gibson the builder. Two fatal weaknesses in Gourlay become apparent in this second movement. The first is his lack of business subtlety: he falls an easy victim to Gibson's trickery, agreeing to a contract with Gibson that prevents him from competing for a far more lucrative contract with the Coal Company, and – even more galling for him – that binds him to work for Wilson. His pride – the second and greater weakness – drives him into further trouble: he refuses to honour his agreement, is involved in breach of contract, and thus begins to slide to financial ruin. This second movement is important too for showing how the device of the chorus – the bodies – can be used positively to goad the protagonist to further disastrous action. On a journey by brake Gourlay is obliged to listen to the malicious comments of Brodie, Allardyce, Toddle and Connal: Wilson's rising prosperity is thrown against Gourlay's decline:

> "He goes up the brae as fast as some other folk are going down't".

This illustrates the purely commenting function of the chorus; then comes an example of its more dynamic use: here they become the instrument that causes a disastrous decision. It is given out that Wilson is sending his son to the University of Edinburgh. Gourlay manages to restrain himself throughout the ordeal in the brake; but, as the author says—

> . . . the evil was done. Enough had been said to influence Gourlay to the most disastrous resolution of his life.

Gourlay decides his son too must go to College. The concluding chapter in this second movement has a pointed commentary that foreshadows the particular tragic weakness of young Gourlay. The "bitter dominie" ("Old Bleach-the-boys") takes over the function of chorus to make the illuminating and prophetic comment:

> "They're making a great mistake . . . yon boy's the last young-ster on earth who should go to College . . . The fault of young Gourlay . . . is a sensory perceptiveness in gross excess of his intellectuality".

The second movement of the novel has played out the Wilson-Gourlay conflict: Wilson has triumphed but the emphasis moves to concentrate itself more on the rapidly increasing ruin of the Gourlay family. Attention now focusses for a time on the son on whom Gourlay has pinned his hopes.

The third movement is therefore concerned mostly with the fortunes of young John in Edinburgh. He goes to the university reluctantly, but he eventually finds solace in drink. The dinners at Jock Allan's rescue him from his solitariness and melancholy but set him well on the road to ruin. Yet in this part there is a gleam of happiness and false prosperity for John: because of his one doubtful skill – his sensory perceptiveness – he wins the Raeburn prize and thus is briefly reconciled to his father. As counterpoint to John's adventures at the university there is the steady degeneration of the Gourlay family – Janet's illness, the development of Mrs Gourlay's breast cancer, the dismissal of Gourlay's last employee. But the climax of this third movement returns us to its main theme – young Gourlay and his misfortunes. He insults a lecturer, refuses to apologise, and is expelled from the university. The end of Chapter 23, interweaving the two themes (Gourlay's coming financial ruin and young John's disgrace) brings this third movement to a close with attention concentrated on John as he returns to the setting where the final tragedy is to be played out:

> He would not have to face his father the moment he went in. He would be able to get home before him. He crept on through the gloaming to the House with the Green Shutters.

So far what we have had in this First Part is a novel constructed in three inter-related movements and developed in a fairly expansive manner with details of life in the community filled in and the drama and its harshness toned down at times by humour and social commentary. What we have in the last four chapters is by way of contrast a highly concentrated tragedy in five acts. There is no room here for character cameos or detailed descriptions: here the pace increases and the move towards tragedy is swift and inexorable.

The first act of this final part is a kind of preliminary. The bodies, more generalised here and given Morality-type names – Certainty, Curiosity – present a kind of gloating prologue. We see the Gourlay family disintegrating; Gourlay fails to get financial backing; and the whole of this first act (Chapter 24) leads to Gourlay's homecoming and confronting his son in the House:

> The first thing he saw on entering the kitchen was his son –
> sitting muffled in his coat by the great fender.

(There is an interesting piece of structural overlapping between Chapter 23 and Chapter 24 – the end of the First Part and the beginning of the Second. The scene of John's slinking past his father during the abortive negotiations – marked by the words "I'll be on the street for another half-hour" – is presented first from John's viewpoint and then from Gourlay's.)

We move now into the high drama of the second act of the Gourlay tragedy. After the peripheral reference to Jenny's troubles comes Gourlay's opening conversation with his son on prizes – bitter, sarcastic, demoniac. Then a pause, a suspension of action before Gourlay in a mounting humour of wildness calls for drinks. This is formal ritual – the libation; and it is the more effective for being performed as a great satirical act. We have the impression of a build-up of fury and frenzy just kept in control. As the father plays cat-and-mouse with the boy, within the mind of the boy another kind of wrath begins to simmer:

> Another voice . . . seemed to whisper with dull iteration, "I'll
> *kill* him . . ."

After the smashing of the brandy bottle comes another pause, another cat-and-mouse ballet, and then the relief of John's escape from the House.

The third act – still within Chapter 25 – begins in a more relaxed mood with a chorus scene at the Red Lion, dominated by Allardyce, lightened by Webster's drunken humour, and marked by an act of violence by Brodie which prepares John to face his father again. Meantime at home too there is a moment of relaxation: to embellish the House, Gourlay is up a ladder fixing a pair of steel rests for his gun. Enter young Gourlay: the conflict quickly flares up to the point where John strikes his father with the poker as Gourlay leaps from the ladder and strikes the fender:

Gourlay thudded on the fender, his brow crashing on the rim.

This climactic act of violence in this third act is marked by such comments as "One terrible fact had changed the Universe", and "The effect was that of an unholy spell". Ironically it is the mother who recovers first and her flash of resourcefulness brings the act to a conclusion:

"Run, John; run for the doctor", she screamed. "Oh, Mrs Webster, . . . I'm glad to see ye. Mr Gourlay fell from the top o' the ladder, and smashed his brow on the muckle fender".

The last two chapters represent the last two acts of the tragedy. There is a slackening of tension in the fourth act: the fall of the House is stressed further by the letter from the solicitors demanding money or eviction; the chorus of bodies begin to talk in terms of the killing of the father by the son; and young John begins to break down mentally: like Orestes he is haunted by his Furies – seeing eyes glower at him from various corners.

The final act (Chapter 27) rises steadily to its ritualistic end. John returns from Glasgow to announce the ruin of the family; after another visit to the pub he disappears into the parlour. Gradually the women realise something has happened: John is found dead of poisoning with the whisky bottle alongside him. The climax is the more effective for being muted: Mrs Gourlay's reaction is calm, fatalistic, almost noble: "Aye, he's deid . . . he winna be hanged now". The threads are drawn together: the abscess on the mother's breast is revealed; and the past is thrown up. In her pride Mrs Gourlay returns to her youth as Miss Richmond; in her clear sight she becomes a prophetess of doom – a Cassandra figure. The final ironical touch is the reading from Corinthians with its emphasis on the quality lacking in Gourlay – "Though I speak with the tongues of men and of angels, and have not charity . . ." The reading brings the novel to a moment of high ritual before the women go into the parlour to destroy themselves.

The coda to the whole tragic play is short: we return to the matter-of-fact note in the post's description and in the resumption of the bodies' gossip. The post, finding the door to the House open and the place silent, unwittingly marks the tragedy:

"God, they sleep sound after all their misfortunes".

When he penetrates the sanctuary-mortuary and learns the truth, his hysteria takes him out and up the street. The final impression is of silence; the last shot is of the House – the symbol of pride now become a symbol of nemesis:

No man dared to speak. They gazed with blanched faces at the House with the Green Shutters, sitting dark there and terrible, beneath the radiant arch of the dawn.

If we are looking for weaknesses in the novel, we could say that the work is split in two – the first part up to Chapter 23 with its three movements a fully developed novel realistic and satiric that has its lighter moments as a contrast to its prevailing harsh tone; and a second part from Chapter 24 a tragedy in five concentrated acts. But these two main parts are linked together by structure, symbol and method; and if we object to the occasional authorial commentary, we have to remember that Greek drama had its commentary firmly built into the structure. It is interesting that J. B. Priestley in his introduction to the Travellers' Library edition should say that the weakness of the work lies in its trying to be two different kinds of novel at the same time – a novel of social life and a tragic drama. It seems to me that this is not so much a weakness as an interesting structural experiment.

Characterisation

Is the novel dominated by The House as a symbol of pride and isolation, or by John Gourlay as a character who exemplifies that pride and isolation? Certainly Gourlay is the chief and dominating character of the book, yet there is a sense in which he is dominated and broken by the environment and the events which he tries to control. In this there may be a key to understanding his tragedy.

The character of Gourlay may have been based, as Cuthbert Lennox suggests, on a man who was at one time called the village king of Ochiltree[1]; he may have been based on impressions of the author's father George Douglas Brown of Drumsmudden, a large, powerful, perhaps at times overbearing man, who yet found himself at the mercy of other forces and was eventually evicted from his farm. On the other hand, in Gourlay's tendency to isolate himself from others there is something of the author's own make-up: in a letter to Tom Smith, Brown wrote:

> I have got to be that I can live in absolute loneliness with tremendous satisfaction to myself.

Reading the critical note in which Lang says that Gourlay was "worthy of the hand that drew Weir of Hermiston", one wonders if Brown had read Robert Louis Stevenson's *Weir of Hermiston* (published 1896). There are certain similarities in the protagonists: both Gourlay and Weir are overpowering men of influence who have scant regard for other people's feelings or opinions; they are harsh to their wives and contemptuous of their sons. Each has a fierce pride in his social position; and each is impatient of the ideas or ways of others. J. D. Scott points out also they have a demoniac quality in common[2]. The great difference is of course in the matter of intellect. Weir is a brilliant jurist, sharp and calculating; Gourlay is a poor strategist, at his best when posing as the great man, but an easy prey to schemers like Gibson and Wilson, and too easily pushed into disastrous decisions by malicious gossip.

We may gain a superficial impression that Gourlay is harsh, tense and self-regarding *throughout the whole work*. It is true that his harshness is an important flaw, leading to

[1] *George Douglas Brown*, Hodder and Stoughton, 1903, p. 146.
[2] "R. L. Stevenson and G. D. Brown: the myth of Lord Braxfield" – article in *Horizon*, May, 1946.

acts of cruelty on the one hand and isolation on the other; and it is true that in public or private confrontations he becomes too tense and self-regarding to be able to see straight and come to reasonable decisions. Yet the author does indicate touches of humanity and moments of relaxation. With Templandmuir he can be friendly and jocose; with Peter Riney, his longest serving employee, he can be light-hearted, human, generous, and compassionate. At the news of the death of Tam the pony he shows that love of animals that links him with his fellow countrymen. In the family circle he is kindest to Jenny his ailing daughter, and he shows that kindness in the climactic scene in Chapter 25 when he is least composed.

The author indicates Gourlay's greatest weakness in character in a direct commentary in Chapter 4:

Stupidity and pride provoked the brute in him.

As Gourlay's fortunes decline, this brutish quality becomes more and more pronounced, more and more demoniac. (J. D. Scott believes Brown was inspired by what he calls "the Braxfield myth," particularly in portraying Gourlay in the penultimate interview with his son.) There is something awesome, terrifying and dramatically fascinating in the spectacle of a man abandoning himself so completely and so systematically to an evil, non-human course of action that leads inevitably to his own destruction. In the final part of the novel Gourlay becomes less of a character and more of an impersonal force working towards an inevitable tragedy:

quem deus perdere vult, prius dementat.

Pride is the driving force behind Gourlay's personality. It is pride that drives him from his prosperity, that makes him take disastrous decisions, and that puts him at the mercy of enemies and hostile forces.

Gourlay *père* does not entirely dominate the novel. Gourlay *fils* is the chief character in what I have called the third movement of the first part of the novel. Into this section he takes with him a psychology moulded by his parents. On the one hand he is cowed by his father, bullied, fearful, lacking self-confidence; on the other he is indulged by his mother and inclined to boast and show off. In that third movement he superimposes on these qualities an uneasy sociability and a taste for drink (cultivated at Jock Allan's); and also in that third movement he exercises his fatal gift – the ability to visualise – "the power of seeing things vividly inside your mind". This gift enables him to win the Raeburn Prize and thus gain a moment of triumph, a brief prosperity. The balancing weakness is his inability to intellectualise the gift – a weakness analysed by the dominie at the end of Chapter 15. This becomes the tragic flaw that brings about his madness and suicide. Yet his final desperate acts – particularly the killing of his father – are not so much illustrations of character as actions into which he is precipitated by the developing tragic pattern of the Gourlays' life. He lacks the strength finally to be anything but the plaything of the gods.

Curiously enough it is Mrs Gourlay, of all the mainstream characters, who seems to grow rather than diminish in stature in the closing stages. True she is presented as a "gey feckless" woman, keeping an untidy house, spoiling her son, scorned by her husband for her uncomely appearance. Again we find a resemblance between *The House* and *Weir:* in each novel the woman is weak and downtrodden but towards the end gains a strength in re-asserting herself – mainly through the power of her religion. Mrs Gourlay is more impressive in this respect than Mrs Weir. As mentioned earlier, near the end Mrs Gourlay shows legitimate pride in remembering her position as Miss Richmond of Tenshillingland, and she demonstrates a sense of fitness and a high resolve in the way she prepares for and carries out the joint suicide. Nor is Janet the daughter to be dismissed as a mere fill-in of a character. She is depicted as a much more intelligent and honest person than her brother; and the compassion she shows for her mother at the end impresses as a final illustration of her humanity.

The "bodies" are intended basically to function as a

corporate character or force commenting on Gourlay's declining fortunes, on his conflict with Wilson, and on young John's weaknesses. The author does succeed in using the bodies in that way; but he also contrives to break from the Greek tragic mould and give us individual character sketches. Of the malevolent bodies Tam Brodie, leather merchant and Conservative, stands out as the loudest-tongued, most outspoken and blustering member. He is most vividly portrayed in the scene in the brake in Chapter 15. The nastiest and smarmiest bodie is the lisping Deacon Allardyce who can both gossip and flatter, who is capable of malicious talk against the Gourlays and of treacherously fraternising with Gilmour and young John Gourlay. The baker sums him up as "an artist in spite": he is, in his insidious methods, a sharp contrast to Brodie. Sandy Toddle is the affected member of the chorus: he subscribes equally to the malice and the gossip but is himself frequently mocked for his English accent. Connal is the provost who becomes the ex-provost in the course of the novel – a pompous man who is careful to avoid frontal action but who can be as spiteful as the others. These four are the "nesty bodies" – "the sons of scandal". The other three – Johnny Coe, Tam Wylie and the baker – are the "decent" or harmless bodies. Johnny Coe is the "sage philosopher" who has charity enough to see strength of character in Gourlay, and maintains in the teeth of Sandy Toddle's scorn that Gourlay is a kind of aristocrat with possibilities. Tam Wylie is described as "a wealthy old hunks": he is good-natured but sly, and likes to annoy Connal by pretending to support Gourlay. Of the three decent bodies he is the most detached and most relaxed. The baker is by far the most pleasant and most charitable of the bodies. He is a Burnsomaniac: he it is who quotes from two of Burns's poems. He is broad-minded enough to see possibilities in young Gourlay; and he shows his sympathy for him in the scene at the station in Chapter 14. He expresses the philosophy that is a complete antithesis to all that Gourlay and the nesty bodies stand for: "folk should be kind to folk". He is not given a full name, although his wife calls him Tom. His relationship with his wife is tersely suggested in the brief scene when she interrupts a meeting of the bodies. He calls her a "great muckle fat hotch o' a decent bodie", but at her request "gangs in" to have a dish of tea with her. Between these two hemi-choruses – the "nesty" four and the "decent" three—there are tussles and arguments that illustrate the two points of view about Gourlay and the two aspects of the Scottish character. The cleavage is indicated not only in Chapter 21 where Coe and Wylie support Gourlay, but also in Chapter 26 where the Deacon's malevolence brings out Wylie's comment: "Dean Allardyce, your heart's black-rotten".

Something of the chorus technique may be traced also in the handling of the group that surrounds young John in Edinburgh (Chapters 17 and 18). This group is dominated by Jock Allan, a sentimental, hospitable man whose skill in mathematics had transformed him from Ayrshire herd to Edinburgh actuary. His early love for Mrs Gourlay makes him sympathetic to young John; and it is part of the novel's tragic irony that Allan's friendship (and character) should prove the means of setting John on the road to ruin. Tarmillan, a doctor and son of Irrendavie, is a forceful second-in-command in this group. He fools and snubs lesser mortals like old Partan and Tozer the Englishman; and he can challenge Allan himself in debate and story-telling. It is Tarmillan who picks up from Allan and illustrates the gift many ordinary Scotsmen have in phrase-making – a gift that has fatal consequences for young Gourlay. Logan the cashier has a more directly baleful influence on John: he it is who introduces John to the Howff – "a snug bit place where . . . West Country billies foregather . . . for a dram and a joke". Logan is described as a "sly cosy man", and "a slug for the drink": he can hold his liquor but likes to see others succumb. A kind of echo of Deacon Allardyce, he functions as an important member of this minor chorus, observing and encouraging young Gourlay in his downward course. Armstrong and Gillespie act as other lesser members of the chorus who let John "run on" and enjoy the spectacle of his "splurging". Outside this group, but figuring as an important person in John's academic world, is the professor of philosophy referred to as "Tam". Possibly based on an academic personality known to the author, Tam delivers a lecture on an aspect of philosophy connected with perceptiveness and its dangers which appeals strongly to young Gourlay, although its implications are clearly beyond his understanding. Even as Tam awards the Raeburn to John, he warns him of the dangers of his "almost morbid perception".

If we pass too quickly over the portrait gallery of minor characters we miss the quality that illustrates the social background, introduces a note of social criticism, and so makes the dark centre of the work stand out. Apart from the seven bodies of the main chorus and the figures surrounding young Gourlay in Edinburgh, there are other briefly but sharply sketched figures. We have already mentioned the baker's wife – a cheerful bossy woman who appears momentarily. A more detailed character is Mrs Wilson, a shrewd, cheerful, bustling go-ahead person described at the end of Chapter 10 as "eastie by nature" (she came from Aberdeen) but with the jovial manner of someone from Kyle. Another carefully observed woman figure is the miller's daughter who marries Templandmuir. She is the harsh shrewish type determined to make her husband break with Gourlay and goading him on to take direct action instead of writing a letter. Her essence comes through vividly in direct speech – in the monologue she screams at Templandmuir in Chapter 12.

Templandmuir himself, "the Laird", one of the few people with whom Gourlay can relax, is described in Chapter 12 as a "rubicund squireen". He is essentially a weak person whose friendship with Gourlay makes him feel important but who is easily driven into the opposite camp by his wife's influence and the changing of public opinion. He is one of three peripheral characters who, in a novel of an earlier period – in Galt or in the Kailyard – would have been at the heart of the community[1]. The

[1] This point is made by John Spiers (*The Scots Literary Tradition*, Chatto & Windus 1940, pp.165-6) specifically about the laird and the minister.

second is the "bitter dominie" who criticises Gourlay for putting his son to the university: he it is who diagnoses young John's weakness as "a sensory perceptiveness in excess of his intellectuality". The third is the minister, the Rev. Mr Struthers, who congratulates young John on winning the Raeburn. Struthers is presented as a rather stupid person who passed his examinations for the ministry only after "a ten years' desperate battle with his heavy brains". He is satirised by George Douglas Brown as pompous and prosy, mouthing clichés in the ministerial manner. These three figures – laird, dominie, minister – would, in a picture of an earlier or idealised Scotland, have dominated the scene or at least have provided some kind of leadership. Here, in the changing society of Barbie, they are minor characters, ineffectual and withdrawn, powerless to influence the course of events.

Two less important but well contrasted characters should be mentioned also. One is Jock Gilmour, the surly servant who antagonises young John and is dismissed by Gourlay. The other is Peter Riney, the faithful servant who cares more for service than reward – like Old Adam in *As You Like It*. Iain Crichton Smith finds the author "at his strongest" in the scene describing Riney's dismissal.[1]

Two much more important characters feature at the heart of the first part of the novel. These are Wilson and Gibson. Wilson is very closely observed as a man of ambition anxious to make friends but even more anxious to take every chance to create for himself a first-class business as merchant and carrier. He is quickly developed as Gourlay's rival, is seen in an unholy alliance with Gibson the builder, and is clever and calculating enough to be accepted eventually as leading man and provost of the town when Gourlay is rapidly moving towards financial ruin. We are given an impression of Wilson from the inside, as it were, in the scene of his conference with Gibson in Chapter 13 where the plot against Gourlay is hatched. This chapter is also remarkable for the impression of Gibson

"The House with the Green Shutters" – article in *Studies in Scottish Literature*, Vol. vii, Nos. 1 and 2, July-October, 1969.

that emerges. The whole interview is presented almost entirely in dialogue form; and out of this dialogue comes the portrait of a completely amoral business man, systematically planning to bring down the leading man in Barbie. Even Wilson himself is staggered at the calculated villainy of Gibson's scheme. Gibson is conceived as lacking in human feeling and possessing a demoniac single-mindedness of purpose; and these are qualities that link him with Gourlay and help to reinforce the idea that the novel has "too much black for the white in it", as George Douglas Brown himself said in a letter to Tom Smith.

The over-all impression of the characterisation in *The House with the Green Shutters* is of a two-fold division within its variety. The minor characters tend to present a picture of the human comedy or the human condition within a Scottish rural setting rather than of human destiny: the flavour is satirical rather than tragic. Even the chorus when broken down gives us the two sides to social life – the malicious and the generous. It is when we return to the major characters and in particular to Gourlay that we find character study reflecting a meanness, a malignity, and a distortion of the psyche that lead to inevitable destruction.

Language and Style: Scots and English

As in the methods of characterisation, there seems to be a variety in the styles of language used in *The House*. In the matter of straight forward English alone, the styles range from the formal and the descriptive to the heightened and the apocalyptic; and in Scots the range is from a thin kind of dialect in parts of the narrative and dialogue to a thick sinewy kind used by Mrs Gourlay and Johnny Coe. The question of the purity of the dialect has been fully discussed by J. Derrick McClure in an important article "Dialect in The House with the Green Shutters".[1] Here I am less concerned with the purity of the Ayrshire Scots than with

In *Studies in Scottish Literature*, Vol. ix, Nos 2-3, October-January, 971-72.

the effect and place of Scots within the whole scope of the novel.

At the beginning of the work, the language is purely English; it is precise and descriptive, but has an aesthetic quality that conveys the pleasantness and beauty of the Scottish summer morning in order to strengthen the impression of a false prosperity that is being deliberately built up:

> The freshness of the air, the smoke rising thin and far above the red chimneys, the sunshine glistering on the roofs and gables, the rosy clearness of everything beneath the dawn, above all the quietness and peace, made Barbie, usually so poor to see, a very pleasant place to look down at on a summer morning.

The note of denigration or criticism is thrown in as an aside – *Barbie, usually so poor to see*. These descriptive touches are used in various parts of the book to contrast the beauty and peace of the scene with the ambition and meanness of the people:

> When Wilson was jogging homeward in the balmy evenings of his first summer at Barbie, no eye had he for the large evening star, tremulous above the woods, or for the dreaming sprays against the yellow west . . . yet Wilson was a dreamer, too . . . When the lights of Barbie twinkled before him in the dusk he used to start from a pleasant dream of some enterprise suggested by the country round . . .

It is a direct impressionistic style that enables us to see the harsh realistic side of human life emerging from an apparently idyllic scene – a contrast to the Kailyard method. It is even more skilfully exploited in the scene of young John's truancy:

> The sun streamed through the skylight window and lay, an oblong patch, in the centre of the floor. John noted the head of a nail that stuck gleaming up. He could hear the pigeons *rooketty-cooing* on the roof, and every now and then a slithering sound, as they lost their footing on the slates and went sliding downward to the rones . . . Once a zinc pail clanked in the yard, and he started with fear, wondering if that was his faither.

The atmosphere is evoked by sight and sound, but it is filtered through the consciousness of John and probes to his latent uneasiness. Here the counterpointing of the impression of the beauty and peace of the scene with the harshness of the human situation is subtle and muted.

An adverse comment could be made on descriptive passages that seem inflated with poetic diction, like the opening of Chapter 21:

> On a beautiful evening in September, when a new crescent moon was pointing through the saffron sky like the lit tip of a finger, the City Fathers had assembled at the corner of the Fleckie Road. Though the moon was peeping, the dying glory of the day was still upon the town. The white smoke rose straight and far in the golden mystery of the heavens, and a line of dark roofs, transfigured against the west, wooed the eye to musing.

But here again we have anti-climax: the poetic description is ironically counterpointed with a touch of realism that ends in Scots:

> For there had been a blitheness in the town that day, and every other man seemed to have been preeing the demijohn.

It is possible George Douglas Brown may here be using the purple passage convention for his own satirical purpose, although he does seem at other points, for example towards the end of chapter 20 ("when eve sheds her spiritual dews . . . "), to be revelling in it for its own sake. On the other hand, Iain Crichton Smith, in his commentary on the descriptive passages in the novel, makes the point that the author "annexes" the landscape "into a specific human consciousness." Brown, he says, has learned "to make landscape a function of human psychology".[1]

In the authorial commentaries on the characters Brown's concise style takes on an aphoristic quality; and this sometimes leads to an elaborating and a flavour of moralising:

---

[1] "The House with the Green Shutters", *Studies in Scottish Literature* Vol. vii, Nos. 1 and 2, pp. 3-4.

Yet he was not wilfully cruel; only a stupid man with a strong character, in which he took a dogged pride. Stupidity and pride provoked the brute in him.

In those early days, to be sure, Gourlay had less occasion for the use of his crude but potent irony, since the sense of his material well-being warmed him and made him less bitter to the world.

This is in direct contrast to the dramatic style developed as the pace increases and the conflicts flare up. George Douglas Brown shows a tendency, as the story takes shape, to end chapters on a heightened note. The ending to Chapter 11 is one of the most effective:

The bodies of Barbie became not only the chorus to Gourlay's tragedy, buzzing it abroad and discussing his downfall; they became also, merely by their maddening tattle, a villain of the piece and an active cause of the catastrophe . . . And so he plunged headlong, while the wary Wilson watched him, smiling at the sight.

There was a pretty hell-broth brewing in the little town.

Later, in the more concentrated final part of the novel, the style becomes even more highly dramatic to convey a sense of inexorable destiny and inevitable tragedy. It reaches its high point in Chapter 25 in the description of the atmosphere after the murder of Gourlay:

There followed an eternity of silence, it seemed, and a haze about the place, yet not a haze, for everything was intensely clear, only it belonged to another world. One terrible fact had changed the Universe. The air was different now; it was full of murder. Everything in the room had a new significance, a sinister meaning. The effect was that of an unholy spell.

We note the cosmic imagery and the suggestion of blasphemy in the reversal of the normal order of things as a result of the death of Gourlay. It is the language of high tragedy; and there is in those references to "a new significance" and "a sinister meaning" a strong flavour of the apocalyptic.

It is one of the outstanding features of this novel of small-town life that the author can combine realism with a note of fate or destiny – a note found in the ballads as well

G.S.—2

as in Greek tragedy. Indeed, George Douglas Brown, it seems to me, achieves a ballad quality in the flash-back sequence in which Johnny Coe tells the story of Gourlay's journey for a doctor at the height of a storm. The Scots used here has a deep-toned ring about it; and its vigour and wild informality are exploited to great dramatic effect:

> . . . the day the brig on the Fleckie Road gaed down, in the year o' the great flood . . . Barbie Water . . . was roaring wide frae bank to brae . . . A' this time Mrs Gourlay was skirling in her pains . . . Ye mind what an awful day it was; the thunder roared as if the heavens were tumbling on the world, and the lichtnin sent the trees daudin on the roads . . .

This sequence in which Johnny Coe's narrative almost transforms Gourlay into a heroic figure is comparable with the sequence narrated by Old Kirsty in *Weir of Hermiston* in which Gib Elliott features as a similar kind of figure. There are similarities in the flash-back technique, the epic quality of the tale, and the vivid manner of the narration.

This illustration of how Scots helps to deepen and extend the scope of the novel raises the question of the total effect of Scots in a work of fiction. Stevenson tends to use English with an occasional flavour of Scots for his narrative, and Scots, where appropriate, for his dialogue, in the manner of Walter Scott; and it would seem on a first impression that George Douglas Brown does the same. The narration of the opening of the novel is almost purely English: there is scarcely a hint of Scots until we hear the voices of the men discussing their last-minute preparations for the departure of the carts; and even then the Scots is thin with only an occasional word like "frae", "bleezes", "glower". For a time the English is mostly kept separate from the Scots, the one setting the scene, the other used for dialogue – the speech of the bodies, of Mrs Gourlay, of Gilmour, of Gourlay himself. But, as the author becomes more involved in his characterisation, he begins to let the Scots overflow into the narrative. In Chapter 11, for instance, where we are told of how Wilson plans to extend his business in dairy produce beyond Barbie, there is a transition from English into Scots as we hear Wilson scheming within himself:

> Another thing played into his hands, too, in that connection.
> It is a cheese-making countryside about Barbie, and the less
> butter produced at a cheese-making place – the better for the
> cheese. Still, a good many pounds are often churned on the
> sly. What need the cheese merchant ken – it keepit the gude-
> wife in bawbees frae week to week – and if she took a little
> cream frae the cheese now and than they werena a pin the
> waur o't, for she aye did it wi' decency and caution! Still it is
> as well to dispose of this kind of butter quietly, to avoid
> gabble among ill-speakers.

In the swift flow of the paragraph the author develops a
flexibility here as he moves between Scots and English and
from the viewpoint of the observer to that of the character.
Sometimes he uses proverbial Scots to mark the character
behind the narration:

> All that he made in this way was not much to be sure – three-
> pence a dozen on the eggs, perhaps, and fourpence on the
> pound of butter – still, you know, every little makes a mickle,
> and hained gear helps weel.

It reminds us of the kind of thing that Lewis Grassic Gibbon
does in *Sunset Song,* except that with George Douglas
Brown there is a greater self-consciousness and formality.
In *Sunset Song* we seem to move freely within the folk
mind; in *The House* we move more obviously from the
narration or the narrator's mind into the character or folk
mind. Here, in Chapter 5, where he parades the typical
"bodie", is another illustration of Brown's method:

> The chief occupation of his idle hours . . . is the discussion of
> his neighbour's affairs. He is generally an 'auld residenter';
> great, therefore, at the redding up of pedigrees. He can tell
> you exactly, for instance, how it is that young Pin-oe's taking
> geyly to the dram: for his grandfather, it seems, was a terrible
> man for the drink – ou, just terrible – why, he went to bed with
> a full jar of whiskey once, and when he left it, he was dead,
> and it was empty. So ye see, that's the reason o't.

We begin with a fairly formal English style, slip into a
quotation in Scots, and then assume the Scots idiom with

the folk voice and rhythm. By the end of the passage we are immersed in the character and situation, and the language and style have become easy and flexible.

On the other hand there are times when George Douglas Brown likes to counterpoint English with Scots sharply and directly. In Chapter 14, which begins in a mock biblical style to point the satire, the tendency is to give the facts of the narrative briskly in English and then bring in the dialogue in Scots. This proves an effective way of presenting the human condition within an objective background. It becomes a kind of alienation device: we are cushioned against too great an impact of the emotional:

> The rain came – a few drops at first, sullen, as if loth to come, that splashed on the pavement wide as a crown-piece – then a white rush of slanting spears. A great blob shot in through the window, open at the top, and spat wide on Gourlay's cheek. It was lukewarm. He started violently – that warmth on his cheek brought the terror so near.
>
> The heavens were rent with a crash and the earth seeemed on fire. Gourlay screamed in terror.
>
> The baker put his arm round him in kindly protection.
>
> "Tuts, man, dinna be feared," he said. "You're John Gourlay's son, ye know. You ought to be a hardy man".
>
> "Aye, but I'm no", chattered John, the truth coming out in his fear. "I just let on to be".

It seems to me there is a great strength and an added power in writing that can use two forms of language so contrasted as Scots and English. It is not that the spoken has always to be marked off in Scots from the English narration, although this is the norm and can be most easily appreciated. The analytical comment fits well into formal English; the personal remark or the homely reference arises naturally out of Scots. But the counterpointing of the one against the other can be done in a variety of ways. One of the most striking is illustrated near the end of the novel. Mrs Gourlay has been reading from I Corinthians 13 – in the English of the Authorised Version. The story is continued in English, the story of how Janet reacts to her mother's reading and how they brace themselves to take the final step towards the parlour and death. Then comes the momentary break from the atmosphere of ritual and impersonal formality:

> She turned and looked at her daughter, and for one fleeting moment she ceased to be above humanity.
> "Janet", she said wistfully, "I have had a heap to thole! Maybe the Lord Jesus Christ'll no be owre sair on me".

The sudden change to Scots is masterly – startling and tremendously moving in its effect. Religion now becomes a homely thing in the form of the living presence of Christ; the human appeal wells up from the depths of Mrs Gourlay's being and only her own Scots can express it for her. This illustrates an outstanding quality of Scots that is exploited throughout the work – its effectiveness in rendering passages of drama and emotion.

A word should be added about George Douglas Brown's feeling for words, phrase-making and imagery. The attempts that he made at formal poetry were on the whole not very successful: he was perhaps best at a kind of pastiche Burns, as we can see from the lines he composed for the occasion of the Forty-seventh Reunion of the Ochiltree Schoolfellows. But in his prose he has a vein of poetry which is best seen in his descriptive passages and in his handling of imagery. The best examples are not restricted to the opening passages and the scene of the truancy; they can also be found in the description of young John's thought processes as he hammers out the Raeburn essay:

> A world of ice groaned round him in the night; bergs ground on each other and were rent in pain; he heard the splash of great fragments tumbled in the deep, and felt the waves of their distant falling lift the vessel beneath him in the darkness. To the long desolate night there came a desolate dawn, and eyes were dazed by the encircling whiteness; yet there flashed green slanting chasms in the ice, and towering pinnacles of sudden rose, lonely and far away. An unknown sea beat upon an unknown shore, and the ship drifted on the pathless waters, a white dead man at the helm.

Introduction

This may first sound like a Coleridgean vision, but underneath the imagery there may also be some kind of psychological pattern. The same combination of decadent romanticism and psychological turmoil seems to be behind the description of John's nightmare in Chapter 23:

> Next moment he was gazing at a ruined castle, its mouldering walls mounded atop with decaying rubble; from a loose crumb of mortar a long, thin film of the spider's weaving stretched bellying away, to a tall weed waving on the crazy brink – Gourlay saw its glisten in the wind. He saw each crack in the wall, each stain of lichen; a myriad details stamped themselves together on his raw mind.

George Douglas Brown's great interest in visualising and phrase-making is illustrated in these passages: there is undoubtedly something of himself in young John at these points. As for his use of imagery and symbol, the most obvious and recurrent is that of the House: one could almost say that the House is the obsessive image that subsumes all in the end. But another, perhaps more subtle image is that of the arch. Near the beginning of the novel attention is drawn to the "smooth round arch of the falling water" from Blowsalinda's pail as it glistens for a moment in mid-air. The symbol is used here to emphasise the beauty of the scene and reinforce the (false) sense of well-being. The image recurs in Chapter 10 in the description of the lettering above the windows of Wilson's Emporium:

> The letters of "James Wilson" made a triumphal arch ...

Here the symbol is used to foreshadow Wilson's victory over Gourlay. Finally, at the very end of the novel the image recurs in the reference to the arch of the dawn; and here it is used with tremendous dramatic irony, for the brightness of the dawn throws into stark relief the horror of the Gourlay tragedy:

> They gazed with blanched faces at the House with the Green Shutters, sitting dark there and terrible, beneath the radiant arch of the dawn.

There is then a fair amount of evidence in *The House* to suggest that George Douglas Brown had gone some way towards developing his powers as an artist in language.

Importance of the Novel: Achievement

IT is generally accepted that *The House with the Green Shutters* was a counterblast to the Kailyard and that it presented the other side of Scottish small-town life, mean and malignant, even terrifying in the evil consequences of its malignancy. It did have that effect: the Kailyard image of the Scot as a couthie individual and of the Scottish community as one dominated by the benign influence of the minister, if it was not destroyed, was badly shattered by the counterblast even if it did survive. But the novel has a significance beyond this: it makes an impact as a work strongly influenced by Scottish, classical, and European traditions, and exerting its own influence on subsequent works.

It is known that George Douglas Brown had read some of the Russian and French novels of the nineteenth century, and that he admired Turgenev and Balzac but criticised Tolstoy and Dostoievsky.[1] In that he probes the life of Barbie realistically with a Balzacian or Flaubertian concern with detail, and in that he explores the psyche of his two Gourlays with a thoroughness worthy of Dostoievsky or Turgenev, George Douglas Brown brings the Scottish novel into the developing European tradition. Above all it is clear he was influenced by the spirit and form of Greek drama: how could he avoid being so, since he had spent so much time studying the classics? Yet when all allowance has been made for literary influence and the intellectual climate of the time, we have to return to the Scottish scene and George Douglas Brown's own home background, upbringing, and language. The novel is firmly rooted in Ayrshire and vividly reflects the Scottish scene. There is the

[1] James Veitch: *George Douglas Brown*, Jenkins, 1952, pp. 70-71.

satirising of the business Scotsman on the make that recalls Galt; the tools of psychology fashioned in France and Russia are used to explore and, as far as possible, to explain the actions and excesses of the local characters; the methods of the Scottish ballad are used in presenting the story; and there is that skill in counterpointing the Scots language against the English that was a feature of writers like Scott and Stevenson and was to be demonstrated in an original way by Lewis Grassic Gibbon. Weaknesses and omissions there are and must be: the relationships between man and woman and between man and man are only partly sketched; the picture is an exaggerated rather than a rounded one;[1] and there are perhaps too many authorial comments and explanations. But the achievement is there: *The House* is a novel that reflects and strengthens the Scottish tradition; and it is a novel that develops a universality that contrasts with the parochial concerns of the Kailyard and enables it to take its place with great novels in Scotland, England, and elsewhere in Europe.

Some of the links and similarities between *Weir of Hermiston* and *The House with the Green Shutters* have already been indicated. It is interesting that J. D. Scott in the *Horizon* article referred to should say that the sixty years' silence in the nineteenth century – "during which no Scottish writer attempted to forge in the smithy of his soul the uncreated conscience of his race" – was broken by Stevenson's last unfinished novel and, a few years later, by George Douglas Brown's work. Both novels, although more realistic or naturalistic than most Scottish works of fiction written during those sixty years, derive their power, according to Mr Scott, from "the Braxfield myth" which attempts to recapture "the repressed, forgotten, demoniac Scotland" (as opposed to nineteenth century hypocritical Scotland). Whatever may be the relative merits of these two works (Mr Scott believes *Weir* to be

---

[1] But I cannot agree with Somerset Maugham when he says in his introduction to the World's Classics edition – "There is not a single character . . . that is not base, cruel, mean, drunken, or stupid". There are some characters to whom this description does not apply, as my section on characterisation indicates.

superior to *The House*), for me the remarkable thing is that George Douglas Brown does not merely reflect the myth or demoniac quality but also builds it firmly into the moral fabric of his work. His novel proves to be a powerful companion-piece to Stevenson's last great work.

There is however another Scottish motif or theme that helps to give *The House* its universality. This links it with the novels of Neil Gunn, and is dealt with at some length by Kurt Wittig.[1] This theme is the Scottish talent for phrase-making, for seeing something vividly inside the mind, for flashing ideas together – a gift possessed by young John Gourlay in *The House*, and discussed by the Jock Allan circle in Chapter 17. It is illustrated elsewhere in the novel – particularly in Chapters 18 and 23 (see pp. xxxvii - xxxviii). This flashing together of images is seen by Kurt Wittig as being related to Neil Gunn's animism – which can place the swallow of life in the hands of a small boy (*Butcher's Broom*), or envisage thought mushrooming up "until it was the dome of the sky" (*The Other Landscape*), or describe the kind of audible silence that enables Jeems to hear "the chuckle that was Tullach's dark smile" (*The Grey Coast*).

These links with Stevenson and Gunn illustrate the more subtle aspects of George Douglas Brown's achievement in *The House*. On a more obvious and straightforward level he can be seen to have prepared the way for J. MacDougall Hay's *Gillespie* (1914), a study of a demoniac lowlander who preys on his highland neighbours, and for Lewis Grassic Gibbon's *Sunset Song* (1932), in which the black and white of Scottish society are more fully represented and better balanced. *The House* may also be said to have inspired minor works like A. J. Cronin's *Hatter's Castle* (1931) and Willa Muir's *Mrs Ritchie* (1933). The Cronin novel is a full-blooded study of Brodie the hatter who is obviously based on Gourlay, but it lacks the stark, unblurred quality of the original. Mrs Muir's novel is an interesting variant of the theme in which the demoniac quality is embodied in a religious bigot of a woman who systemati-

[1] *Neil Gunn: the Man and the Writer*, Blackwood, 1973, pp. 316-340.

cally and self-righteously destroys husband and son. (Here
we may have also something of the influence of James
Hogg's *Confessions of a Justified Sinner*.)

F. R. Leavis says that out of Emily Brontë and *Wuthering
Heights* comes a minor tradition "to which belongs, most
notably, *The House with the Green Shutters*".[1] Certainly
Wuthering Heights and *The House with the Green Shutters*
have in common overpowering psychological developments
and a demoniac energy that go far beyond surface realism.
The House may be grouped with *Wuthering Heights* as
belonging to a minor tradition as far as the English novel is
concerned. What there is no doubt about in my mind is
that George Douglas Brown's work, firmly placed within
the Scottish tradition, reflecting European developments
and influencing later Scottish works, makes an important
and original contribution to the novel of the twentieth
century.

[1] *The Great Tradition*, Penguin Books, reprint 1966, p. 38.

The House with the Green Shutters

CHAPTER 1

THE frowsy chamber-maid of the "Red Lion" had just finished washing the front door steps. She rose from her stooping posture, and, being of slovenly habit, flung the water from her pail, straight out, without moving from where she stood. The smooth round arch of the falling water glistened for a moment in mid-air. John Gourlay, standing in front of his new house at the head of the brae, could hear the swash of it when it fell. The morning was of perfect stillness.

The hands of the clock across "The Square" were pointing to the hour of eight. They were yellow in the sun.

Blowsalinda, of the Red Lion, picked up the big bass that usually lay within the porch and, carrying it clumsily against her breast, moved off round the corner of the public house, her petticoat gaping behind. Halfway she met the ostler with whom she stopped in amorous dalliance. He said something to her, and she laughed loudly and vacantly. The silly *tee-hee* echoed up the street.

A moment later a cloud of dust drifting round the corner, and floating white in the still air, shewed that she was pounding the bass against the end of the house. All over the little town the women of Barbie were equally busy with their steps and door-mats. There was scarce a man to be seen either in the Square, at the top of which Gourlay stood, or in the long street descending from its near corner. The men were at work; the children had not yet appeared; the women were busy with their household cares.

The freshness of the air, the smoke rising thin and far above the red chimneys, the sunshine glistering on the roofs and gables, the rosy clearness of everything beneath the dawn, above all the quietness and peace, made Barbie, usually so poor to see, a very pleasant place to look down at on a summer morning. At this hour there was an unfamiliar

1

delicacy in the familiar scene, a freshness and purity of aspect – almost an unearthliness – as though you viewed it through a crystal dream. But it was not the beauty of the hour that kept Gourlay musing at his gate. He was dead to the fairness of the scene, even while the fact of its presence there before him wove most subtly with his mood. He smoked in silent enjoyment because on a morning such as this, everything he saw was a delicate flattery to his pride. At the beginning of a new day to look down on the petty burgh in which he was the greatest man, filled all his being with a consciousness of importance. His sense of prosperity was soothing and pervasive; he felt it all round him like the pleasant air, as real as that and as subtle; bathing him, caressing. It was the most secret and intimate joy of his life to go out and smoke on summer mornings by his big gate, musing over Barbie ere he possessed it with his merchandise.

He had growled at the quarry carters for being late in setting out this morning (for like most resolute dullards he was sternly methodical), but in his heart he was secretly pleased. The needs of his business were so various that his men could rarely start at the same hour, and in the same direction. To-day, however, because of the delay, all his carts would go streaming through the town together, and that brave pomp would be a slap in the face to his enemies. "I'll shew them," he thought, proudly. "Them" was the town-folk, and what he would shew them was what a big man he was. For, like most scorners of the world's opinion, Gourlay was its slave, and shewed his subjection to the popular estimate by his anxiety to flout it. He was not great enough for the carelessness of perfect scorn.

Through the big green gate behind him came the sound of carts being loaded for the day. A horse, weary of standing idle between the shafts, kicked ceaselessly and steadily against the ground with one impatient hinder foot, clink, clink, clink upon the paved yard. "Easy, damn ye; ye'll smash the bricks!" came a voice. Then there was the smart slap of an open hand on a sleek neck, a quick start, and the rattle of chains as the horse quivered to the blow.

"Run a white tarpaulin across the cheese, Jock, to keep

2

them frae melting in the heat," came another voice. "And canny on the top there wi' thae big feet o' yours; d'ye think a cheese was made for *you* to dance on wi' your mighty brogues?" Then the voice sank to the hoarse warning whisper of impatience; loudish in anxiety, yet throaty from fear of being heard. "Hurry up, man—hurry up, or he'll be down on us like bleezes for being so late in getting off!"

Gourlay smiled, grimly, and a black gleam shot from his eye as he glanced round to the gate and caught the words. His men did not know he could hear them.

The clock across the Square struck the hour, eight soft slow strokes, that melted away in the beauty of the morning. Five minutes passed. Gourlay turned his head to listen, but no further sound came from the yard. He walked to the green gate, his slippers making no noise.

"Are ye sleeping, my pretty men?" he said, softly. . ."*Eih*?"

The "*Eih*" leapt like a sword, with a slicing sharpness in its tone, that made it a sinister contrast to the first sweet question to his "pretty men." "*Eih*?" he said again, and stared with open mouth and fierce dark eyes.

"Hurry up, Peter," whispered the gaffer, "hurry up, for Godsake. He has the black glower in his e'en."

"Ready, sir; ready now!" cried Peter Riney, running out to open the other half of the gate. Peter was a wizened little man, with a sandy fringe of beard beneath his chin, a wart on the end of his long, slanting-out nose, light blue eyes, and bushy eyebrows of a reddish gray. The bearded red brows, close above the pale blueness of his eyes, made them more vivid by contrast; they were like pools of blue light amid the brownness of his face. Peter always ran about his work with eager alacrity. A simple and willing old man, he affected the quick readiness of youth to atone for his insignificance.

"Hup horse; hup then!" cried courageous Peter, walking backwards with curved body through the gate, and tugging at the reins of a horse the feet of which struck sparks from the paved ground as they stressed painfully on edge to get weigh on the great waggon behind. The cart rolled through, then another, and another, till twelve of them had passed. Gourlay stood aside to watch them. All the horses were

3

brown; "he makes a point of that," the neighbours would have told you. As each horse passed the gate the driver left its head, and took his place by the wheel, cracking his whip, with many a "hup horse; yean horse; woa lad; steady!"

In a dull little country town the passing of a single cart is an event, and a gig is followed with the eye till it disappears. Anything is welcome that breaks the long monotony of the hours, and suggests a topic for the evening's talk. "Any news?" a body will gravely enquire; "Ou aye," another will answer with equal gravity, "I saw Kennedy's gig going past in the forenoon." "Aye, man, where would *he* be off till? He's owre often in his gig, I'm thinking—" and then Kennedy and his affairs will last them till bedtime.

Thus the appearance of Gourlay's carts woke Barbie from its morning lethargy. The smith came out in his leather apron, shoving back, as he gazed, the grimy cap from his white-sweating brow; bowed old men stood in front of their doorways, leaning with one hand on short trembling staffs, while the slaver slid unheeded along the cutties which the left hand held to their toothless mouths; white-mutched grannies were keeking past the jambs; an early urchin, standing wide-legged to stare, waved his cap and shouted, "Hooray!"— and all because John Gourlay's carts were setting off upon their morning rounds, a brave procession for a single town! Gourlay, standing great-shouldered in the middle of the road, took in every detail, devoured it grimly as a homage to his pride. "Ha! ha! ye dogs," said the soul within him. Past the pillar of the Red Lion door he could see a white peep of the landlord's waistcoat— though the rest of the mountainous man was hidden deep within his porch. (On summer mornings the vast totality of the landlord was always inferential to the town from the tiny white peep of him revealed.) Even fat Simpson had waddled to the door to see the carts going past. It was fat Simpson—might the Universe blast his adipose— who had once tried to infringe Gourlay's monopoly as the sole carrier in Barbie. There had been a rush to him at first, but Gourlay set his teeth and drove him off the road, carrying stuff for nothing till Simpson had nothing to carry, so that the local wit suggested "a wee parcel in a big cart" as a new sign for his hotel. The twelve browns prancing past would be a pill to Simpson! There was no smile about Gourlay's mouth—a fiercer glower was the only sign of his pride—but it put a bloom on his morning, he felt, to see the suggestive round of Simpson's waistcoat, down yonder at the porch. Simpson, the swine! He had made short work o' *him*!

Ere the last of the carts had issued from the yard at the House with the Green Shutters the foremost was already near the Red Lion. Gourlay swore beneath his breath when Miss Toddle—described in the local records as "a spinster of independent means"—came fluttering out with a silly little parcel to accost one of the carriers. Did the auld fool mean to stop Andy Gow about *her* petty affairs—and thus break the line of carts on the only morning they had ever been able to go down the brae together? But no. Andy tossed her parcel carelessly up among his other packages, and left her bawling instructions from the gutter, with a portentous shaking of her corkscrew curls. Gourlay's men took their cue from their master, and were contemptuous of Barbie, most unchivalrous scorners of its old maids.

Gourlay was pleased with Andy for snubbing Sandy Toddle's sister. When he and Elshie Hogg reached the Cross they would have to break off from the rest to complete their loads, but they had been down Main Street over night as usual picking up their commissions, and until they reached the Bend o' the Brae it was unlikely that any business should arrest them now. Gourlay hoped that it might be so, and he had his desire, for, with the exception of Miss Toddle, no customer appeared. The teams went slowly down the steep side of the Square in an unbroken line, and slowly down the street leading from its near corner. On the slope the horses were unable to go fast—being forced to stell themselves back against the heavy propulsion of the carts behind; and thus the procession endured for a length of time worthy its surpassing greatness. When it disappeared round the Bend o' the Brae the watching bodies disappeared too; the event of the day had passed and vacancy resumed her reign. The street and the Square lay empty to the morning sun. Gourlay

5

alone stood idly at his gate, lapped in his own satisfaction.

It had been a big morning, he felt. It was the first time for many a year that all his men, quarry-men and carriers, carters of cheese and carters of grain, had led their teams down the brae together in the full view of his rivals. "I hope they liked it!" he thought, and he nodded several times at the town beneath his feet, with a slow up and down motion of the head, like a man nodding grimly to his beaten enemy. It was as if he said, "See what I have done to ye!"

CHAPTER 2

ONLY a man of Gourlay's brute force of character could have kept all the carrying trade of Barbie in his own hands. Even in these days of railways, nearly every parish has a pair of carriers at the least, journeying once or twice a week to the nearest town. In the days when Gourlay was the great man of Barbie, railways were only beginning to thrust themselves among the quiet hills, and the bulk of inland commerce was still being drawn by horses along the country roads. Yet Gourlay was the only carrier in the town. The wonder is diminished when we remember that it had been a decaying burgh for thirty years, and that its trade, at the best of times, was of meagre volume. Even so, it was astonishing that he should be the only carrier. If you asked the natives how he did it, "Ou," they said, "he makes the one hand wash the other, doan't ye know?"—meaning thereby that he had so many horses travelling on his own business, that he could afford to carry other people's goods at rates that must cripple his rivals.

"But that's very stupid, surely," said a visitor once, who thought of entering into competition. "It's cutting off his nose to spite his face! Why is he so anxious to be the only carrier in Barbie that he carries stuff for next to noathing the moment another man tries to work the roads? It's a daft-like thing to do!"

"To be sure is't, to be sure is't! Just the stupeedity o' spite! Oh, there are times when Gourlay makes little or noathing from the carrying; but then, ye see, it gies him a fine chance to annoy folk! If you ask him to bring ye ocht, 'Oh,' he growls, 'I'll see if it suits my own convenience.' And ye have to be content. He has made so much money of late that the pride of him's not to be endured."

It was not the insolence of sudden wealth however that

7

made Gourlay haughty to his neighbours; it was a repressiveness natural to the man and a fierce contempt of their scoffing envy. But it was true that he had made large sums of money during recent years. From his father (who had risen in the world) he inherited a fine trade in cheese; also the carrying to Skeighan on the one side and Fleckie on the other. When he married Miss Richmond of Tenshillingland, he started as a corn broker with the snug dowry that she brought him, Then, greatly to his own benefit, he succeeded in establishing a valuable connection with Templandmuir.

It was partly by sheer impact of character that Gourlay obtained his ascendancy over hearty and careless Templandmuir, and partly by a bluff joviality which he—so little cunning in other things—knew to affect among the petty lairds. The man you saw trying to be jocose with Templandmuir, was a very different being from the autocrat who "downed" his fellows in the town. It was all "How are ye the day, Templandmuir?" and "How d'ye doo-oo, Mr Gourlay?" and the immediate production of the big decanter.

More than ten years ago now, Templandmuir gave this fine dour upstanding friend of his a twelve-year tack of the Red Quarry—and that was the making of Gourlay. The quarry yielded the best building stone in a circuit of thirty miles, easy to work and hard against wind and weather. When the main line went north through Skeighan and Poltandie, there was a great deal of building on the far side, and Gourlay simply coined the money. He could not have exhausted the quarry had he tried—he would have had to howk down a hill—but he took thousands of loads from it for the Skeighan folk; and the commission he paid the laird on each was ridiculously small. He built wooden stables out on Templandmuir's estate—the Templar had seven hundred acres of hill land—and it was there the quarry horses generally stood. It was only rarely—once in two years, perhaps—that they came into the House with the Green Shutters. Last Saturday they had brought several loads of stuff for Gourlay's own use; and that is why they were present at the great procession on the Monday following.

8

It was their feeling that Gourlay's success was out of all proportion to his merits that made other great-men-in-a-small-way so bitter against him. They were an able lot, and scarce one but possessed fifty times his weight of brain. Yet he had the big way of doing, though most of them were well enough to pass. Had they not been aware of his stupidity they would never have minded his triumphs in the countryside, but they felt it with a sense of personal defeat that he—the donkey, as they thought him—should scoop every chance that was going, and leave them, the long-headed ones, still muddling in their old concerns. They consoled themselves with sneers, he retorted with brutal scorn, and the feud kept increasing between them.

They were standing at the Cross, to enjoy their Saturday at e'en, when Gourlay's "quarriers"—as the quarry horses had been named— came through the town last week-end. There were groups of bodies in the streets, washed from toil to enjoy the quiet air; dandering slowly or gossiping at ease; and they all turned to watch the quarriers stepping bravely up, their heads tossing to the hill. The big-men-in-a-small-way glowered and said nothing.

"I wouldn't mind," said Sandy Toddle at last, "I wouldn't mind of he weren't such a demned ess!"

"Ess?" said the Deacon unpleasantly. He puckered his brow and blinked, pretending not to understand.

"Oh, a cuddy, ye know," said Toddle, colouring.

"Gourlay'th stupid enough," lisped the Deacon. "We all know that. But there'th one thing to be said on hith behalf. He's not such a 'demned ess' as to try and thpeak fancy English!"

When the Deacon was not afraid of a man he stabbed him straight. When he was afraid of him he stabbed him on the sly. He was annoyed by the passing of Gourlay's carts, and he took it out of Sandy Toddle.

"It's extr'ornar!" blurted the Provost (who was a man of brosey speech, large-mouthed and fat of utterance). "It's extr'ornar. Yass; it's extr'ornar! I mean the luck of that man —for gumption he has noan. Noan whatever! But if the railway came hereaway I wager Gourlay would go down," he added, less in certainty of knowledge than as prophet of the thing desired. "I wager he'd go down, sirs."

"Likely enough," said Sandy Toddle; "he wouldn't be quick enough to jump at the new way of doing."

"Moar than that!" cried the Provost, spite sharpening his insight, "moar than that! He'd be owre dour to abandon the auld way. *I'm* talling ye. He would just be left out entirely! It's only those, like myself, who approach him on the town's affairs that know the full extent of his stupeedity."

"Oh, he's a 'demned ess,' " said the Deacon, rubbing it into Toddle and Gourlay at the same time.

"A-ah, but then, ye see, he has the abeelity that comes from character," said Johnny Coe, who was a sage philosopher. "For there are two kinds of abeelity, don't ye understaand? There's a scattered abeelity that's of no use! Auld Randie Donaldson was good at fifty different things, and he died in the poorhouse! There's a dour kind of abeelity, though, that has no cleverness, but just gangs trampling on; and that's—"

"The easiest beaten by a flank attack," said the Deacon, snubbing him.

CHAPTER 3

WITH the sudden start of a man roused from a daydream Gourlay turned from the green gate and entered the yard. Jock Gilmour, the "orra" man, was washing down the legs of a horse beside the trough. It was Gourlay's own cob, which he used for driving round the countryside. It was a black— Gourlay "made a point" of driving with a black. "The brown for sturdiness, the black for speed," he would say, making a maxim of his whim to give it the sanction of a higher law.

Gilmour was in a wild temper because he had been forced to get up at five o'clock in order to turn several hundred cheeses, to prevent them bulging out of shape owing to the heat, and so becoming cracked and spoiled. He did not raise his head at his master's approach. And his head being bent, the eye was attracted to a patent leather collar which he wore, glazed with black and red stripes. It is a collar much affected by ploughmen, because a dip in the horse-trough once a month suffices for its washing. Between the striped collar and his hair (as he stooped) the sunburned redness of his neck struck the eye vividly—the cropped fair hairs on it shewing whitish on the red skin.

The horse quivered as the cold water swashed about its legs, and turned playfully to bite its groom. Gilmour, still stooping, dug his elbow up beneath its ribs. The animal wheeled in anger, but Gilmour ran to its head with most manful blasphemy and led it to the stable door. The off hind leg was still unwashed.

"Has the horse but the three legs?" said Gourlay suavely.

Gilmour brought the horse back to the trough, muttering sullenly.

"Were ye saying anything?" said Gourlay. "*Eih*?"

Gilmour sulked out and said nothing; and his master smiled grimly at the sudden redness that swelled his neck

11

and ears to the verge of bursting.

A boy, standing in his shirt and trousers at an open window of the house above, had looked down at the scene with craning interest—big-eyed. He had been alive to every turn and phase of it—the horse's quiver of delight and fear, his skittishness, the groom's ill-temper, and Gourlay's grinding will. Eh, but his father was a caution! How easy he had downed Jock Gilmour! The boy was afraid of his father himself, but he liked to see him send other folk to the right about. For he was John Gourlay, too.—Hokey, but his father could down them!

Mr Gourlay passed on to the inner yard, which was close to the scullery door. The paved little court, within its high wooden walls, was curiously fresh and clean. A cock-pigeon strutted round, puffing his gleaming breast and *rooketty-cooing* in the sun. Large clear drops fell slowly from the spout of a wooden pump, and splashed upon a flat stone. The place seemed to enfold the stillness. There was a sense of inclusion and peace.

There is a distinct pleasure to the eye in a quiet brick court where everything is fresh and prim; in sunny weather you can lounge in a room and watch it through an open door, in a kind of lazy dream. The boy, standing at the window above to let the fresh air blow round his neck, was alive to that pleasure; he was intensely conscious of the pigeon swelling in its bravery, of the clean yard, the dripping pump, and the great stillness. His father on the step beneath had a different pleasure in the sight. The fresh indolence of morning was round him too, but it was more than that that kept him gazing in idle happiness. He was delighting in the sense of his own property around him, the most substantial pleasure possible to man. His feeling, deep though it was, was quite vague and inarticulate. If you had asked Gourlay what he was thinking of he could not have told you, even if he had been willing to answer you civilly—which is most unlikely. Yet his whole being, physical and mental (physical, indeed, rather than mental), was surcharged with the feeling that the fine buildings around him were his, that he had won them by his own effort and built them large and significant before the world. He was lapped in the thought of it.

All men are suffused with that quiet pride in looking at the houses and lands which they have won by their endeavours— in looking at the houses more than at the lands, for the house which a man has built seems to express his character and stand for him before the world, as a sign of his success. It is more personal than cold acres, stamped with an individuality. All men know that soothing pride in the contemplation of their own property. But in Gourlay's sense of property there was another element, an element peculiar to itself, which endowed it with its warmest glow. Conscious always that he was at a disadvantage among his cleverer neighbours, who could achieve a civic eminence denied to him, he felt nevertheless that there was one means, a material means, by which he could hold his own and reassert himself; by the bravery of his business, namely, and all the appointments thereof—among which his dwelling was the chief. That was why he had spent so much money on the House. That was why he had such keen delight in surveying it. Every time he looked at the place he had a sense of triumph over what he knew in his bones to be an adverse public opinion. There was anger in his pleasure, and the pleasure that is mixed with anger often gives the keenest thrill. It is the delight of triumph in spite of opposition. Gourlay's house was a material expression of that delight, stood for it in stone and lime.

It was not that he reasoned deliberately when he built the house. But every improvement that he made—and he was always spending money on improvements—had for its secret motive a more or less vague desire to score off his rivals. "*That*'ll be a slap in the face to the Provost!" he smiled, when he planted his great mound of shrubs. "There's noathing like *that* about the Provost's! Ha, ha!"

Encased as he was in his hard and insensitive nature he was not the man who in new surroundings would be quick to every whisper of opinion. But he had been born and bred in Barbie, and he knew his townsmen—oh, yes, he knew them. He knew they laughed because he had no gift of the gab, and could never be Provost, or Bailie, or Elder—or even Chairman of the Gasworks! Oh, verra well, verra well; let Connal and Brodie and Allardyce have the talk, and manage the town's affairs (he was damned if they should manage his!)—he, for his part, preferred the substantial reality. He could never aspire to the Provostship, but a man with a house like that, he was fain to think, could afford to do without it. Oh, yes; he was of opinion he could do without it! It had run him short of cash to build the place so big and braw, but, Lord! it was worth it. There wasn't a man in the town who had such accommodation!

And so, gradually, his dwelling had come to be a passion of Gourlay's life. It was a by-word in the place that if ever his ghost was seen, it would be haunting the House with the Green Shutters. Deacon Allardyce, trying to make a phrase with him, once quoted the saying in his presence. "Likely enough!" said Gourlay. "It's only reasonable I should prefer my own house to you rabble in the graveyard!"

Both in appearance and position the house was a worthy counterpart of its owner. It was a substantial two-story dwelling, planted firm and gawcey on a little natural terrace that projected a considerable distance into the Square. At the foot of the steep little bank shelving to the terrace ran a stone wall, of no great height, and the iron railings it uplifted were no higher than the sward within. Thus the whole house was bare to the view from the ground up, nothing in front to screen its admirable qualities. From each corner, behind, flanking walls went out to the right and left, and hid the yard and the granaries. In front of these walls the dwelling seemed to thrust itself out for notice. It took the eye of a stranger the moment he entered the Square—"Whose place is that?" was his natural question. A house that challenges regard in that way should have a gallant bravery in its look; if its aspect be mean, its assertive position but directs the eye to its infirmities. There is something pathetic about a tall, cold, barn-like house set high upon a brae; it cannot hide its naked shame; it thrusts its ugliness dumbly on your notice, a manifest blotch upon the world, a place for the winds to whistle round. But Gourlay's house was worthy its commanding

14

station. A little dour and blunt in the outlines like Gourlay himself, it drew and satisfied your eye as he did.

And its position, "cockit up there on the brae," made it the theme of constant remark, to men because of the tyrant who owned it, and to women because of the poor woman who mismanaged its affairs. "'Deed, I don't wonder that gurly Gourlay, as they ca' him, has an ill temper," said the gossips gathered at the pump, with their big bare arms akimbo; "whatever led him to marry that dishclout of a woman clean beats *me*! I never could make head nor tail o't!" As for the men, they twisted every item about Gourlay and his domicile into fresh matter of assailment. "What's the news?" asked one, returning from a long absence—to whom the smith, after smoking in silence for five minutes, said, "Gourlay has got new rones!" "Ha—aye, man, Gourlay has got new rones!" buzzed the visitor, and then their eyes, diminished in mirth, twinkled at each other from out their ruddy wrinkles, as if wit had volleyed between them. In short, the House with the Green Shutters was on every tongue—and with a scoff in the voice if possible.

15

CHAPTER 4

GOURLAY went swiftly to the kitchen from the inner yard.
He had stood so long in silence on the step, and his coming
was so noiseless, that he surprised a long thin trollop of a
woman, with a long thin scraggy neck, seated by the slat-
ternly table, and busy with a frowsy paper-covered volume,
over which her head was bent in intent perusal.

"At your novelles?" said he. "Aye, woman; will it be a
good story?"

She rose in a nervous flutter when she saw him; yet
needlessly shrill in her defence, because she was angry at
detection.

"Ah, well!" she cried, in weary petulance, "it's an unco
thing if a body's not to have a moment's rest after such a
morning's darg! I just sat down wi' the book for a little, till
John should come till his breakfast!"

"So?" said Gourlay.

"God aye!" he went on, "you're making a nice job of *him*.
He'll be a credit to the House. Oh, it's right, no doubt, that
you should neglect your work till *he* consents to rise."

"Eh, the puir la-amb," she protested, dwelling on the
vowels in fatuous maternal love, "the bairn's wearied, man!
He's ainything but strong, and the schooling's owre sore on
him."

"Poor lamb, atweel," said Gourlay. "It was a muckle
sheep that dropped him."

It was Gourlay's pride in his house that made him harsher
to his wife than others, since her sluttishness was a constant
offence to the order in which he loved to have his dear pos-
sessions. He, for his part, liked everything precise. His claw-
toed hammer always hung by the head on a couple of nails
close together near the big clock; his gun always lay across
a pair of wooden pegs, projecting from the brown rafters,
just above the hearth. His bigotry in trifles expressed his

16

character. Strong men of a mean understanding often deliberately assume, and passionately defend, peculiarities of no importance, because they have nothing else to get a repute for, "No, no," said Gourlay; you'll never see a brown cob in *my* gig—I wouldn't take one in a present!" He was full of such fads, and nothing should persuade him to alter the crochets, which, for want of something better, he made the marks of his dour character. He had worked them up as part of his personality, and his pride of personality was such that he would never consent to change them. Hence the burly and gurly man was prim as an old maid with regard to his belongings. Yet his wife was continually infringing the order on which he set his heart. If he went forward to the big clock to look for his hammer, it was sure to be gone—the two bright nails staring at him vacantly. "Oh," she would say in weary complaint, "I just took it to break a wheen coals";—and he would find it in the coal-hole, greasy and grimy finger-marks engrained on the handle which he loved to keep so smooth and clean. Innumerable her offences of the kind. Independent of these, the sight of her general incompetence filled him with a seething rage, which found vent not in lengthy tirades but in the smooth venom of his tongue. Let him keep the outside of the House never so spick and span, inside was awry with her untidiness. She was unworthy of the House with the Green Shutters— that was the gist of it. Every time he set eyes on the poor trollop, the fresh perception of her incompetence which the sudden sight of her flashed, as she trailed aimlessly about, seemed to fatten his rage and give a coarser birr to his tongue.

Mrs Gourlay had only four people to look after, her husband, her two children, and Jock Gilmour, the orra man. And the wife of Dru'cken Wabster—who had to go charing because she was the wife of Dru'cken Wabster—came in every day, and all day long, to help her with the work. Yet the house was always in confusion. Mrs Gourlay had asked for another servant, but Gourlay would not allow that; "one's enough," said he, and what he once laid down, he never went back on. Mrs Gourlay had to muddle along as best she could, and having no strength either of mind or body, she let things drift and took refuge in reading silly fiction.

As Gourlay shoved his feet into his boots, and stamped to make them easy, he glowered at the kitchen from under his heavy brows with a huge disgust. The table was littered with unwashed dishes, and on the corner of it next to him was a great black sloppy ring, showing where a wet saucepan had been laid upon the bare board. The sun streamed through the window in yellow heat right on to a pat of melting butter. There was a basin of dirty water beneath the table, with the dishcloth slopping over on the ground.

"It's a tidy house!" said he.

"Ach well," she cried, "you and your kitchen-range! It was that that did it! The masons could have redd out the fireplace to make room for't in the afternoon before it comes hame. They could have done't brawly, but ye wouldna hear o't—oh, no—ye bude to have the whole place gutted out yestreen. I had to boil everything on the parlour fire this morning—no wonder I'm a little tousy!"

The old fashioned kitchen grate had been removed and the jambs had been widened on each side of the fireplace; it yawned, empty and cold. A little rubble of mortar, newly dried, lay about the bottom of the square recess. The sight of the crude, unfamiliar scraps of dropped lime in the gaping space where warmth should have been, increased the discomfort of the kitchen.

"Oh, that's it!" said Gourlay. "I see! It was want of the fireplace that kept ye from washing the dishes that we used yestreen. That was terrible! However, ye'll have plenty of boiling water when I put in the grand new range for ye; there winna be its equal in the parish! We'll maybe have a clean house *than*."

Mrs Gourlay leaned, with the outspread thumb and red raw knuckles of her right hand, on the sloppy table, and gazed away through the back window of the kitchen in a kind of mournful vacancy. Always when her first complaining defence had failed to turn aside her husband's tongue, her mind became a blank beneath his heavy sarcasms, and sought refuge by drifting far away. She would fix her eyes on the distance in dreary contemplation, and her mind would follow her eyes, in a vacant and wistful regard. The preoccupation of her mournful gaze enabled her to meet her husband's sneers with a kind of dumb unheeding acquiescence. She scarcely heard them.

Her head hung a little to one side as if too heavy for her wilting neck. Her hair, of a dry red brown, curved low on either side of her brow, in a thick untidy mass, to her almost transparent ears. As she gazed in weary and dreary absorption her lips had fallen heavy and relaxed, in unison with her mood; and through her open mouth her breathing was quick, and short, and noiseless. She wore no stays, and her slack cotton blouse shewed the flatness of her bosom, and the faint outlines of her withered and pendulous breasts hanging low within.

There was something tragic in her pose, as she stood, sad and abstracted, by the dirty table. She was scraggy helplessness, staring in sorrowful vacancy. But Gourlay eyed her with disgust—why, by Heaven, even now her petticoat was gaping behind, worse than the sloven's at the Red Lion. She was a pr-r-retty wife for John Gourlay! The sight of her feebleness would have roused pity in some: Gourlay it moved to a steady and seething rage. As she stood helpless before him he stung her with crude, brief irony.

Yet he was not wilfully cruel; only a stupid man with a strong character, in which he took a dogged pride. Stupidity and pride provoked the brute in him. He was so dull—only dull is hardly the word for a man of his smouldering fire—he was so dour of wit that he could never hope to distinguish himself by anything in the shape of cleverness. Yet so resolute a man must make the strong personality of which he was proud, tell in some way. How, then, should he assert his superiority and hold his own? Only by affecting a brutal scorn of everything said and done unless it was said and done by John Gourlay. His lack of understanding made his affectation of contempt the easier. A man can never sneer at a thing which he really understands. Gourlay, understanding nothing, was able to sneer at everything. "Hah! I don't

19

understand that; it's damned nonsense!"—that was his attitude to life. If "that" had been an utterance of Shakespeare or Napoleon it would have made no difference to John Gourlay. It would have been damned nonsense just the same. And he would have told them so, if he had met them.

The man had made dogged scorn a principle of life to maintain himself, at the height which his courage warranted. His thickness of wit was never a bar to the success of his irony. For the irony of the ignorant Scot is rarely the outcome of intellectual qualities. It depends on a falsetto voice and the use of a recognized number of catchwords. "Dee-ee-ar me, dee-ee-ar me"; "Just so-a, just so-a"; "Im-phm!" "D'ye tell me that?" "Wonderful, serr, wonderful"; "Ah, well, may-ay-be, may-ay-be,"—these be words of potent irony when uttered with a certain birr. Long practice had made Gourlay an adept in their use. He never spoke to those he despised or disliked without "the birr". Not that he was voluble of speech; he wasn't clever enough for lengthy abuse. He said little and his voice was low, but every word from the hard, clean lips was a stab. And often his silence was more withering than any utterance. It struck life like a black frost.

In those early days, to be sure, Gourlay had less occasion for the use of his crude but potent irony, since the sense of his material well-being warmed him and made him less bitter to the world. To the substantial farmers and petty squires around he was civil, even hearty, in his manner—unless they offended him. For they belonged to the close corporation of "bien men" and his familiarity with them was a proof to the world of his greatness. Others, again, were far too far beneath him already for him to "down" them. He reserved his jibes for his immediate foes, the assertive bodies his rivals in the town—and for his wife, who was a constant eyesore. As for her, he had baited the poor woman so long that it had become a habit; he never spoke to her without a sneer. "Aye, where have *you* been stravaiging to?" he would drawl, and if she answered meekly, "I was taking a dander to the linn owre-bye," "The linn!" he would take her up;

"ye had a heap to do to gang there; your Bible would fit you better on a bonny Sabbath afternune!" Or it might be: "What's that you're burying your nose in now?" and if she faltered, "It's the Bible," "Hi!" he would laugh, "you're turning godly in your auld age. Weel, I'm no saying but it's time."

"Where's Janet?" he demanded, stamping his boots once more, now he had them laced.

"Eh?" said his wife vaguely, turning her eyes from the window. "Wha-at?"

"Ye're not turning deaf, I hope. I was asking ye where Janet was."

"I sent her down to Scott's for a can o' milk," she answered him wearily.

"No doubt ye had to send *her*," said he. "What ails the lamb that ye couldna send *him*? Eh?"

"Oh, she was about when I wanted the milk, and she volunteered to gang. Man, it seems I never do a thing to please ye! What harm will it do her to run for a drop milk?"

"Noan," he said gravely, "noan. And it's right, no doubt, that her brother should still be a-bed—oh, it's right that he should get the privilege—seeing he's the eldest!"

Mrs Gourlay was what the Scotch call "browdened* on her boy." In spite of her slack grasp on life—perhaps, because of it—she clung with a tenacious fondness to him. He was all she had, for Janet was a thowless† thing, too like her mother for her mother to like her. And Gourlay had discovered that it was one way of getting at his wife to be hard upon the thing she loved. In his desire to nag and annoy her, he adopted a manner of hardness and repression to his son—which became permanent. He was always "down" on John. The more so because Janet was his own favourite—perhaps, again, because her mother seemed to neglect her. Janet was a very unlovely child, with a long tallowy face and a pimply brow, over which a stiff fringe of whitish hair came down almost to her staring eyes, the eyes themselves being

---

Browdened: a Scot devoted to his children is said to be "browdened on his bairns".

†*Thowless,* weak, useless.

large, pale blue, and saucer-like, with a great margin of unhealthy white. But Gourlay, though he never petted her, had a silent satisfaction in his daughter. He took her about with him in the gig, on Saturday afternoons, when he went to buy cheese and grain at the outlying farms. And he fed her rabbits when she had the fever. It was a curious sight to see the dour silent man mixing oatmeal and wet tea-leaves in a saucer at the dirty kitchen table, and then marching off to the hutch, with the ridiculous dish in his hand, to feed his daughter's pets.

A sudden yell of pain and alarm rang through the kitchen. It came from the outer yard.

When the boy, peering from the window above, saw his father disappear through the scullery door, he stole out. The coast was clear at last.

He passed through to the outer yard. Jock Gilmour had been dashing water on the paved floor, and was now sweeping it out with a great whalebone besom. The hissing whalebone sent a splatter of dirty drops showering in front of it. John set his bare feet wide (he was only in his shirt and knickers) and eyed the man whom his father had "downed" with a kind of silent swagger. He felt superior. His pose was instinct with the feeling: "*My* father is *your* master, and ye daurna stand up till him." Children of masterful sires often display that attitude towards dependants. The feeling is not the less real for being subconscious.

Jock Gilmour was still seething with a dour anger because Gourlay's quiet will had ground him to the task. When John came out and stood there, he felt tempted to vent on him the spite he felt against his father. The subtle suggestion of criticism and superiority in the boy's pose intensified the wish. Not that Gilmour acted from deliberate malice; his irritation was instinctive. Our wrath against those whom we fear is generally wreaked upon those whom we don't.

John, with his hands in his pockets, strutted across the yard, still watching Gilmour with that silent offensive look. He came into the path of the whalebone. "Get out, you smeowt!" cried Gilmour, and with a vicious shove of the brush he sent a shower of dirty drops spattering about the boy's bare legs.

"Hallo you! what are ye after?" bawled the boy. "Don't you try that on again, I'm telling ye. What are *you*, anyway. Ye're just a servant. Hay-ay-ay, my man, my faither's the boy for ye. *He* can put ye in your place."

Gilmour made to go at him with the head of the whale-bone besom. John stopped and picked up the wet lump of cloth with which Gilmour had been washing down the horse's legs.

"Would ye?" said Gilmour, threateningly.

"Would I no?" said John, the wet lump poised for throwing, level with his shoulder.

But he did not throw it for all his defiant air. He hesitated. He would have liked to slash it into Gilmour's face, but a swift vision of what would happen if he did, withheld his craving arm. His irresolution was patent in his face; in his eyes there was both a threat and a watchful fear. He kept the dirty cloth poised in mid-air.

"Drap the clout," said Gilmour.

"I'll no," said John.

Gilmour turned sideways and whizzed the head of the besom round so that its dirty spray rained in the boy's face and eyes. John let him have the wet lump slash in his mouth. Gilmour dropped the besom and hit him a sounding thwack on the ear. John hullabalooed. Murther and desperation!

Ere he had gained breath for a second roar his mother was present in the yard. She was passionate in defence of her cub, and rage transformed her. Her tense frame vibrated in anger; you would scarce have recognized the weary trollop of the kitchen.

"What's the matter, Johnny dear?" she cried, with a fierce glance at Gilmour.

"Gilmour hut me!" he bellowed angrily.

"Ye muckle lump!" she cried shrilly, the two scraggy muscles of her neck standing out long and thin as she screamed; "ye muckle lump—to strike a defenceless wean! —Dinna greet, my lamb, I'll no let him meddle ye.—Jock Gilmour, how daur ye lift your finger to a wean of mine.—

23

But I'll learn ye the better o't! Mr Gourlay'll gie *you* the order to travel ere the day's muckle aulder. I'll have no servant about *my* hoose to ill-use *my* bairn."

She stopped, panting angrily for breath, and glared at her darling's enemy.

"*Your* servant!" cried Gilmour in contempt. "Ye're a nice-looking object to talk about servants." He pointed at her slovenly dress and burst into a blatant laugh: "Huh, huh, huh!"

Mr Gourlay had followed more slowly from the kitchen as befitted a man of his superior character. He heard the row well enough, but considered it beneath him to hasten to a petty squabble.

"What's this?" he demanded, with a widening look. Gilmour scowled at the ground.

"This!" shrilled Mrs Gourlay, who had recovered her breath again; "this! Look at him there, the muckle slabber," and she pointed to Gilmour who was standing with a red-lowering, downcast face; "look at him! A man of that size to even himsell to a wean!"

"He deserved a' he got," said Gilmour sullenly. "His mother spoils him at ony rate. And I'm damned if the best Gourlay that ever dirtied leather's gaun to trample owre *me*."

Gourlay jumped round with a quick start of the whole body. For a full minute he held Gilmour in the middle of his steady glower.

"Walk," he said, pointing to the gate.

"Oh, I'll walk," bawled Gilmour, screaming now that anger gave him courage. "Gie me time to get *my* kist, and I'll walk mighty quick. And damned glad I'll be, to get redd o' you and your hoose. The Hoose wi' the Green Shutters," he laughed, "hi, hi, hi! the Hoose wi' the Green Shutters!"

Gourlay went slowly up to him, opening his eyes on him black and wide. "You swine!" he said with quiet vehemence; "for damned little I would kill ye wi' a glower!" Gilmour shrank from the blaze in his eyes.

"Oh, dinna be fee-ee-ared," said Gourlay quietly, "dinna be fee-ee-ared. I wouldn't dirty my hand on 'ee! But get your

24

bit kist, and I'll see ye off the premises. Suspeecious characters are worth the watching."

"Suspeecious!" stuttered Gilmour, "suspeecious! Wh-wh-
whan was I ever suspeecious? I'll have the law of ye for that.
I'll make ye answer for your wor-rds."

"Imphm!" said Gourlay. "In the meantime, look slippy
wi' that bit box o' yours. I don't like daft folk about *my*
hoose."

"There'll be dafter folk as me[1] in your hoose yet," spluttered Gilmour angrily as he turned away.

He went up to the garret where he slept and brought down
his trunk. As he passed through the scullery, bowed beneath
the clumsy burden on his left shoulder, John, recovered
from his sobbing, mocked at him.

"Hay-ay-ay," he said in throaty derision, "my faither's the
boy for ye. Yon was the way to put ye down!"

[1]The reading of all editions except the Memorial Edition which prints
nor me for *as me.*

25

CHAPTER 5

IN every little Scotch community there is a distinct type known as "the bodie". "What does he do, that man?" you may ask, and the answer will be, "Really, I could hardly tell ye what he does—he's juist a bodie!" The "bodie" may be a gentleman of independent means (a hundred a year from the Funds) fussing about in spats and light check breeches; or he may be a jobbing gardener; but he is equally a "bodie." The chief occupation of his idle hours (and his hours are chiefly idle) is the discussion of his neighbour's affairs. He is generally an "auld residenter"; great, therefore, at the redding up of pedigrees. He can tell you exactly, for instance, how it is that young Pin-oe's taking geyly to the dram: for his grandfather, it seems, was a terrible man for the drink— ou, just terrible—why, he went to bed with a full jar of whiskey once, and when he left it, he was dead, and it was empty. So ye see, that's the reason o't.

The genus "bodie" is divided into two species: the "harmless bodies" and the "nesty bodies." The bodies of Barbie mostly belonged to the second variety. Johnny Coe, and Tam Wylie, and the baker, were decent enough fellows in their way, but the others were the sons of scandal. Gourlay spoke of them as a "wheen damned auld wives."—But Gourlay, to be sure, was not an impartial witness.

The Bend o' the Brae was the favourite stance of the bodies; here they foregathered every day to pass judgment on the town's affairs. And, indeed, the place had many things to recommend it. Among the chief it was within an easy distance of the Red Lion, farther up the street, to which it was really very convenient to adjourn nows and nans. Standing at the Bend o' the Brae, too, you could look along two roads to the left and right, or down upon the Cross beneath, and the three low streets that guttered away from it. Or you might turn and look up Main Street, and past the side of the Square, to the House with the Green Shutters, the highest in the town. The Bend o' the Brae, you will gather, was a fine post for observation. It had one drawback, true; if Gourlay turned to the right in his gig he disappeared in a moment, and you could never be sure where he was off to. But even that afforded matter for pleasant speculation which often lasted half an hour.

It was about nine o'clock when Gourlay and Gilmour quarrelled in the yard, and that was the hour when the bodies foregathered for their morning dram.

"Good moarning, Mr Wylie!" said the Provost.—When the Provost wished you good morning, with a heavy civic eye, you felt it was going to be good.

"Mornin', Provost, mornin'! Fine weather for the fields," said Tam, casting a critical glance at the blue dome in which a soft white-bosomed cloud floated high above the town. "If this weather hauds, it'll be a blessing for us poor farming bodies."

Tam was a wealthy old hunks, but it suited his humour to refer to himself constantly as "a poor farming bodie." And he dressed in accordance with his humour. His clean old crab-apple face was always grinning at you from over a white-sleeved moleskin waistcoat, as if he had been no better than a breaker of road-metal.

"Faith aye!" said the Provost, cunning and quick— "fodder should be cheap"— and he shot the covetous glimmer of a bargain-making eye at Mr Wylie.

Tam drew himself up. He saw what was coming.

"We're needing some hay for the burgh horse," said the Provost. "Ye'll be willing to sell at fifty shillings the ton, since it's like to be so plentiful."

"Oh," said Tam solemnly, "that's on-possible! Gourlay's seeking the three pound! And where he leads we maun a' gang. Gourlay sets the tune and Barbie dances till't."

That was quite untrue so far as the speaker was concerned. It took a clever man to make Tam Wylie dance to his piping. But Thomas, the knave, knew that he could always take a rise out of the Provost by cracking up the Gourlays, and that to do it now was the best way of fobbing him off about

27

the hay.

"Gourlay!" muttered the Provost in disgust. And Tam winked at the baker.

"Losh!" said Sandy Toddle, "yonder's the Free Kirk Minister going past the Cross! Where'll *he* be off till, at this hour of the day? He's not often up so soon."

"They say he sits late studying," said Johnny Coe.

"H'mph, studying!" grunted Tam Brodie, a big heavy wall-cheeked man, whose little side-glancing eyes seemed always alert for scandal amid the massive insolence of his smooth face. "I see few signs of studying in *him*. He's noathing but a stink wi' a skin on't."

T. Brodie was a very important man, look you, and wrote "Leather Mercht." above his door, though he cobbled with his own hands. He was a staunch Conservative, and down on the Dissenters.

"What road'th he taking?" lisped Deacon Allardyce, craning past Brodie's big shoulder to get a look.

"He's stoppit to speak to Widow Wallace. What will he be saying to *her*?"

"She's a greedy bodie that Mrs Wallace; I wouldna wonder but she's speiring him for bawbees."

"Will he take the Skeighan Road, I wonder?"

"Or the Fechars?"

"He's a great man for gathering gowans and other sic trash. He's maybe for a dander up the burn juist. They say he's a great botanical man."

"Aye," said Brodie, "paidling in a burn's the ploy for him. He's a weanly gowk."

"A-a-ah!" protested the baker who was a Burnsomaniac, "there's waur than a walk by the bank o' a bonny burn. Ye ken what Mossgiel said:

" 'The Muse nae poet ever fand her,
　　Till by himsel he learned to wander,
　　Adown some trottin burn's meander,
　　　　And no think[1] lang;
　　O sweet, to muse and pensive ponder
　　　　A heartfelt sang.' "

[1] A correction. *Thick* in other editions.

Poetical quotations however made the Provost uncomfortable. "Aye," he said drily in his throat; "verra good, baker, verra good!—Whose yellow doag's that? I never saw the beast about the town before!"

"Nor me either. It's a perfect stranger!"

"It's like a herd's doag!"

"Man you're right! That's just what it will be. The morn's Fleckie lamb fair, and some herd or other'll be in about the town."

"He'll be drinking in some public house, I'se warrant, and the doag will have lost him."

"Imph, that'll be the way o't."

"I'm demned if he hasn't taken the Skeighan Road!" said Sandy Toddle, who had kept his eye on the minister.— Toddle's accent was a varying quality. When he remembered he had been a packman in England it was exceedingly fine. But he often forgot.

"The Skeighan Road! The Skeighan Road! Who'll he be going to see in that airt? Will it be Templandmuir?"

"Gosh, it canna be Templandmuir. He was there no later than yestreen!"

"Here's a man coming down the brae!" announced Johnny Coe in a solemn voice, as if a man "coming down the brae" was something unusual. In a moment every head was turned to the hill.

"What's yon he's carrying on his shouther?" pondered Brodie.

"It looks like a boax," said the Provost, slowly, bending every effort of eye and mind to discover what it really was. He was giving his profoundest cogitations to the "boax."

"It *is* a boax! But who is it though? I canna make him out."

"Dod, I canna tell either; his head's so bent with his burden!"

At last the man, laying his "boax" on the ground, stood up to ease his spine, so that his face was visible.

"Losh, it's Jock Gilmour, the orra man at Gourlay's! What'll *he* be doing out on the street at this hour of the day? I thocht he was always busy on the premises! Will Gourlay

29

be sending him off with something to somebody? But no; that canna be. He would have sent it with the carts."

"I'll wager ye," cried Johnny Coe quickly, speaking more loudly than usual in the animation of discovery, "I'll wager ye Gourlay has quarrelled him and put him to the door!"

"Man, you're right! That'll just be it, that'll just be it! Aye; aye; faith aye; and yon'll be his kist he's carrying! Man, you're right, Mr Coe; you have just put your finger on't. We'll hear news *this* morning."

They edged forward to the middle of the road, the Provost in front, to meet Gilmour coming down.

"Ye've a heavy burden this morning, John," said the Provost graciously.

"No wonder, sir," said Gilmour with big-eyed solemnity, and set down the chest; "it's no wonder, seeing that I'm carrying my a-all."

"Aye, man, John. How's that na?"

To be the centre of interest and the object of gracious condescension was balm to the wounded feelings of Gilmour. Gourlay had lowered him, but this reception restored him to his own good opinion. He was usually called "Jock" (except by his mother, to whom, of course, he was "oor Johnny") but the best merchants in the town were addressing him as "John." It was a great occasion. Gilmour expanded in gossip beneath its influence benign.

He welcomed, too, this first and fine opportunity of venting his wrath on the Gourlays.

"Oh, I just telled Gourlay what I thocht of him, and took the door ahint me. I let him have it hot and hardy, I can tell ye. He'll no' forget *me* in a hurry"—Gilmour bawled angrily, and nodded his head significantly, and glared fiercely, to show what good cause he had given Gourlay to remember him—"he'll no forget *me* for a month of Sundays."

"Aye, man, John, what did ye say till him?"

"Na, man, what did he say to you?"

"Wath he angry, Dyohn?"

"How did the thing begin?"

"Tell us, man, John."

"What was it a-all about, John?"

30

"Was Mrs. Gourlay there?"

Bewildered by this pelt of questions Gilmour answered the last that hit his ear. "There, aye; faith, she was there. It was her was the cause o't."

"D'ye tell me that, John? Man, you surprise me. I would have thocht the thowless trauchle* hadna the smeddum† left to interfere."

"Oh, it was yon boy of hers. He's aye swaggerin' aboot, interferin' wi' folk at their wark—he follows his faither's example in that, for as the auld cock craws the young ane learns—and his mither's that daft aboot him that ye daurna give a look! He came in my road when I was sweeping out the close, and some o' the dirty jaups splashed about his shins; but was I to blame for that?—ye maun walk wide o' a whale-bone besom if ye dinna want to be splashed. Afore I kenned where I was, he up wi' a dirty washing-clout and slashed me in the face wi't! I hit him a thud in the ear—as wha wadna? Out come his mother like a fury, skirling about *her* hoose, and *her* servants, and *her* weans. 'Your servant!' says I, 'your servant! You're a nice-looking trollop to talk aboot servants,' says I."

"Did ye really, John?"

"Man, that wath bauld o' ye."

"And what did *she* say?"

"Oh, she just kept skirling! And then, to be sure, Gourlay must come out and interfere! But I telled him to his face what I thocht of *him*! 'The best Gourlay that ever dirtied leather,' says I, ''s no gaun to make dirt of me,' says I."

"Aye man, Dyohn!" lisped Deacon Allardyce, with bright and eagerly enquiring eyes. "And what did he thay to that, na? *That* wath a dig for him! I'the warrant he wath angry."

"Angry? He foamed at the mouth! But I up and says to him, 'I have had enough o' you,' says I, 'you and your Hoose wi' the Green Shutters,' says I, 'you're no fit to have a decent servant,' says I. 'Pay *me my* wages and I'll be redd o' ye,' says I. And wi' that I flang my kist on my shouther and slapped the gate ahint me."

Trauchle, a poor trollop who trails about.

†*Smeddum,* grit.

"And *did* he pay ye your wages?" Tam Wylie probed him slily, with a sideward glimmer in his eye.

"Ah, well, no; not exactly," said Gilmour drawing in. "But I'll get them right enough for a'that. He'll no get the better o' *me*." Having grounded unpleasantly on the question of the wages he thought it best to be off ere the bloom was dashed from his importance, so he shouldered his chest and went. The bodies watched him down the street.

"He's a lying brose, that," said the baker. "We a' ken what Gourlay is. He would have flung Gilmour out by the scruff o' the neck, if he had daured to set his tongue against him!"

"Faith, that's so," said Tam Wylie and Johnny Coe together.

But the others were divided between their perception of the fact and their wish to believe that Gourlay had received a thrust or two. At other times they would have been the first to scoff at Gilmour's swagger. Now their animus against Gourlay prompted them to back it up.

"Oh, I'm not so sure of tha-at, baker," cried the Provost, in the false loud voice of a man defending a position which he knows to be unsound. "I'm no so sure of that, at a-all. A-a-ah, mind ye," he drawled persuasively, "he's a hardy fallow that Gilmour. I've no doubt he gied Gourlay a good dig or two. Let us howp they will do him good."

For many reasons intimate to the Scot's character, envious scandal is rampant in petty towns such as Barbie. To go back to the beginning, the Scot, as pundits will tell you, is an individualist. His religion alone is enough to make him so. For it is a scheme of personal salvation significantly described once by the Reverend Mr Struthers of Barbie. "At the Day of Judgment, my frehnds," said Mr Struthers; "at the Day of Judgment every herring must hang by its own tail!" Self-dependence was never more luridly expressed. History, climate, social conditions, and the national beverage have all combined (the pundits go on) to make the Scot an individualist, fighting for his own hand. The better for him if it be so; from that he gets the grit that tells.

From their individualism, however, comes inevitably a

keen spirit of competition (the more so because Scotch democracy gives fine chances to compete), and from their keen spirit of competition comes, inevitably again, an envious belittlement of rivals. If a man's success offends your individuality, to say everything you can against him is a recognized weapon of the fight. It takes him down a bit. And (inversely) elevates his rival.

It is in a small place like Barbie that such malignity is most virulent, because in a small place like Barbie every man knows everything to his neighbour's detriment. He can redd up his rival's pedigree, for example, and lower his pride (if need be) by detailing the disgraces of his kin. "I have grand news the day!" a big-hearted Scot will exclaim (and when their hearts are big they are big to hypertrophy)—"I have grand news the day! Man, Jock Goudie has won the C.B." —"Jock Goudie," an envious bodie will pucker as if he had never heard the name; "Jock Goudie? Wha's *he* for a Goudie? Oh, aye, let me see now. He's a brother o'—eh, a brother o'—eh (tit-tit-titting on his brow)—oh, just a brother o' Dru'cken Will Goudie o' Auchterwheeze! Oo-ooh I ken *him* fine. His grannie keepit a sweetie-shop in Strathbungo." —There you have the "nesty" Scotsman.

Even if Gourlay had been a placable and inoffensive man, then, the malignants of the petty burgh (it was scarce bigger than a village) would have fastened on his character, simply because he was above them. No man has a keener eye for behaviour than the Scot (especially when spite wings his intuition), and Gourlay's thickness of wit, and pride of place, would in any case have drawn their sneers. So, too, on lower grounds, would his wife's sluttishness. But his repressiveness added a hundred-fold to their hate of him. That was the particular cause, which acting on their general tendency to belittle a too-successful rival, made their spite almost monstrous against him. Not a man among them but had felt the weight of his tongue—for edge it had none. He walked among them like the dirt below his feet. There was no give and take in the man; he could be verra jocose with the lairds, to be sure, but he never dropped in to the Red Lion for a crack and a dram with the town-folk; he just glowered as if he could devour them! And who was he, I should like to know? His grandfather had been noathing but a common carrier!

Hate was the greater on both sides because it was often impotent. Gourlay frequently suspected offence, and seethed because he had no idea how to meet it—except by driving slowly down the brae in his new gig and never letting on when the Provost called to him. That was a wipe in the eye for the Provost! The "bodies," on their part, could rarely get near enough Gourlay to pierce his armour; he kept them off him by his brutal dourness. For it was not only pride and arrogance, but a consciousness, also, that he was no match for them at their own game, that kept Gourlay away from their society. They were adepts at the under stroke and they would have given him many a dig if he had only come amongst them. But, oh, no; not he; he was the big man; he never gave a body a chance! Or if you did venture a bit jibe when you met him, he glowered you off the face of the earth with thae black e'en of his. Oh, how they longed to get at him! It was not the least of the evils caused by Gourlay's black pride that it perverted a dozen characters. The "bodies" of Barbie may have been decent enough men in their own way, but against him their malevolence was monstrous. It shewed itself in an insane desire to seize on every scrap of gossip they might twist against him. That was why the Provost lowered municipal dignity to gossip in the street with a discharged servant. As the baker said afterwards, it was absurd for a man in his "poseetion." But it was done with the sole desire of hearing something that might tell against Gourlay. Even Countesses, we are told, gossip with malicious maids, about other Countesses. Spite is a great leveller.

"Shall we adjourn?" said Brodie, when they had watched Jock Gilmour out of sight. He pointed across his shoulder to the Red Lion.

"Better noat just now," said the Provost, nodding in slow authority; "better noat just now! I'm very anxious to see Gourlay about yon matter we were speaking of, doan't ye understa-and? But I'm determined not to go to his house!

On the other hand if we go into the Red Lion the now, we may miss him on the street. We'll noat have loang to wait, though; he'll be down the town directly, to look at the horses he has at the gerse out the Fechars Road. But *I'm* talling ye, I simply will noat go to his house—to put up with a wheen damned insults!" he puffed in angry recollection.

"To tell the truth," said Wylie, "I don't like to call upon Gourlay, either. I'm aware of his eyes on my back when I slink beaten through his gate—and I feel that my hurdies are wanting in dignity!"

"Huh!" spluttered Brodie, "that never affects me. I come stunting out in a bleeze of wrath and slam the yett ahint me!"

"Oh, well," said the Deacon, "that'th one way of being dignified."

"I'm afraid," said Sandy Toddle, "that he won't be in a very good key to consider our request this morning, after his quarrel with Gilmour."

"No," said the Provost, "he'll be blazing angry! It's most unfoartunate. But we maun try to get his consent be his temper what it will. It's a matter of importance to the town, doan't ye see, and if he refuses, we simply can-noat proceed wi' the improvement."

"It was Gilmour's jibe at the House wi' the Green Shutters that would anger him the most—for it's the perfect god of his idolatry. Eh, sirs, he has wasted an awful money upon yon house!"

"Wasted's the word!" said Brodie with a blatant laugh. "Wasted's the word! They say he has verra little lying cash! And I shouldna be surprised at all. For, ye see, Gibson the builder diddled him owre the building o't."

"Oh, I'se warrant Cunning Johnny would get the better of an ass like Gourlay. But how in particular, Mr Brodie? Have ye heard ainy details?"

"I've been on the track o' the thing for a while back, but it was only yestreen I had the proofs o't. It was Robin Wabster that told me. He's a jouking bodie, Robin, and he was ahint a dyke up the Skeighan Road when Gibson and Gourlay foregathered—they stoppit just forenenst him! Gourlay began to curse at the size of Gibson's bill, but Cunning

Johnny kenned the way to get round him brawly. 'Mr Gourlay,' says he, 'there's not a thing in your house that a man in your poseetion can afford to be without—and ye needn't expect the best house in Barbie for an oald song!' And Gourlay was pacified at once! It appeared frae their crack, however, that Gibson has diddled him tremendous. 'Verra well then,' Robin heard Gourlay cry, 'you must allow me a while ere I pay that!' I wager, for a' sae muckle as he's made of late, that his balance at the bank's a sma' yin."

"More thyow than thubstanth," said the Deacon.

"Well, I'm sure!" said the Provost, "he needn't have built such a gra-and house to put a slut of a wife like yon in!"

"I was surprised," said Sandy Toddle, "to hear about her firing up. I wouldn't have thought she had the spirit, or that Gourlay would have come to her support!"

"Oh," said the Provost, "it wasn't her he was thinking of! It was his own pride, the brute. He leads the woman the life of a doag. I'm surprised that he ever married her!"

"I ken fine how he married her," said Johnny Coe. "I was acquaint wi' her faither, auld Tenshillingland owre at Fechars —a grand farmer he was, wi' land o' his nain, and a gey pickle bawbees. It was the bawbees, and not the woman, that Gourlay went after! It was *her* money, as ye ken, that set him on his feet, and made him such a big man. He never cared a preen for *her*, and then when she proved a dirty trollop, he couldna endure her look! That's what makes him so sore upon her now. And yet I mind her a braw lass, too," said Johnny the sentimentalist, "a braw lass she was," he mused, "wi' fine, brown glossy hair, I mind, and,—ochonee! ochonee!—as daft as a yett in a windy day. She had a cousin, Jenny Wabster, that dwelt in Tenshillingland than, and mony a summer nicht up the Fechars Road, when ye smelled the honey-suckle in the gloaming, I have heard the two o' them tee-heeing owre the lads thegither, skirling in the dark and lauching to themselves. They were of the glaikit kind ye can always hear loang before ye see. Jock Allan (that has done so well in Embro) was a herd at Tenshillingland than, and he likit her, and I think she likit him, but Gourlay came wi' his gig and whisked her away. She doesna lauch sae muckle now,

36

puir bodie! But a braw lass she—"

"It's you maun speak to Gourlay, Deacon," said the Provost, brushing aside the reminiscent Coe.

"How can it be that, Provost? It'th *your* place, surely. You're the head of the town!"

When Gourlay was to be approached there was always a competition for who should be hindmost.

"Yass, but you know perfectly well, Deacon, that I cannot thole the look of him. I simply cannot thole the look! And he knows it too. The thing'll gang smash at the outset—*I'm* talling ye, now—it'll go smash at the outset if it's left to me.— And than, ye see, you have a better way of approaching folk!"

"Ith that tho?" said the Deacon drily. He shot a suspicious glance to see if the Provost was guying him.

"Oh, it must be left to you, Deacon," said the baker and Tam Wylie in a breath.

"Certainly, it maun be left to the Deacon," assented Johnny Coe, when he saw how the others were giving their opinion.

"Tho be it, then," snapped the Deacon.

"Here he comes," said Sandy Toddle.

Gourlay came down the street towards them, his chest big, his thumbs in the armholes of his waistcoat. He had the power of staring steadily at those whom he approached without the slightest sign of recognition or intelligence appearing in his eyes. As he marched down upon the bodies he fixed them with a wide-open glower that was devoid of every expression but courageous steadiness. It gave a kind of fierce vacancy to his look.

The Deacon limped forward on his thin shanks to the middle of the road.

"It'th a fine morning, Mr Gourlay," he simpered.

"There's noathing wrong with the morning," grunted Gourlay, as if there was something wrong with the Deacon.

"We wath wanting to thee ye on a very important matter, Mithter Gourlay," lisped the Deacon, smiling up at the big man's face, with his head on one side, and rubbing his fingers in front of him. "It'th a matter of the common good, you thee; and we all agreed that we should speak to *you*, ath the foremost merchant of the town!"

Allardyce meant his compliment to fetch Gourlay. But Gourlay knew his Allardyce and was cautious. It was well to be on your guard when the Deacon was complimentary. When his language was most flowery there was sure to be a serpent hidden in it somewhere. He would lisp out an innocent remark and toddle away, and Gourlay would think nothing of the matter till a week afterwards, perhaps, when something would flash a light—then "Damn him, did he mean '*that*'?" he would seethe, starting back and staring at the '*that*' while his fingers strangled the air in place of the Deacon.

He glowered at the Deacon now till the Deacon blinked.

"You thee, Mr Gourlay," Allardyce shuffled uneasily, "it's for your own benefit just ath much ath ourth. We were thinking of you ath well ath of ourthelves! Oh, yeth, oh, yeth!"

"Aye , man!" said Gourlay, "that was kind of ye! I'll be the first man in Barbie to get ainy benefit from the fools that mismanage our affairs."

The gravel grated beneath the Provost's foot. The atmosphere was becoming electric, and the Deacon hastened to the point.

"You thee, there'th a fine natural supply of water—a perfect reservore the Provost sayth—on the brae-face just above *your* garden, Mr Gourlay. Now, it would be easy to lead that water down and alang through all the gardenth on the high side of Main Street—and, 'deed, it might feed a pump at the Cross, too, to supply the lower portionth o' the town. It would really be a grai-ait convenience—Every man on the high side o' Main Street would have a running spout at his own back door! If your garden didna run tho far back, Mr Gourlay, and ye hadna tho muckle land about your place"—*that* should fetch him, thought the Deacon!—"if it werena for that, Mr Gourlay, we could easily lead the water round to the other gardenth without interfering with your property. But, ath it ith, we simply can-noat move without ye. The water must come through your garden, if it comes at

38

a-all."

"The most o' you important men live on the high side o' Main Street," birred Gourlay. "Is it the poor folk at the Cross, or your ain bits o' back doors that you're thinking o'?"

"Oh—oh, Mr Gourlay!" protested Allardyce, head flung back and palms in air, to keep the thought of self-interest away, "oh—oh, Mr Gourlay! We're thinking of noathing but the common good, I do assure ye."

"Aye, man! You're dis-in-ter-ested!" said Gourlay, but he stumbled on the big word and spoiled the sneer. That angered him, and, "it's likely," he rapped out, "that I'll allow the land round *my* house to be howked and trenched and made a mudhole of, to oblige a wheen things like you!"

"Oh—oh, but think of the convenience to uth—eh—eh—I mean to the common good," said Allardyce.

"I howked wells for myself," snapped Gourlay. "Let others do the like."

"Oh, but we haven't all the enterprithe of you, Mr Gourlay. You'll surely accommodate the town!"

"I'll see the town damned first," said Gourlay, and passed on his steady way.

CHAPTER 6

THE bodies watched Gourlay in silence until he was out of ear-shot. Then, "It's monstrous!" the Provost broke out in solemn anger; "I declare it's perfectly monstrous! But I believe we could get Pow-ers to compel him. Yass; I believe we could get Pow-ers. I do believe we could get Pow-ers."

The Provost was fond of talking about "Pow-ers" because it implied that he was intimate with the great authorities who might delegate such "Pow-ers" to him. To talk of "Pow-ers," mysteriously, was a tribute to his own importance. He rolled the word on his tongue as if he enjoyed the sound of it.

On the Deacon's cheek bones two red spots flamed, round and big as a Scotch penny. His was the hurt silence of the baffled diplomatist, to whom a defeat means reflections on his own ability.

"Demn him!" he skirled, following the solid march of his enemy with fiery eyes.

Never before had his Deaconship been heard to swear. Tam Wylie laughed at the shrill oath till his eyes were buried in his merry wrinkles, a suppressed snirt, a continuous gurgle in the throat and nose, in beaming survey the while of the withered old creature dancing in his rage. (It was all a good joke to Tam, because, living on the outskirts of the town, he had no spigot of his own to feed.) The Deacon turned the eyes of hate on him. Demn Wylie too!—what was he laughing at!

"Oh, I darethay you could have got round him!" he snapped.

"In my opinion, Allardyce," said the baker, "you mismanaged the whole affair. Yon wasna the way to approach him!"

"It'th a pity you didna try your hand, then, I'm sure! No doubt a clever man like *you* would have worked wonderth!"

So the bodies wrangled among themselves. Somehow or

other Gourlay had the knack of setting them by the ears. It was not till they hit on a common topic of their spite in railing at him, that they became a band of brothers and a happy few.

"Whisht!" said Sandy Toddle, suddenly, "here's his boy!"

John was coming towards them on his way to school. The bodies watched him as he passed, with the fixed look men turn on a boy of whose kinsmen they were talking even now. They affect a stony and deliberate regard, partly to include the new-comer in their critical survey of his family, and partly to banish from their own eyes any sign that they have just been running down his people. John, as quick as his mother to feel, knew in a moment they were watching *him*. He hung his head sheepishly and blushed, and the moment he was past he broke into a nervous trot, the bag of books bumping on his back as he ran.

"He's getting a big boy, that son of Gourlay's," said the Provost, "how oald will he be?"

"He's approaching twelve," said Johnny Coe, who made a point of being able to supply such news because it gained him consideration where he was otherwise unheeded. "He was born the day the brig on the Fleckie Road gaed down, in the year o' the great flood; and since the great flood it's twelve year come Lammas. Rab Tosh o' Fleckie's wife was heavy-footed at the time, and Doctor Munn had been a' nicht wi' her, and when he cam to Barbie Water in the morning it was roaring wide frae bank to brae; where the brig should have been there was naething but the swashing of the yellow waves. Munn had to drive a' the way round to the Fechars brig, and in parts o' the road the water was so deep that it lapped his horse's bellyband. A' this time Mrs Gourlay was skirling in her pains and praying to God she micht dee. Gourlay had been a great crony o' Munn's, but he quarrelled him for being late; he had trysted him, ye see, for the occasion, and he had been twenty times at the yett to look for him,—ye ken how little he would stomach that; he was ready to brust wi' anger. Munn, mad for the want of sleep and wat to the bane, swüre back at him; and than Gourlay wadna let him near his wife! Ye mind what an

41

awful day it was; the thunder roared as if the heavens were tumbling on the world, and the lichtnin sent the trees daudin on the roads, and folk hid below their beds and prayed—they thocht it was the Judgment! But Gourlay rammed his black stepper in the shafts, and drave like the devil o' hell to Skeighan Drone, where there was a young doctor. The lad was feared to come, but Gourlay swore by God that he should, and he garred him. In a' the countryside driving like his that day was never kenned or heard tell o'; they were back within the hour! I saw them gallop up Main Street; lichtnin struck the ground before them; the young doctor covered his face wi' his hands, and the horse nichered wi' fear and tried to wheel, but Gourlay stood up in the gig and lashed him on through the fire. It was thocht for lang that Mrs Gourlay would die; and she was never the same woman after. Atweel aye sirs, Gourlay has that morning's work to blame for the poor wife he has now. Him and Munn never spoke to each other again, and Munn died within the twelvemonth,—he got his death that morning on the Fleckie Road. But, for a' so pack's they had been, Gourlay never looked near him."

Coe had told his story with enjoying gusto, and had told it well—for Johnny, though constantly snubbed by his fellows, was in many ways the ablest of them all. His voice and manner drove it home. They knew, besides, he was telling what himself had seen. For they knew he was lying prostrate with fear in the open smiddyshed from the time Gourlay went to Skeighan Drone to the time that he came back; and that he had seen him both come and go. They were silent for a while, impressed, in spite of themselves, by the vivid presentment of Gourlay's manhood on the day that had scared them all. The baker felt inclined to cry out on his cruelty for keeping his wife suffering to gratify his wrath; but the sudden picture of the man's courage changed that feeling to another of admiring awe; a man so defiant of the angry heavens might do anything. And so with the others; they hated Gourlay, but his bravery was a fact of nature which they could not disregard; they knew themselves smaller and said nothing for a while. Tam Brodie, the most brutal among them, was the first to recover. Even he did not try to belittle at once, but he felt the subtle discomfort of the situation, and relieved it by bringing the conversation back to its usual channel.

"That was at the boy's birth, Mr Coe?" said he.

"Ou, aye, just the laddie. It was a' richt when the lassie came. It was Doctor Dandy brought *her* hame, for Munn was deid by that time, and Dandy had his place."

"What will Gourlay be going to make of him?" the Provost asked. "A doctor or a minister or wha-at?"

"Deil a fear of that," said Brodie; "he'll take him into the business! It's a' that he's fit for. He's an infernal dunce, just his father owre again, and the Dominie thrashes him remorseless! I hear my own weans speaking o't. Ou, it seems he's just a perfect numbskull!"

"Ye couldn't expect ainything else from a son of Gourlay," said the Provost.

Conversation languished. Some fillip was needed to bring it to an easy flow, and the simultaneous scrape of their feet turning round shewed the direction of their thoughts.

"A dram would be very acceptable now," murmured Sandy Toddle, rubbing his chin.

"Ou, we wouldna be the waur o't," said Tam Wylie.

"We would all be the better of a little drope," smirked the Deacon.

And they made for the Red Lion for the matutinal dram.

CHAPTER 7

JOHN GOURLAY, the younger, was late for school, in spite of the nervous trot he fell into when he shrank from the bodies' hard stare at him. There was nothing unusual about that; he was late for school every other day. To him it was a howling wilderness where he played a most appropriate rôle. If his father was not about he would hang round his mother till the last moment, rather than be off to old "Bleach-the-boys"—as the master had been christened by his scholars. "Mother, I have a pain in *my* heid," he would whimper, and she would condole with him and tell him she would keep him at home with her—were it not for dread of her husband. She was quite sure he was ainything but strong, poor boy, and that the schooling was bad for him; for it was really remarkable how quickly the pain went if he was allowed to stay at home; why, he got better just directly! It was not often she dared to keep him from school, however, and if she did, she had to hide him from his father.

On school mornings the boy shrank from going out with a shrinking that was almost physical. When he stole through the Green Gate with his bag slithering at his hip (not braced between the shoulders like a birkie scholar's) he used to feel ruefully that he was in for it now—and the Lord alone knew what he would have to put up with ere he came home! And he always had the feeling of a freed slave when he passed the gate on his return, never failing to note with delight the clean smell of the yard after the stuffiness of school, sucking it in through glad nostrils, and thinking to himself, "Oh, crickey, it's fine to be home!" On Friday nights, in particular, he used to feel so happy that, becoming arrogant, he would try his hand at bullying Jock Gilmour in imitation of his father. John's dislike of school, and fear of its trampling bra-voes, attached him peculiarly to the House with the Green Shutters; there was his doting mother, and she gave him stories to read, and the place was so big that it was easy to avoid his father and have great times with the rabbits and the doos. He was as proud of the sonsy house as Gourlay himself, if for a different reason, and he used to boast of it to his comrades. And he never left it, then or after, without a foreboding.

As he crept along the School Road with a rueful face, he was alone, for Janet, who was cleverer than he, was always earlier at school. The absence of children in the sunny street lent to his depression. He felt forlorn; if there had been a chattering crowd marching along, he would have been much more at his ease.

Quite recently the school had been fitted up with varnished desks, and John, who inherited his mother's nervous senses with his father's lack of wit, was always intensely alive to the smell of the desks the moment he went in; and as his heart always sank when he went in, the smell became associated in his mind with that sinking of the heart—to feel it, no matter where, filled him with uneasiness. As he stole past the joiner's on that sunny morning, when wood was resinous and pungent of odour, he was suddenly conscious of a varnishy smell, and felt a misgiving without knowing why. It was years after, in Edinburgh, ere he knew the reason; he found that he never went past an upholsterer's shop, on a hot day in spring, without being conscious of a vague depression, and feeling like a boy slinking into school.

In spite of his forebodings nothing more untoward befell him that morning than a cut over the cowering shoulders for being late, as he crept to the bottom of his class. He reached "leave", the ten minutes' run at twelve o'clock, without misadventure. Perhaps it was this unwonted good fortune that made him boastful, when he crouched near the pump among his cronies, sitting on his hunkers with his back to the wall. Half a dozen boys were about him, and Swipey Broon was in front, making mud pellets in a trickle from the pump.

He began talking of the new range.

"Yah! Auld Gemmell needn't have let welp at *me* for being late this morning," he spluttered big-eyed, nodding his head in aggrieved and solemn protest. "It wasna *my*

45

faut! We're getting in a grand new range, and the whole of
the kitchen fireplace has been gutted out to make room for't,
and my mother couldna get my breakfast in time this morning, because, ye see, she had to boil everything in the parlour
—and here, when she gaed ben the house, the parlour fire
was out!"

"It's to be a splendid range, the new one," he went on,
with a conceited jerk of the head. "Peter Riney's bringin't
from Skeighan in the afternune. My father says there winna
be its equal in the parish!"

The faces of the boys lowered uncomfortably. They felt it
was a silly thing of Gourlay to blow his own trumpet in this
way, but, being boys, they could not prick his conceit with
a quick rejoinder. It is only grown-ups who can be ironical;
physical violence is the boy's repartee. It had scarcely gone
far enough for that yet, so they lowered in uncomfortable
silence.

"We're aye getting new things up at our place," he went
on. "I heard my father telling Gibson the builder he must
have everything of the best! Mother says it'll all be mine
some day. I'll have the fine times when I leave the schule,—
and that winna be long now, for I'm clean sick o't; I'll no
bide a day longer than I need! I'm to go into the business,
and then I'll have the times; I'll dash about the country in a
gig wi' two dogs walloping ahin'. I'll have the great life o't."

"Ph-tt!" said Swipey Broon, and planted a gob of mud
right in the middle of his brow.

"Hoh! hoh! hoh!" yelled the others. They hailed Swipey's
action with delight because, to their minds, it exactly met the
case. It was the one fit retort to his bouncing.

Beneath the wet plunk of the mud John started back,
bumping his head against the wall behind him. The sticky
pellet clung to his brow, and he brushed it angrily aside. The
laughter of the others added to his wrath against Swipey.

"What are you after?" he bawled. "Don't try your tricks
on me, Swipey Broon. Man, I could kill ye wi' a glower!"

In a twinkling Swipey's jacket was off and he was dancing
in his shirt sleeves, inviting Gourlay to come on and try't.

"G'way, man," said John, his face as white as the wall;

"g'way, man! Don't have *me* getting up to ye, or I'll knock the fleas out of your duds!"

Now the father of Swipey—so called because he always swiped when batting at rounders—the father of Swipey was the rag and bone merchant of Barbie, and it was said (with what degree of truth I know not) that his home was verminous in consequence. John's taunt was calculated, therefore, to sting him to the quick.

The scion of the Broons, fired for the honour of his house, drove straight at the mouth of the insulter. But John jouked to the side, and Swipey skinned his knuckles on the wall.

For a moment he rocked to and fro, doubled up in pain, crying "*Ooh!*" with a rueful face, and squeezing his hand between his thighs to dull its sharper agonies. Then, with redoubled wrath bold Swipey hurled him at the foe. He grabbed Gourlay's head and, shoving it down between his knees, proceeded to pummel his bent back, while John bellowed angrily (from between Swipey's legs), "Let me up, see!"

Swipey let him up. John came at him with whirling arms, but Swipey jouked and gave him one on the mouth that split his lip. In another moment Gourlay was grovelling on his hands and knees, and triumphant Swipey, astride his back, was bellowing "Hurroo!"—Swipey's father was an Irishman.

"Let him up, Broon!" cried Peter Wylie. "Let him up, and meet each other square!"

"Oh, I'll let him up," cried Swipey and leapt to his feet with magnificent pride. He danced round Gourlay with his fists sawing the air. "I could fight ten of him! Come on, Gourlay!" he cried, "and I'll poultice the road wi' your brose."

John rose, glaring. But when Swipey rushed he turned and fled. The boys ran into the middle of the street, pointing after the coward and shouting, "Yeh! Yeh! Yeh!" with the infinite cruel derision of boyhood.

"Yeh! Yeh! Yeh!" the cries of execration and contempt pursued him as he ran.

Ere he had gone a hundred yards he heard the shrill

whistle with which Mr Gemmell summoned his scholars
from their play.

CHAPTER 8

ALL the children had gone into school. The street was lonely in the sudden stillness. The joiner slanted across the road, brushing shavings and sawdust from his white apron. There was no other sign of life in the sunshine. Only from the smiddy, far away, came at times the tink of an anvil.

John crept on up the street, keeping close to the wall. It seemed unnatural being there at that hour; everything had a quiet unfamiliar look. The white walls of the houses reproached the truant with their silent faces.

A strong smell of wallflowers oozed through the hot air. John thought it a lonely smell and ran to get away.

"Johnny dear, what's wrong wi' ye?" cried his mother, when he stole in through the scullery at last. "Are ye ill, dear?"

"I wanted to come hame," he said. It was no defence; it was the sad and simple expression of his wish.

"What for, my sweet?"

"I hate the school," he said, bitterly; "I aye want to be at hame."

His mother saw his cut mouth.

"Johnny," she cried in concern, "what's the matter with your lip, dear? Has ainybody been meddling ye?"

"It was Swipey Broon," he said.

"Did ever a body hear?" she cried. "Things have come to a fine pass when decent weans canna go to the school without a wheen rag-folk yoking on them! But what can a body ettle? Scotland's not what it used to be! It's owrerun wi' the dirty Eerish!"

In her anger she did not see the sloppy dishclout on the scullery chair, on which she sank exhausted by her rage.

"Oh, but I let him have it," swaggered John. "I threatened to knock the fleas off him. The other boys were on *his* side, or I would have walloped him."

49

"Atweel, they would a' be on his side," she cried. "But it's juist envy, Johnny. Never mind, dear; you'll soon be left the school, and there's not wan of them has the business that you have waiting ready to step intil."

"Mother," he pleaded, "let me bide here for the rest o' the day!"

"Oh, but your father, Johnny? If *he* saw ye?"

"If you gie me some o' your novelles to look at, I'll go up to the garret and hide, and ye can ask Jenny no to tell."

She gave him a hunk of nuncheon and a bundle of her novelettes, and he stole up to an empty garret and squatted on the bare boards. The sun streamed through the skylight window and lay, an oblong patch, in the centre of the floor. John noted the head of a nail that stuck gleaming up. He could hear the pigeons *rooketty-cooing* on the roof, and every now and then a slithering sound, as they lost their footing on the slates and went sliding downward to the rones. But for that, all was still, uncannily still. Once a zinc pail clanked in the yard, and he started with fear, wondering if that was his faither!

If young Gourlay had been the right kind of a boy he would have been in his glory, with books to read and a garret to read them in. For to snuggle close beneath the slates is as dear to the boy as the bard, if somewhat diverse their reasons for seclusion. Your garret is the true kingdom of the poet, neighbouring the stars; side-windows tether him to earth, but a skylight looks to the heavens. (That is why so many poets live in garrets, no doubt.) But it is the secrecy of a garret for him and his books that a boy loves; there he is lord of his imagination; there, when the impertinent world is hidden from his view, he rides with great Turpin at night beneath the glimmer of the moon. What boy of sense would read about Turpin in a mere respectable parlour? A hayloft's the thing, where you can hide in a dusty corner, and watch through a chink the baffled minions of Bow Street, and hear Black Bess—good jade!—stamping in her secret stall, and be ready to descend when a friendly ostler cries, "Jericho!" But if there is no hayloft at hand a mere garret will do very well. And so John should have been in his glory,—as indeed for a

50

while he was. But he shewed his difference from the right kind of a boy by becoming lonely. He had inherited from his mother a silly kind of interest in silly books, but to him reading was a painful process, and he could never remember the plot. What he liked best (though he could not have told you about it) was a vivid physical picture. When the puffing steam of Black Bess's nostrils cleared away from the moonlit pool, and the white face of the dead man stared at Turpin through the water, John saw it and shivered, staring big-eyed at the staring horror. He was alive to it all; he heard the seep of the water through the mare's lips, and its hollow glug as it went down, and the creak of the saddle beneath Turpin's hip; he saw the smear of sweat roughening the hair on her slanting neck, and the great steaming breath she blew out when she rested from drinking, and then that awful face glaring from the pool.—Perhaps he was not so far from being the right kind of boy, after all, since that was the stuff that *he* liked.—He wished he had some Turpin with him now, for his mother's periodicals were all about men with impossibly broad shoulders and impossibly curved waists who asked Angelina if she loved them. Once, it is true, a somewhat too florid sentence touched him on the visual nerve: "Through a chink in the Venetian blind a long pencil of yellow light pierced the beautiful dimness of the room and pointed straight to the dainty bronze slipper peeping from under Angelina's gown; it became a slipper of vivid gold amid the gloom." John saw that and brightened, but the next moment they began to talk about love and he was at sea immediately. "Dagon them and their love!" quoth he.

To him, indeed, reading was never more than a means of escape from something else; he never thought of a book so long as there were things to see. Some things were different from others, it is true. Things of the outer world, where he swaggered among his fellows and was thrashed, or bungled his lessons and was thrashed again, imprinted themselves vividly on his mind, and he hated the impressions. When Swipey Broon was hot the sweat pores always glistened distinctly on the end of his mottled nose—John, as he thought angrily of Swipey this afternoon, saw the glistening sweat pores before him and wanted to bash them. The varnishy smell of the desks, the smell of the wallflowers at Mrs Manzie's on the way to school, the smell of the school itself—to all these he was morbidly alive, and he loathed them. But he loved the impressions of his home. His mind was full of perceptions of which he was unconscious, till he found one of them recorded in a book, and that was the book for him. The curious physical always drew his mind to hate it or to love. In summer he would crawl into the bottom of an old hedge, among the black mould and the withered sticks, and watch a red-ended beetle creep slowly up a bit of wood till near the top, and fall suddenly down, and creep patiently again,—this he would watch with curious interest and remember always. "Johnny," said his mother once, "what do you breenge into the bushes to watch those nasty things for?"

"They're queer," he said musingly.

Even if he *was* a little dull wi' the book, she was sure he would come to something, for, eh, he was such a noticing boy.

But there was nothing to touch him in "The Wooing of Angeline"; he was moving in an alien world. It was a complicated plot, and, some of the numbers being lost, he was not sharp enough to catch the idea of the story. He read slowly and without interest. The sounds of the outer world reached him in his loneliness and annoyed him, because, while wondering what they were, he dared not look out to see. He heard the rattle of wheels entering the big yard; that would be Peter Riney back from Skeighan with the range. Once he heard the birr of his father's voice in the lobby and his mother speaking in shrill protest, and then—oh, horror!— his father came up the stair. Would he come into the garret? John, lying on his left side, felt his quickened heart thud against the boards, and he could not take his big frighted eyes from the bottom of the door. But the heavy step passed and went into another room. John's open mouth was dry, and his shirt was sticking to his back.

The heavy steps came back to the landing.

"Whaur's *my* gimlet?" yelled his father down the stair.

"Oh, I lost the corkscrew, and took it to open a bottle," cried his mother wearily. "Here it is, man, in the kitchen drawer."

"*Hah!*" his father barked, and he knew he was infernal angry. If he should come in!

But he went tramping down the stair, and John, after waiting till his pulses were stilled, resumed his reading. He heard the masons in the kitchen, busy with the range, and he would have liked fine to watch them, but he dared not go down till after four. It was lonely up here by himself. A hot wind had sprung up, and it crooned through the keyhole drearily; "*oo-woo-oo*," it cried, and the sound drenched him in a vague depression. The splotch of yellow light had shifted round to the fireplace; Janet had kindled a fire there last winter, and the ashes had never been removed, and now the light lay, yellow and vivid, on a red clinker of coal, and a charred piece of stick. A piece of glossy white paper had been flung in the untidy grate, and in the hollow curve of it a thin silt of black dust had gathered—the light shewed it plainly. All these things the boy marked and was subtly aware of their unpleasantness. He was forced to read to escape the sense of them. But it was words, words, words that he read; the substance mattered not at all. His head leaned heavy on his left hand and his mouth hung open, as his eye travelled dreamily along the lines. He succeeded in hypnotizing his brain at last, by the mere process of staring at the page.

At last he heard Janet in the lobby. That meant that school was over. He crept down the stair.

"*You* were playing the truant," said Janet, and she nodded her head in accusation. "I've a good mind to tell my faither."

"If ye wud—" he said, and shook his fist at her threateningly. She shrank away from him. They went into the kitchen together.

The range had been successfully installed, and Mr Gourlay was shewing it to Grant of Loranogie, the foremost farmer of the shire. Mrs Gourlay, standing by the kitchen table, viewed her new possession with a faded simper of approval. She was pleased that Mr Grant should see the grand new thing that they had gotten. She listened to the talk of the men with a faint smile about her weary lips, her eyes upon the sonsy range.

"Dod, it's a handsome piece of furniture," said Loranogie. "How did ye get it brought here, Mr Gourlay?"

"I went to Glasgow and ordered it special. It came to Skeighan by the train, and my own beasts brought it owre. That fender's a feature," he added, complacently; "it's onusual wi' a range."

The massive fender ran from end to end of the fireplace, projecting a little in front; its rim, a square bar of heavy steel, with bright sharp edges.

"And that poker, too; man, there's a history wi' that. I made a point o' the making o't. He was an ill-bred little whalp, the bodie in Glasgow. I happened to say till um I would like a poker-heid just the same size as the rim of the fender! 'What d'ye want wi' a heavy-heided poker?' says he, 'a' ye need's a bit sma' thing to rype the ribs wi'.' 'Is that so?' says I. 'How do *you* ken what *I* want?' I made short work o' *him*! The poker-heid's the identical size o' the rim; I had it made to fit!"

Loranogie thought it a silly thing of Gourlay to concern himself about a poker. But that was just like him, of course. The moment the body in Glasgow opposed his whim, Gourlay, he knew, would make a point o't.

The grain merchant took the bar of heavy metal in his hand. "Dod, it's an awful weapon," he said, meaning to be jocose. "You could murder a man wi't."

"Deed you could," said Loranogie; "you could kill him wi' the one lick."

The elders, engaged with more important matters, paid no attention to the children, who had pushed between them to the front and were looking up at their faces, as they talked, with curious watching eyes. John, with his instinct to notice things, took the poker up when his father laid it down, to see if it was really the size of the rim. It was too heavy for him to raise by the handle; he had to lift it by the middle. Janet was at his elbow, watching him. "You could kill a man with that," he told her, importantly, though she had heard it for herself. Janet stared and shuddered. Then the boy laid the poker-head along the rim, fitting edge to edge with a nice precision.

"Mother," he cried, turning towards her in his interest, "Mother, look here! It's exactly the same size!"

"Put it down, sir," said his father with a grim smile at Loranogie. "You'll be killing folk next."

55

CHAPTER 9

"Are ye packit, Peter?" said Gourlay.

"Yes, sir," said Peter Riney, running round to the other side of a cart, to fasten a horse's bellyband to the shaft. "Yes, sir, we're a' ready."

"Have the carriers a big load?"

"Andy has just a wheen parcels, but Elshie's as fu' as he can haud. And there's a gey pickle stuff waiting at the Cross."

The hot wind of yesterday had brought lightning through the night, and this morning there was the gentle drizzle that sometimes follows a heavy thunderstorm. Hints of the further blue shewed themselves in a lofty sky of delicate and drifting grey. The blackbirds and thrushes welcomed the cooler air with a gush of musical piping, as if the liquid tenderness of the morning had actually got into their throats and made them softer.

"You had better snoove away then," said Gourlay. "Donnerton's five mile ayont Fleckie, and by the time you deliver the meal there, and load the ironwork, it'll be late ere you get back. Snoove away, Peter; snoove away!"

Peter shuffled uneasily, and his pale blue eyes blinked at Gourlay from beneath their grizzled crow nests of red hair.

"Are we a' to start thegither, sir?" he hesitated. "D'ye mean—d'ye mean the carriers, too?"

"Atweel, Peter!" said Gourlay. "What for no?"

Peter took a great old watch, with a yellow case, from his fob, and, "It wants a while o' aicht, sir," he volunteered.

"Aye, man, Peter, and what of that?" said Gourlay.

There was almost a twinkle in his eye. Peter Riney was the only human being with whom he was ever really at his ease. It is only when a mind feels secure in itself that it can laugh unconcernedly at others. Peter was so simple that in his presence Gourlay felt secure; and he used to banter him.

"The folk at the Cross winna expect the carriers till aicht, sir," said Peter, "and I doubt their stuff won't be ready."

"Aye, man, Peter!" Gourlay joked lazily, as if Peter was a little boy. "Aye, man, Peter! You think the folk at the Cross winna be prepared?"

"No, sir," said Peter, opening his eyes very solemnly, "they winna be prepared."

"It'll do them good to hurry a little for once," growled Gourlay, humour yielding to spite at the thought of his enemies. "It'll do them good to hurry a little for once! Be off, the lot of ye!"

After ordering his carriers to start, to back down and postpone their departure, just to suit the convenience of his neighbours, would derogate from his own importance. His men might think he was afraid of Barbie.

He strolled out to the big gate and watched his teams going down the brae.

There were only four carts this morning because the two that had gone to Fechars yesterday with the cheese would not be back till the afternoon; and another had already turned west to Auchterwheeze, to bring slates for the flesher's new house. Of the four that went down the street two were the usual carrier's carts, the other two were off to Fleckie with meal, and Gourlay had started them the sooner since they were to bring back the ironwork which Templandmuir needed for his new improvements. Though the Templar had reformed greatly since he married his birkie wife, he was still far from having his place in proper order, and he had often to depend on Gourlay for the carrying of stuff which a man in his position should have had horses of his own to bring.

As Gourlay stood at his gate he pondered with heavy cunning how much he might charge Templandmuir for bringing the ironwork from Fleckie. He decided to charge him for the whole day, though half of it would be spent in taking his own meal to Donnerton. In that he was carrying out his usual policy—which was to make each side of his business help the other.

As he stood puzzling his wits over Templandmuir's

account, his lips worked in and out, to assist the slow process of his brain. His eyes narrowed between peering lids, and their light seemed to turn inward as he fixed them abstractedly on a stone in the middle of the road. His head was tilted that he might keep his eyes upon the stone; and every now and then, as he mused, he rubbed his chin slowly between the thumb and fingers of his left hand. Entirely given up to the thought of Templandmuir's account he failed to see the figure advancing up the street.

At last the scrunch of a boot on the wet road struck his ear. He turned with his best glower on the man who was approaching; more of the "Wha-the-bleezes-are-you?" look than ever in his eyes—because he had been caught unawares.

The stranger wore a light yellow overcoat, and he had been walking a long time in the rain, apparently, for the shoulders of the coat were quite black with the wet, these black patches showing in strong contrast with the dryer, therefore, yellower, front of it. Coat and jacket were both hanging slightly open, and between was seen the slight bulge of a dirty white waistcoat. The newcomer's trousers were turned high at the bottom, and the muddy spats he wore looked big and ungainly in consequence. In his appearance there was an air of dirty and pretentious well-to-do-ness. It was not shabby gentility. It was like the gross attempt at dress of your well-to-do publican who looks down on his soiled white waistcoat with complacent and approving eye.

"It's a fine morning, Mr Gourlay!" simpered the stranger. His air was that of a forward tenant who thinks it a great thing to pass remarks on the weather with his laird.

Gourlay cast a look at the dropping heavens.

"Is that *your* opinion?" said he. "I fail to see't mysell."

It was not in Gourlay to see the beauty of that grey wet dawn. A fine morning to him was one that burnt the back of your neck.

The stranger laughed; a little deprecating giggle. "I meant it was fine weather for the fields," he explained. He had meant nothing of the kind, of course; he had merely been talking at random in his wish to be civil to that important man, John Gourlay.

58

"Imphm," he pondered, looking round on the weather with a wise air; "Imphm; it's fine weather for the fields!"

"Are *you* a farmer then?" Gourlay nipped him, with his eye on the white waistcoat.

"Oh—oh, Mr Gourlay! A farmer, no. Hi—hi! I'm not a farmer. I daresay, now, you have no mind of *me*!"

"No," said Gourlay, regarding him very gravely and steadily with his dark eyes. "I cannot say, sir, that I have the pleasure of remembering *you*!"

"Man, I'm a son of auld John Wilson of Brigabee!"

"Oh, auld Wilson, the mole-catcher!" said contemptuous Gourlay. "What's this they christened him now? 'Toddling Johnnie,' was it noat?"

Wilson coloured. But he sniggered to gloss over the awkwardness of the remark. A coward always sniggers when insulted, pretending that the insult is only a joke of his opponent, and therefore to be laughed aside. So he escapes the quarrel which he fears a show of displeasure might provoke.

But, though Wilson was not a hardy man, it was not timidity only that caused his tame submission to Gourlay.

He had come back after an absence of fifteen years, with a good deal of money in his pocket, and he had a fond desire that he, the son of the mole-catcher, should get some recognition of his prosperity from the most important man in the locality. If Gourlay had said, with solemn and fat-lipped approval, "Man, I'm glad to see that you have done so well!" he would have swelled with gratified pride. For it is often the favourable estimate of their own little village— "What they'll think of me at home"—that matters most to Scotsmen who go out to make their way in the world. No doubt that is why so many of them go home and cut a dash when they have made their fortunes; they want the cronies of their youth to see the big men they have become. Wilson was not exempt from that weakness. As far back as he remembered Gourlay had been the big man of Barbie; as a boy he had viewed him with admiring awe; to be received by him now, as one of the well-to-do, were a sweet recognition of his greatness. It was a fawning desire for that recognition that caused his smirking approach to the grain merchant. So strong was the desire that, though he coloured and felt awkward at the contemptuous reference to his father, he sniggered and went on talking, as if nothing untoward had been said. He was one of the band impossible to snub, not because they are endowed with superior moral courage, but because their easy self-importance is so great, that an insult rarely pierces it enough to divert them from their purpose. They walk through life wrapped comfortably round in the wool of their own conceit. Gourlay, though a dull man—perhaps because he was a dull man—suspected insult in a moment. But it rarely entered Wilson's brain (though he was cleverer than most) that the world could find anything to scoff at in such a fine fellow as James Wilson. A less ironic brute than Gourlay would never have pierced the thickness of his hide. It was because Gourlay succeeded in piercing it that morning, that Wilson hated him for ever—with a hate the more bitter because he was rebuffed so seldom.

"Is business brisk?" he asked, irrepressible.

Business! Heavens, did ye hear him talking? What did Toddling Johnny's son know about business? What was the world coming to? To hear him setting up his face there, and asking the best merchant in the town whether business was brisk! It was high time to put him in his place, the conceited upstart, shoving himself forward like an equal!

For it was the assumption of equality implied by Wilson's manner that offended Gourlay—as if mole-catcher's son and monopolist were discussing, on equal terms, matters of interest to them both.

"Business!" he said gravely. "Well, I'm not well acquainted with your line, but I believe mole traps are cheap—if ye have any idea of taking up the oald trade!"

Wilson's eyes flickered over him, hurt and dubious. His mouth opened—then shut—then he decided to speak after all. "Oh, I was thinking Barbie would be very quiet," said he, "compared wi' places where they have the railway! I was thinking it would need stirring up a bit."

"Oh, ye was thinking that, was ye?" birred Gourlay, with

a stupid man's repetition of his jibe. "Well; I believe there's
a grand opening in the moleskin line, so *there's* a chance for
ye! My quarrymen wear out their breeks in no time!"

Wilson's face, which had swelled with red shame, went
a dead white. "Good-morning!" he said, and started rapidly
away with a vicious dig of his stick upon the wet road.

"Goo-ood mor-r-ning, serr!" Gourlay birred after him;
"Goo-ood mor-r-ning, serr!" He felt he had been bright this
morning. He had put the branks on Wilson!

Wilson was as furious at himself as at Gourlay. Why the
devil had he said "Good morning"? It had slipped out of
him unawares, and Gourlay had taken it up with an ironic
birr that rang in his ears now, poisoning his blood. He felt
equal in fancy to a thousand Gourlays now—so strong was
he in wrath against him. He had gone forward to pass
pleasant remarks about the weather, and why should he
noat?—he was no disgrace to Barbie, but a credit rather. It
was not every working man's son that came back with five
hundred in the bank. And here Gourlay had treated him like
a doag! Ah, well, he would maybe be upsides with Gourlay
yet, so he might!

CHAPTER 10

"SUCH a rickle of furniture I never saw!" said the Provost.

"Whose is it?" said Brodie.

"Oh, have ye noat heard?" said the Head of the Town with eyebrows in air. "It beloangs to that fellow Wilson, doan't ye know? He's a son of oald Wilson, the mowdie-man of Brigabee. It seems we're to have him for a neighbour, or all's bye wi't. I declare I doan't know what this world's coming to!"

"Man, Provost," said Brodie, "d'ye tell me tha-at? I've been over at Fleckie for the last ten days—my brother Rab's dead and won away, as I daresay you have heard—oh, yes, we must all go—so, ye see, I'm scarcely abreast o' the latest intelligence. What's Wilson doing here? I thought he had been a pawnbroker in Embro."

"Noat he! It's *whispered* indeed, that he left Brigabee to go and help in a pawnbroker's, but it seems he married an Aberdeen lass and sattled there after a while, the manager of a store, I have been given to understand. He has taken oald Rab Jamieson's barn at the bottom of the Cross—for what purpose it beats even me to tell! And that's his furniture—"

"I declare!" said the astonished Brodie. "He's a smart-looking boy that. Will that be a son of his?"

He pointed to a sharp-faced urchin of twelve who was busy carrying chairs round the corner of the barn, to the tiny house where Wilson meant to live. He was a red-haired boy with an upturned nose, dressed in shirt and knickerbockers only. The cross of his braces came comically near his neck—so short was the space of shirt between the top line of his breeches and his shoulders. His knickers were open at the knee, and the black stockings below them were wrinkled slackly down his thin legs, being tied loosely above the calf with dirty white strips of cloth instead of garters. He had no cap, and it was seen that his hair had a "cow-lick" in front;

it slanted up from his brow, that is, in a sleek kind of tuft. There was a violent squint in one of his sharp grey eyes, so that it seemed to flash at the world across the bridge of his nose. He was so eager at his work that his clumsy-looking boots—they only *looked* clumsy because the legs they were stuck to were so thin—skidded on the cobbles as he whipped round the barn with a chair inverted on his poll. When he came back for another chair, he sometimes wheepled a tune of his own making, in shrill disconnected jerks, and sometimes wiped his nose on his sleeve. And the bodies watched him.

"Faith, he's keen," said the Provost.

"But what on earth has Wilson ta'en auld Jamieson's house and barn for? They have stude empty since I kenna whan," quoth Alexander Toddle, forgetting his English in surprise.

"They say he means to start a business! He's made some bawbees in Aiberdeen, they're telling me, and he thinks he'll set Barbie in a lowe wi't."

"Ou, he means to work a perfect revolution," said Johnny Coe.

"In Barbie!" cried astounded Toddle.

"In Barbie e'en't," said the Provost.

"It would take a heap to revolutionize *hit*," said the baker, the ironic man.

"There's a chance in that hoose," Brodie burst out, ignoring the baker's jibe. "Dod, there's a chance, sirs. I wonder it never occurred to me before."

"Are ye thinking ye have missed a gude thing?" grinned the Deacon.

But Brodie's lips were working in the throes of commercial speculation, and he stared, heedless of the jibe. So Johnny Coe took up his sapient parable.

"Atweel," said he, "there's a chance, Mr Brodie. That road round to the back's a handy thing. You could take a horse and cart brawly through an opening like that. And there's a gey bit ground at the back, too, when a body comes to think o't."

"What line's he meaning to purshoo?" queried Brodie,

whose mind, quickened by the chance he saw at No. 1, The Cross, was hot on the hunt of its possibilities.

"He's been very close about that," said the Provost. "I asked Johnny Gibson—it was him had the selling o't—but he couldn't give me ainy satisfaction. All he could say was that Wilson had bought it and paid it. 'But, losh!' said I, 'he maun 'a' lat peep what he wanted the place for!' But na; it seems he was owre auld-farrant for the like of that. 'We'll let the folk wonder for a while, Mr Gibson,' he had said. 'The less we tell them, the keener they'll be to ken; and they'll advertise me for noathing by spiering one another what I'm up till."

"Cunning!" said Brodie. breathing the word low in expressive admiration.

"Demned cute!" said Sandy Toddle.

"Very thmart!" said the Deacon.

"But the place has been falling down since ever I have mind o't," said Sandy Toddle. "He's a very clever man if he makes anything out of *that*."

"Well, well," said the Provost, "we'll soon see what he's meaning to be at. Now that his furniture's in, he surely canna keep us in the dark much loanger!"

Their curiosity was soon appeased. Within a week they were privileged to read the notice here appended:

"Mr. James Wilson begs to announce to the inhabitants of Barbie and surrounding neighbourhood that he has taken these commodious premises, No. 1, The Cross, which he intends to open shortly as a Grocery, Ironmongery, and General Provision Store. J.W. is apprised that such an Emporium has long been a felt want in the locality. To meet this want is J.W.'s intention. He will try to do so, not by making large profits on a small business, but by making small profits on a large business. Indeed, owing to his long acquaintance with the trade, Mr. Wilson will be able to supply all commodities at a very little over cost price. For J.W. will use those improved methods of business which have been confined hitherto to the larger centres of population. At his Emporium you will be able, as the saying goes, to buy everything from a needle to an anchor. Moreover, to meet the convenience of his customers, J.W. will deliver goods at your own doors, distributing them with his own carts either in the town of Barbie or at any convenient distance from the same. Being a native of the district, his business hopes to secure a due share of your esteemed patronage. Thanking you, in anticipation, for the favour of an early visit,

"Believe me, Ladies and Gentlemen,

"Yours faithfully,

"JAMES WILSON."

Such was the poster with which "Barbie and surrounding neighbourhood" were besprinkled within a week of "J. W.'s" appearance on the scene. He was known as "J. W." ever after. To be known by your initials is sometimes a mark of affection, and sometimes a mark of disrespect. It was not a mark of affection in the case of our "J. W." When Donald Scott slapped him on the back and cried "Hullo, J. W., how are the anchors selling?" Barbie had found a cue which it was not slow to make use of. Wilson even received letters addressed to "J. W., Anchor Merchant, No. 1, The Cross." Ours is a nippy locality.

But Wilson, cosy and cocky in his own good opinion, was impervious to the chilly winds of scorn. His posters, in big blue letters, were on the smiddy door and on the sides of every brig within a circuit of five miles; they were pasted in smaller red letters, on the gateposts of every farm; and Robin Tam, the bellman, handed them about from door to door. The folk could talk of nothing else.

"Dod!" said the Provost when he read the bill, "we've a new departure here! This is an unco splutter, as the oald sow said when she tumbled in the gutter."

"Aye," said Sandy Toddle, a fuff in the pan, I'm thinking. He promises owre muckle to last long! He lauchs owre loud to be merry at the end o't. For the loudest bummler's no the best bee, as my father, honest man, used to tell the minister."

"Ah-ah, I'm no so sure o' that," said Tam Brodie. "I foregathered wi' Wilson on Wednesday last, and I tell ye, sirs, he's worth the watching. They'll need to stand on a baikie that put the branks on him. He has the considering eye in his head—yon lang far-away glimmer at a thing from out the end of the eyebrow. He turned it on mysell twa-three times, the cunning devil, trying to keek into me, to see if he could use me. And look at the chance he has! There's two stores in Barbie, to be sure; but Kinnikum's a dirty beast, and folk have a scunner at his goods, and Catherwood's a dru'cken swine, and his place but sairly guided. That's a great stroke o' policy, too, promising to deliver folk's goods on their own doorstep to them. There's a whole jing-bang of out-lying clachans round Barbie that he'll get the trade of by a dodge like that. The like was never tried hereaway before. I wadna wonder but it works wonders."

It did.

It was partly policy and partly accident that brought Wilson back to Barbie. He had been managing a wealthy old merchant's store for a long time in Aberdeen, and he had been blithely looking forward to the goodwill of it, when jink, at the old man's death, in stepped a nephew, and ousted the poo-oor fellow. He had bawled shrilly, but to no purpose; he had to be travelling. When he rose to greatness in Barbie it was whispered that the nephew discovered he was feathering his own nest, and that this was the reason of his sharp dismissal. But perhaps we should credit that report to Barbie's disposition rather than to Wilson's misdemeanour.

Wilson might have set up for himself in the nippy northern town. But it is an instinct with men who have met with a rebuff in a place, to shake its dust from their shoes, and be off to seek their fortunes in the larger world. We take a scunner at the place that has ill-used us. Wilson took a scunner at Aberdeen, and decided to leave it and look around him. Scotland was opening up, and there were bound to be heaps of chances for a man like him! "A man like me," was a frequent phrase of Wilson's retired and solitary speculation. "Aye," he said, emerging from one of his business reveries, "there's bound to be heaps o' chances for a man like me, if I only look about me."

He was "looking about him" in Glasgow when he fore-gathered with his cousin William—the borer he! After many "How are ye, Jim"s and mutual speirings over a "bit mouthful of yill"—so they phrased it, but that was a meiosis, for they drank five quarts—they fell to a serious discussion of the commercial possibilities of Scotland. The borer was of the opinion that the Braes of Barbie had a future yet, "for a' the gaffer was so keen on keeping his men in the dark about the coal."

Now Wilson knew (as what Scotsman does not?) that in the middle-fifties coal-boring in Scotland was not the honourable profession that it now is. More than once, speculators procured lying reports that there were no minerals, and after landowners had been ruined by their abortive preliminary experiments, stepped in, bought the land and boomed it. In one notorious case a family, now great in the public eye, bribed a laird's own borers to conceal the truth, and then buying the Golconda from its impoverished owner, laid the basis of a vast fortune.

"D'ye mean—to tell—*me*, Weelyum Wilson," said James, giving him his full name in the solemnity of the moment, "d'ye mean—to tell—*me*, sir"—here he sank his voice to a whisper—"that there's joukery-pawkery at work?"

"A declare to God A div," said Weelyum with equal solemnity, and he nodded with alarmed sapience across his beer jug.

"You believe there's plenty of coal up Barbie Valley, and that they're keeping it dark in the meantime for some purpose of their own?"

"I do," said Weelyum.

"God!" said James, gripping the table with both hands in his excitement, "God, if that's so, what a chance there's in Barbie! It has been a dead town for twenty year, and twenty to the end o't. A verra little would buy the hauf o't. But property 'ull rise in value like a puddock stool at dark, serr, if the pits come round it! It will that. If I was only sure o' your suspeecion, Weelyum, I'd invest every bawbee I have in't. You're going home the night, are ye not?"

"I was just on my road to the station when I met ye," said Weelyum.

"Send me a scrape of your pen to-morrow, man, if what you see on getting back keeps you still in the same mind o't. And directly I get your letter, I'll run down and look about me."

The letter was encouraging, and Wilson went forth to spy the land, and initiate the plan of campaign. It was an important day for him. He entered on his feud with Gourlay, and bought Rab Jamieson's house and barn (with the field behind it) for a trifle. He had five hundred of his own, and he knew where more could be had for the asking.

Rab Jamieson's barn was a curious building to be stranded in the midst of Barbie. In quaint villages and little towns of England you sometimes see a mellow red-tiled barn, with its rich yard, close upon the street; it seems to have been hemmed in by the houses round, while dozing, so that it could not escape with the fields fleeing from the town. There it remains and gives a ripeness to the place, matching fitly with the great horse-chestnut yellowing before the door, and the old inn further down, mantled in its blood-red creepers. But that autumnal warmth and cosiness is rarely seen in the barer streets of the north. How Rab Jamieson's barn came to be stuck in Barbie nobody could tell. It was a gaunt grey building with never a window, but a bole high in one corner for the sheaves, and a door low in another corner for auld Rab Jamieson. There was no mill inside, and the place had not been used for years. But the roof was good, and the walls stout and thick, and Wilson soon got to work on his new possession. He had seen all that could be made of the place the moment he clapped an eye on it, and he knew that he had found a good thing, even if the pits should never come near Barbie. The bole and door next the street were walled up, and a fine new door opened in the middle, flanked on either side by a great window. The interior was fitted up with a couple of counters and a wooden floor; and above the new wood ceiling there was a long loft for a store room, lighted by skylights in the roof. That loft above the rafters, thought the provident Wilson, will come in braw and handy for storing things, so it will. And there, hey presto! the transformation was achieved, and Wilson's Emporium stood before you. It was crammed with merchandise. On the white flapping slant of a couple of awnings, one over each window, you might read in black letters, "JAMES WILSON: EMPORIUM." The letters of "James Wilson" made a triumphal arch, to which "Emporium" was the base. It seemed symbolical.

Now, the shops of Barbie (the drunken man's shop and the dirty man's shop always excepted, of course) had usually been low-browed little places with faded black scrolls above the door, on which you might read in dim gilt letters (or it might be, in white)

"LICENS'D TO SELL TEA & TOBACCO." "LICENS'D" was on one corner of the ribboned scroll, "TO SELL TEA &" occupied the flowing arch above, with "TOBACCO" in the other corner. When you mounted two steps and opened the door, a bell of some kind went "*ping*" in the interior, and an old woman in a mutch, with big specs slipping down her nose, would come up a step from a dim little room behind, and wiping her sunken mouth with her apron—she had just left her tea— would say, "What's your wull the day, sur?" And if you said your "wull" was tobacco, she would answer, "Ou, sir, I dinna sell ocht now but the tape and sweeties." And then you went away, sadly.

With the exception of the dirty man's shop and the drunken man's shop, that kind of shop was the Barbie kind of shop. But Wilson changed all that. One side of the Emporium was crammed with pots, pans, pails, scythes, gardening implements, and saws, with a big barrel of paraffin partitioned off in a corner. The rafters on that side were bristling and hoary with brushes of all kinds dependent from the roof, so that the minister's wife (who was a six-footer) went off with a brush in her bonnet once. Behind the other counter were canisters in goodly rows, barrels of flour and bags of meal, and great yellow cheeses in the window. The rafters here were heavy with their wealth of hams, brown-skinned flitches of bacon interspersed with the white tight-corded home-cured—"Barbie's Best," as Wilson christened it. All along the back, in glass cases to keep them unsullied, were bales of cloth, layer on layer to the roof. It was a pleasure to go into the place, so big and bien was it, and to smell it on a frosty night set your teeth watering. There was always a big barrel of American apples just inside the door, and their homely fragrance wooed you from afar, the mellow savour cuddling round you half a mile off. Barbie boys had despised the provision trade, heretofore, as a mean and meagre occupation, but now the imagination of each gallant youth was fired and radiant; he meant to be a grocer.

Mrs Wilson presided over the Emporium. Wilson had a treasure in his wife. She was Aberdeen born and bred, but her manner was the manner of the South and West. There is a broad difference of character between the peoples of East and West Scotland. The East throws a narrower and a nippier breed. In the West they take Burns for their exemplar, and affect the jovial and robustious—in some cases it is affectation only, and a mighty poor one at that. They claim to be bigger men and bigger fools than the Eastern billies. And the Eastern billies are very willing to yield one half of the contention.

Mrs Wilson, though Eastie by nature, had the jovial manner that you find in Kyle. More jovial, indeed, than was common in nippy Barbie, which, in general character, seems to have been transplanted from some sand dune looking out upon the German ocean. She was big of hip and bosom, with sloe-black hair and eyes, and a ruddy cheek, and when she flung back her head for the laugh her white teeth flashed splendid on the world. That laugh of hers became one of the well-known features of Barbie. "Lo'd-sake!" a startled visitor would cry, "whatna skirl's tha-at!" "Oh, dinna be alarmed," a native would comfort him, "it's only Wilson's wife lauchin at the Cross!"

Her manner had a hearty charm. She had a laugh and a joke for every customer, quick as a wink with her answer; her jibe was in you and out again, before you knew you were wounded. Some, it is true, took exception to the loudness of her skirl; the Deacon, for instance, who "gave her a good one" the first time he went in for snuff. But "Tut!" quoth she, "a mim cat's never gude at the mice," and she lifted him out by the scruff of his neck, crying, "Run, mousie, or I'll catch ye!" On that day her popularity in Barbie was assured for ever. But she was as keen on the penny as a penurious weaver, for all her heartiness and laughing ways. She combined the commercial merits of the East and West. She could coax you to the buying like a Cumnock quean, and fleece you in the selling like the cadgers o' Kincardine. When Wilson was abroad on his affairs he had no need to be afraid that things were mismanaging at home. During his first year in Barbie Mrs Wilson was his sole helper. She had the brawny arm of a giantess, and could toss a bag of meal like a baby; to see her twirl a big ham on the counter was to see a thing done as it should be. When Dru'cken Wabster came in and was offensive once, "Poo-oor fellow!" said she (with a wink to a customer) "I declare he's in a high fever," and she took him kicking to the pump and cooled him.

With a mate like that at the helm every sail of Wilson's craft was trimmed for prosperity. He began to "look about" him to increase the fleet.

CHAPTER 11

THAT the Scot is largely endowed with the commercial imagination his foes will be ready to acknowledge. Imagination may consecrate the world to a man, or it may merely be a visualising faculty which sees that, as already perfect, which is still lying in the raw material. The Scot has the lower faculty in full degree; he had the forecasting leap of the mind which sees what to make of things—more, sees them made and in vivid operation. To him there is a railway through the desert where no railway exists, and mills along the quiet stream. And his *perfervidum ingenium* is quick to attempt the realizing of his dreams. That is why he makes the best of colonists. Galt is his type—Galt, dreaming in boyhood of the fine water power a fellow could bring round the hill, from the stream where he went a-fishing (they have done it since), dreaming in manhood of the cities yet to rise amid Ontario's woods (they are there to witness to his foresight). Indeed, so flushed and riotous can the Scottish mind become over a commercial prospect that it sometimes sends native caution by the board, and a man's really fine idea becomes an empty balloon, to carry him off to the limbo of vanities. There is a megalomaniac in every parish of Scotland. Well, not so much as that; they're owre canny for that to be said of them. But in every district, almost, you may find a poor creature who for thirty years has cherished a great scheme by which he means to revolutionize the world's commerce, and amass a fortune in monstrous degree. He is generally to be seen shivering at the Cross, and (if you are a nippy man) you shout carelessly in going by, "Good morning, Tamson; how's the scheme?" And he would be very willing to tell you, if only you would wait to listen. "Man," he will cry eagerly behind you, "if I only had anither wee wheel in my invention —she would do, the besom! I'll sune have her ready noo." Poor Tamson!

But these are the exceptions. Scotsmen, more than other men perhaps, have the three great essentials of commercial success—imagination to conceive schemes, common sense to correct them, and energy to push them through. Common sense, indeed, so far from being wanting, is in most cases too much in evidence, perhaps, crippling the soaring mind and robbing the idea of its early radiance; in quieter language, she makes the average Scotsman to be over-cautious. His combinations are rarely Napoleonic until he becomes an American. In his native dales he seldom ventures on a daring policy. And yet his forecasting mind is always detecting "possibeelities". So he contents himself by creeping cautiously from point to point, ignoring big reckless schemes and using the safe and small, till he arrives at a florid opulence. He has expressed his love of *festina lente* in business in a score of proverbs—"bit-by-bit's the better horse, though big-by-big's the baulder"; "ca' canny or ye'll cowp"; "many a little makes a mickle"; and "creep before ye gang." This mingling of caution and imagination is the cause of his stable prosperity. And its characteristic is a sure progressiveness. That sure progressiveness was the characteristic of Wilson's prosperity in Barbie. In him, too, imagination and caution were equally developed. He was always foreseeing "chances" and using them, gripping the good and rejecting the dangerous (had he not gripped the chance of auld Rab Jamieson's barn?—there was caution in that, for it was worth the money whatever happened, and there was imagination in the whole scheme, for he had a vision of Barbie as a populous centre and streets of houses in his holm). And every "chance" he seized led to a better one, till almost every "chance" in Barbie was engrossed by him alone. This is how he went to work. Note the "bit-by-bit-ness" of his great career.

When Mrs Wilson was behind the counter, Wilson was out "distributing." He was not always out, of course—his volume of trade at first was not big enough for that, but in the mornings, and the long summer dusks, he made his way to the many outlying places of which Barbie was the centre. There, in one and the same visit, he distributed goods and collected orders for the future. Though his bill had spoken of "carts," as if he had several, that was only a bit of splurge on his part; his one conveyance at the first was a stout spring cart, with a good brown cob between the shafts. But with this he did such a trade as had never been known in Barbie. The Provost said it was "shtupendous."

When Wilson was jogging homeward in the balmy evenings of his first summer at Barbie no eye had he for the large evening star, tremulous above the woods, or for the dreaming sprays against the yellow west. It wasn't his business—he had other things to mind. Yet Wilson was a dreamer, too. His close musing eye, peering at the dusky-brown nodge of his pony's hip through the gloom, saw not that, but visions of chances, opportunities, occasions. When the lights of Barbie twinkled before him in the dusk he used to start from a pleasant dream of some commercial enterprise suggested by the country round. "Yon holm would make a fine bleaching green—pure water, fine air, labour cheap, and everything handy. Or the Lintie's Linn among the woods—water power running to waste yonder—surely something could be made of that." He would follow his idea through all its mazes and developments, oblivious of the passing miles. His delight in his visions was exactly the same as the author's delight in the figments of his brain. They were the same good company along the twilight roads. The author, happy with his thronging thoughts (when they are kind enough to throng) is no happier than Wilson was on nights like these.

He had not been a week on his rounds when he saw a "chance" waiting for development. When out "delivering" he used to visit the upland farms to buy butter and eggs for the Emporium. He got them cheaper so. But more eggs and butter could be had than were required in the neighbourhood of Barbie. Here was a chance for Wilson! He became a collector for merchants at a distance. Barbie, before it got the railway, had only a silly little market once a fortnight, which was a very poor outlet for stuff. Wilson provided a better one. Another thing played into his hands, too, in that connection. It is a cheese-making countryside about Barbie, and the less butter produced at a cheese-making place—the better for the cheese. Still, a good many pounds are often churned on the sly. What need the cheese merchant ken—if keepit the gudewife in bawbees frae week to week—and it she took a little cream frae the cheese now and than they werena a pin the waur o't, for she aye did it wi' decency and caution! Still it is as well to dispose of this kind of butter quietly, to avoid gabble among ill-speakers. Wilson, slithering up the back road with his spring cart in the gloaming, was the man to dispose of it quietly. And he got it dirt cheap, of course, seeing it was a kind of contraband. All that he made in this way was not much to be sure—threepence a dozen on the eggs, perhaps, and fourpence on the pound of butter—still, you know, every little makes a mickle, and hained gear helps weel*. And more important than the immediate profit was the ultimate result. For Wilson, in this way, established with merchants, in far-off Fechars and Poltandie, a connection for the sale of country produce which meant a great deal to him in future, when he launched out as cheese-buyer in opposition to Gourlay.

It "occurred" to him also (things were always occurring to Wilson) that the "Scotch Cuddy" business had as fine a chance in "Barbie and surrounding neighbourhood" as ever it had in North and Middle England. The "Scotch Cuddy" is so called because he is a beast of burden, and not from the nature of his wits. He is a travelling packman, who infests communities of working men, and disposes of his goods on the credit system, receiving payment in instalments. You go into a working man's house (when he is away from home for preference) and, laying a swatch of cloth across his wife's knee, "What do you think of that, mistress?" you enquire, watching the effect keenly. Instantly all her covetous heart is in her eye and, thinks she to herself, "Oh, but John would look well in that, at the Kirk on Sunday!" She has no ready money, and would never have the cheek to go into a draper's and order the suit, but when she sees it lying there across her knee, she just cannot resist it. (And fine you knew that when you clinked it down before her!) Now that the goods are in the house she cannot bear to let them out the door again. But she hints a scarcity of cash. "Tut, woman!"

* *Hained gear:* saved money.

75

quoth you, bounteous and kind, "there's no obstacle in *that*!
—You can pay me in instalments!" How much would the
instalments be, she enquires. "Oh a mere trifle—half-a
crown a week, say." She hesitates and hankers. "John's
Sunday coat's getting quite shabby, so it is, and Tam Macalister has a new suit, she was noticing—the Macalisters are
always flaunting in their braws! And, there's that Paisley
shawl for herself, too; eh, but they would be the canty pair,
cocking down the road on Sunday in *that* rig!—they would
take the licht frae Meg Macalister's e'en, thae Macalisters
are always so en-vy-fu'!" Love, vanity, covetousness, present
opportunity, are all at work upon the poor body. She succumbs. But the half-crown weekly payments have a habit of
lengthening themselves out till the packman has made fifty
per cent by the business. And why not?—a man must have
some interest on his money! Then there's the risk of bad
debts, too—that falls to be considered. But there was little
risk of bad debts when Wilson took to cloth-distributing.
For success in that game depends on pertinacity in pursuit
of your victim and Wilson was the man for that.

He was jogging home from Brigabee, where he had been
distributing groceries at a score of wee houses, when there
flashed on his mind a whole scheme for cloth-distribution on
a large scale—for mining villages were clustering in about
Barbie by this time, and he saw his way to a big thing.

He was thinking of Sandy Toddle, who had been a Scotch
Cuddy in the Midlands and had retired to Barbie on a snug
bit fortune—he was thinking of Sandy when the plan rose
generous on his mind. He would soon have more horses
than one on the road—why shouldn't they carry swatches of
cloth as well as groceries? If he had responsible men under
him, it would be their own interest, for a small commission
on the profits, to see that payments were levied correctly
every week. And those colliers were reckless with their cash,
far readier to commit themselves to buying than the cannier
country bodies round. Lord! there was money in the scheme.
No sooner thought of than put in practice. Wilson gave up
the cloth-peddling after five or six years—he had other fish
to fry by that time—but while he was at it he made money

hand over fist at the job.

But what boots it to tell of all his schemes? He had the lucky eye—and everything he looked on prospered.

Before he had been a week in Barbie he met Gourlay, just at the Bend o' the Brae, in full presence of the bodies. Remembering their first encounter the grocer tried to out-stare him, but Gourlay hardened his glower and the grocer blinked. When the two passed, "I declare!" said the bodies, "did ye see yon?—they're not on speaking terms!" And they hotched with glee to think that Gourlay had another enemy.

Judge of their delight when they saw one day about a month later, just as Gourlay was passing up the street, Wilson come down it with a load of coals for a customer! For he was often out Auchterwheeze road in the early morning, and what was the use of an empty journey back again, especially as he had plenty of time in the middle of the day to attend to other folk's affairs—so here he was, started as a carrier, in full opposition to Gourlay.

"Did you see Gourlay's face?" chuckled the bodies when the cart went by. "Yon was a bash in the eye to him. Ha, ha! —he's not to have it all his own way now!"

Wilson had slid into the carrying in the natural develop-ment of business. It was another of the possibilities which he saw and turned to his advantage. The two other chief grocers in the place, Cunningham the dirty, and Calderwood the drunken, having no carts or horses of their own, were dependent on Gourlay for conveyance of their goods from Skeighan. But Wilson brought his own. Naturally, he was asked by his customers to bring a parcel now and then, and naturally, being the man he was, he made them pay for the privilege. With that for a start the rest was soon accom-plished. Gourlay had to pay now for his years of insolence and tyranny; all who had irked beneath his domineering ways got their carrying done by Wilson. Ere long that prosperous gentleman had three carts on the road, and two men under him to help in his various affairs.

Carting was only one of several new developments in the business of J. W. When the navvies came in about the town and accommodation was ill to find, Wilson rigged up an old

shed in the corner of his holm as a hostelry for ten of them—
and they had to pay through the nose for their night's
lodging. Their food they obtained from the Emporium, and
thus the Wilsons bled them both ways. Then there was the
scheme for supplying milk—another of the "possibeelities."
Hitherto in winter, Barbie was dependent for its milk supply
on heavy farm-carts that came lumbering down the street,
about half-past seven in the morning, jangling bells to waken
sleepy customers, and carrying lanterns that carved circles
of hairy[1] yellow out the raw air. But Mrs Wilson got four
cows, back-calvers who would be milking strong in Decem-
ber, and supplied milk to all the folk about the Cross.

She had a lass to help her in the house now, and the red-
headed boy was always to be seen, jinking round corners
like a weasel, running messages hot-foot, errand boy to the
"bisness" in general. Yet, though everybody was busy and
skelping at it, such a stress of work was accompanied with
much disarray. Wilson's yard was the strangest contrast to
Gourlay's. Gourlay's was a pleasure to the eye, everything
of the best and everything in order, since the master's pride
would not allow it to be other. But, though Wilson's Emporium was clean, his back yard was littered with dirty
straw, broken boxes, old barrels, stable refuse, and the sky-
pointing shafts of carts, uptilted in between. When boxes
and barrels were flung out of the Emporium they were
generally allowed to lie on the dunghill, until they were
converted into firewood. "Mistress, you're a trifle mixed,"
said the Provost in grave reproof, when he went round to
the back to see Wilson on a matter of business. But "Tut,"
cried Mrs Wilson, as she threw down a plank, to make a path
for him across a dub—"Tut," she laughed, "the clartier the
cosier!" And it was as true as she said it. The thing went
forward splendidly in spite of its confusion.

Though trade was brisker in Barbie than it had ever been
before, Wilson had already done injury to Gourlay's business as general conveyer. But, hitherto, he had not infringed
on the gurly one's other monopolies. His chance came at

[1] The reading of all editions consulted except Travellers' Library and
Nelson, which have *fairy yellow*.

last.

He appeared on a market day in front of the Red Lion, a piece of pinkey-brown paper in his hand. That was the first telegram ever seen in Barbie, and it had been brought by special messenger from Skeighan. It was short and to the point. It ran: "Will buy 300 stone cheese 8 shillings stone* delivery at once," and was signed by a merchant in Poltandie.

Gourlay was talking to old Tarmillan of Irrendavie, when Wilson pushed in and addressed Tarmillan, without a glance at the grain-merchant.

"Have you a kane o' cheese to sell, Irrendavie?" was his blithe salutation.

"I have," said Irrendavie, and he eyed him suspiciously. For what was Wilson speiring for? *He* wasna a cheese-merchant.

"How much the stane are ye seeking for't?" said Wilson.

"I have just been asking Mr Gourlay here for seven and six," said Irrendavie, "but he winna rise a penny on the seven!"

"*I'll* gi'e ye seven and six," said Wilson, and slapped his long thin flexible bank-book far too ostentatiously against the knuckles of his left hand.

"But—but," stammered Irrendavie, suspicious still, but melting at the offer, "*you* have no means of storing cheese."

"Oh," said Wilson, getting in a fine one at Gourlay, "there's no drawback in that! The ways o' business have changed greatly since steam came close to our doors. It's nothing but vanity nowadays when a country merchant wastes money on a ramshackle of buildings for storing— there's no need for that if he only had brains to develop quick deliveries. Some folk, no doubt, like to build monuments to their own pride, but I'm not one of that kind; there's not enough sense in that to satisfy a man like me. My offer doesna hold, you understand, unless you deliver the cheese at Skeighan Station. Do you accept the condition?"

* That is for the stone of fourteen pounds. At that time Scotch cheese was selling, *roughly*, at from fifty to sixty shillings the hundredweight.

"Oh, yes," said Irrendavie, "I'm willing to agree to that."

"C'way into the Red Lion then, said Wilson, "and we'll wet the bargain with a drink to make it hold the tighter!"

Then a strange thing happened. Gourlay had a curious stick of foreign wood (one of the trifles he fed his pride on) the crook of which curved back to the stem and inhered, leaving space only for the fingers. The wood was of wonderful toughness, and Gourlay had been known to bet that no man could break the handle of his stick by a single grip over the crook and under it. Yet now, as he saw his bargain whisked away from him and listened to Wilson's jibe, the thing snapped in his grip like a rotten twig. He stared down at the broken pieces for a while, as if wondering how they came there, then dashed them on the ground while Wilson stood smiling by. And then he strode—with a look on his face that made the folk fall away.

"He's hellish angry," they grinned to each other when their foe was gone, and laughed when they heard the cause of it. "Ha, ha, Wilson's the boy to diddle him!" And yet they looked queer when told that the famous stick had snapped in his grasp like a worm-eaten larch-twig. "Lord!" cried the baker in admiring awe, "did he break it with the ae chirt? It's been tried by scores of fellows for the last twenty years, and never a man of them was up till't! Lads, there's something splendid about Gourlay's wrath. What a man he is when the paw-sion grups him!"

"Thplendid, d'ye ca't?" said the Deacon. "He may thwing in a towe for his thplendid wrath yet."

From that day Wilson and Gourlay were a pair of gladiators for whom the people of Barbie made a ring. They pitted the protagonists against each other and hounded them on to rivalry by their comments and remarks, taking the side of the newcomer, less from partiality to him than from hatred of their ancient enemy. It was strange that a thing so impalpable as gossip should influence so strong a man as John Gourlay to his ruin. But it did. The bodies of Barbie became not only the chorus to Gourlay's tragedy, buzzing it abroad and discussing his downfall; they became also, merely by their maddening tattle, a villain of the piece and an active cause of the catastrophe. Their gossip seemed to materialize into a single entity, a something propelling, that spurred Gourlay on to the schemes that ruined him. He was not to be done, he said; he would show the dogs what he thought of them. And so he plunged headlong, while the wary Wilson watched him, smiling at the sight.

There was a pretty hell-broth brewing in the little town.

CHAPTER 12

"AYE man, Templandmuir, it's you!" said Gourlay, coming forward with great heartiness. "Aye man, and how are ye? C'way into the parlour!"

"Good evening, Mr Gourlay," said the Templar. His manner was curiously subdued.

Since his marriage there was a great change in the rubicund squireen. Hitherto he had lived in sluttish comfort on his own land, content with the little it brought in, and proud to be the friend of Gourlay whom everybody feared. If it ever dawned on his befuddled mind that Gourlay turned the friendship to his own account, his vanity was flattered by the prestige he acquired because of it. Like many another robustious big toper, the Templar was a chicken at heart, and "to be in with Gourlay" lent him a consequence that covered his deficiency. "Yes, I'm sleepy," he would yawn in Skeighan Mart, "I had a sederunt yestreen wi' John Gourlay," and he would slap his boot with his riding-switch, and feel like a hero. "I know how it is, I know how it is!" Provost Connal of Barbie used to cry; "Gourlay both courts and cowes him —first he courts and then he cowes—and the Templar hasn't the courage to break it off!" The Provost hit the mark.

But when the Templar married the miller's daughter of the Mill o' Blink (a sad come-down, said foolish neighbours, for a Halliday of Templandmuir) there was a sudden change about the laird. In our good Scots proverb, "A miller's daughter has a shrill voice", and the new leddy of Templandmuir ("a leddy she is!" said the frightened housekeeper) justified the proverb. Her voice went with the skirl of an East wind through the rat-riddled mansion of the Hallidays. She was nine-and-twenty, and a birkie woman of nine-and-twenty can make a good husband out of very unpromising material. The Templar wore a scared look in those days and went home betimes. His cronies knew the fun was over when

they heard what had happened to the great punch-bowl—
she made it a swine-trough. It was the heirloom of a hundred
years, and as much as a man could carry with his arms out,
a massive curio in stone; but to her husband's plaint about its
degradation, "Oh," she cried, "it'll never know the difference!
It's been used to swine!"

But she was not content with the cessation of the old,
she was determined on bringing in the new. For a twelvemonth now she had urged her husband to be rid of Gourlay.
The country was opening up, she said, and the quarry ought
to be their own. A dozen times he had promised her to warn
Gourlay that he must yield the quarry when his tack ran
out at the end of the year, and a dozen times he had shrunk
from the encounter.

"I'll write," he said feebly.

"Write!" said she, lowered in her pride to think her husband was a coward. "Write, indeed! Man, have ye no spunk?
Think what he has made out o' ye! Think o' the money that
has gone to him that should have come to you! You should
be glad o' the chance to tell him o't. My certy, if I was you I
wouldn't miss it for the world—just to let him know of his
cheatry! Oh, it's very right that *I*"—she sounded the *I* big
and brave—"it's very right that *I* should live in this tumble-
down hole while *he* builds a palace from your plunder! It's
right that *I* should put up with this"—she flung hands of
contempt at her dwelling—"it's right that *I* should put up
with this, while yon trollop has a splendid mansion on the
top o' the brae! And every bawbee of his fortune has come
out of you—the fool makes nothing from his other business
—he would have been a pauper if he hadn't met a softie like
you that he could do what he liked with. Write, indeed! I
have no patience with a wheen sumphs of men! Them do the
work o' the world! They may wear the breeks, but the
women wear the brains, I trow. I'll have it out with the black
brute myself," screamed the hardy dame, "if you're feared
of his glower. If you havena the pluck for it, *I* have. Write
indeed! In you go to the meeting that oald ass of a Provost
has convened, and don't show your face in Templandmuir
till you have had it out with Gourlay!"

No wonder the Templar looked subdued.

When Gourlay came forward with his usual calculated heartiness, the laird remembered his wife and felt very uncomfortable. It was ill to round on a man who always imposed on him a hearty and hardy goodfellowship. Gourlay, greeting him so warmly, gave him no excuse for an outburst. In his dilemma he turned to the children, to postpone the evil hour.

"Aye, man, John!" he said, heavily, "you're there!" Heavy Scotsmen are fond of telling folk that they are where they are. "You're there!" said Templandmuir.

"Aye," said John, the simpleton, "I'm here."

In the grime of the boy's face there were large white circles round the eyes, showing where his fists had rubbed off the tears through the day.

"How are you doing at the school?" said the Templar.

"Oh, he's an ass!" said Gourlay. "He takes after his mother in that! The lassie's more smart—she favours our side o' the house! Eh, Jenny?" he enquired, and tugged her pigtail, smiling down at her in grim fondness.

"Yes," nodded Janet, encouraged by the petting, "John's always at the bottom of the class. Jimmy Wilson's always at the top, and the dominie set him to teach John his 'counts the day—after he had thrashed him!"

She cried out, at a sudden tug on her pigtail, and looked up, with tears in her eyes, to meet her father's scowl.

"You eediot!" said Gourlay, gazing at his son with a savage contempt, "have you no pride to let Wilson's son be your master?"

John slunk from the room.

"Bide where you are, Templandmuir," said Gourlay, after a little, "I'll be back directly."

He went through to the kitchen and took a crystal jug from the dresser. He "made a point" of bringing the water for his whiskey. "I like to pump it up *cold*," he used to say, "cold and cold, ye know, till there's a mist on the outside of the glass like the bloom on a plum, and then, by Goad, ye have the fine drinking! Oh, no—ye needn't tell me, I wouldn't lip drink if the water wasna ice-cold." He never varied from the tipple he approved. In his long sederunts with Templandmuir he would slip out to the pump, before every brew, to get water of sufficient coldness.

To-night he would birl the bottle with Templandmuir as usual, till the fuddled laird should think himself a fine big fellow as being the intimate of John Gourlay—and then, sober as a judge himself, he would drive him home in the small hours. And when next they met, the pot-valiant squireen would chuckle proudly, "Faith, yon was a night." By a crude cunning of the kind Gourlay had maintained his ascendancy for years, and to-night he would maintain it still. He went out to the pump, to fetch water with his own hands, for their first libation.

But when he came back and set out the big decanter Templandmuir started to his feet.

"Noat to-night, Mr Gourlay," he stammered—and his unusual flutter of refusal might have warned Gourlay— "noat to-night, if *you* please, noat to-night, if *you* please. As a matter of fact—eh—what I really came into the town for, doan't you see, was—eh—to attend the meeting the Provost has convened about the railway. You'll come down to the meeting, will ye noat?"

He wanted to get Gourlay away from the House with the Green Shutters. It would be easier to quarrel with him out of doors.

But Gourlay gaped at him across the table, his eyes big with surprise and disapproval.

"Huh!" he growled, "I wonder at a man like you giving your head to that! It's a wheen damned nonsense."

"Oh, I'm no so sure of that," drawled the Templar. "I think the railway means to come."

The whole country was agog about the new railway. The question agitating solemn minds was whether it should join the main line at Fechars, thirty miles ahead, or pass to the right, through Fleckie and Barbie, to a junction up at Skeighan Drone. Many were the reasons spluttered in vehement debate for one route or the other. "On the one side, ye see, Skeighan was a big place a'readys, and look what a centre it would be, if it had three lines of rail running

85

out and in! Eh, my, what a centre! Then there was Fleckie
and Barbie—they would be the big towns! Up the valley,
too, was the shortest road; it would be a daft-like thing to
build thirty mile of rail, when fifteen was enough to establish
the connection! And was it likely—I put it to ainy man of
sense—was it likely the Coal Company wouldn't do everything in their power to get the railway up the valley, seeing
that if it didn't come that airt, they would need to build a
line of their own?"—"Ah, but then, ye see, Fechars was a
big place, too, and there was lots of mineral up there as
well! And though it was a longer road to Fechars and part
of it lay across the moors, there were several wee towns that
airt just waiting for a chance of growth! I can tell ye, sirs,
this was going to be a close question!"

Such was the talk in pot-house and parlour, at kirk and
mart and tryst and fair, and wherever potentates did gather
and abound. The partisans on either side began to canvass
the country in support of their contentions. They might have
kept their breath to cool their porridge, for these matters,
we know, are settled in the great Witenagemot. But petitions
were prepared and meetings were convened. In those days
Provost Connal of Barbie was in constant communion with
the "Pow-ers." "Yass," he nodded gravely—only "nod" is a
word too swift for the grave inclining of that mighty pow—
"Yass, ye know, the great thing in matters like this is to get
at the Pow-ers, doan't you see? Oh, yass, yass; we must get
at the Pow-ers!"—and he looked as if none but he were
equal to the job. He even went to London (to interrogate the
"Pow-ers") and simple bodies, gathered at the Cross for
their Saturday at e'en, told each other with bated breath that
the Provost was away to the "seat of Goaver'ment to see
about the railway". When he came back and shook his head,
hope drained from his fellows and left them hollow in an
empty world. But when he smacked his lips on receiving an
important letter, the heavens were brightened and the land-
scapes smiled.

The Provost walked about the town nowadays with the
air of a man on whose shoulders the weight of empires did
depend. But for all his airs it was not the Head o' the Town

who was the ablest advocate of the route up the Water of
Barbie. It was that public-spirited citizen, Mr James Wilson
of the Cross! Wilson championed the cause of Barbie with
an ardour that did infinite credit to his civic heart. For one
thing, it was a grand way of recommending himself to his
new townsfolk, as he told his wife, "and so increasing the
circle of our present trade, don't ye understand?"—for
another, he was as keen as the keenest that the railway
should come and enhance the value of his property. "We
must agitate," he cried, when Sandy Toddle murmured a
doubt whether anything they could do would be of much
avail. "It's not settled yet what road the line's to follow, and
who knows but a trifle may turn the scale on our behalf?
Local opinion ought to be expressed! They're sending a
monster petition from the Fechars side; we'll send the
Company a bigger one from ours! Look at Skeighan and
Fleckie and Barbie—three towns at our back, and the new
Coal Company, forbye! A public opinion of that size ought
to have a great weight—if put forward properly! We must
agitate, sirs, we must agitate—we maun scour the country
for names in our support. Look what a number of things
there are, to recommend *our* route. It's the shortest, and
there's no need for heavy cuttings such as are needed on the
other side; the road's there a'ready—Barbie Water has cut
it through the hills. It's the manifest design of Providence
that there should be a line up Barbie Valley! What a position
for't!—And, oh," thought Wilson, "what a site for building
houses in my holm!—Let a meeting be convened at wunst!"

The meeting was convened with Provost Connal in the
chair, and Wilson as general factotum.

"You'll come down to the meeting?" said Templandmuir
to Gourlay.

Go to a meeting for which Wilson had sent out the bills!
At another, Gourlay would have hurled his usual objur-
gation that he would see him condemned to eternal agonies
ere he granted his request! But Templandmuir was different.
Gourlay had always flattered this man (whom he inwardly
despised) by a companionship which made proud the other.
He had always yielded to Templandmuir in small things,

for the sake of the quarry, which was a great thing. He yielded to him now.

"Verra well," he said shortly, and rose to get his hat.

When Gourlay put on his hat, the shallow meanness of his brow was hid, and nothing was seen to impair his dark strong gravity of face. He was a man you would have turned to look at, as he marched in silence by the side of Templandmuir. Though taller than the laird, he looked shorter because of his enormous breadth. He had a chest like the heave of a hill. Templandmuir was afraid of him. And fretting at the necessity he felt to quarrel with a man of whom he was afraid, he had an unreasonable hatred of Gourlay whose conduct made this quarrel necessary at the same time that his character made it to be feared; and he brooded on his growing rage that, with it for a stimulus, he might work his cowardly nature to the point of quarrelling. Conscious of the coming row, then, he felt awkward in the present, and was ignorant what to say. Gourlay was silent, too. He felt it an insult to the House with the Green Shutters that the laird should refuse its proffered hospitality. He hated to be dragged to a meeting he despised. Never before was such irritation between them.

When they came to the hall, where the meeting was convened, there were knots of bodies grouped about the floor. Wilson fluttered from group to group, an important man, with a roll of papers in his hand. Gourlay, quick for once in his dislike, took in every feature of the man he loathed.

Wilson was what the sentimental women of the neighbourhood called a "bonny man." His features were remarkably regular, and his complexion was remarkably fair. His brow was so delicate of hue that the blue veins running down his temples could be traced distinctly beneath the whiteness of the skin. Unluckily for him he was so fair, that in a strong light (as now beneath the gas) the suspicion of his unwashedness became a certainty—"as if he got a bit idle slaik now and than, and never a good rub," thought Gourlay in a clean disgust. Full lips showed themselves bright red in the middle between the two wings of a very blonde and very symmetrical moustache. The ugly feature of the face was the blue calculating eyes. They were tender round the lids, so that the white lashes stuck out in little peaks. And in conversation he had a habit of peering out of these eyes as if he were constantly spying for something to emerge that he might twist to his advantage. As he talked to a man close by, and glimmered (not at the man beside him, but far away in the distance of his mind at some chance of gain suggested by the other's words) Gourlay heard him say musingly, "Imphm; imphm; imphm; there might be something *in* that!" nodding his head and stroking his moustache, as he uttered each meditative "imphm."

It was Wilson's unconscious revelation that his mind was busy with a commercial hint which he had stolen from his neighbour's talk. "The damned sneck-drawer!" thought Gourlay, enlightened by his hate, "he's sucking Tam Finlay's brains, to steal some idea himsell!" And still as Wilson listened he murmured swiftly, "Imphm! I see, Mr Finlay; imphm! imphm! imphm!" nodding his head and pulling his moustache and glimmering at his new "opportunity."

Our insight is often deepest into those we hate, because annoyance fixes our thought on them to probe. We cannot keep our minds off them—"Why do they do it?" we snarl, and wondering why, we find out their character. Gourlay was not an observant man, but every man is in any man somewhere, and hate tonight driving his mind into Wilson, helped him to read him like an open book. He recognized with a vague uneasiness—not with fear, for Gourlay did not know what it meant, but with uneasy anger—the superior cunning of his rival. Gourlay, a strong block of a man cut off from the world by impotence of speech, could never have got out of Finlay what Wilson drew from him in two minutes' easy conversation.

Wilson ignored Gourlay, but he was very blithe with Templandmuir and inveigled him off to a corner. They talked together very briskly, and Wilson laughed once with uplifted head, glancing across at Gourlay as he laughed. Curse them, were they speaking of him?

The hall was crammed at last, and the important bodies

took their seats upon the front benches. Gourlay refused to be seated with the rest, but stood near the platform, with his back to the wall, by the side of Templandmuir.

After what the Provost described as "a few preliminary remarks"—they lasted half an hour—he called on Mr Wilson to address the meeting. Wilson descanted on the benefits that would accrue to Barbie if it got the railway, and on the needcessity for a "long pull and a strong pull and a pull altogether"—a phrase which he repeated many times in the course of his address. He sat down at last amid thunders of applause.

"There's no needcessity for me to make a loang speech," said the Provost.

"Hear, hear!" said Gourlay, and the meeting was unkind enough to laugh.

"Order, order!" cried Wilson perkily.

"As I was saying when I was grossly interrupted," fumed the Provost, "there's no needcessity for me to make a loang speech. I had thoat we were a-all agreed on the desirabeelity of the rileway coming in our direction. I had thoat, after the able—I must say the very able—speech of Mr Wilson, that there wasn't a man in this room so shtupid as to utter a word of dishapproval. I had thoat we might prosheed at woance to elect a deputation. I had thoat we would get the name of everybody here for the great petition we mean to send the Pow-ers. I had thoat it was all, so to shpeak, a foregone conclusion. But it seems I was mistaken, ladies and gentle-men—or rather, I oat to say gentleman, for I believe there are no ladies present. Yass, it seems I was mistaken. It may be there are some who would like to keep Barbie going on in the oald way which they found so much to their advan-tage. It may be there are some who regret a change that will put an end to their chances of tyraneezin'. It may be there are some who know themselves so shtupid that they fear the new condeetions of trade the railway's bound to bring."— Here Wilson rose and whispered in his ear, and the people watched them, wondering what hint J.W. was passing to the Provost. The Provost leaned with pompous gravity toward his monitor, hand at ear to catch the treasured words. He nodded and resumed.—"Now, gentlemen, as Mr. Wilson said,—this is a case that needs a loang pull, and a stroang pull, and a pull altogether. We must be unanimous. It will *noat* do to show ourselves divided among ourselves. Therefore, I think, we oat to have expressions of opinion from some of our leading townsmen. That will show how far we are unanimous. I had thoat there could be only one opinion, and that we might prosheed at once with the petition. But it seems I was wroang. It is best to enquire first exactly where we stand. So I call upon Mr. John Gourlay who has been the foremost man in the town for mainy years—at least he used to be that—I call upon Mr. Gourlay as the first to express an opinion on the subjeck."

Wilson's hint to the Provost placed Gourlay in a fine dilemma. Stupid as he was he was not so stupid as not to perceive the general advantage of the railway. If he approved it, however, he would seem to support Wilson and the Provost whom he loathed. If he disapproved, his opposition would be set down to a selfish consideration for his own trade, and he would incur the anger of the meeting, which was all for the coming of the railway. Wilson had seized the chance to put him in a false position. He knew Gourlay could not put forty words together in public, and that in his dilemma he would blunder and give himself away.

Gourlay evaded the question.

"It would be better to convene a meeting," he bawled to the Provost, "to consider the state of some folk's back-doors."—That was a nipper to Wilson!—"There's a stink at the Cross that's enough to kill a cuddy!"

"Evidently not," yelled Wilson, "since you're still alive!"

A roar went up against Gourlay. All he could do was to scowl before him, with hard-set mouth and gleaming eyes, while they bellowed him to scorn.

"I would like to hear what Templandmuir has to say on the subject," said Wilson getting up. "But no doubt he'll follow his friend, Mr Gourlay."

"No, I don't follow Mr. Gourlay," bawled Templand-muir with unnecessary loudness. The reason of his vehemence was twofold. He was nettled (as Wilson meant he should be)[1] by the suggestion that he was nothing but Gourlay's henchman. And, being eager to oppose Gourlay, yet a coward, he yelled to supply in noise what he lacked in resolution.

"I don't follow Mr. Gourlay at all," he roared. "I follow nobody but myself! Every man in the district's in support of this petition. It would be absurd to suppose anything else. I'll be glad to sign't among the first, and do everything I can in its support."

"Verra well," said the Provost, "it seems we're agreed after all. We'll get some of our foremost men to sign the petition at this end of the hall, and then it'll be placed in the anteroom for the rest to sign as they go out."

"Take it across to Gourlay," whispered Wilson to the two men who were carrying the enormous tome. They took it over to the grain-merchant, and one of them handed him an inkhorn. He dashed it to the ground.

The meeting hissed like a cellarful of snakes. But Gourlay turned and glowered at them, and somehow the hisses died away. His was the high courage that feeds on hate, and welcomes rather than shrinks from its expression. He was smiling as he faced them.

"Let *me* pass," he said, and shouldered his way to the door, the bystanders falling back to make room. Templandmuir followed him out.

"I'll walk to the head o' the brae," said the Templar.

He must have it out with Gourlay at once, or else go home to meet the anger of his wife. Having opposed Gourlay already, he felt that now was the time to break with him for good. Only a little was needed to complete the rupture. And he was the more impelled to declare himself to-night because he had just seen Gourlay discomfited, and was beginning to despise the man he had formerly admired. Why the whole meeting had laughed at his expense! In quarrelling with Gourlay, moreover, he would have the whole locality behind him. He would range himself on the popular side. Every impulse of mind and body pushed him forward to the brink of speech; he would never get a better occasion to bring out

[1] As in Memorial edition. Other editions omit *be*.

his grievance.

They trudged together in a burning silence. Though nothing was said between them, each was in wrathful contact with the other's mind. Gourlay blamed everything that had happened on Templandmuir, who had dragged him to the meeting and deserted him. And Templandmuir was longing to begin about the quarry, but afraid to start.

That was why he began at last with false unnecessary loudness. It was partly to encourage himself (as a bull bellows to increase his rage) and partly because his spite had been so long controlled. It burst the louder for its pent fury.

"Mr. Gourlay!" he bawled suddenly, when they came opposite the House with the Green Shutters, "I've had a crow to pick with you for more than a year!"

It came on Gourlay with a flash that Templandmuir was slipping away from him. But he must answer him civilly for the sake of the quarry.

"Aye man," he said quietly, "and what may that be?"

"I'll damned soon tell you what it is," said the Templar. "Yon was a monstrous overcharge for bringing my ironwork from Fleckie. I'll be damned if I put up with that!"

And yet it was only a trifle. He had put up with fifty worse impositions and never said a word. But when a man is bent on a quarrel any spark will do for an explosion.

"How do ye make that out?" said Gourlay, still very quietly, lest he should alienate the quarry laird.

"Damned fine do I make that out," yelled Templandmuir, and louder than ever was the yell. He was the brave man now, with his bellow to hearten him. "Damned fine do I make that out. You charged me for a whole day, though half o't was spent upon your own concerns. I'm tired o' you and your cheatry. You've made a braw penny out o' me in your time. But curse me if I endure it loanger. I give you notice this verra night that your tack o' the quarry must end at Martinmas."

He was off, glad to have it out and glad to escape the consequence, leaving Gourlay a cauldron of wrath in the darkness. It was not merely the material loss that maddened him. But for the first time in his life he had taken a rebuff without a word or a blow in return. In his desire to conciliate he had let Templandmuir get away unscathed. His blood rocked him where he stood.

He walked blindly to the kitchen door—never knowing how he reached it. It was locked—at this early hour!—and the simple inconvenience let loose the fury of his wrath. He struck the door with his clenched fist till the blood streamed on his knuckles.

It was Mrs. Gourlay who opened the door to him. She started back before his awful eyes.

"John!" she cried, "what's wrong wi' ye?"

The sight of the she-tatterdemalion there before him, whom he had endured so long and must endure forever, was the crowning burden of his night. Damn her, why didn't she get out of the way, why did she stand there in her dirt and ask silly questions? He struck her on the bosom with his great fist, and sent her spinning on the dirty table.

She rose from among the broken dishes, and came towards him, with slack lips and great startled eyes. "John," she panted, like a pitiful frightened child, "what have I been doing? . . . Man, what did you hit me for?"

He gaped at her with hanging jaw. He knew he was a brute —knew she had done nothing to-night more than she had ever done, knew he had vented on her a wrath that should have burst on others. But his mind was at a stick; how could he explain—to *her*? He gaped and glowered for a speechless moment, then turned on his heel and went into the parlour, slamming the door till the windows rattled in their frames.

She stared after him a while in a large-eyed stupor, then flung herself in her old nursing chair by the fire, and spat blood in the ribs, hawking it up coarsely—we forget to be delicate in moments of supremer agony. And then she flung her apron over her head and rocked herself to and fro in the chair where she had nursed his children, wailing: "It's a pity o' me, it's a pity o' me! My God, aye, it's a geyan pity o' me!"

The boy was in bed, but Janet had watched the scene with a white scared face and tearful cries. She crept to her mother's side.

The sympathy of children with those who weep is innocently selfish. The sight of tears makes them uncomfortable, and they want them to cease, in the interests of their own happiness. If the outward signs of grief would only vanish, all would be well. They are not old enough to appreciate the inward agony.

So Janet tugged at the obscuring apron, and whimpered, "Don't greet, mother, don't greet. Woman, I dinna like to see ye greetin'."

But Mrs. Gourlay still rocked herself and wailed, "It's a pity o' me, it's a pity o' me; my God, aye, it's a geyan pity o' me!"

CHAPTER 13

"Is he in himself?" asked Gibson the builder, coming into the Emporium.

Mrs. Wilson was alone in the shop. Since trade grew so brisk she had an assistant to help her, but he was out for his breakfast at present, and as it happened she was all alone.

"No," she said, "he's no in! We're terribly driven this twelve-month back, since trade grew so thrang, and he's aye hunting business in some corner. He's out the now after a carrying affair. Was it ainything particular?"

She looked at Gibson with a speculation in her eyes that almost verged on hostility. Wives of the lower classes who are active helpers in a husband's affairs often direct that look upon strangers who approach him in the way of business. For they are enemies whatever way you take them; come to be done by the husband or to do him—in either case, therefore, the object of a sharp curiosity. You may call on an educated man, either to fleece him or be fleeced, and his wife, though she knows all about it, will talk to you charmingly of trifles, while you wait for him in her parlour. But a wife of the lower orders, active in her husband's affairs, has not been trained to dissemble so prettily—though her face be a mask, what she is wondering comes out in her eye. There was suspicion in the big round stare that Mrs. Wilson directed at the builder. What was *he* speiring for "himsell" for? What could he be up to? Some end of his own, no doubt. Anxious curiosity forced her to enquire.

"Would I do instead?" she asked.

"Well, hardly," said Gibson, clawing his chin, and gazing at a corded round of "Barbie's Best" just above his head. "Dod, it's a fine ham that," he said, to turn the subject. "How are ye selling it the now?"

"Tenpence a pound retail, but ninepence only if ye take a whole one. Ye had better let me send you one, Mr. Gibson, now that winter's drawing on! It's a heartsome thing, the smell of frying ham on a frosty morning—" and her laugh went skelloching up the street.

"Well, ye see," said Gibson with a grin, "I expect Mr. Wilson to present me with one, when he hears the news that I have brought him."

"Aha!" said she, "it's something good then," and she stuck her arms akimbo. "James!" she shrilled, "James!"— and the red-haired boy shot from the back premises.

"Run up to the Red Lion, and see if your father has finished his crack wi' Templandmuir. Tell him Mr. Gibson wants to see him on important business."

The boy squinted once at the visitor, and scooted, the red head of him foremost.

While Gibson waited and clawed his chin she examined him narrowly. Suspicion as to the object of his visit fixed her attention on his face.

He was a man with mean brown eyes. Brown eyes may be clear and limpid as a mountain pool, or they may have the fine black flash of anger and the jovial gleam, or they may be mean things—little and sly and oily. Gibson's had the depth of cunning, not the depth of character, and they glistened like the eyes of a lustful animal. He was a reddish man, with a fringe of sandy beard, and a perpetual grin which showed his yellow teeth, with green deposit round their roots. It was more than a grin, it was a rictus, semicircular from cheek to cheek, and the beady eyes, ever on the watch up above it, belied its false benevolence. He was not florid, yet that grin of his seemed to intensify his reddishness (perhaps because it brought out and made prominent his sandy valance and the ruddy round of his cheeks) so that the baker christened him long ago "the man with the sandy smile." "Cunning Johnny" was his other nickname. Wilson had recognized a match in him the moment he came to Barbie, and had resolved to act with him if he could, but never to act against him. They had made advances to each other. Birds of a feather, in short.

The grocer came in hurriedly, white-waistcoated today, and a perceptibly bigger bulge in his belly than when we first saw him in Barbie, four years ago now.

"Good morning, Mr. Gibson," he panted. "Is it private that ye wanted to see me on?"

"Verra private," said the sandy smiler.

"We'll go through to the house then," said Wilson, and ushered his guest through the back premises. But the voice of his wife recalled him. "James!" she cried. "Here for a minute just!" and he turned to her, leaving Gibson in the yard.

"Be careful what you're doing," she whispered in his ear. "It wisna for nothing they christened Gibson 'Cunning Johnny.' Keep the dirt out your e'en."

"There's no fear of that," he assured her pompously. It was a grand thing to have a wife like that, but her advice nettled him now just a little, because it seemed to imply a doubt of his efficiency—and that was quite onnecessar. He knew what he was doing. They would need to rise very early that got the better o' a man like him!

"You'll take a dram?" said Wilson when they reached a pokey little room where the most conspicuous and dreary object was a large bare flowerpot of red earthenware, on a green woollen mat, in the middle of a round table. Out of the flowerpot rose gauntly a three-sticked frame, up which two lonely stalks of a climbing plant tried to scramble, but failed miserably to reach the top. The round little rickety table with the family album on one corner (placed at what Mrs Wilson considered a beautiful artistic angle to the window), the tawdry cloth, the green mat, the shiny horse-hair sofa, and the stuffy atmosphere, were all in a perfect harmony of ugliness. A sampler on the wall informed the world that there was no place like home.

Wilson pushed the flowerpot to one side, and "You'll take a dram?" he said blithely.

"Oh, aye," said Gibson with a grin, "I never refuse drink when I'm offered it for nothing."

"Hi! hi!" laughed Wilson at the little joke, and produced a cut decanter and a pair of glasses. He filled the glasses so brimming full that the drink ran over on the table.

"Canny, man, for God's sake canny!" cried Gibson

starting forward in alarm. "Don't ye see you're spilling the mercies?" He stooped his lips to the rim of his glass, and sipped, lest a drop of Scotia's nectar should escape him.

They faced each other, sitting. "Here's pith!" said Gibson —"Pith!" said the other in chorus, and they nodded to each other in amity, primed glasses up and ready. And then it was eyes heavenward and the little finger uppermost.

Gibson smacked his lips once and again when the fiery spirit tickled his uvula.

"Ha!" said he, "that's the stuff to put heart in a man."

"It's no bad whiskey," said Wilson complacently.

Gibson wiped the sandy stubble round his mouth with the back of his hand, and considered for a moment. Then, leaning forward, he tapped Wilson's knee in whispering importance.

"Have you heard the news?" he murmured, with a watchful glimmer in his eyes.

"No!" cried Wilson glowering, eager and alert. "Is't ocht in the business line? Is there a possibeelity for me in't?"

"Oh, there might," nodded Gibson, playing his man for a while.

"Aye man!" cried Wilson briskly, and brought his chair an inch or two forward. Gibson grinned and watched him with his beady eyes.—"What green teeth he has!" thought Wilson who was not fastidious.

"The Coal Company are meaning to erect a village for five hundred miners a mile out the Fleckie Road, and they're running a branch line up the Lintie's Burn, that'll need the building of a dozen brigs. I'm happy to say I have nabbed the contract for the building."

"Man, Mr. Gibson, d'ye tell me that! I'm proud to hear it, sir; I am that!" Wilson was hotching in his chair with eagerness. For what could Gibson be wanting with *him* if it wasna to arrange about the carting? "Fill up your glass, Mr. Gibson, man; fill up your glass! You're drinking nothing at all. Let *me* help you!"

"Aye, but I havena the contract for the carting," said Gibson. "That's not mine to dispose of. They mean to keep it in their own hand."

Wilson's mouth forgot to shut, and his eyes were big and round as his mouth in staring disappointment. Was it this he was wasting his drink for?

"Where do I come in?" he asked blankly.

Gibson tossed off another glassful of the burning heartener of men, and leaned forward with his elbows on the table.

"D'ye ken Goudie, the Company's Manager? He's worth making up to, I can tell ye. He has complete control of the business, and can airt you the road of a good thing. I made a point of helping him in everything, ever since he came to Barbie, and I'm glad to say that he hasna forgotten't. Man, it was through him I got the building contract—they never threw't open to the public. But they mean to contract separate for carting the material. That means that they'll need the length of a dozen horses on the road for a twelvemonth to come; for it's no only the building—they're launching out on a big scale, and there's lots of other things forbye. Now Goudie's as close as a whin and likes to keep everything dark till the proper time comes for sploring o't. Not a whisper has been heard so far about this village for the miners—there's a rumour, to be sure, about a wheen houses going up, but nothing *near* the reality. And there's not a soul, either, that kens there's a big contract for carting to be had 'ceptna Goudie and mysell. But or a month's bye, they'll be advertising for estimates for a twelvemonth's carrying. I thocht a hint aforehand would be worth something to you, and that's the reason of my visit."

"I see," said Wilson briskly. "You're verra good, Mr. Gibson. You mean you'll give me an inkling in private of the other estimates sent in, and help to arrange mine according?"

"Na," said Gibson. Goudie's owre close to let me ken! I'll speak a word in his ear on your behalf, to be sure, if you agree to the proposal I mean to put before you. But Gourlay's the man you need to keep your eye on. It's you or him for the contract—there's nobody else to compete wi' the two o' ye."

"Imphm, I see," said Wilson, and tugged his moustache in

meditation. All expression died out of his face while his brain churned within. What Brodie had christened "the considering keek" was in his eyes; they were far away, and saw the distant village in process of erection; busy with its chances and occasions. Then an uneasy thought seemed to strike him and recall him to the man by his side. He stole a shifty glance at the sandy smiler.

"But I thought *you* were a friend of Gourlay's," he said slowly.

"Friendship!" said Gibson. "We're speaking of business! And there's sma-all friendship atween me and Gourlay. He was nebby owre a bill I sent in the other day; and I'm getting tired of his bluster. Besides, there's little more to be made of him. Gourlay's bye wi't. But you're a rising man, Mr Wilson, and I think that you and me might work thegither to our own advantage, don't ye see? Yes; just so; to the advantage of us both. Oom?"

"I hardly see what you're driving at," said Wilson.

"I'm driving at this," said Gibson. "If Gourlay kens you're against him for the contract, he'll cut his estimate down to a ruinous price, out o' sheer spite—yes, out o' sheer spite—rather than be licked by *you* in public competition. And if he does that, Goudie and I may do what we like, but we canna help you. For it's the partners that decide the estimates sent in, d'ye see? Imphm, it's the partners. Goudie has noathing to do wi' that. And if Gourlay once gets round the partners, you'll be left out in the cold for a very loang time. Shivering, sir, shivering! You will that!"

"Dod, you're right. There's a danger of that. But I fail to see how we can prevent it!"

"We can put Gourlay on a wrong scent," said Gibson.

"But how though?"

Gibson met one question by another.

"What was the charge for a man and a horse and a day's carrying when ye first came hereaway?" he asked.

"Only four shillings a day," said Wilson promptly. "It has risen to six now," he added.

"Exactly!" said Gibson; "and with the new works coming in about the town it'll rise to eight yet! I have it for a fact that the Company's willing to gie that! Now if you and me could procure a job for Gourlay at the lower rate, before the news o' this new industry gets scattered—a job that would require the whole of his plant, you understand, and prevent his competing for the Company's business—we would clear" —he clawed his chin to help his arithmetic—"we could clear three hundred and seventy-four pounds o' difference on the twelvemonth. At least *you* would make that," he added, "but you would allow me a handsome commission of course —the odd hundred and seventy, say—for bringing the scheme before ye! I don't think there's ocht unreasonable in tha-at! For it's not the mere twelvemonth's work that's at stake, you understand, it's the valuable connection for the fee-yuture! Now, I have influence wi' Goudie; I can help you there. But if Gourlay gets in there's just a chance that you'll never be able to oust him."

"I see," said Wilson. "Before he knows what's coming, we're to provide work for Gourlay at the lower rate, both to put money in our own pocket and prevent him competing for the better business."

"You've summed it to the nines," said Gibson.

"Yes," said Wilson blankly, "but how on earth are *we* to provide work for him?"

Gibson leaned forward a second time and tapped Wilson on the knee.

"Have you never considered what a chance for building there's in that holm of yours?" he asked. "You've a fortune there, lying undeveloped!"

That was the point to which Cunning Johnny had been leading all the time. He cared as little for Wilson as for Gourlay; all he wanted was a contract for covering Wilson's holm with jerry-built houses, and a good commission on the year's carrying. It was for this he evolved the conspiracy to cripple Gourlay.

Wilson's thoughts went to and fro like the shuttle of a weaver. He blinked in rapidity of thinking, and stole shifty glances at his comrade. He tugged his moustache and said "Imphm" many times. Then his eyes went off in their long preoccupied stare, and the sound of the breath, coming heavy through his nostrils, was audible in the quiet room. Wilson was one of the men whom you hear thinking.

"I see," he said slowly. "You mean to bind Gourlay to cart building material to my holm, at the present price of work. You'll bind him in general terms so that he canna suspect, till the time comes, who in particular he's to work for. In the meantime I'll be free to offer for the Company's business at the higher price."

"That's the size o't," said Gibson.

Wilson was staggered by the rapid combinations of the scheme. But Cunning Johnny had him in the toils. The plan he proposed stole about the grocer's every weakness, and tugged his inclinations to consent. It was very important, he considered, that he, and no other, should obtain this contract, which was both valuable in itself and an earnest of other business in the future. And Gibson's scheme got Gourlay, the only possible rival, out of the way. For it was not possible for Gourlay to put more than twelve horses on the road, and if he thought he had secured a good contract already, he would never dream of applying for another. Then, Wilson's malice was gratified by the thought that Gourlay, who hated him, should have to serve, as helper and underling, in a scheme for his aggrandizement. That would take down his pride for him! And the commercial imagination, so strong in Wilson, was inflamed by the vision of himself as a wealthy house-owner which Gibson put before him. Cunning Johnny knew all this when he broached the scheme—he foresaw the pull of it on Wilson's nature. Yet Wilson hesitated. He did not like to give himself to Gibson quite so rapidly.

"You go fast, Mr Gibson," said he. "Faith, you go fast! This is a big affair, and needs to be looked at for a while."

"Fast!" cried Gibson. "Damn it, we have no time to waste. We maun act on the spur of the moment."

"I'll have to borrow money," said Wilson slowly, "and it's verra dear at the present time."

"It was never worth more in Barbie than it is at the present time. Man, don't ye see the chance you're neglecting? Don't ye see what it means? There's thousands lying at

103

your back door if ye'll only reach to pick them up! Yes, thousands! Thousands, I'm telling ye! Thousands!"

Wilson saw himself provost and plutocrat. Yet was he cautious.

"*You*'ll do well by the scheme," he said tartly, "if you get the sole contract for building these premises of mine, and a fat commission on the carrying forbye!"

"Can you carry the scheme without me?" said Gibson. "A word from me to Goudie means a heap." There was a veiled threat in the remark.

"Oh, we'll come to terms," said the other. "But how will you manage Gourlay?"

"Aha!" said Gibson, "I'll come in handy for that, you'll discover! There's been a backset in Barbie for the last year— things went owre quick at the start and were followed by a wee lull; but it's only for a time, sir, it's only for a time. Hows'ever, it and you thegither have damaged Gourlay— he's both short o' work and scarce o' cash, as I found to my cost when I asked him for my siller! So when I offer him a big contract for carting stones atween the quarry and the town foot, he'll swallow it without question. I'll insert a clause that he must deliver the stuff at such places as I direct within four hundred yards of the Cross, in ainy direction—for I've several jobs near the Cross, doan't ye see, and how's he to know that yours is one o' them? Man, it's easy to bamboozle an ass like Gourlay! Besides, he'll think my principals have trusted me to let the carrying to ainyone I like, and, as I let it to him, he'll fancy I'm on his side, doan't ye see?— he'll never jalouse that I mean to diddle him. In the meantime we'll spread the news that you're meaning to build on a big scale upon your own land—we'll have the ground levelled, the foundations dug, and the drains and everything seen to. Now, it'll never occur to Gourlay, in the present slackness o' trade, that you would contract wi' another man to cart your material, and go hunting for other work yoursell.That'll throw him off the scent till the time comes to put his nose on't. When the Company advertise for estimates he canna compete wi' you, because he's pre-engaged to me, and he'll think you're out o't, too, because you're busy wi' your own woark. You'll be free to nip the eight shillings. Then we'll force him to fulfil his bargain and cart for us at six!"

"If he refuses?" said Wilson.

"I'll have the contract stamped and signed in the presence of witnesses," said Gibson. "Not that that's necessary, I believe, but a double knot's aye the safest."

Wilson looked at him with admiration.

"Gosh, Mr Gibson," he cried, "you're a warmer! Ye deserve your name. Ye ken what the folk ca' you?"

"Oh, yes," said Gibson complacently. "I'm quite proud o' the description."

"I've my ain craw to pick wi' Gourlay." he went on. "He was damned ill-bred yestreen when I asked him to settle my account, and talked about extortion. But bide a wee, bide a wee! I'll enjoy the look on his face when he sees himself forced to carry for you, at a rate lower than the market price."

When Gibson approached Gourlay on the following day he was full of laments about the poor state of trade.

"Aye," said he, "the grand railway they boasted o' hasna done muckle for the town!"

"Atweel aye," quoth Gourlay with pompous wisdom; "they'll maybe find, or a's bye, that the auld way wasna the warst way. There was to be a great boom, as they ca't, but I see few signs o't."

"I see few signs o't, either," said Gibson, "it's the slackest time for the last twa years."

Gourlay grunted his assent.

"But I've a grand job for ye, for a' that," said Gibson, slapping his hands. "What do ye say to the feck of a year's carting tweesht the quarry and the town foot?"

"I might consider that," said Gourlay, "if the terms were good."

"Six shillins," said Gibson and went on in solemn protest: "In the present state o' trade, doan't ye see, I couldna give a penny more." Gourlay, who had denounced the present state of trade even now, was prevented by his own words from asking for a penny more.

"At the town foot, you say?" he asked.

"I've several jobs thereaway," Gibson explained hurriedly; "and you must agree to deliver stuff ainy place I want it within four hundred yards o' the Cross!—It's all one to you, of course," he went on, "seeing you're paid by the day."

"Oh, it's all one to me," said Gourlay.

Peter Riney and the new "orra" man were called in to witness the agreement. Cunning Johnny had made it as cunning as he could.

"We may as well put a stamp on't," said he, "A stamp costs little, and means a heap."

"You're damned particular the day," cried Gourlay in a sudden heat.

"Oh, nothing more than my usual, nothing more than my usual," said Gibson blandly. "Good morning, Mr Gourlay," and he made for the door, buttoning the charter of his dear revenge in the inside pocket of his coat. Gourlay ignored him.

When Gibson got out he turned to the House with the Green Shutters, and "Curse you!" said he, "you may refuse to answer me the day, but wait till this day eight weeks. You'll be roaring than."

On that day eight weeks Gourlay received a letter from Gibson requiring him to hold himself in readiness to deliver stone, lime, baulks of timber, and iron girders in Mr Wilson's holm, in terms of his agreement, and in accordance with the orders to be given him from day to day. He was apprised that a couple of carts of lime and seven loads of stone were needed on the morrow.

He went down the street with grinding jaws, the letter crushed to a white pellet in his hand. It would have gone ill with Gibson had he met him. Gourlay could not tell why, or to what purpose, he marched on and on with forward staring eyes. He only knew vaguely that the anger drove him.

When he came to the Cross a long string of carts was filing from the Skeighan Road, and passing across to the street leading Fleckie-ward. He knew them to be Wilson's. The Deacon was there of course, hobbling on his thin shanks, and cocking his eye to see everything that happened.

"What does this mean?" Gourlay asked him, though he loathed the Deacon.

"Oh, haven't ye heard?" quoth the Deacon blithely. "That's the stuff for the new mining village out the Fleckie Road. Wilson has nabbed the contract for the carting. They're saying it was Gibson's influence wi' Goudie that helped him to the getting o't!"

Amid his storm of anger at the trick, Gourlay was conscious of a sudden pity for himself, as for a man most unfairly worsted. He realized for a moment his own inefficiency as a business man, in conflict with cleverer rivals, and felt sorry to be thus handicapped by nature. Though wrath was uppermost, the other feeling was revealed, shewing itself by a gulping in the throat and a rapid blinking of the eyes. The Deacon marked the signs of his chagrin.

"Man!" he reported to the bodies, "but Gourlay was cut to the quick. His face shewed how gunkit he was. Oh, but he was chawed. I saw his breist give the great heave."

"Were ye no sorry?" cried the baker.

"Thorry, hi!" laughed the Deacon. "Oh, I was thorry, to be sure," he lisped, "but I didna thyow't. I'm glad to thay I've a grand control of my emotionth. Not like thum folk we know of," he added slily, giving the baker a "good one."

All next day Gibson's masons waited for their building material in Wilson's holm. But none came. And all day seven of Gourlay's horses champed idly in their stalls.

Barbie had a weekly market now, and, as it happened, that was the day it fell on. At two in the afternoon Gourlay was standing on the gravel outside the Red Lion, trying to look wise over a sample of grain which a farmer had poured upon his great palm. Gibson approached with false voice and smile.

"Gosh, Mr Gourlay!" he cried protestingly; "have ye forgotten whatna day it is? Ye havena gi'en my men a ton o' stuff to gang on wi'!"

To the farmer's dismay his fine sample of grain was scattered on the gravel by a convulsive movement of Gourlay's arm. As Gourlay turned on his enemy, his face was frightfully distorted; all his brow seemed gathered in a knot above his nose, and he gaped on his words, yet ground them out like a labouring mill, each word solid as plug shot.

"I'll see Wil-son. . . . and Gib-son . . . . and every other man's son . . . . frying in hell," he said slowly, "ere a horse o' mine draws a stane o' Wilson's property. Be damned to ye, but there's your answer!"

Gibson's cunning deserted him for once. He put his hand on Gourlay's shoulder in pretended friendly remonstrance.

"Take your hand off my shouther!" said Gourlay in a voice the tense quietness of which should have warned Gibson to forbear.

But he actually shook Gourlay with a feigned playfulness.

Next instant he was high in air; for a moment the hobnails in the soles of his boots gleamed vivid to the sun; then Gourlay sent him flying through the big window of the Red Lion, right on to the middle of the great table where the market-folk were drinking.

For a minute he lay stunned and bleeding among the broken crockery, in a circle of white faces and startled cries.

Gourlay's face appeared at the jagged rent, his eyes narrowed to fiercely gleaming points, a hard, triumphant devilry playing round his black lips. "You damned treacherous rat!" he cried, "that's the game John Gourlay can play wi' a thing like you."

Gibson rose from the ruin on the table and came bleeding to the window, his grin a rictus of wrath, his green teeth wolfish with anger.

"By God, Gourlay," he screamed, "I'll make you pay for this; I'll fight you through a' the law courts in Breetain, but you'll implement your bond."

"Damn you for a measled swine, would you grunt at me," cried Gourlay, and made to go at him through the window. Though he could not reach him, Gibson quailed at his look. He shook his fist in impotent wrath, and spat threats of justice through his green teeth.

"To hell wi' your law-wers!" cried Gourlay, "I'd throttle ye like the dog you are on the floor o' the House o' Lords."

But that day was to cost him dear. Ere six months passed he was cast in damages and costs for a breach of contract aggravated by assault. He appealed, of course. He was not to be done; he would shew the dogs what he thought of them.

CHAPTER 14

IN those days it came to pass that Wilson sent his son to the High School of Skeighan, even James, the red-haired one, with the squint in his eye. Whereupon Gourlay sent *his* son to the High School of Skeighan, too, of course, to be upsides with Wilson. If Wilson could afford to send his boy to a distant and expensive school, then, by the Lord, so could he! And it also came to pass that James, the son of James, the grocer, took many prizes. But John, the son of John, took no prizes. Whereat there were ructions in the House of Gourlay.

Gourlay's resolve to be equal to Wilson in everything he did was his main reason for sending his son to the High School of Skeighan. That he saw his business decreasing daily was a reason, too. Young Gourlay was a lad of fifteen now, undersized for his age at that time, though he soon shot up to be a swaggering youngster. He had been looking forward with delight to helping his father in the business— how grand it would be to drive about the country and see things!—and he had irked at being kept for so long under the tawse of old Bleach-the-boys. But if the business went on at this rate there would be little in it for the boy. Gourlay was not without a thought of his son's welfare when he packed him off to Skeighan. He would give him some book-lear, he he said; let him make a kirk or a mill o't.

But John shrank, chicken-hearted, from the prospect. Was he still to drudge at books? Was he to go out among strangers whom he feared? His imagination set to work on what he heard of the High School of Skeighan and made it a bugbear. They had to do mathematics—what could *he* do wi' thae whigmaleeries? They had to recite Shakespeare in public—how could *he* stand up and spout, before a whole jing-bang o' them?

"I don't want to gang," he whined.

"Want?" flamed his father. "What does it matter what

110

you want? Go you shall."

"I thocht I was to help in the business," whimpered John.

"Business!" sneered his father. "A fine help *you* would be in business."

"Aye man, Johnnie," said his mother, maternal fondness coming out in support of her husband, "you should be glad your father can allow ye the opportunity. Eh, but it's a grand thing, a gude education! You may rise to be a minister."

Her ambition could no further go. But Gourlay seemed to have formed a different opinion of the sacred calling. "It's a' he's fit for," he growled.

So John was put to the High School of Skeighan, travelling backwards and forwards night and morning by the train, after the railway had been opened. And he discovered, on trying it, that the life was not so bad as he had feared. He hated his lessons, true, and avoided them whenever he was able. But his father's pride and his mother's fondness saw that he was well-dressed and with money in his pocket; and he began to grow important. Though Gourlay was no longer the only "big man" of Barbie, he was still one of the "big men," and a consciousness of the fact grew upon his son. When he passed his old classmates (apprentice-grocers now and carters and ploughboys) his febrile insolence led him to swagger and assume. And it was fine to mount the train at Barbie on the fresh cool mornings, and be off past the gleaming rivers and the woods. Better still was the home-coming—to board the empty train at Skeighan when the afternoon sun came pleasant through the windows, to loll on the fat cushions, and read the novelettes. He learned to smoke too, and that was a source of pride. When the train was full on market days he liked to get in among the jovial farmers who encouraged his assumptions. Meanwhile Jimmy Wilson would be elsewhere in the train, busy with his lessons for the morrow—for Jimmy had to help in the Emporium of nights—his father kept him to the grindstone. Jimmy had no more real ability than young Gourlay, but infinitely more caution. He was one of the gimlet characters who, by diligence and memory, gain prizes in their schooldays—and are fools for the remainder of their lives.

The bodies of Barbie, seeing young Gourlay at his pranks, speculated over his future, as Scotch bodies do about the future of every youngster in their ken.

"I wonder what that son o' Gourlay's 'ull come till," said Sandy Toddle, musing on him with the character-reading eye of the Scots peasant.

"To no good—you may be sure of that," said ex-Provost Connal. "He's a regular splurge! When Drunk Dan Kennedy passed him his flask in the train the other day he swigged it, just for the sake of showing off! And he's a coward, too, for all his swagger. He grew ill-bred when he swallowed the drink, and Dan, to frighten him, threatened to hang him from the window by the heels! He didn't mean it, to be sure; but young Gourlay grew white at the very idea o't—he shook like a dog in a wet sack. 'Oh!' he cried, shivering, 'how the ground would go flying past your eyes; how quick the wheel opposite ye would buzz—it would blind ye by its quickness—how the grey slag would flash below ye!' Those were his very words. He seemed to see the thing as if it were happening before his eyes, and stared like a fellow in hysteerics, till Dan was obliged to give him another drink! 'You would spue with the dizziness,' said he, and he actually bocked himsell."

Young Gourlay seemed bent on making good the prophecy of Barbie. Though his father was spending money he could ill afford on his education, he fooled away his time. His mind developed a little, no doubt, since it was no longer dazed by brutal and repeated floggings. In some of his classes he did fairly well. But others he loathed. It was the rule at Skeighan High School to change rooms every hour, the classes tramping from one to another through a big lobby. Gourlay got a habit of stealing off at such times—it was easy to slip out—and playing truant in the bye-ways of Skeighan. He often made his way to the station, and loafed in the waiting room. He had gone there on a summer afternoon, to avoid his mathematics and read a novel, when a terrible thing befell him.

For a while he swaggered round the empty platform and smoked a cigarette. Milk-cans clanked in a shed, mournfully. Gourlay had a congenital horror of eerie sounds—he was his mother's son for that—and he fled to the waiting room, to avoid the hollow clang. It was a June afternoon, of brooding heat, and a band of yellow sunshine was lying on the glazed table, showing every scratch in its surface. The place oppressed him—he was sorry he had come. But he plunged into his novel and forgot the world.

He started in fear when a voice addressed him. He looked up—and here it was only the baker!—the baker smiling at him with his fine grey eyes, the baker with his reddish fringe of beard and his honest grin, which wrinkled up his face to his eyes in merry and kindly wrinkles. He had a wonderful hearty manner with a boy.

"Aye man, John; it's you," said the baker. "Dod, I'm just in time. The storm's at the burstin!"

"Storm!" said Gourlay. He had a horror of lightning since the day of his birth.

"Aye, we're in for a pelter. What have you been doing that you didna see't?"

They went to the window. The fronting heavens were a black purple. The thunder, which had been growling in the distance, swept forward and roared above the town. The crash no longer rolled afar, but cracked close to the ear, hard, crepitant. Quick lightning stabbed the world in vicious and repeated hate. A blue-black moistness lay heavy on the cowering earth. The rain came—a few drops at first, sullen, as if loth to come, that splashed on the pavement wide as a crown-piece—then a white rush of slanting spears. A great blob shot in through the window, open at the top, and spat wide on Gourlay's cheek. It was lukewarm. He started violently—that warmth on his cheek brought the terror so near.

The heavens were rent with a crash and the earth seemed on fire. Gourlay screamed in terror.

The baker put his arm round him in kindly protection.

"Tuts, man, dinna be feared," he said. "You're John Gourlay's son, ye know. You ought to be a hardy man."

"Aye, but I'm no," chattered John, the truth coming out in his fear. "I just let on to be."

But the worst was soon over. Lightning, both sheeted

and forked, was vivid as ever, but the thunder slunk growling away.

"The heavens are opening and shutting like a man's eye," said Gourlay; "oh, it's a terrible thing the world—" and he covered his face with his hands.

A flash shot into a mounded wood far away. "It stabbed it like a dagger!" stared Gourlay.

"Look, look, did ye see yon? It came down in a broad flash—then jerked to the side—then ran down to a sharp point again. It was like the coulter of a plough."

Suddenly a blaze of lightning flamed wide, and a fork shot down its centre.

"That," said Gourlay, "was like a red crack in a white-hot furnace door."

"Man, you're a noticing boy," said the baker.

"Aye," said John, smiling in curious self-interest, "I notice things too much. They give me pictures in my mind. I'm feared of them, but I like to think them over when they're bye."

Boys are slow of confidence to their elders, but Gourlay's terror and the baker's kindness moved him to speak. In a vague way he wanted to explain.

"I'm no feared of folk," he went on, with a faint return to his swagger. "But things get in on me. A body seems so wee compared with that—" he nodded to the warring heavens.

The baker did not understand. "Have you seen your faither?" he asked.

"My faither!" John gasped in terror. If his father should find him playing truant!

"Yes; did ye no ken he was in Skeighan? We come up thegither by the ten train, and are meaning to gang hame by this. I expect him every moment."

John turned to escape. In the doorway stood his father.

When Gourlay was in wrath he had a widening glower that enveloped the offender; yet his eye seemed to stab— a flash shot from its centre to transfix and pierce. Gaze at a tiger through the bars of his cage, and you will see the look. It widens and concentrates at once.

"What are you doing here?" he asked, with the wild-beast glower on his son.

"I—I—I," John stammered and choked.

"What are you doing here?" said his father.

John's fingers worked before him; his eyes were large and aghast on his father; though his mouth hung open no words would come.

"How lang has he been here, baker?"

There was a curious regard between Gourlay and the baker. Gourlay spoke with a firm civility.

"Oh, just a wee whilie," said the baker.

"I see! You want to shield him.—You have been playing the truant, have 'ee? Am I to throw away gude money on *you* for this to be the end o't?"

"Dinna be hard on him, John," pleaded the baker. "A boy's but a boy. Dinna thrash him."

"Me thrash him!" cried Gourlay. "I pay the High School of Skeighan to thrash him, and I'll take damned good care I get my money's worth. I don't mean to hire dowgs and bark for mysell!"

He grabbed his son by the coat-collar and swung him out the room. Down High Street he marched, carrying his cub by the scruff of the neck as you might carry a dirty puppy to an outhouse. John was black in the face; time and again in his wrath Gourlay swung him off the ground. Grocers coming to their doors, to scatter fresh yellow sawdust on the old, now trampled black and wet on the sills, stared sideways, chins up and mouths open, after the strange spectacle. But Gourlay splashed on amid the staring crowd, never looking to the right or left.

Opposite The Fiddler's Inn whom should they meet but Wilson! A snigger shot to his features at the sight. Gourlay swung the boy up—for a moment a wild impulse surged within him to club his rival with his own son.

He marched into the vestibule of the High School, the boy dangling from his great hand.

"Where's your gaffer?" he roared at the janitor.

"Gaffer?" blinked the janitor.

"Gaffer, dominie, whatever the damn you ca' him, the fellow that runs the business."

"The Headmaster!" said the janitor.

"Heid-maister, aye!" said Gourlay in scorn, and went trampling after the janitor down a long wooden corridor. A door was flung open showing a class-room where the Headmaster was seated teaching Greek.

The sudden appearance of the great-chested figure in the door, with his fierce gleaming eyes, and the rain-beads shining on his frieze coat, brought into the close academic air the sharp strong gust of an outer world.

"I believe I pay *you* to look after that boy," thundered Gourlay; "is this the way you do your work?" And with the word he sent his son spinning along the floor like a curling-stone, till he rattled, a wet huddled lump, against a row of chairs. John slunk bleeding behind the master.

"Really!" said MacCandlish, rising in protest.

"Don't 'really' me, sir! I pay *you* to teach that boy, and you allow him to run idle in the streets! What have you to seh?"

"But what can I do?" bleated MacCandlish, with a white spread of deprecating hands. The stronger man took the grit from his limbs.

"Do? Do? Damn it, sir, am *I* to be *your* dominie? Am *I* to teach *you* your duty? Do! Flog him, flog him, flog him—if you don't send him hame wi' the welts on him as thick as that forefinger, I'll have a word to say to you-ou, Misterr MacCandlish!"

He was gone—they heard him go clumping along the corridor.

Thereafter young Gourlay had to stick to his books. And, as we know, the forced union of opposites breeds the greater disgust between them. However, his schooldays would soon be over, and meanwhile it was fine to pose on his journeys to and fro as Young Hopeful of the Green Shutters.

He was smoking at Skeighan Station on an afternoon, as the Barbie train was on the point of starting. He was staying on the platform till the last moment, in order to shew the people how nicely he could bring the smoke down his nostrils—his "Prince of Wales's feathers" he called the great curling puffs. As he dallied, a little aback from an open

window, he heard a voice which he knew mentioning the
Gourlays. It was Templandmuir who was speaking.

"I see that Gourlay has lost his final appeal in that law-
suit of his," said the Templar.

"D'ye tell me that?" said a strange voice. Then—"Gosh,
he must have lost infernal!"

"Atweel has he that," said Templandmuir. "The costs
must have been enormous, and then there's the damages. He
would have been better to settle't and be done wi't, but his
pride made him fight it to the hindmost! It has made touch
the boddom of his purse, I'll wager ye. Weel, weel, it'll help
to subdue his pride a bit, and muckle was the need o' that."

Young Gourlay was seized with a sudden fear. The
prosperity of the House with the Green Shutters had been a
fact of his existence; it had never entered his boyish mind to
question its continuance. But a weakening doubt stole
through his limbs. What would become of him, if the Gourlays were threatened with disaster? He had a terrifying
vision of himself as a lonely atomy, adrift on a tossing world,
cut off from his anchorage.

"Mother, are *we* ever likely to be ill off?" he asked his
mother that evening.

She ran her fingers through his hair, pushing it back from
his brow fondly. He was as tall as herself now.

"No, no, dear; what makes ye think that? Your father has
always had a grand business, and I brought a hantle money
to the house."

"Hokey!" said the youth, "when Ah'm in the business,
Ah'll have the times!"

CHAPTER 15

GOURLAY was hard up for money. Every day of his life taught him that he was nowhere in the stress of modern competition. The grand days—only a few years back, but seeming half a century away, so much had happened in between—the grand days when he was the only big man in the locality, and carried everything with a high hand, had disappeared for ever. Now all was bustle, hurry and confusion, the getting and sending of telegrams, quick despatches by railway, the watching of markets at a distance, rapid combinations that bewildered Gourlay's duller mind. At first he was too obstinate to try the newer methods; when he did, he was too stupid to use them cleverly. When he plunged it was always at the wrong time, for he plunged at random, not knowing what to do. He had lost heavily of late both in grain and cheese, and the law-suit with Gibson had crippled him. It was well for him that property in Barbie had increased in value; the House with the Green Shutters was to prove the buttress of his fortune. Already he had borrowed considerably upon that security. He was now dressing to go to Skeighan and get more.

"Brodie, Gurney, and Yarrowby," of Glasgow were the lawyers who financed him, and he had to sign some papers at Goudie's office ere he touched the cash.

He was meaning to drive of course; Gourlay was proud of his gig, and always kept a spanking roadster. "What a fine figure of a man!" you thought, as you saw him coming swiftly towards you, seated high on his driving cushion. That driving cushion was Gourlay's pedestal from which he looked down on Barbie for many a day.

A quick step, yet shambling, came along the lobby. There was a pause, as of one gathering heart for a venture; then a clumsy knock on the door.

"Come in," snapped Gourlay.

Peter Riney's queer little old face edged timorously into the room. He only opened the door the width of his face, and looked ready to bolt at a word.

"Tam's deid!" he blurted.

Gourlay gashed himself frightfully with his razor, and a big red blob stood out on his cheek.

"Deid!" he stared.

"Yes," stammered Peter. "He was right enough when Elshie gae him his feed this morning, but when I went in enow, to put the harness on, he was lying deid in the loose-box. The batts—it's like."

For a moment Gourlay stared with the open mouth of an angry surprise, forgetting to take down his razor.

"Aweel, Peter," he said at last, and Peter went away.

The loss of his pony touched Gourlay to the quick. He had been stolid and dour in his other misfortunes, had taken them as they came, calmly; he was not the man to whine and cry out against the angry heavens. He had neither the weakness, not the width of nature, to indulge in the luxury of self-pity. But the sudden death of his gallant roadster, his proud pacer through the streets of Barbie, touched him with a sense of quite personal loss and bereavement. Coming on the heels of his other calamities it seemed to make them more poignant, more sinister, prompting the question if misfortune would never have an end.

"Damn it, I have enough to thole," Gourlay muttered; "surely there was no need for this to happen." And when he looked in the mirror to fasten his stock, and saw the dark strong clean-shaven face, he stared at it for a moment, with a curious compassion for the man before him, as for one who was being hardly used. The hard lips could never have framed the words, but the vague feeling in his heart, as he looked at the dark vision, was: "It's a pity of you, sir."

He put on his coat rapidly, and went out to the stable. An instinct prompted him to lock the door.

He entered the loose-box. A shaft of golden light, aswarm with motes, slanted in the quietness. Tam lay on the straw, his head far out, his neck unnaturally long, his limbs sprawling, rigid. What a spanker Tam had been! What gallant drives they had had together! When he first put Tam between the shafts five years ago, he had been driving his world before him, plenty of cash and a big way of doing.—Now Tam was dead, and his master netted in a mesh of care.

"I was always gude to the beasts at any rate," Gourlay muttered, as if pleading in his own defence.

For a long time he stared down at the sprawling carcass, musing. "Tam the powney," he said twice, nodding his head each time as he said it; "Tam the powney"; and he turned away.

How was he to get to Skeighan? He plunged at his watch. The ten o'clock train had already gone, the express did not stop at Barbie; if he waited till one o'clock he would be late for his appointment. There was a brake, true, which ran to Skeighan every Tuesday. It was a downcome, though, for a man who had been proud of driving behind his own horse-flesh to pack in among a crowd of the Barbie sprats. And if he went by the brake, he would be sure to rub shoulders with his stinging and detested foes. It was a fine day; like enough the whole jing-bang of them would be going with the brake to Skeighan. Gourlay, who shrank from nothing, shrank from the winks that would be sure to pass when they saw him, the haughty, the aloof, forced to creep among them cheek for jowl. Then his angry pride rushed towering to his aid. Was John Gourlay to turn tail for a wheen o' the Barbie dirt? Damn the fear o't! It was a public conveyance; he had the same right to use it as the rest o' folk!

The place of departure for the brake was the "Black Bull," at the Cross, nearly opposite to Wilson's. There were winks and stares and elbow-nudgings when the folk hanging round saw Gourlay coming forward; but he paid no heed. Gourlay, in spite of his mad violence when roused, was a man at all other times of a grave and orderly demeanour. He never splurged. Even his bluster was not bluster, for he never threatened the thing which he had not it in him to do. He walked quietly into the empty brake, and took his seat in the right-hand corner, at the top, close below the driver.

As he had expected, the Barbie bodies had mustered in strength for Skeighan. In a country brake it is the privilege of the important men to mount beside the driver, in order to take the air and show themselves off to an admiring world. On the dickey were ex-Provost Connal and Sandy Toddle, and between them the Deacon, tightly wedged. The Deacon was so thin (the bodie) that though he was wedged closely, he could turn and address himself to Tam Brodie, who was seated next the door.

The fun began when the horses were crawling up the first brae.

The Deacon turned with a wink to Brodie, and dropping a glance on the crown of Gourlay's hat, "Tummuth", he lisped, "what a dirty place that ith!" pointing to a hovel by the wayside.

Brodie took the cue at once. His big face flushed with a malicious grin. "Aye," he bellowed, "the owner o' that maun be married to a dirty wife, I'm thinking!"

"It must be terrible," said the Deacon, "to be married to a dirty trollop."

"Terrible," laughed Brodie; it's enough to give ainy man a gurly temper."

They had Gourlay on the hip at last. More than arrogance had kept him off from the bodies of the town; a consciousness also that he was not their match in malicious innuendo. The direct attack he could meet superbly, downing his opponent with a coarse birr of the tongue; to the veiled gibe he was a quivering hulk, to be prodded at your ease. And now the malignants were around him (while he could not get away); talking *to* each other, indeed, but *at* him, while he must keep quiet in their midst.

At every brae they came to (and there were many braes) the bodies played their malicious game, shouting remarks along the brake, to each other's ears, to his comprehension.

The new house of Templandmuir was seen above the trees.

"What a splendid house Templandmuir has built!" cried the ex-Provost.

"Splendid!" echoed Brodie. "But a laird like the Templar has a right to a fine mansion such as that! He's no' like some merchants we ken o' who throw away money on a house for no other end but vanity. Many a man builds a grand

121

house for a show-off, when he has verra little to support it. But the Templar's different. He has made a mint of money since he took the quarry in his own hand."

"He's verra thick wi' Wilson, I notice," piped the Deacon, turning with a grin, and a gleaming droop of the eye on the head of his tormented enemy. The Deacon's face was alive and quick with the excitement of the game, his face flushed with an eager grin, his eyes glittering. Decent folk in the brake behind felt compunctious visitings when they saw him turn with the flushed grin and the gleaming squint on the head of his enduring victim. "Now for another stab!" they thought.

"You may well say that," shouted Brodie. "Wilson has procured the whole of the Templar's carterage. Oh, Wilson has become a power! Yon new houses of his must be bringing in a braw penny.—I'm thinking, Mr Connal, that Wilson ought to be the Provost!"

"Strange!" cried the former Head of the Town, "that *you* should have been thinking that! I've just been in the same mind o't. Wilson's by far and away the most progressive man we have. What a business he has built in two or three years!"

"He has that!" shouted Brodie. "He goes up the brae as fast as some other folk are going down't. And yet they tell me he got a verra poor welcome from some of us the first morning he appeared in Barbie!"

Gourlay gave no sign. Others would have shown by the moist glisten of self-pity in the eye, or the scowl of wrath, how much they were moved; but Gourlay stared calmly before him, his chin resting on the head of his staff, resolute, immobile, like a stone head at gaze in the desert. Only the larger fulness of his fine nostril betrayed the hell of wrath seething within him. And when they alighted in Skeighan an observant boy said to his mother, "I saw the marks of his chirted teeth through his jaw."

But they were still far from Skeighan, and Gourlay had much to thole.

"Did ye hear?" shouted Brodie, "that Wilson is sending his son to the College at Embro' in October?"

"D'ye tell me that?" said the Provost. "What a successful lad that has been! He's a credit to moar than Wilson, he's a credit to the whole town."

"Aye," yelled Brodie, "the money wasna wasted on *him*! It must be a terrible thing when a man has a splurging ass for his son, that never got a prize!"

The Provost began to get nervous. Brodie was going too far. It was all very well for Brodie who was at the far end of the waggonette, and out of danger; but if he provoked an outbreak, Gourlay would think nothing of tearing Provost and Deacon from their perch, and tossing them across the hedge.

"What does Wilson mean to make of his son?" he enquired—a civil enough question surely.

"Oh, a minister. That'll mean six or seven years at the University."

"Indeed!" said the Provost. "That'll cost an enormous siller!"

"Oh," yelled Brodie, "but Wilson can afford it! It's not everybody can! It's all verra well to send your son to Skeighan High School, but when it comes to sending him to College, it's time to think twice of what you're doing—especially if you've little money left to come and go on."

"Yeth," lisped the Deacon, "if a man canna afford to College his son he had better put him in hith business—if he hath ainy business left to thpeak o', that ith!"

The brake swung on through merry cornfields where reapers were at work, past happy brooks flashing to the sun, through the solemn hush of ancient and mysterious woods, beneath the great white-moving clouds and blue spaces of the sky. And amid the suave enveloping greatness of the world, the human pismires stung each other and were cruel, and full of hate and malice and a petty rage.

"Oh, damn it, enough of this!" said the baker at last.

"Enough of what?" blustered Brodie.

"Of you and your gibes," said the baker with a wry mouth of disgust. "Damn it, man, leave folk alane!"

Gourlay turned to him quietly. "Thank you, baker," he said slowly. "But don't interfere on my behalf! John Gourla"

—he dwelt on his name in ringing pride—"John Gourla can fight for his own hand—if so there need to be. And pay no heed to the thing before ye. The mair ye tramp on a dirt it spreads the wider!"

"Who was referring to *you*?" bellowed Brodie.

Gourlay looked over at him in the far corner of the brake, with the wide open glower that made people blink. Brodie blinked rapidly, trying to stare fiercely the while.

"Maybe ye werena referring to me," said Gourlay slowly. "But if *I* had been in your end o' the brake *ye* would have been in hell or this!"

He had said enough. There was silence in the brake till it reached Skeighan. But the evil was done. Enough had been said to influence Gourlay to the most disastrous resolution of his life.

"Get yourself ready for the College in October," he ordered his son that evening.

"The College!" cried John, aghast.

"Yes! Is there ainything in that to gape at?" snapped his father, in sudden irritation at the boy's amaze.

"But I don't want to gang!" John whimpered as before.

"Want! What does it matter what *you* want? You should be damned glad of the chance! I mean to make ye a minister —they have plenty of money and little to do—a grand easy life o't. MacCandlish tells me you're a stupid ass, but have some little gift of words. You have every qualification!"

"It's against *my* will," John bawled angrily.

"*Your* will!" sneered his father.

To John the command was not only tyrannical, but treacherous. There had been nothing to warn him of a coming change, for Gourlay was too contemptuous of his wife and children to inform them how his business stood. John had been brought up to go into the business, and now, at the last moment he was undeceived, and ordered off to a new life, from which every instinct of his being shrank afraid. He was cursed with an imagination in excess of his brains, and in the haze of the future he saw two pictures with uncanny vividness—himself in bleak lodgings raising his head from Virgil, to wonder what they were doing at home tonight, and, contrasted with that loneliness, the others, his cronies, laughing along the country roads beneath the glimmer of the stars. They would be having the fine ploys while he was mewed up in Edinburgh. Must he leave loved Barbie and the House with the Green Shutters, must he still drudge at books which he loathed, must he venture on a new life where everything terrified his mind?

"It's a shame!" he cried. "And I refuse to go. I don't want to leave Barbie! I'm feared of Edinburgh"—and there he stopped in conscious impotence of speech. How could he explain his forebodings to a rock of a man like his father?

"No more o't!" roared Gourlay, flinging out his hand. "Not another word! You go to College in October!"

"Aye man, Johnny," said his mother, "think o' the future that's before ye!"

"Aye!" howled the youth in silly anger, "it's like to be a braw future!"

"It's the best future you can have!" growled his father.

For while rivalry, born of hate, was the propelling influence in Gourlay's mind, other reasons whispered that the course suggested by hate was a good one on its merits. His judgment, such as it was, supported the impulse of his blood. It told him that the old business would be a poor heritage for his son and that it would be well to look for another opening. The boy gave no sign of aggressive smartness to warrant a belief that he would ever pull the thing together. Better make him a minister. Surely there was enough money left about the House for tha-at! It was the best that could befall him.

Mrs Gourlay, for her part, though sorry to lose her son, was so pleased at the thought of sending him to College, and making him a minister, that she ran on in foolish maternal gabble to the wife of Drucken Wabster. Mrs Webster informed the gossips and they discussed the matter at the Cross.

"Dod," said Sandy Toddle, "Gourlay's better off than I supposed!"

"Huts!" said Brodie, "it's just a wheen bluff to blind folk!"

"It would fit him better," said the Doctor, "if he spent some money on his daughter. She ought to pass the winter in a warmer locality than Barbie. The lassie has a poor chest! I told Gourlay, but he only gave a grunt. And 'oh,' said Mrs Gourlay, 'it would be a daft-like thing to send *her* away, when John maun be weel-provided for the College.' D'ye know, I'm beginning to think there's something seriously wrong with yon woman's health! She seemed anxious to consult me on her own account, but when I offered to sound her, she wouldn't hear of it—'Na,' she cried, 'I'll keep it to mysell!'—and put her arm across her breast as if to keep me off. I do think she's hiding some complaint! Only a woman whose mind was weak with disease could have been so callous as yon about her lassie."

"Oh, her mind's weak enough," said Sandy Toddle. "It was always that! But it's only because Gourlay has tyraneezed her verra soul. I'm surprised, however, that *he* should be careless of the girl. He was aye said to be browdened upon *her.*"

"Men-folk are often like that about lassie-weans," said Johnny Coe. "They like well enough to pet them when they're wee, but when once they're big they never look the road they're on! They're a' very fine when they're pets, but they're no sae fine when they're pretty misses. And, to tell the truth, Janet Gourlay's ainything but pretty!"

Old Bleach-the-boys, the bitter dominie (who rarely left the studies in political economy which he found a solace for his thwarted powers) happened to be at the Cross that evening. A brooding and taciturn man, he said nothing till others had their say. Then he shook his head.

"They're making a great mistake," he said gravely, "they're making a great mistake! Yon boy's the last youngster on earth who should go to College."

"Aye man, dominie, he's an infernal ass, is he noat?" they cried, and pressed for his judgment.

At last, partly in real pedantry, partly with humerous intent to puzzle them, he delivered his astounding mind.

"The fault of young Gourlay," quoth he, "is a sensory perceptiveness in gross excess of his intellectuality."

126

They blinked and tried to understand.

"Aye man, dominie!" said Sandy Toddle. "That means he's an infernal cuddy, dominie! Does it na, dominie?"

But Bleach-the-boys had said enough. "Aye," he said drily, "there's a wheen gey cuddies in Barbie!"—and he went back to his stuffy little room to study *The Wealth of Nations*.

CHAPTER 16

THE scion of the house of Gourlay was a most untravelled sprig when his father packed him off to the University. Of the world beyond Skeighan he had no idea. Repression of his children's wishes to see something of the world was a feature of Gourlay's tyranny, less for the sake of the money which a trip might cost (though that counted for something in his refusal) than for the sake of asserting his authority. "Wants to gang to Fechars, indeed! Let him bide at home," he would growl, and at home the youngster had to bide. This had been the more irksome to John since most of his companions in the town were beginning to peer out, with their mammies and daddies to encourage them. To give their cubs a "cast o' the world" was a rule with the potentates of Barbie; once or twice a year young Hopeful was allowed to accompany his sire to Fechars or Poltandie, or—oh, rare joy!—to the city on the Clyde. To go farther, and get the length of Edinburgh, was dangerous, because you came back with a halo of glory round your head which banded your fellows together in a common attack on your pretensions. It was his lack of pretension to travel, however, that banded them against young Gourlay. "Gunk" and "chaw" are the Scots for a bitter and envious disappointment which shows itself in face and eyes. Young Gourlay could never conceal that envious look when he heard of a glory which he did not share; and the youngsters noted his weakness with the unerring precision of the urchin to mark simple difference of character. Now the boy presses fiendishly on an intimate discovery in the nature of his friends, both because it gives him a new and delightful feeling of power over them, and also because he has not learned charity from a sense of his deficiencies, the brave ruffian having none. He is always coming back to probe the raw place, and Barbie boys were always coming back to "do a gunk" and "play a chaw" on

128

young Gourlay by boasting their knowledge of the world, winking at each other the while to observe his grinning anger. They were large on the wonders they had seen and the places they had been to, while he grew small (and they saw it) in envy of their superiority. Even Swipey Broon had a crow at him. For Swipey had journeyed in the company of his father to far-off Fechars, yea even to the groset-fair; and came back with an epic tale of his adventures. He had been in fifteen taverns, and one hotel (a Temperance Hotel where old Brown bashed the proprietor for refusing to supply him gin); one Pepper's Ghost; one Wild Beasts' Show; one Exhibition of the Fattest Woman on the Earth; also in the precincts of one gaol, where Mr Patrick Brown was cruelly incarcerate for wiping the floor with the cold refuser of the gin. "Criffens! Fechars!" said Swipey for a twelvemonth after, stunned by the mere recollection of that home of the glories of the earth. And then he would begin to expatiate for the benefit of young Gourlay—for Swipey, though his name was the base Teutonic Brown, had a Celtic contempt for brute facts that cripple the imperial mind. So well did he expatiate that young Gourlay would slink home to his mother and say, "Yah, even Swipey Broon has been to Fechars, though my faither 'ull no allow *me*!" "Never mind, dear," she would soothe him, "when once you're in the business, you'll gang a'where. And nut wan o' them has sic a business to gang intill!"

But though he longed to go here and there for a day, that he might be able to boast of it at home, young Gourlay felt that leaving Barbie for good would be a cutting of his heart-strings. Each feature of it, town and landward, was a crony of old years. In a land like Barbie of quick hill and dale, of tumbled wood and fell, each facet of nature has an individuality so separate and so strong, that if you live with it a little it becomes your friend, and a memory so dear that you kiss the thought of it in absence. The fields are not similar as pancakes; they have their difference; each leaps to the eye with a remembered and peculiar charm. That is why the heart of the Scot dies in flat Southern lands; he lives in a vacancy; at dawn there is no Ben Agray to nod recognition through the mists. And that is why when he gets north of Carlisle he shouts with glee as each remembered object sweeps on the sight; yonder's the Nith with a fisherman hip-deep jigging at his rod, and yonder's Corsoncon with the mist on his brow. It is less the totality of the place than the individual feature that pulls at the heart, and it was the individual feature that pulled at young Gourlay. With intellect little or none, he had a vast sensational experience, and each aspect of Barbie was working in his blood and brain. Was there ever a Cross like Barbie Cross; was there ever a burn like the Lintie? It was blithe and heartsome to go birling to Skeighan in the train; it was grand to jouk round Barbie on the nichts at e'en! Even people whom he did not know he could locate with warm sure feelings of superiority. If a poor work-man slouched past him on the road he set him down in his heart as one of that rotten crowd from the Weaver's Vennel or the Tinker's Wynd. Barbie was in subjection to the mind of the son of the important man. To dash about Barbie in a gig with a big dog walloping behind, his coat-collar high about his ears and the reek of a meerschaum pipe floating white and blue many yards behind him, jovial and sordid nonsense about home—that had been his ideal. His father, he thought angrily, had encouraged the ideal, and now he forbade it, like the brute he was. From the earth in which he was rooted so deeply his father tore him, to fling him on a world he had forbidden him to know. His heart presaged disaster.

Old Gourlay would have scorned the sentimentality of seeing him off from the station, and Mrs Gourlay was too feckless to propose it for herself. Janet had offered to convoy him, but when the afternoon came she was down with a racking cold. He was alone as he strolled on the platform; a youth well-groomed and well-supplied, but for once in his life not a swaggerer—though the chance to swagger was unique. He was pointed out as "Young Gourlay off to the College." But he had no pleasure in the rôle, for his heart was in his boots.

He took the slow train to Skeighan, where he boarded the express. Few sensational experiences were unknown to his too-impressionable mind, and he knew the animation of railway travelling. Coming back from Skeighan in an empty compartment on nights of the past, he had sometimes shouted and stamped and banged the cushions till the dust flew, in mere joy of his rush through the air; the constant rattle, the quick-repeated noise, getting at his nerves, as they get at the nerves of savages and Englishmen on Bank Holidays. But any animation of the kind which he felt today was soon expelled by the slow uneasiness welling through his blood. He had no eager delight in the unknown country rushing past; it inspired him with fear. He thought with a feeble smile of what Mysie Monk said when they took her at the age of sixty (for the first time in her life) to the top of Milmannoch Hill. " Eh," said Mysie, looking round her in amaze, "eh, sirs, it's a lairge place the world when you see it all!" Gourlay smiled because he had the same thought, but feebly, because he was cowering at the bigness of the world. Folded nooks in the hills swept past, enclosing their lonely farms; then the open straths where autumnal waters gave a pale gleam to the sky. Sodden moors stretched away in vast patient loneliness. Then a grey smear of rain blotted the world, penning him in with his dejection. He seemed to be rushing through unseen space, with no companion but his own foreboding. "Where are you going to?" asked his mind, and the wheels of the train repeated the question all the way to Edinburgh, jerking it out in two short lines and a long one: "Where are you going to? Where are you going to? Ha, ha, Mr Gourlay, where are you going to?"

It was the same sensitiveness to physical impression which won him to Barbie that repelled him from the outer world. The scenes round Barbie, so vividly impressed, were his friends because he had known them from his birth; he was a somebody in their midst and had mastered their familiarity; they were the ministers of his mind. Those other scenes were his foes because, realizing them morbidly in relation to himself, he was cowed by their big indifference to him, and felt puny, a nobody before them. And he could not pass them like more manly and more callous minds; they came burdening in on him whether he would or no. Neither could he get above them. Except when lording it at Barbie he had never a quick reaction of the mind on what he saw; it possessed him, not he it.

About twilight, when the rain had ceased, his train was brought up with a jerk between the stations. While the rattle and bang continued it seemed not unnatural to young Gourlay (though depressing) to be whirling through the darkening land; it went past like a panorama in a dream. But in the dead pause following the noise he thought it "queer" to be sitting here in the intense quietude and looking at a strange and unfamiliar scene—planted in its midst by a miracle of speed and gazing at it closely through a window! Two ploughmen from the farmhouse near the line were unyoking at the end of the croft; he could hear the muddy noise ("splorroch" is the Scotch of it) made by the big hoofs on the squashy head-rig. "Bauldy" was the name of the shorter ploughman, so yelled to by his mate, and two of the horses were "Prince and Rab" just like a pair in Loranogie's stable. In the curtainless window of the farmhouse shone a leaping flame, not the steady glow of a lamp, but the tossing brightness of a fire, and thought he to himself, "'They're getting the porridge for the men!'" He had a vision of the woman stirring in the meal, and of the homely interior in the dancing firelight. He wondered who the folk were, and would have liked to know them. Yes, it was "queer," he thought, that he who left Barbie only a few hours ago should be in intimate momentary touch with a place and people he had never seen before. The train seemed arrested by a spell that he might get his vivid impression.

When ensconced in his room that evening, he had a brighter outlook on the world. With the curtains drawn, and the lights burning, its shabbiness was unrevealed. After the whirling strangeness of the day he was glad to be in a place that was his own; here at least was a corner of earth of which he was master; it reassured him. The firelight dancing on the tea things was pleasant and homely, and the enclosing cosiness shut out the black roaring world that threatened to engulf his personality. His spirits rose, ever ready to jump at a trifle.

The morrow, however, was the first of his lugubrious time. If he had been an able man he might have found a place in his classes to console him. Many youngsters are conscious of a vast depression when entering the portals of a University; they feel themselves inadequate to cope with the wisdom of the ages garnered in the solid walls. They envy alike the smiling sureness of the genial charlatan (to whom Professors are a set of fools), and the easy mastery of the man of brains. They have a cowering sense of their own inefficiency. But the feeling of uneasiness presently disappears. The first shivering dip is soon forgotten by the hearty breaster of the waves. But ere you breast the waves you must swim; and to swim through the sea of learning was more than heavy-headed Gourlay could accomplish. His mind, finding no solace in work, was left to prey upon itself.

If he had been the ass total and complete he might have loafed in the comfortable haze which surrounds the average intelligence, and cushions it against the world. But in Gourlay was a rawness of nerve, a sensitiveness to physical impression, which kept him fretting and stewing, and never allowed him to lapse on a sluggish indifference.

Though he could not understand things, he could not escape them; they thrust themselves forward on his notice. We hear of poor genius cursed with perceptions which it can't express; poor Gourlay was cursed with impressions which he couldn't intellectualize. With little power of thought, he had a vast power of observation; and as everything he observed in Edinburgh was offensive and depressing, he was constantly depressed—the more because he could not understand. At Barbie his life, though equally void of mental interest, was solaced by surroundings which he loved. In Edinburgh his surroundings were appalling to his timid mind. There was a greengrocer's shop at the corner of the street in which he lodged, and he never passed it without being conscious of its trodden and decaying leaves. They were enough to make his morning foul. The middle-aged woman, who had to handle carrots with her frozen fingers, was less wretched than he who saw her, and thought of her after he went by. A thousand such impressions came boring in upon his mind, and made him squirm. He could not toss them aside like the callous and manly; he could not see them in their due relation, and think them unimportant, like the able; they were always recurring and suggesting woe. If he fled to his room, he was followed by his morbid sense of an unpleasant world. He conceived a rankling hatred of the four walls wherein he had to live. Heavy Biblical pictures, in frames of gleaming black like the splinters of a hearse, were hung against a dark ground. Every time Gourlay raised his head he scowled at them with eyes of gloom. It was curious that, hating his room, he was loth to go to bed. He got a habit of sitting till three in the morning, staring at the dead fire in sullen apathy.

He was sitting at nine o'clock one evening, wondering if there was no means of escape from the wretched life he had to lead, when he received a letter from Jock Allan, asking him to come and dine.

CHAPTER 17

THAT dinner was a turning-point in young Gourlay's career. It is lucky that a letter describing it has fallen into the hands of the patient chronicler. It was sent by young Jimmy Wilson to his mother. As it gives an idea—which is slightly mistaken —of Jock Allan, and an idea—which is very unmistakable— of young Wilson, it is here presented in the place of pride. It were a pity not to give a human document of this kind all the honour in one's power.

"Dear mother," said the wee sma' Scoatchman—so the hearty Allan dubbed him—"Dear mother, I just write to inform you that I've been out to a grand dinner at Jock Allan's. He met me on Princes Street, and made a great how-d'ye-do. 'Come out on Thursday night, and dine with me,' says he, in his big way. So here I went out to see him. I can tell you he's a warmer! I never saw a man eat so much in all my born days—but I suppose he would be having more on his table than usual, to shew off a bit, knowing us Barbie boys would be writing home about it all. And drink! D'ye know?—he began with a whole half tumbler of whiskey, and how many more he had I really should *not* like to say! And he must be used to it, too, for it seemed to have no effect on him whatever. And then he smoked and smoked—two great big cigars after we had finished eating, and then 'damn it' says he—he's an awful man to swear—'damn it' he says, 'there's no satisfaction in cigars; I must have a pipe,' and he actually smoked *four* pipes before I came away! I noticed the cigars were called 'Estorellas—Best Quality,' and when I was in last Saturday night getting an ounce of shag at the wee shoppie round the corner, I asked the price of 'these Estorellas.' 'Ninepence a piece!' said the bodie. Just imagine Jock Allan smoking eighteenpence—and not being satisfied! He's up in the world since he used to shaw turnips at Loranogie for sixpence a day! But he'll come down as

135

quick if he keeps on at yon rate. He made a great phrase with me, but though it keeps down one's weekly bill to get a meal like yon—I declare I wasn't hungry for two days—for all that I'll go very little about him. He'll be the kind that borrows money very fast—one of those harum-scarum ones!"

Criticism like that is a boomerang that comes back to hit the emitting skull with a hint of its kindred woodenness. It reveals the writer more than the written of. Allan was a bigger man than you would gather from Wilson's account of his Gargantuan revelry. He had a genius for mathematics —a gift which crops up, like music, in the most unexpected corners—and from ploughboy and herd he had become an actuary in Auld Reekie. Wilson had no need to be afraid, the meagre fool, for his host could have bought him and sold him.

Allan had been in love with young Gourlay's mother when she herself was a gay young fliskie at Tenshillingland, but his little romance was soon ended when Gourlay came and whisked her away. But she remained the one romance of his life. Now in his gross and jovial middle-age he idealized her in memory (a sentimentalist, of course. . he was Scotch); he never saw her in her scraggy misery to be disillusioned; to him she was still the wee bit lairdie's dochter, a vision that had dawned on his wretched boyhood, a pleasant and pathetic memory. And for that reason he had a curious kindness to her boy. That was why he introduced him to his boon companions. He thought he was doing him a good turn.

It was true that Allan made a phrase with a withered wisp of humanity like young Wilson. Not that he failed to see through him, for he christened him "a dried washing-clout." But Allan, like most great-hearted Scots far from their native place, saw it through a veil of sentiment; harsher features that would have been ever-present to his mind if he had never left it, disappeared from view, and left only the finer qualities bright within his memory. And idealizing the place he idealized its sons. To him they had a value not their own, just because they knew the brig and the burn and the brae, and had sat upon the school benches. He would have welcomed a dog from Barbie. It was from a like generous emotion that he greeted the bodies so warmly on his visits home—he thought they were as pleased to see him, as he was to see them. But they imputed false motives to his hearty greetings. Even as they shook his hand the mean ones would think to themselves: "What does he mean by this, now? What's he up till? No doubt he'll be wanting something off me!" They could not understand the gusto with which the returned exile cried, "Aye man, Jock Tamson, and how are ye?" They thought such warmth must have a sinister intention.—A Scot revisiting his native place ought to walk very quietly. For the parish is sizing him up.

There were two things to be said against Allan, and two only—unless, of course, you consider drink an objection. Wit with him was less the moment's glittering flash than the anecdotal bang; it was a fine old crusted blend which he stored in the cellars of his mind to bring forth on suitable occasions, as cobwebby as his wine. And it tickled his vanity to have a crowd of admiring youngsters round him to whom he might retail his anecdotes, and play the brilliant *raconteur*. He had cronies of his own years and he was lordly and jovial amongst them—yet he wanted another *entourage*. He was one of those middle-aged bachelors who like a train of youngsters behind them, whom they favour in return for homage. The wealthy man who had been a peasant lad delighted to act the jovial host to sons of petty magnates from his home. Batch after batch as they came up to College were drawn around him—partly because their homage pleased him and partly because he loved anything whatever that came out of Barbie. There was no harm in Allan— though when his face was in repose you saw the look in his eye at times of a man defrauding his soul. A robustious young fellow of sense and brains would have found in this lover of books and a bottle not a bad comrade. But he was the worst of cronies for a weak swaggerer like Gourlay. For Gourlay, admiring the older man's jovial power, was led on to imitate his faults, to think them virtues and a credit—and he lacked the clear cool head that kept Allan's faults from flying away with him.

At dinner that night there were several braw braw lads of Barbie Water. There was Tarmillan the doctor (a son of Irrendavie), Logan the cashier, Tozer the Englishman, old Partan—a guileless and enquiring mind—and half-a-dozen students raw from the West. The students were of the kind that goes up to College with the hay-seed sticking in its hair. Two are in a Colonial Cabinet now, two are in the poor-house. So they go.

Tarmillan was the last to arrive. He came in sucking his thumb into which he had driven a splinter while conducting an experiment.

"I've a morbid horror of lockjaw," he explained. "I never get a jag from a pin but I see myself in the shape of a hoop, semicircular, with my head on one end of a table my heels on the other, and a doctor standing on my navel trying to reduce the curvature."

"Gosh!" said Partan, who was a literal fool, "is that the treatment they purshoo?"

"That's the treatment!" said Tarmillan, sizing up his man. "Oh, it's a queer thing, lockjaw! I remember when I was goldmining in Tibet, one of our carriers who died of lockjaw had such a circumbendibus in his body, that we froze him and made him the hoop of a bucket to carry our water in. You see he was a thin bit man, and iron was scarce."

"Aye man!" cried Partan, "you've been in Tibet?"

"Often," waved Tarmillan, "often! I used to go there every summer."

Partan, who liked to extend his geographical knowledge, would have talked of Tibet for the rest of the evening—and Tarmie would have told him news—but Allan broke in.

"How's the book, Tarmillan?" he enquired.

Tarmillan was engaged on a treatise which those who are competent to judge consider the best thing of its kind ever written.

"Oh, don't ask me," he writhed. "Man, it's an irksome thing to write, and to be asked about it makes you squirm. It's almost as offensive to ask a man when his book will be out, as to ask a woman when she'll be delivered. I'm glad you invited me—to get away from the confounded thing.

It's become a blasted tyrant. A big work's a mistake; it's a
monster that devours the brain. I neglect my other work
for that fellow of mine; he bags everything I think. I never
light on a new thing, but 'Hullo!' I cry, 'here's an idea
for the book!' If you are engaged on a big subject all your
thinking works into it or out of it."

"M'yes," said Logan, "but that's a swashing way of
putting it."

"It's the danger of the aphorism," said Allan, "that it
states too much in trying to be small. Tozer, what do you
think?"

"I never was engaged on a big subject," sniffed Tozer.

"We're aware o' that!" said Tarmillan.

Tozer went under, and Tarmillan had the table. Allan was
proud of him.

"Courage is the great thing," said he. "It often succeeds by
the mere show of it. It's the timid man that a dog bites. Run
at him and he runs."

He was speaking to himself rather than the table, admiring
the courage that had snubbed Tozer with a word. But his
musing remark rang a bell in young Gourlay. By Jove, he
had thought that himself, so he had! He was a hollow thing,
he knew, but a buckram pretence prevented the world from
piercing to his hollowness. The son of his courageous sire
(whom he equally admired and feared) had learned to play
the game of bluff. A bold front was half the battle. He had
worked out his little theory, and it was with a shock of
pleasure the timid youngster heard great Allan give it forth.
He burned to let him know that he had thought that, too.

To the youngsters, fat of face and fluffy of its circling
down, the talk was a banquet of the gods. For the first time
in their lives they heard ideas (such as they were) flung round
them royally. They yearned to show that they were thinkers,
too. And Gourlay was fired with the rest.

"I heard a very good one the other day from old Bauldy
Johnston," said Allan, opening his usual wallet of stories
when the dinner was in full swing.—At a certain stage of
the evening "I heard a good one" was the invariable keynote
of his talk. If you displayed no wish to hear the "good one"

he was huffed.—"Bauldy was up in Edinburgh," he went on, "and I met him near the Scott Monument and took him to Lockhart's for a dram. You remember what a friend he used to be of old Will Overton. I wasn't aware, by the bye, that Will was dead till Bauldy told me. '*He was a great fellow my friend Will,*' he rang out in yon deep voice of his. '*The thumb mark of his Maker was wet in the clay of him.*' Man, it made a quiver go down my spine."

"Oh, Bauldy has been a kenned phrase-maker for the last forty year," said Tarmillan. "But every other Scots peasant has the gift. To hear Englishmen talk, you would think Carlyle was unique for the word that sends the picture home —they give the man the credit of his race. But I've heard fifty things better than 'willowy man', in the stable a-hame on a wat day in hairst—fifty things better!—from men just sitting on the cornkists and chowing beans".

"I know a better one than that," said Allan. Tarmillan had told no story, you observe, but Allan was so accustomed to saying "I know a better one than that," that it escaped him before he was aware. "I remember when Bauldy went off to Paris on the spree. He kept his mouth shut when he came back, for he was rather ashamed o' the outburst. But the bodies were keen to hear. 'What's the incense like in Notre Dame?' said Johnny Coe with his e'en big. '*Burning stink!*' said Bauldy."

"I can cap that with a better one, still," said Tarmillan, who wasn't to be done by any man. "I was with Bauldy when he quarrelled Tam Gibb of Hoochan-doe. Hoochan-doe's a yelling ass, and he threatened Bauldy—oh, he would do this, and he would do that, and he would do the other thing. '*Damn ye, would ye threaten me?*' cried Bauldy. '*I'll gar your brains jaup red to the heavens!*' And, I 'clare to God, sirs, a nervous man looked up to see if the clouds werena spattered with the gore!"

Tozer cleared a sarcastic windpipe.

"Why do you clear your throat like that?" said Tarmillan —"like a craw with the croup, on a bare branch, against a grey sky in November! If I had a throat like yours, I'd cut it and be done wi't."

"I wonder what's the cause of that extraordinary vividness in the speech of the Scotch peasantry?" said Allan—more to keep the blades from bickering than from any wish to know.

"It comes from a power of seeing things vividly inside your mind," said a voice, timorous and wheezy, away down the table.

What cockerel was this crowing?

They turned and beheld the blushing Gourlay.

But Tarmillan and Tozer were at it again, and he was snubbed. Jimmy Wilson sniggered, and the other youngsters enjoyed his discomfiture. Huh! What right has *he* to set up his pipe?

His shirt stuck to his back. He would have liked the ground to open and swallow him.

He gulped a huge swill of whiskey to cover his vexation— and, oh, the mighty difference! A sudden courage flooded his veins. He turned with a scowl on Wilson, and, "What the devil are *you* sniggering at?" he growled. Logan, the only senior who marked the by-play, thought him a hardy young spunkie.

The moment the whiskey had warmed the cockles of his heart, Gourlay ceased to care a rap for the sniggerers. Drink deadened his nervous perception of the critics on his right and left, and set him free to follow his idea undisturbed. It was an idea he had long cherished—being one of the few that ever occurred to him. He rarely made phrases himself— though, curiously enough, his father often did without knowing it—the harsh grind of his character producing a flash. But Gourlay was aware of his uncanny gift of visualization—or of "seeing things in the inside of his head," as he called it—and vanity prompted the inference, that this was the faculty that sprang the metaphor. His theory was now clear and eloquent before him. He was realizing for the first time in his life (with a sudden joy in the discovery) the effect of whiskey to unloose the brain; sentences went hurling through his brain with a fluency that thrilled. If he had the ear of the company, now he had the drink to hearten him, he would show Wilson and the rest that he wasn't such a

blasted fool! In a room by himself he would have spouted
to the empty air.

Some such point he had reached in the hurrying jumble of
his thoughts, when Allan addressed him.

Allan did not mean his guest to be snubbed. He was a
gentleman at heart, not a cad like Tozer; and this boy was
the son of a girl whose laugh he remembered in the
gloamings at Tenshillingland.

"I beg your pardon, John," he said in heavy benevolence
—he had reached that stage—"I beg your pardon. I'm
afraid you was interrupted."

Gourlay felt his heart a lump in his throat, but he rushed
into speech.

"Metaphor comes from the power of seeing things in the
inside of your head," said the unconscious disciple of
Aristotle—"seeing them so vivid that you see the likeness
between them. When Bauldy Johnston said 'the thumb-mark
of his Maker was wet in the clay of him,' he *saw* the print of a
thumb in wet clay, and he *saw* the Almighty making a man
out of mud, the way He used to do in the Garden of Eden
langsyne—so Bauldy flashed the two ideas together and the
metaphor sprang! A man'll never make phrases unless he
can see things in the middle of his brain. *I* can see things in
the middle of my brain," he went on cockily—"anything I
want to! I don't need to shut my eyes, either. They just
come up before me."

"Man, you're young to have noticed these things, John,"
said Jock Allan. "I never reasoned it out before, but I'm
sure you're in the right o't."

He spoke more warmly than he felt, because Gourlay had
flushed and panted and stammered (in spite of inspiring bold
John Barleycorn) while airing his little theory, and Allan
wanted to cover him. But Gourlay took it as a tribute to his
towering mind. Oh, but he was the proud mannikin. "Pass
the watter!" he said to Jimmy Wilson, and Jimmy passed it
meekly.

Logan took a fancy to Gourlay on the spot. He was a slow
sly cosy man, with a sideward laugh in his eye, a humid
gleam. And because his blood was so genial and so slow,

he liked to make up to brisk young fellows, whose wilder outbursts might amuse him. They quickened his sluggish blood. No bad fellow, and good-natured in his heavy way, he was what the Scotch call a "slug for the drink." A "slug for the drink" is a man who soaks and never succumbs. Logan was the more dangerous a crony on that account. Remaining sober while others grew drunk, he was always ready for another dram, always ready with an oily chuckle for the sploring nonsense of his satellites. He would see them home in the small hours, taking no mean advantage over them, never scorning them because they "couldn't carry it," only laughing at their daft vagaries. And next day he would gurgle: "So-and-so was screwed last night, and, man, if you had heard his talk!" Logan had enjoyed it. He hated to drink by himself, and liked a splurging youngster with whom to go the rounds.

He was attracted to Gourlay by the manly way he tossed his drink, and by the false fire it put into him. But he made no immediate advance. He sat smiling in creeshy benevolence, beaming on Gourlay but saying nothing. When the party was ended, however, he made up to him going through the door.

"I'm glad to have met you, Mr Gourlay," said he. "Won't you come round to the Howff for a while?"

"The Howff?" said Gourlay.

"Yes," said Logan, "haven't ye heard o't! It's a snug bit house, where some of the West Country billies foregather for a nicht at e'en. Oh, nothing to speak of, ye know—just a dram and a joke to pass the time now and then!"

"Aha!" laughed Gourlay, "there's worse than a drink, by Jove. It puts smeddum in your blood!"

Logan nipped the guard of his arm in heavy playfulness, and led him to the Howff.

CHAPTER 18

YOUNG Gourlay had found a means of escaping from his
foolish mind. By the beginning of his second session he was
as able a toper as a publican could wish. The somewhat
sordid joviality of Allan's ring, their wit-combats that were
somewhat crude, appeared to him the very acme of social
intercourse. To emulate Logan and Allan was his aim. But
drink appealed to him in many ways, besides. Now when his
too-apprehensive nerves were frightened by bugbears in his
lonely room he could be off to the Howff and escape them.
And drink inspired him with false courage to sustain his
pose as a hardy rollicker. He had acquired a kind of prestige
since the night of Allan's party, and two of the fellows
whom he met there, Armstrong and Gillespie, became his
friends at College and the Howff. He swaggered before them
as he had swaggered at school both in Barbie and Skeighan
—and now there was no Swipey Broon to cut him over the
coxcomb. Armstrong and Gillespie—though they saw
through him—let him run on, for he was not bad fun when
he was splurging. He found, too, when with his cronies that
drink unlocked his mind, and gave a free flow to his ideas.
Nervous men are often impotent of speech from very excess
of perception—they realize not merely what they mean to
say, but with the nervous antennae of their minds they
feel the attitude of every auditor. Distracted by lateral
perceptions from the point ahead, they blunder, where
blunter minds would go forward undismayed. That was the
experience of young Gourlay. If he tried to talk freely when
sober, he always grew confused. But drink deadened the
outer rim of his perception and left it the clearer in the
middle for its concentration. In plainer language, when he
was drunk, he was less afraid of being laughed at, and free
of that fear, he was a better speaker. He was driven to drink,
then, by every weakness of his character. As nervous

hypochondriac, as would-be swaggerer, as a dullard requiring stimulus, he found that drink, to use his own language, gave his "smeddum!"

With his second year he began the study of philosophy, and that added to his woes. He had nerves to feel the Big Conundrum, but not the brains to solve it—small blame to him for that since philosophers have cursed each other black in the face over it for the last five thousand years. But it worried him. The strange and sinister detail of the world, that had always been a horror to his mind, became more horrible, beneath the stimulus of futile thought. But whiskey was the mighty cure. He was the gentleman who gained notoriety on a memorable occasion, by exclaiming— "Metaphysics be damned: let us drink!" Omar and other bards have expressed the same conclusion in more dulcet wise. But Gourlay's was equally sincere. How sincere is another question.

Curiously, an utterance of "Auld Tam," one of his professors, half confirmed him in his evil ways.

"I am speaking now," said Tam, "of the comfort of a true philosophy, less of its higher aspect than its comfort to the mind of man. Physically, each man is highest on the globe; intellectually, the philosopher alone dominates the world. To him are only two entities that matter, himself and the Eternal; or, if another, it is his fellow-man, whom serving he serves the ultimate of being. But he is master of the outer world. The mind, indeed, in its first blank outlook on life is terrified by the demoniac force of nature and the swarming misery of man; by the vast totality of things, the cold remoteness of the starry heavens and the threat of the devouring seas. It is puny in their midst."

Gourlay woke up, and the sweat broke on him. Great Heaven, had Tam been through it, too!

"At that stage," quoth the wise man, "the mind is dispersed in a thousand perceptions and a thousand fears; there is no central greatness in the soul. It is assailed by terrors which men sunk in the material never seem to feel. Phenomena, uninformed by thought, bewilder and depress."

"Just like me!" thought Gourlay, and listened with a

thrilling interest because it was "just like him."

"But the labyrinth," said Tam, with a ring in his voice as of one who knew—"the labyrinth cannot appal the man who has found a clue to its windings. A mind that has attained to thought lives in itself, and the world becomes its slave. Its formerly distracted powers rally home; it is central, possessing not possessed. The world no longer frightens, being understood. Its sinister features are accidents that will pass away, and they gradually cease to be observed. For real thinkers know the value of a wise indifference. And that is why they are often the most genial men; unworried by the transient, they can smile and wait, sure of their eternal aim. The man to whom the infinite beckons is not to be driven from his mystic quest by the ambush of a temporal fear— there is no fear; it has ceased to exist. That is the comfort of a true philosophy—if a man accepts it not merely mechanically, from another, but feels it in breath and blood and every atom of his being. With a warm surety in his heart, he is undaunted by the outer world. That, gentlemen, is what thought can do for a man."

"By Jove," thought Gourlay, "that's what whiskey does for me!"

And that, on a lower level, was what whiskey did. He had no conception of what Tam really meant—there were people indeed who used to think that Tam never knew what he meant himself. They were as little able as Gourlay to appreciate the mystic, through the radiant haze of whose mind thoughts loomed on you sudden and big, like mountain tops in a sunny mist, the grander for their dimness. But Gourlay, though he could not understand, felt the fortitude of whiskey was somehow akin to the fortitude described. In the increased vitality it gave, he was able to tread down the world. If he walked on a wretched day in a wretched street, when he happened to be sober, his mind was hither and yon in a thousand perceptions and a thousand fears, fastening to (and fastened to) each squalid thing around. But with whiskey humming in his blood, he paced onward in a happy dream. The wretched puddles by the way, the frowning rookeries where misery squalled, the melancholy noises of the street, were passed unheeded by. His distracted powers rallied home; he was concentrate, his own man again, the hero of his musing mind. For, like all weak men of a vivid fancy, he was constantly framing dramas of which he was the towering lord. The weakling who never "downed" men in reality, was always "downing" them in thought. His imaginary triumphs consoled him for his actual rebuffs. As he walked in a tipsy dream, he was "standing up" to somebody, hurling his father's phrases at him, making short work of *him!* If imagination paled, the nearest tavern supplied a remedy, and flushed it to a radiant glow. Whereupon he had become the master of his world, and not its slave.

"Just imaigine," he thought, "whiskey doing for me what philosophy seems to do for Tam. It's a wonderful thing, the drink!"

His second session wore on, and when near its close, Tam gave out the subject for the Raeburn.

The Raeburn was a poor enough prize, a few books for an "essay in the picturesque," but it had a peculiar interest for the folk of Barbie. Twenty years ago it was won four years in succession by men from the valley; and the unusual run of luck fixed it in their minds. Thereafter when an unsuccessful candidate returned to his home, he was sure to be asked very pointedly, "Who won the Raeburn the year?" to rub into him their perception that he at least had been a failure. A bodie would dander slowly up, saying, "Aye, man, ye've won hame!" then, having mused awhile, would casually ask, "By-the-bye, who won the Raeburn the year?—Oh, it was a Perthshire man! It used to come our airt, but we seem to have lost the knack o't! Oh, yes, sir, Barbie bred writers in those days, but the breed seems to have decayed." Then he would murmur dreamily, as if talking to himself, "Jock Goudie was the last that got it hereaway. But *he* was a clever chap."

The caustic bodie would dander away with a grin, leaving a poor writhing soul. When he reached the Cross, he would tell the Deacon blithely of the "fine one he had given him," and the Deacon would lie in wait to give him a fine one, too.

In Barbie, at least, your returning student is never met at the station with a brass band, whatever may happen in more emotional districts of the North, where it pleases them to shed the tear.

"An Arctic Night" was the inspiring theme which Tam set for the Raeburn.

"A very appropriate subject!" laughed the fellow; "quite in the style of his own lectures." For Tam, though wise and a humorist, had his prosy hours. He used to lecture on the fifteen characteristics of Lady Macbeth (so he parcelled the unhappy Queen), and he would announce quite gravely, "We will now approach the discussion of the eleventh feature of the lady."

Gourlay had a shot at the Raeburn. He could not bring a radiant fulness of mind to bear upon his task (it was not in him to bring), but his morbid fancy set to work of its own accord. He saw a lonely little town far off upon the verge of Lapland night, leagues and leagues across a darkling plain, dark itself and little and lonely in the gloomy splendour of a Northern sky. A ship put to sea, and Gourlay heard in his ears the skirl of the man who went overboard—struck dead by the icy water on his brow, which smote the brain like a tomahawk.

He put his hand to his own brow when he wrote that, and, "Yes," he cried eagerly, "it would be the *cold* would kill the brain! Ooh-ooh, how it would go in!"

A world of ice groaned round him in the night; bergs ground on each other and were rent in pain; he heard the splash of great fragments tumbled in the deep, and felt the waves of their distant falling lift the vessel beneath him in the darkness. To the long desolate night came a desolate dawn, and eyes were dazed by the encircling whiteness; yet there flashed green slanting chasms in the ice, and towering pinnacles of sudden rose, lonely and far away. An unknown sea beat upon an unknown shore, and the ship drifted on the pathless waters, a white dead man at the helm.

"Yes, by Heaven," cried Gourlay, "I can see it all, I can see it all—that fellow standing at the helm, frozen white and as stiff's an icicle!"

Yet, do what he might, he was unable to fill more than half a dozen small pages. He hesitated whether he should send them in, and held them in his inky fingers, thinking he would burn them. He was full of pity for his own inability. "I wish I was a clever chap," he said mournfully.

"Ach, well, I'll try my luck," he muttered at last, "though Tam may guy me before the whole class, for doing so little o't."

The Professor, however (unlike the majority of Scotch Professors), rated quality higher than quantity.

"I have learned a great deal myself," he announced on the last day of the session, "I have learned a great deal myself from the papers sent in on the subject of an 'Arctic Night'."

"Hear, hear!" said an insolent student at the back.

"Where, where?" said the Professor, "stand up, sir!"

A gigantic Borderer rose blushing into view, and was greeted with howls of derision by his fellows. Tam eyed him, and he winced.

"You will apologize in my private room at the end of the hour," said Aquinas, as the students used to call him. "Learn that this is not a place to bray in."

The giant slunk down, trying to hide himself.

"Yes," said Tam, "I have learned what a poor sense of proportion some of you students seem to have. It was not to see who could write the most, but who could write the best, that I set the theme. One gentleman—he has been careful to give me his full name and address—" twinkled Tam, and picking up a huge manuscript he read it from the outer page—"Mr Alexander MacTavish, of Benmacstronachan, near Auchnapeterhoolish, in the island of South Uist, has sent me in no less than a hundred and fifty-three closely written pages! I daresay it's the size of the adjectives he uses that makes the thing so heavy," quoth Tam, and dropped it thudding on his desk. "Life is short, the art of the MacTavish long, and to tell the truth, gentlemen"—he gloomed at them humorously—"to tell the truth, I stuck in the middle o't!" (Roars of laughter, and a reproving voice, "Oh, ta pold MacTa-avish!" whereat there was pandemonium.) MacTavish was heard to groan, "Oh, why tid

I leave my home!" to which a voice responded in mocking antiphone, "Why tid you cross ta teep?" The noise they made was heard at Holyrood.

When the tumult and the shouting died, Tam resumed with a quiver in his voice, for "ta pold MacTavish" had tickled him too. "Now, gentlemen," he said, "I don't judge essays by their weight, though I'm told they sometimes pursue that method in Glasgow!"

(Groans for the rival University, cries of "Oh-oh-oh!" and a weary voice, "Please sir, don't mention that place—it makes me feel quite ill.")

The Professor allayed the tumult with dissuasive palm.

"I believe," he said drily, "you call that noise of yours 'the College Tramp;' in the Senatus we speak o't as 'the Cuddies' Trudge.'—Now, gentlemen, I'm not unwilling to allow a little noise on the last day of the session, but really you must behave more quietly.—So little does that method of judging essays commend itself to me, I may tell you, that the sketch which I consider the best barely runs to half a dozen short pages."

Young Gourlay's heart gave a leap within him; he felt it thudding on his ribs. The skin crept on him, and he breathed with quivering nostrils. Gillespie wondered why his breast heaved.

"It's a curious sketch," said the Professor. "It contains a serious blunder in grammar, and several mistakes in spelling, but it shows, in some ways, a wonderful imagination."

"Ho, ho!" thought Gourlay.

"Of course there are various kinds of imagination," said Tam. "In its lowest form it merely recalls something which the eyes have already seen, and brings it vividly before the mind. A higher form pictures something which you never saw, but only conceived as a possible existence. Then there's the imagination which not only sees but hears—actually hears what a man would say on a given occasion, and entering into his blood, tells you exactly why he does it. The highest form is both creative and consecrative, if I may use the word, merging in diviner thought. It irradiates the world. Of that high power there is no evidence in the essay before me. To be sure there was little occasion for its use."

Young Gourlay's thermometer went down.

"Indeed," said Aquinas, "there's a curious want of bigness in the sketch—no large nobility of phrase. It is written in gaspy little sentences, and each sentence begins 'and'—'and' —'and,' like a schoolboy's narrative. It's as if a number of impressions had seized the writer's mind, which he jotted down hurriedly, lest they should escape him. But, just because it's so little wordy, it gets the effect of the thing— faith, sirs, it's right on to the end of it every time! The writing of some folk is nothing but a froth of words—lucky if it glistens without, like a blobber of iridescent foam. But in this sketch there's a perception at the back of every sentence. It displays, indeed, too nervous a sense of the external world."

"Name, name!" cried the students, who were being deliberately worked by Tam to a high pitch of curiosity.

"I would strongly impress on the writer," said the shepherd, heedless of his bleating sheep, "I would strongly impress on the writer, to set himself down for a spell of real, hard, solid, and deliberate thought. That almost morbid perception, with philosophy to back it, might create an opulent and vivid mind. Without philosophy, it would stimply be a curse. With philosophy, it would bring thought the material to work on. Without philosophy it would simply distract and irritate the mind."

"Name, name!" cried the fellows.

"The winner of the Raeburn," said Thomas Aquinas, "is Mr John Gourlay."

Gourlay and his friends made for the nearest public house. The occasion, they thought, justified a drink. The others chaffed Gourlay about Tam's advice.

"You know, Jack," said Gillespie, mimicking the sage, "what you have got to do next summer is to set yourself down for a spell of real, hard, solid and deliberate thought. That was Tam's advice, you know."

"Him and his advice!" said Gourlay.

CHAPTER 19

THERE were only four other passengers dropped by the eleven o'clock express at Skeighan station, and, as it happened, young Gourlay knew them all. They were petty merchants of the neighbourhood whom he had often seen about Barbie. The sight of their remembered faces, as he stepped on to the platform, gave him a delightful sense that he was nearing home. He had passed from the careless world where he was nobody at all, to the familiar circle where he was a somebody, a mentioned man, and the son of a mentioned man—young Mr Gourlay!

He had a feeling of superiority to the others, too, because they were mere local journeyers while he had travelled all the way from mighty Edinburgh by the late express. He was returning from the outer world while they were bits of bodies who had only been to Fechars. As Edinburgh was to Fechars so was he to them. Round him was the halo of distance and the mystery of night-travelling. He felt big.

"Have you a match, Robert?" he asked very graciously of Robin Gregg, one of the porters whom he knew. Getting his match, he lit a cigarette; and when it was lit, after one quick puff, turned it swiftly round to examine its burning end. "Rotten!" he said, and threw it away to light another. The porters were watching him, and he knew it. When the station-master appeared yawning from his office, as he was passing through the gate, and asked who it was, it flattered his vanity to hear Robin's answer, that it was "young Mr Gourlay of Barbie, just back from the Univ-ai-rsity!"

He had been so hot for home that he had left Edinburgh at twilight, too eager to wait for the morrow. There was no train for Barbie at this hour of the night; and, of course, there was no gig to meet him. Even if he had sent word of his coming: "There's no need for travelling so late," old Gourlay would have growled—"let him shank it! We're in no hurry to have him home."

He set off briskly, eager to see his mother and tell her he
had won the Raeburn. The consciousness of his achievement
danced in his blood, and made the road light to his feet. His
thoughts were not with the country around him, but entirely
in the moment of his entrance, when he should proclaim his
triumph, with proud enjoyment of his mother's pride. His
fancy swept to his journey's end, and took his body after, so
that the long way was as nothing, annihilate by the leap
forward of his mind.

He was too vain, too full of himself and his petty triumph,
to have room for the beauty of the night. The sky was one
sea of lit cloud, foamy ridge upon ridge over all the heavens,
and each wave was brimming with its own whiteness,
seeming unborrowed of the moon. Through one peep-hole,
and only one, shone a distant star, a faint white speck far
away, dimmed by the nearer splendours of the sky. Sometimes the thinning edge of a cloud brightened in spume,
and round the brightness came a circle of umber, making a
window of fantastic glory for Dian the queen; there her
white vision peeped for a moment on the world—and the
next she was hid behind a fleecy veil, witching the heavens.
Gourlay was alone with the wonder of the night. The light
from above him was softened in a myriad boughs, no
longer mere light and cold, but a spirit as indwelling as
their soul, and they were boughs no longer, but a woven
dream. He walked beneath a shadowed glory. But he was
dead to it all. One only fact possessed him. He had won the
Raeburn, he had won the Raeburn! the road flew beneath
him.

Almost before he was aware, the mean grey streets of
Barbie had clipped him round. He stopped, panting from the
hurry of his walk, and looked at the quiet houses, all still
among the gloom. He realized with a sudden pride that he
alone was in conscious possession of the town. Barbie
existed to no other mind. All the others were asleep; while
he had a thrilling consciousness of them, and of their future
attitude to him, they did not know that he, the returning
great one, was present in their midst. They all knew of the

Raeburn, however, and ere long they would know that it was his. He was glad to hug his proud secret in presence of the sleeping town, of which he would be the talk to-morrow. How he would surprise them! He stood for a little, gloating in his own sensations. Then a desire to get home tugged him, and he scurried up the long brae.

He stole round the corner of the House with the Green Shutters. Roger, the collie, came at him with a bow-wow-wow. "Roger!" he whispered, and cuddled him, and the old loyalist fawned on him and licked his hand. The very smell of the dog was couthie in his nose.

The window of the bedroom went up with a crash.

"Now, then, who the devil are you?" came the voice of old Gourlay.

"It's me, faither," said John.

"Oh, it's you, is it? This is a fine time o' night to come home."

"Faither, I have—I have won the Raeburn!"

"It'll keep, my mannie, it'll keep"—and the window slammed.

Next moment it was up.

"Did young Wilson get onything?" came the eager cry.

"Nut him!" said John.

"Fine, man! Dam'd, sir, I'm proud o' ye!"

John went round the corner treading on air. For the first time in his life his father had praised him.

He peeped through a kink at the side of the kitchen-blind, where its descent was arrested by a flowerpot, in the corner of the window-sill. As he had expected, though it was long past midnight, his mother was not yet in bed. She was folding a white cloth over her bosom, and about her, on the backs of chairs, there were other such cloths, drying by the fire. He watched her curiously—once he seemed to hear a whimpering moan. When she buttoned her dress above the cloth, she gazed sadly at the dying embers, the look of one who had gained short respite from a task of painful tendance on the body, yet is conscious that the task and the pain are endless, and will have to be endured, to-morrow and to-morrow, till she dies. It was the fixed gaze of utter

154

weariness and apathy. A sudden alarm for his mother made John cry her name.

She flew to the door, and in a moment had him in her arms. He told his news and basked in her adoration.

She came close to him, and "John," she said in a smiling whisper, big-eyed, "John," she breathed, "would ye like a dram?" It was as if she was propounding a roguish plan in some dear conspiracy.

He laughed. "Well," he said, "seeing we have won the Raeburn, you and I, I think we might!"

He heard her fumbling in the distant pantry. He smiled to himself as he listened to the clinking glass, and, "By Jove," said he, "a mother's a fine thing!"

"Where's Janet?" he asked when she returned. He wanted another worshipper.

"Oh, she gangs to bed the moment it's dark," his mother complained, like one aggrieved. "She's always saying that she's ill! I thocht when she grew up that she might be a wee help, but she's no use at all. And I'm sure, if a' was kenn Ied, have more to complain o' than she has. Atweel aye," she said, and stared at the embers.

It rarely occurs to young folk who have never left their homes that their parents may be dying soon; from infancy they have known them as established facts of nature like the streams and hills; they expect them to remain. But the young who have been away for six months are often struck by a tragic difference in their elders on returning home. To young Gourlay there was a curious difference in his mother. She was almost beautiful tonight. Her blue eyes were large and glittering; her ears waxen and delicate; and her brown hair swept low on her blue-veined temples. Above and below her lips there was a narrow margin of the purest white.

"Mother," he said anxiously, "you're not ill, are ye? What do ye need so many wee clouts for?"

She gasped and started. "They're just a wheen clouts I was sorting out," she faltered.—"No, no, dear, there's noathing wrong wi' me."

"There's one sticking in your blouse," said he, and pointed to her slack breast.

She glanced nervously down and pushed it further in. "I daresay I put it there when I wasna thinking," she explained. But she eyed him furtively to see if he were still looking.

CHAPTER 20

THERE is nothing worse for a weakling than a small success. The strong man tosses it beneath his feet, as a step to rise higher on. He squeezes it into its proper place as a layer in the life he is building. If his memory dwells on it for a moment it is only because of its valuable results, not because in itself it is a theme for vanity. And if he be higher than strong he values not it, but the exercise of getting it; viewing his actual achievement, he is apt to reflect: "Is this pitiful thing, then, all that I toiled for?" Finer natures often experience a keen depression and sense of littleness in the pause that follows a success. But the fool is so swollen by thought of his victory that he is unfit for all healthy work till somebody jags him and lets the gas out. He never forgets the great thing he fancies he did thirty years ago, and expects the world never to forget it either. The more of a weakling he is, and the more incapable of repeating his former triumph, the more he thinks of it; and the more he thinks of it the more it satisfies his meagre soul and prevents him essaying another brave venture in the world. His petty achievement ruins him. The memory of it never leaves him, but swells to a huge balloon that lifts him off his feet and carries him heavens-high—till it lands him on a dunghill. Even from that proud eminence he oft cock-a-doodles his former triumph to the world. "Man, you wouldn't think to see me here that I once held a great position! Thirty year back, I did a big thing. It was like this, ye see." And then follows a recital of his faded glories—generally ending with a hint that a drink would be very acceptable.

Even such a weakling was young Gourlay. His success in Edinburgh, petty as it was, turned his head, and became one of the many causes working to destroy him. All that summer at Barbie, he swaggered and drank on the strength of it.

On the morning after his return he clothed himself in fine raiment (he was always well-dressed till the end came), and sallied forth to dominate the town. As he swaggered past the Cross, smoking a cigarette, he seemed to be conscious that the very walls of the houses watched him with unusual eyes, as if even they felt that yon was John Gourlay whom they had known as a boy, proud wearer now of the academic wreath, the conquering hero returned to his home. So Gourlay figured them. He, the disconsidered, had shed a lustre on the ancient walls. They were tributaries to his new importance—somehow their attitude was different from what it had ever been before. It was only his self-conscious bigness, of course, that made even inanimate things seem the feeders of his greatness. As Gourlay, always alive to obscure emotions which he could never express in words, mused for a moment over the strange new feeling that had come to him, a gowsterous voice hailed him from the Black Bull door. He turned, and Peter Wylie, hearty and keen like his father, stood him a drink in honour of his victory—which was already buzzed about the town.

Drucken Wabster's wife had seen to that. "Ou," she cried, "his mother's daft about it, the silly auld thing; she can speak o' noathing else. Though Gourlay gies her very little to come and go on, she slipped him a whole sovereign this morning, to keep his pooch! Think o' that, kimmers; heard ye ever sic extravagance! I saw her doin'd wi' my own eyes. It's aince wud and aye waur* wi' her, I'm thinking. But the wastfu' wife's the waefu' widow, she should keep in mind. She's far owre browdened upon yon boy. I'm sure I howp good may come o't, but—" and with an ominous shake of the head she ended the Websterian harangue.

When Peter Wylie left him Gourlay lit a cigarette and stood at the Cross, waiting for the praises yet to be. The Deacon toddled forward on his thin shanks.

"Man Dyohn, you're won hame, I thee! Aye man! And how are ye?"

Gourlay surveyed him with insolent, indolent eyes. "Oh, I'm all rai-ight, Deacon," he swaggered, "how are

*"*Aince wud and aye waur*"; silly for once and silly for always.

ye-ow?" and he sent a puff of tobacco-smoke down through his nostrils.

"I declare!" said the Deacon. "I never thaw onybody thmoke like that before! That'll be one of the thingth ye learn at College, no doubt."

"Ya-as," yawned Gourlay; "it gives you the full flavour of the we-eed."

The Deacon glimmered over him with his eyes. "The weed," said he. "Jutht tho! Imphm. The weed."

Then worthy Mister Allardyce tried another opening. "But, dear me!" he cried, "I'm forgetting entirely. I must congratulate ye! Ye've been doing wonderth, they tell me, up in Embro."

"Just a little bit," swaggered Gourlay, right hand on outshot hip, left hand flaunting a cigarette in air most delicate, tobacco-smoke curling from his lofty nose. He looked down his face at the Deacon. "Just a little bit, Mr Allardyce, just a little bit. I tossed the thing off in a twinkling."

"Aye man, Dyohn," said the Deacon with great solicitude, "but you maunna work that brain o' yours too hard, though. A heid like yours doesna come through the hatter's hand ilka day o' the week; you mutht be careful not to put too great a thtrain on't. Aye, aye; often the best machine's the easiest broken and the warst to mend. You should take a rest and enjoy yourself. But there! what need I be telling *you* that? A College-bred man like you kenth far better about it than a thilly auld country bodie! You'll be meaning to have a grand holiday and lots o' fun—a dram now and then, eh? and mony a rattle in the auld man's gig?"

At this assault on his weak place Gourlay threw away his important manner with the end of his cigarette. He could never maintain the lofty pose for more than five minutes at a time.

"You're *right,* Deacon," he said, nodding his head with splurging sincerity. "I mean to have a dem'd good holiday. One's glad to get back to the old place after six months in Edinburgh."

"Atweel," said the Deacon. "But, man, have you tried the new whiskey at the Black Bull—I thaw ye in wi' Pate Wylie? It'th extr'ornar gude—thaft as the thang o' a mavis on a nicht at e'en, and fiery as a Highland charge."—It was not in character for the Deacon to say such a thing, but whiskey makes the meanest of Scots poetical. He elevates the manner to the matter, and attains the perfect style.—"But no doubt," the cunning old pryer went on, with a smiling suavity in his voice, "but no doubt a man who knowth Edinburgh tho well as you, will have a favourite blend of hith own. I notice that University men have a fine taste in thpirits."

"I generally prefer 'Kinblythmont's Cure'," said Gourlay with the air of a connoisseur. "But 'Anderson's Sting o' Delight' 's very good, and so's 'Balsillie's Brig o' the Mains.'"

"Aye," said the Deacon. "Aye, aye! 'Brig o' the Mains' ith what Jock Allan drinks. He'll pree noathing else. I dare thay you thee a great deal of him in Embro."

"Oh, every week," swaggered Gourlay. "We're always together, he and I."

"Alwayth thegither!" said the Deacon.

It was not true that Allan and Gourlay were together at all times. Allan was kind to Jean Richmond's son (in his own ruinous way) but not to the extent of being burdened with the cub half a dozen times a week. Gourlay was merely boasting—as young blades are apt to do of acquaintance with older roisterers. They think it makes them seem men of the world. And in his desire to vaunt his comradeship with Allan, John failed to see that Allardyce was scooping him out like an oyster.

"Aye man," resumed the Deacon; "he's a hearty fellow, Jock. No doubt you have great thprees?"

"Sprees!" gurgled Gourlay, and flung back his head with a laugh. "I should think we have. There was a great foy at Allan's the night before I left Edinburgh. Tarmillan was there—d'ye know, yon's the finest fellow I ever met in my life!—and Bauldy Logan—he's another great chap. Then there was Armstrong and Gillespie—great friends of mine—

and damned clever fellows they are, too, I can tell you. Besides us three there were half a dozen more from the College. You should have heard the talk! And every man-jack was as drunk as a lord. The last thing I remember is some of us students dancing round a lamp-post while Logan whistled a jig."

Though Gourlay the elder hated the Deacon, he had never warned his son to avoid him. To have said "Allardyce is dangerous" would have been to pay the old malignant too great a compliment; it would have been beneath John Gourlay to admit that a thing like Allardyce could harm him and his. Young Gourlay, therefore, when once set a-going by the Deacon's deft management, blurted everything without a hanker. Even so, however, he felt that he had gone too far. He glanced anxiously at his companion. "Mum's the word about this, of course," he said with a wink. "It would never do for this to be known about the 'Green Shutters.'"

"Oh, I'm ath thound ath a bell, Dyohn, I'm ath thound ath a bell," said the Deacon. "Aye man! You jutht bear out what I have alwayth underthood about the men o' brainth. They're the heartiest devilth after a'. Burns, that the baker raves so muckle o', was jutht another o' the thame. Jutht another o' the thame! We'll be hearing o' you boys—Pate Wylie and you and a wheen mair—having rare ploys in Barbie through the thummer."

"Oh, we'll kick up a bit of a dust," Gourlay sniggered, well-pleased. Had not the Deacon ranked him in the robustious great company of Burns! "I say, Deacon, come in and have a nip."

"There's your faither," grinned the Deacon.

"Eh? What?" cried Gourlay in alarm, and started round, to see his father and the Rev Mr Struthers advancing up the Fechars Road. "Eh—eh—Deacon—I—I'll see you again about the nip."

"Jutht tho!" grinned the Deacon. "We'll postpone the drink to a more convenient opportunity."

He toddled away, having no desire that old Gourlay should find him talking to his son. If Gourlay suspected him of pulling the young fellow's leg, likely as not he would give an exhibition of his dem'd unpleasant manners!

Gourlay and the minister came straight towards the student. Of the Rev Mr Struthers it may be said with truth that he would have cut a remarkable figure in any society. He had big splay feet, short stout legs, and a body of such bulging bulbosity, that all the droppings of his spoon—which were many—were caught on the round of his black waistcoat, which always looked as if it had just been spattered by a grey shower. His eye-brows were bushy and white, and the hairs slanting up and out rendered the meagre brow even narrower than it was. His complexion, more expecially in cold weather, was a dark crimson. The purply colour of his face was intensified by the pure whiteness of the side whiskers projecting stiffly by his ears, and in mid-week, when he was unshaven, his redness revealed more plainly, in turn, the short gleaming stubble that lay like rime on his chin. His eyes goggled, and his manner at all times was that of a staring and earnest self-importance. "Puffy Importance" was one of his nicknames.

Struthers was a man of lowly stock who, after a ten years' desperate battle with his heavy brains, succeeded at the long last of it in passing the examinations required for the ministry. The influence of a wealthy patron then presented him to Barbie. Because he had taken so long to get through the University himself, he constantly magnified the place in his conversation, partly to excuse his own slowness in getting through it, partly that the greater glory might redound on him who had conquered it at last, and issued from its portals a fat and prosperous alumnus. Stupid men who have mastered a system, not by intuition but by a plodding effort of slow years, always exaggerate its importance—did it not take them ten years to understand it?— Whoso has passed the system, then, is to their minds one of a close corporation, of a select and intellectual few, and entitled to pose before the uninitiate. Because their stupidity made the thing difficult, their vanity leads them to exalt it. Woe to him that shall scoff at any detail! To Struthers the Senatus Academicus was an august assemblage worthy of the Roman

Curia, and each petty academic rule was a law sacrosanct and holy. He was forever talking of the "Univairsity." "Mind ye," he would say, "it takes a loang time to understand even the workings of the Univairsity—the Senatus and suchlike; it's not for everyone to criticize." He implied, of course, that he had a right to criticize, having passed triumphant through the mighty test. This vanity of his was fed by a peculiar vanity of some Scots peasants, who like to discuss Divinity Halls, and so on, because to talk of these things shews that they, too, are intelligent men, and know the awful intellectual ordeal required of a "Meenister." When a peasant says "He went through his Arts course in three years, and got a kirk the moment he was licensed," he wants you to see that he's a smart man himself, and knows what he's talking of. There were several men in Barbie who liked to talk in that way, and among them Puffy Importance, when graciously inclined, found ready listeners to his pompous blether about the "Univairsity." But what he liked best of all was to stop a newly-returned student in full view of the people, and talk learnedly of his courses—dear me, aye—of his courses, and his matriculations, and his lectures, and his graduations, and his thingumbobs. That was why he bore down upon our great essayist.

"Allow me to congratulate you, John," he said, with heavy solemnity—for Struthers always made a congregation of his listener, and droned as if mounted for a sermon. "Ye have done excellently well this Session; ye have indeed. Ex-cellently well! Ex-cellently well!"

Gourlay blushed and thanked him.

"Tell me now," said the cleric, "do you mean to take your Arts course in three years or four? A loang Arts course is a grand thing for a clairgyman. Even if he spends half a dozen years on't he won't be wasting his time!"

Gourlay glanced at his father. "I mean to try't in three," he said. His father had threatened him that he must get through his Arts in three years—without deigning, of course, to give any reason for the threat.

"We'ell," said Mr Struthers, gazing down the Fechars

Road, as if visioning great things, "it will require a strenuous and devoted application—a strenuous and devoted
application—even from the man of abeelity you have shown
yourself to be. Tell me now," he went on, "have ye heard
ainything of the new Professor of Exegesis? D'ye know
how he's doing?"

Young Gourlay knew nothing of the new Professor of
Exegesis, but he answered, "Very well, I believe," at a
venture.

"Oh, he's sure to do well, he's sure to do well! He's one
of the best men we have in the Church. I have just finished
his book on the Epheesians. It's most profound! It has taken
me a whole year to master it." (*Garvie on the Ephesians* is
a book of a hundred and eighty pages.) "And, by the way,"
said the parson, stooping to Scotch in his ministerial
jocoseness, "how's auld Tam, in whose class you were a
prizewinner? He was appointed to the Professoriate the
same year that I obtained my license. I remember to have
heard him deliver a lecture on German philosophy, and I
thought it excellently good. But perhaps," he added, with
solemn and pondering brows, "perhaps he was a little too
fond of Hegel.—Yess, I am inclined to think that he was a
little too fond of Hegel." Mrs Eccles, listening from the
Black Bull door, wondered if Hegel was a drink.

"He's very popular," said young Gourlay.

"Oh, he's sure to be popular, he merits the very greatest
popple-arity. And he would express himself as being
excellently well pleased with your theme? What did he say
of it, may I venture to enquire?

Beneath the pressure of his father's presence young
Gourlay did not dare to splurge. "He seemed to think there
was something in it," he answered, modestly enough.

"Oh, he would be sure to think there was something in it,"
said the minister, staring, and wagging his pow. "Not a
doubt of tha-at, not a doubt of tha-at! There must have been
something in it, to obtain the palm of victory in the face of
such prodigious competeetion. It's the see-lect intellect of
Scotland that goes to the Univairsity, and only the ee-lect of
the see-lect win the palm. And it's an augury of great good

for the future. Abeelity to write is a splendid thing for the Church. Good-bye, John, and allow me to express once moar my great satisfaction that a pareeshioner of mine is a la-ad of such brilliant promise!"

Though the elder Gourlay disconsidered the Church, and thought little of Mr Struthers, he swelled with pride to think that the minister should stop his offspring in the Main Street of Barbie, to congratulate him on his prospects. They were close to the Emporium; and with the tail of his eye he could **see** Wilson peeping from the door, and listening to every word. This would be a hair in Wilson's neck! There were no clerical compliments for *his* son! The tables were turned at last.

His father had a generous impulse to John for the bright triumph he had won the Gourlays. He fumbled in his trouser-pocket, and passed him a sovereign.

"I'm kind o' hard-up," he said with grim jocosity, "but there's a pound to keep your pouch.—No nonsense now!" he shot at the youth with a loaded eye. "That's just for use if you happen to be in company. A Gourlay maun spend as much as the rest o' folk."

"Yes, faither," said the youngster, and Gourlay went away.

That grimly-jocose reference to his poverty was a feature of Gourlay's talk now, when he spoke of money to his family. It excused the smallness of his doles, yet led them to believe that he was only joking, that he had plenty of money if he would only consent to shell it out. And that was what he wished them to believe. His pride would not allow him to confess, even to his nearest, that he was a failure in business, and hampered with financial trouble. Thus his manner of warning them to be careful had the very opposite effect. "He has heaps o' cash," thought the son, as he watched the father up the street; "there's no need for a fellow to be mean."

Flattered (as he fondly imagined) by the Deacon, flattered by the minister, tipped by his mother, tipped by his father, hail-fellow-well-met with Pate Wylie—Lord, but young Gourlay was the fine fellow! Symptoms of swell-head set in

with alarming rapidity. He had a wild tendency to splurge.
And, that he might show in a single afternoon all the crass
stupidity of which he was capable, he immediately allowed
himself a veiled insult towards the daughters of the ex-
Provost. They were really nice girls, in spite of their paren-
tage, and, as they came down the street, they glanced with
shy kindness at the student from under their broad-brimmed
hats. Gourlay raised his in answer to their nod. But the
moment after, and in their hearing, he yelled blatantly to
Swipey Broon, to come on and have a drink of beer. Swipey
was a sweep now, for Brown the ragman had added
chimney-cleaning to his other occupations—plurality of
professions you observe, being one of the features of the life
of Barbie. When Swipey turned out of the Fleckie Road,
he was as black as the ace of spades, a most disreputable
phiz. And when Gourlay yelled his loud welcome to that
grimy object, what he wanted to convey to the two girls
was: "Ho, ho, my pretty misses; I'm on bowing terms with
you, and yet when I might go up and speak to ye, I prefer
to go off and drink with a sweep, d'ye see? That shows
what I think o' ye!" All that summer John took an oblique
revenge on those who had disconsidered the Gourlays—but
would have liked to make up to him now when they thought
he was going to do well—he took a paltry revenge by
patently rejecting their advances and consorting instead,
and in their presence, with the lowest of low company.
Thus he vented a spite which he had long cherished against
them for their former neglect of Janet and him. For, though
the Gourlay children had been welcome at well-to-do
houses in the country, their father's unpopularity had
cut them off from the social life of the town. When the
Provost gave his grand spree on Hogmanay there was never
an invitation for the Gourlay youngsters. The slight had
rankled in the boy's mind. Now, however, some of the local
bigwigs had an opinion (with very little to support it) that
he was going to be a successful man, and they shewed a
disposition to be friendly. John, with a rankling memory of
their former coldness, flouted every overture, by letting them
see plainly that he preferred to their company—that of

Swipey Broon, Jock McCraw, and every ragamuffin of the town. It was a kind of backhanded stroke at them. That was the paltry form which his father's pride took in him. He did not see that he was harming himself rather than his father's enemies. Harm himself he did, for you could not associate with Jock McCraw and the like, without drinking in every howff you came across.

When the bodies assembled next day for their "morning," the Deacon was able to inform them that young Gourlay was back from the College, dafter than ever, and that he had pulled his leg as far as he wanted it. "Oh," he said, "I played him like a kitten wi' a cork and found out ainything and everything I wished. I dithcovered that he's in wi' Jock Allan and that crowd—I edged the conversation round on purpoth! Unless he wath blowing his trump—which I greatly doubt—they're as thick as thieveth. Ye ken what that meanth. He'll turn hith wee finger to the ceiling oftener than he puts hith forefinger to the pen, I'm thinking. It theemth he drinkth enormuth! He took a gey nip last thummer, and this thummer I wager he takes mair o't. He avowed his plain intention! 'I mean to kick up a bit of a dust,' thays he. Oh, but he's the splurge!"

"Aye, aye," said Sandy Toddle; "thae students are a gey squad. Especially the young ministers."

"Ou," said Tam Wylie, "dinna be hard on the ministers. Ministers are just like the rest o' folk. They mind me o' last year's early tatties. They're grand when they're gude, but the feck o' them's frostit."

"Aye," said the Deacon, "and young Gourlay's frostit in the shaw already. I doubt it'll be a poor ingathering."

"Weel, weel," said Tam Wylie, "the mair's the pity o' that, Deacon."

"Oh, it'th a grai-ait pity," said the Deacon, and he bowed his body solemnly with outspread hands. "No doubt it'th a grai-ait pity!" and he wagged his head from side to side, the picture of a poignant woe.

"I saw him in the Black Bull yestreen," said Brodie, who had been silent hitherto in utter scorn of the lad they were speaking of—too disgusted to open his mouth. "He was standing drinks to a crowd that were puffing him up about that prize o' his."

"It's alwayth the numskull hath the most conceit," said the Deacon.

"And yet there must be something in him too, to get that prize," mused the ex-Provost.

"A little ability's a dangerous thing," said Johnny Coe, who could think at times. "To be safe you should be a genius winged and flying, or a crawling thing that never leaves the earth. It's the half-and-half that hell gapes for. And owre they flap."

But nobody understood him. "Drink and vanity'll soon make end of *him*," said Brodie curtly, and snubbed the philosopher.

Before the summer holiday was over (it lasts six months in Scotland) young Gourlay was a habit-and-repute tippler. His shrinking abhorrence from the scholastic life of Edinburgh flung him with all the greater abandon into the conviviality he had learned to know at home. His mother (who always seemed to sit up now, after Janet and Gourlay were in bed) often let him in during the small hours, and, as he hurried past her in the lobby, he would hold his breath lest she should smell it. "You're unco late, dear," she would say wearily, but no other reproach did she utter. "I was taking a walk," he would answer thickly; "there's a fine moon!" It was true that when his terrible depression seized him, he was sometimes tempted to seek the rapture and peace of a moonlight walk upon the Fleckie Road. In his crude clay there was a vein of poetry; he could be alone in the country, and not lonely; had he lived in a green quiet place, he might have learned the solace of nature for the wounded when eve sheds her spiritual dews. But the mean pleasures to be found at the Cross satisfied his nature, and stopped him midway to that soothing beauty of the woods and streams, which might have brought healing and a wise quiescence. His success—such as it was—had gained him a circle—such as it was—and the assertive nature proper to his father's son gave him a kind of lead amongst them. Yet even his henchmen saw through his swaggering.

Swipey Broon turned on him one night, and threatened to
split his mouth, and he went as white as the wall behind him.

Among his other follies, he assumed the pose of a man
who could an he would, who had it in him to do great
things, if he would only set about them. In this, he was
partly playing up to a foolish opinion of his more ignorant
associates; it was they who suggested the pose to him.
"Devilish clever!" he heard them whisper one night as he
stood in the door of a tavern; "he could do it if he liked,
only he's too fond o' the fun." Young Gourlay flushed
where he stood in the darkness, flushed with pleasure at the
criticism of his character which was, nevertheless, a compliment to his wits. He felt that he must play up at once to the
character assigned him. "Ho, ho, my lads!" he cried,
entering with a splurge, "let's make a night o't. I should be
working for my degree to-night, but I suppose I can get it
easy enough when the time comes." "What did I tell ye?"
said McCraw, nudging an elbow—and Gourlay saw the
nudge. Here at last he had found the sweet seduction of a
proper pose—that of a *grand homme manqué*, of a man who
would be a genius were it not for the excess of his qualities.
Would he continue to appear a genius, then he must continue to display that excess which—so he wished them to
believe—alone prevented his brilliant achievements. It was
all a curious vicious inversion. "You could do great things
if you didn't drink," crooned the fools. "See how I drink,"
Gourlay seemed to answer—"that is why I don't do great
things. But, mind you, I could do them, were it not for this."
Thus every glass he tossed off seemed to hint in a roundabout
way at the glorious heights he might attain if he didn't
drink it. His very roystering became a pose, and his vanity
made him royster the more, to make the pose more
convincing.

CHAPTER 21

ON a beautiful evening in September, when a new crescent moon was pointing through the saffron sky like the lit tip of a finger, the City Fathers had assembled at the corner of the Fleckie Road. Though the moon was peeping, the dying glory of the day was still upon the town. The white smoke rose straight and far in the golden mystery of the heavens, and a line of dark roofs, transfigured against the west, wooed the eye to musing. But though the bodies felt the fine evening bathe them in a sensuous content, as they smoked and dawdled, they gave never a thought to its beauty. For there had been a blitheness in the town that day, and every other man seemed to have been preeing the demijohn.

Drucken Wabster and Brown the ragman came around the corner, staggering.

"Young Gourlay's drunk!" blurted Wabster—and reeled himself as he spoke.

"Is he a wee fou?" said the Deacon eagerly.

"Wee be damned," said Wabster; "he's as fou as the Baltic Sea! If you wait here, you'll be sure to see him! He'll be round the corner directly."

"De-ar, me, is he so bad as that?" said the ex-Provost, raising his hands in solemn reprobation. He raised his eyes to heaven at the same time, as if it pained them to look on a world that endured the burden of a young Gourlay. "In broad daylight, too!" he sighed. "De-ar me, has he come to this?"

"Yis, Pravast," hiccupped Brown, "he has! He's as phull of drink as a whelk-shell's phull of whelk. He's nearly as phull as meself.—And begorra, that's mighty phull." He stared suddenly, scratching his head solemnly as if the fact had just occurred to him. Then he winked.

"You could set fire to his braith!" cried Wabster. "A match to his mouth would send him in a lowe."

"A living gas jet!" said Brown.

They staggered away, sometimes rubbing shoulders as they lurched together, sometimes with the road between them.

"I kenned young Gourlay was on the fuddle when I saw him swinging off this morning in his greatcoat," cried Sandy Toddle. "There was debauch in the flap o' the tails o't."

"Man, have you noticed that, too!" cried another eagerly. "He's aye warst wi' the coat on!"

"Clothes undoubtedly affect the character," said Johnny Coe. "It takes a gentleman to wear a lordly coat without swaggering."

"There's not a doubt o' tha-at!" approved the baker, who was merry with his day's carousal; "there's not a doubt o' tha-at! Claes affect the disposeetion. I mind when I was a young chap I had a grand pair o' breeks—Wull I ca'ed them —unco decent breeks they were, I mind, lang and swankie like a ploughman—and I aye thocht I was a tremendous honest and hamely fallow when I had them on! And I had a verra disreputable hat," he added—"Rab I christened him for he was a perfect devil—and I never cocked him owre my lug on nichts at e'en but 'Baker!' he seemed to whisper, 'Baker! Let us go out and do a bash!'—And we generally went."

"You're a wonderful man!" piped the Deacon.

"We may as well wait and see young Gourlay going bye," said the ex-Provost. "He'll likely be a sad spectacle."

"Ith auld Gourlay on the threet the nicht?" cried the Deacon eagerly. "I wonder will he thee the youngster afore he gets hame! Eh, man—" he bent his knees with staring delight—"eh, man, if they would only meet forenenst uth! Hoo!"

"He's a regular waster," said Brodie. "When a silly young blood takes a fancy to a girl in a public house he's always done for—I've observed it times without number. At first he lets on that he merely gangs in for a drink; what he really wants, however, is to see the girl. Even if he's no great toper to begin with, he must show himself fond o' the dram, as a means of getting to his jo. Then, before he kens where he is, the habit has gripped him. That's a gate mony a ane gangs."

"That's verra true—now that ye mention't," gravely assented the ex-Provost. His opinion of Brodie's sagacity, high already, was enhanced by the remark. "Indeed, that's verra true. But how does't apply to young Gourlay in particular, Thomas? Is *he* after some damsel o' the gill-stoup?"

"Ou aye—he's ta'en a fancy to yon bit shilp in the bar-room o' the Red Lion. He's always hinging ower the counter talking till her, a cigarette dropping from his face, and a half-fu' tumbler at his elbow. When a young chap takes to hinging round bars, ae elbow on the counter and a hand on his other hip, I have verra bad brows o' him always; verra bad brows, indeed. Oh—oh, young Gourlay's just a goner! a goner, sirs; a goner!"

"Have ye heard about him at the Skeighan Fair?" said Sandy Toddle.

"No, man!" said Brodie, bowing down and keeking at Toddle in his interest; "I hadna heard about tha-at! Is this a *new* thing?"

"Oh, just at the fair; the other day, ye know!"

"Aye, man, Sandy!" said big Brodie, stooping down to Toddle to get near the news; "and what was it, Sandy?"

"Ou, just drinking, ye know; wi'—wi' Swipey Broon—and, eh, and that McCraw, ye know—and Sandy Hull—and a wheen mair o' that kind—ye ken the kind; a verra bad lot!" said Sandy, and wagged a disapproving pow. "Here they all got as drunk as drunk could be, and started fighting wi' the colliers! Young Gourlay got a bloodied nose! Then nothing would serve him but he must drive back wi' young Pin-oe, who was even drunker than himsell. They drave at sic a rate that when they dashed from this side o' Skeighan Drone, the stour o' their career was rising at the far-end. They roared and sang till it was a perfect affront to God's day, and frae sidie to sidie they swung till the splash-brods were skreighing on the wheels. At a quick turn o' the road they wintled owre; and there they were, sitting on their dowps in the atoms o' the gig, and glowering frae them! When young Gourlay slid hame at dark, he was in such a state that his mother had to hide him frae the auld man. She had that, puir body! The twa women were obliged to carry the drunk lump to his bedroom—and yon lassie far ga'en in consumption, too, they tell me! Ou, he was in a perfectly awful condition; perfectly awful!"

"Aye, man," nodded Brodie. "I hadna heard o't. Curious that I didna hear o' that!"

"It was Drucken Wabster's wife that telled it. There's not a haet that happens at the Gourlays but she clypes. I speired her mysell, and she says young Gourlay has a black eye."

"Aye, aye; there'th thmall hope for the Gourlayth in *him!*" said the Deacon.

"How do *you* ken?" cried the baker. "He's no the first youngster I've seen the wiseacres o' the world wagging their sagacious pows owre; and, eh, but he was *this* waster!—according to their way of it—and, oh, but he was the *other* waster! and, ochonee, but he was the *wild* fellow!—and a' the while they werena fit to be his door mat; for it was only the fire in the ruffian made him seem sae daft."

"True!" said the ex-Provost; "true! Still there's a decency in daftness. And there's no decency in young Gourlay. He's just a mouth! 'Start canny and you'll steer weel,' my mother used to say; but he has started unco ill, and he'll steer to ruin."

"Dinna spae ill-fortune!" said the baker, "dinna spae ill-fortune! And never despise a youngster for a random start. It's the blood makes a breenge."

"Well, I like young men to be quiet," said Sandy Toddle. "I would rather have them a wee soft than rollickers."

"Not I!" said the baker. "If I had a son, I would rather an ill deil sat fornenst me at the table, than parratch in a poke. Burns (God rest his banes!) struck the he'rt o't. Ye mind what he said o' Prince Geordie:

" 'Yet mony a ragged cowte's been known
To mak a noble aiver;
And ye may doucely fill a Throne,
For a' their clishmaclaver;
There Him at Agincourt wha shone,
Few better were or braver;

173

And yet wi' funny queer Sir John
He was an unco shaver
For monie a day.' "
"Dam't, but Burns is gude."

"Huts man, dinna sweer sae muckle!" frowned the old Provost.

"Ou, there's waur than an oath now and than," said the baker. "Like spice in a bun it lends a briskness. But it needs the hearty manner wi't. The Deacon there couldna let blatter wi' a hearty oath to save his withered sowl. I kenned a trifle o' a fellow that got in among a jovial gang lang-syne that used to sweer tremendous, and he bude to do the same the bit bodie!—so he used to say '*Dim it!*' in a wee sma voice that was clean rideec'lous. He was a lauchable dirt, that."

"What was his name?" said Sandy Toddle.

"Your ain," said the baker. (To tell the truth, he was gey fou.) "Alexander Toddle was his name: '*Dim it!*' he used to squeak, for he had been a Scotch cuddy in the Midlands, and whiles he used the English. '*Dim it!!*' said he. I like a man that says '*Dahm't*'."

"Aye, but then, you thee, *you're* an artitht in wordth," said the Deacon.

"Ye're an artist in spite," said the baker.

"Ah, well," said the ex-Provost, "Burns proved to be wrang in the end o't, and you'll maybe be the same. George the Fort' didna fill the throne verra doucely for a' their cleishmaclaver, and I don't think young Gourlay'll fill the pulpit verra doucely for a' ours. For he's saftie and daftie baith—and that's the deidly combination. At least, that's my opinion," quoth he, and smacked his lips, the important man.

"Tyuts," said the baker, "folk should be kind to folk. There may be a possibeelity for the Gourlays in the youngster yet!"

He would have said more, but at that moment his sonsy big wife came out, with oh! such a roguish and kindly smile, and, "Tom, Tom," said she, "what are ye havering here for? C'way in, man, and have a dish o' tea wi' me!"

He glanced up at her with comic shrewdness from where he sat on his hunkers—for fine he saw through her—and "Ou aye," said he, "ye great muckle fat hotch o' a dacent bodie, ye—I'll gang in and have a dish o' tea wi' ye." And away went the fine fuddled fellow.

"She's a wise woman, that," said the ex-Provost looking after them. "She kenned no to flyte, and he went like a lamb."

"I believe he'th feared o' her," snapped the Deacon, "or he wudny-un went thae lamb-like!"

"Leave him alone!" said Johnny Coe, who had been drinking too. "He's the only kind heart in Barbie. And Gourlay's the only gentleman."

"Gentleman!" cried Sandy Toddle. "Lord save us! Auld Gourlay a gentleman!"

"Yes, gentleman!" said Johnny, to whom the drink gave a courage. "Brute, if ye like, but aristocrat frae scalp to heel. If he had brains, and a dacent wife, and a bigger field—oh, man," said Johnny, visioning the possibility, "Auld Gourla could conquer the world, if he swalled his neck till't."

"It would be a big conquest that!" said the Deacon.— "Here comes his son taking his ain share o' the earth at ony rate."

Young Gourlay came staggering round the corner, "a little sprung" (as they phrase it in Barbie), but not so bad as they had hoped to see him. Webster and the ragman had exaggerated the condition of their fellow-toper. Probably their own oscillation lent itself to everything they saw. John zig-zagged, it is true, but otherwise he was fairly steady on his pins. Unluckily, however, failing to see a stone before on the road[1], he tripped and went sprawling on his hands and knees. A titter went.

"What the hell are you laughing at?" he snarled, leaping up; quick to feel the slight, blatant to resent it.

"Tyuts man!" Tam Wylie rebuked him in a careless scorn.

With a parting scowl he went swaggering up the street.

"Aye!" said Toddle drily, "that's the Gourlay possi-beelity."

[1]The Memorial edition reads *before him on the road*. All other editions as above.

CHAPTER 22

"Ah, ha, Deacon, my old cock, here you are!" The speaker smote the Deacon between his thin shoulder-blades, till the hat leapt on his startled cranium. "No, not a lengthy stay— just down for a flying visit to see my little girl. Dem'd glad to get back to town again—Barbie's too quiet for my tastes. No life in the place, no life at all!"

The speaker was Davie Aird, draper and buck. "No life at all," he cried, as he shot down his cuffs with a jerk, and swung up and down the bar-room of the Red Lion. He was dressed in a long fawn overcoat reaching to his heels, with two big yellow buttons at the waist behind, in the most approved fashion of the horsey. He paused in his swaggering to survey the backs of his long white delicate hands, holding them side by side before him, as if to make sure they were the same size. He was letting the Deacon see his ring. Then pursing his chin down, with a fastidious and critical regard, he picked a long fair hair off his left coat-sleeve. He held it high as he had seen them do on the stage of the Theatre Royal. "Sweet souvenir!" he cried, and kissed it, "most dear remembrance!"

The Deacon fed on the sight. The richness of his satiric perception was too great to permit of speech. He could only gloat and be dumb.

"Waiting for Jack Gourlay," Aird rattled again. "He's off to College again, and we're driving in his father's trap to meet the express at Skeighan Station. Wonder what's keeping the fellow. I like a man to be punctual. Business training, you see—yes, by Gad, two thousand parcels a week out of our place, and all of 'em up to time! Ah, there he is," he added, as the harsh grind of wheels was heard on the gravel at the door. "Thank God, we'll soon be in civilization."

Young Gourlay entered great-coated and lordly, through

the two halves of that easy-swinging door.

"Good!" he cried. "Just a minute, Aird, till I get my flask filled."

"My weapon's primed and ready," Aird ha-ha'd, and slapped the breast pocket of his coat.

John birled a bright sovereign on the counter, one of twenty old Gourlay had battered his brains to get together for the boy's expenses. The young fellow rattled the change into his trouser-pocket like a master of millions.

The Deacon, and another idler or two, gathered about the steps in the darkness, to see that royal going off. Peter Riney's bunched-up little old figure could be seen on the front seat of the gig; Aird was already mounted behind. The mare (a worthy successor to Spanking Tam) pawed the gravel and fretted in impatience; her sharp ears, seen pricked against the gloom, worked to and fro. A widening cone of light shone out from the leftward lamp of the gig, full on a glistering laurel, which Simpson had growing by his porch. Each smooth leaf of the green bush gave back a separate gleam, vivid to the eye in that pouring yellowness. Gourlay stared at the bright evergreen, and forgot for a moment where he was. His lips parted, and—as they saw in the light from the door—his look grew dreamy and far-away.

The truth was that all the impressions of a last day at home were bitten in on his brain as by acid, in the very middle of his swaggering gusto. That gusto was largely real, true, for it seemed a fine thing to go splurging off to College in a gig; but it was still more largely assumed, to combat the sorrow of departure. His heart was in his boots at the thought of going back to accursed Edinburgh—to those lodgings, those dreary, damnable lodgings. Thus his nature was reduced to its real elements in the hour of leaving home; it was only for a swift moment he forgot to splurge, but for that moment the cloak of his swaggering dropped away and he was his naked self, morbidly alive to the impressions of the world, afraid of life, clinging to the familiar and the known. That was why he gazed with wistful eyes at that laurel clump, so vivid in the pouring rays. So vivid there, it stood for all the dear country round which was now hidden

177

by the darkness; it centred his world among its leaves. It was a last picture of loved Barbie that was fastening on his mind. There would be fine gardens in Edinburgh, no doubt, but, oh, that couthie laurel by the Red Lion door! It was his friend; he had known it always.

The spell lasted but a moment, one of those moments searching a man's nature to its depths, yet flitting like a lonely shadow on the autumn wheat. But Aird was already fidgeting. "Hurry up, Jack," he cried, "we'll need to pelt if we mean to get the train."

Gourlay started. In a moment he had slipped from one self to another, and was the blusterer once more. "Right!" he splurged, "hover a blink till I light my cigar."

He was not in the habit of smoking cigars, but he had bought a packet on purpose, that he might light one before his admiring onlookers ere he went away. Nothing like cutting a dash.

He was seen puffing for a moment with indrawn cheeks, his head to one side, the flame of the flickering vesta lighting up his face, his hat pushed back till it rested on his collar, his fair hair hanging down his brow. Then he sprang to the driving seat and gathered up the reins. "Ta-ta, Deacon; see and behave yourself!" he flung across his shoulder, and they were off with a bound.

"Im-pidenth!" said the outraged Deacon.

Peter Riney was quite proud to have the honour of driving two such bucks to the station. It lent him a consequence; he would be able to say when he came back that he had been "awa wi' the young mester"—for Peter said "mester," and was laughed at by the Barbie wits who knew that "maister" was the proper English. The splurging twain rallied him and drew him out in talk, passed him their flasks at the Brownie's Brae, had him tee-heeing at their nonsense. It was a full-blooded night to the withered little man.

That was how young Gourlay left Barbie for what was to prove his last session at the University.

All Gourlay's swankie chaps had gone with the going of his trade; only Peter Riney, the queer little oddity, remained.

There was a loyal simplicity in Peter which never allowed him to question the Gourlays. He had been too long in their service to be of use to any other; while there was a hand's turn to be done about the House with the Green Shutters, he was glad to have the chance of doing it. His respect for his surly tyrant was as great as ever; he took his pittance of a wage and was thankful. Above all he worshipped young Gourlay; to be in touch with a College-bred man was a reflected glory; even the escapades noised about the little town, to his gleeful ignorance, were the signs of a man of the world. Peter chuckled when he heard them talked of. "Terr'ble clever fallow, the young mester!" the bowed little man would say, sucking his pipe of an evening, "terr'ble clever fallow, the young mester—and hardy, too; infernal hardy!" Loyal Peter believed it.

But ere four months had gone, Peter was discharged. It was on the day after Gourlay sold Black Sally, the mare, to get a little money to go on with.

It was a bright spring day, of enervating softness, a fosie day, a day when the pores of everything seemed opened. People's brains felt pulpy, and they sniffed as with winter's colds. Peter Riney was opening a pit of potatoes in the big garden, shovelling aside the foot-deep mould, and tearing off the inner covering of yellow straw—which seemed strange and unnatural, somehow, when suddenly revealed in its glistening dryness, beneath the moist dark earth. Little crumbles of mould trickled down, in among the flattened shining straws. In a tree near Peter, two pigeons were gurgling and *rooketty-cooing*, mating for the coming year. He fell to sorting out the potatoes, throwing the bad ones on a heap aside—"tattie-walin," as they call it in the north. The enervating softness was at work on Peter's head, too, and from time to time, as he waled, he wiped his nose on his sleeve.

Gourlay watched him for a long time without speaking. Once or twice he moistened his lips, and cleared his throat, and frowned—as one who would broach unpleasant news. It was not like him to hesitate. But the old man, encased in senility, was ill to disturb; he was intent on nothing but the

179

work before him; it was mechanical and soothing and occupied his whole mind. Gourlay, so often the trampling brute without knowing it, felt it brutal to wound the faithful old creature dreaming at his toil. He would have found it much easier to discharge a younger and a keener man.

"Stop, Peter," he said at last; "I don't need you ainy more."

Peter rose stiffly from his knees and shook the mould with a pitiful gesture from his hands. His mouth was fallen slack, and showed a few yellow tusks.

"Eh?" he asked vaguely. The thought that he must leave the Gourlays could not penetrate his mind.

"I don't need you ainy more," said Gourlay again, and met his eye steadily.

"I'm gey auld," said Peter, still shaking his hands with that pitiful gesture, "but I only need a bite and a sup. Man, I'm willin' to tak onything."

"It's no that," said Gourlay sourly, "it's no that. But I'm giving up the business."

Peter said nothing, but gazed away down the garden, his sunken mouth forgetting to munch its straw, which dangled by his chin. "I'm an auld servant," he said at last, "and mind ye," he flashed in pride, "I'm a true ane."

"Oh, you're a' that," Gourlay grunted; "you have been a good servant."

"It'll be the poorhouse, it's like," mused Peter. "Man, have ye noathing for us to do?" he asked pleadingly.

Gourlay's jaw clamped. "Noathing, Peter," he said sullenly, "noathing"; and slipped some money into Peter's heedless palm.

Peter stared stupidly down at the coins. He seemed dazed. "Aye, weel," he said; "I'll feenish the tatties at ony rate."

"No, no, Peter," and Gourlay gripped him by the shoulder as he turned back to his work, "no, no; I have no right to keep you. Never mind about the money—you deserve something, going so suddenly after sic a long service. It's just a bit present to mind you o'—to mind you o'—" he broke off suddenly and scowled across the garden.

Some men, when a feeling touches them, express their

emotion in tears; others by an angry scowl—hating themselves inwardly, perhaps, for their weakness in being moved, hating, too, the occasion that has probed their weakness. It was because he felt parting with Peter so keenly that Gourlay behaved more sullenly than usual. Peter had been with Gourlay's father in his present master's boyhood, had always been faithful and submissive; in his humble way was nearer the grain merchant than any other man in Barbie. He was the only human being Gourlay had ever deigned to joke with; and that, in itself, won him an affection. More, the going of Peter meant the going of everything. It cut Gourlay to the quick. Therefore he scowled.

Without a word of thanks for the money, Peter knocked the mould off his heavy boots, striking one against the other clumsily, and shuffled away across the bare soil. But when he had gone twenty yards, he stopped, and came back slowly. "Good-bye, sir," he said with a rueful smile, and held out his hand.

Gourlay gripped it. "Good-bye, Peter! good-bye; damn ye, man, good-bye!"

Peter wondered vaguely why he was sworn at. But he felt that it was not in anger. He still clung to his master's hand. "I've been fifty year wi' the Gourlays," said he. "Aye, aye; and this, it seems, is the end o't."

"Oh, gang away!" cried Gourlay, "gang away, man!" And Peter went away.

Gourlay went out to the big green gate where he had often stood in his pride, and watched his old servant going down the street. Peter was so bowed that the back of his velveteen coat was half-way up his spine, and the bulging pockets at the corners were mid-way down his thighs. Gourlay had seen the fact a thousand times, but it never gripped him before. He stared till Peter disappeared round the Bend o' the Brae.

"Aye, aye," said he, "aye, aye. There goes the last o' them."

It was a final run of ill-luck that brought Gourlay to this desperate pass. When everything seemed to go against him, he tried several speculations, with a gambler's hope that they might do well, and retrieve the situation. He abandoned the sensible direction of affairs, that is, and trusted entirely to chance, as men are apt to do when despairing. And chance betrayed him. He found himself of a sudden at the end of his resources.

Through all his troubles his one consolation was the fact that he had sent John to the University. That was something saved from the wreck at any rate. More and more, as his other supports fell away, Gourlay attached himself to the future of his son. It became the sheet-anchor of his hopes. If he had remained a prosperous man John's success would have been merely incidental, something to disconsider in speech, at least, however pleased he might have been at heart. But now it was the whole of life to him. For one thing, the son's success would justify the father's past and prevent it being quite useless; it would have produced a minister, a successful man, one of an esteemed profession. Again, that success would be a salve to Gourlay's wounded pride; the Gourlays would show Barbie they could flourish yet, in spite of their present downcome. Thus, in the collapse of his fortunes, the son grew all-important in the father's eyes. Nor did his own poverty seem to him a just bar to his son's prosperity. "I have put him through his Arts," thought Gourlay; "surely he can do the rest himsell. Lots of young chaps, when they warstle through their Arts, teach the sons of swells to get a little money to gang through Diveenity. My boy can surely do the like!" Again and again, as Gourlay felt himself slipping under in the world of Barbie, his hopes turned to John in Edinburgh. If that boy would only hurry up and get through, to make a hame for the lassie and the auld wife!

CHAPTER 23

YOUNG Gourlay spent that winter in Edinburgh pretty much as he had spent the last. Last winter, however, it was simply a weak need for companionship that drew him to the Howff. This winter it was more, it was the need of a formed habit that must have its wonted satisfaction. He had a further impulse to conviviality now. It had become a habit that compelled him.

The diversions of some men are merely subsidiary to their lives, externals easy to be dropped; with others they usurp the man. They usurp a life when it is never happy away from them, when in the midst of other occupations absent pleasures rise vivid to the mind, with an irresistible call. Young Gourlay's too-seeing imagination, always visioning absent delights, combined with his weakness of will, never gripping to the work before him, to make him hate his lonely studies and long for the jolly company of his friends. He never opened his books of an evening but he thought to himself: "I wonder what they're doing at the Howff tonight?" At once he visualized the scene, imagined every detail, saw them in their jovial hours. And, seeing them so happy, he longed to be with them. On that night, long ago, when his father ordered him to College, his cowardly and too vivid mind thought of the ploys the fellows would be having along the Barbie roads, while he was mewed up in Edinburgh. He saw the Barbie rollickers in his mind's eye, and the student in his lonely rooms, and contrasted them mournfully. So now, every night, he saw the cosy companions in their Howff, and shivered at his own isolation. He felt a tugging at his heart to be off and join them. And his will was so weak that, nine times out of ten, he made no resistance to the impulse.

He had always a feeling of depression when he must sit down to his books. It was the start that gravelled him. He would look round his room and hate it, mutter "Damn it, I must work"—and then, with a heavy sigh, would seat himself before an outspread volume on the table, tugging the hair on a puckered forehead. Sometimes the depression left him, when he buckled to his work; as his mind became occupied with other things the vision of the Howff was expelled. Usually, however, the stiffness of his brains made the reading drag heavily, and he rarely attained the sufficing happiness of a student eager and engrossed. At the end of ten minutes he would be gaping across the table, and wondering what they were doing at the Howff. "Will Logan be singing 'Tam Glen'? Or is Gillespie fiddling Highland tunes, by Jing, with his elbow going it merrily? Lord! I would like to hear 'Miss Drummond o' Perth' or 'Gray Daylicht'— they might buck me up a bit. I'll just slip out for ten minutes, to see what they're doing, and be back directly." He came back at two in the morning, staggering.

On a bleak spring evening, near the end of February, young Gourlay had gone to the Howff, to escape the shuddering misery of the streets. It was that treacherous spring weather which blights. Only two days ago, the air had been sluggish and balmy; now an easterly wind nipped the grey city, naked and bare. There was light enough, with the lengthening days, to see, plainly, the rawness of the world. There were cold yellow gleams in windows fronting a lonely west. Uncertain little puffs of wind came swirling round corners, and made dust and pieces of dirty white paper gyrate on the roads. Prosperous old gentlemen pacing home, rotund in their buttoned-up coats, had clear drops at the end of their noses. Sometimes they stopped—their trouser-legs flapping behind them—and trumpeted loudly into red silk handkerchiefs. Young Gourlay had fled the streets. It was the kind of night that made him cower.

By eight o'clock, however, he was merry with the barley-bree, and making a butt of himself to amuse the company. He was not quick-witted enough to banter a comrade readily, nor hardy enough to essay it unprovoked; on the other hand his swaggering love of notice impelled him to some form of talk that would attract attention. So he made a point of always coming with daft stories of things comic that befell him—at least, he said they did. But if his efforts were greeted with too loud a roar, implying not only appreciation of the stories, but also a contempt for the man who could tell them of himself, his sensitive vanity was immediately wounded, and he swelled with sulky anger. And the moment after he would splurge and bluster to reassert his dignity.

"I remember when I was a boy," he hiccuped, "I had a pet goose at home."

There was a titter at the queer beginning.

"I was to get the price of it for myself, and so when Christmas drew near, I went to old MacFarlane, the poulterer in Skeighan. 'Will you buy a goose?' said I. 'Are ye for sale, my man?' was his answer."

Armstrong flung back his head and roared, prolonging the loud *ho-ho!* through his big nose and open mouth long after the impulse to honest laughter was exhausted. He always laughed with false loudness, to indicate his own superiority, when he thought a man had been guilty of a public silliness. The laugh was meant to show the company how far above such folly was Mr Armstrong.

Gourlay scowled. "Damn Armstrong!" he thought, "what did he yell like that for? Does he think I didn't see the point of the joke against myself? Would I have told it if I hadn't? This is what comes of being sensitive. I'm always too sensitive! I felt there was an awkward silence, and I told a story against myself to dispel it in fun, and this is what I get for't. Curse the big brute, he thinks I have given myself away. But I'll show him!"

He was already mellow, but he took another swig to hearten him, as was his habit.

"There's a damned sight too much yell about your laugh, Armstrong," he said, truly enough, getting a courage from his anger and the drink. "No gentleman laughs like that."

" '*Risu inepto res ineptior nulla est,*' " said Tarmillan, who was on one of his rare visits to the Howff. He was too busy and too wise a man to frequent it greatly.

Armstrong blushed; and Gourlay grew big and brave, in the backing of the great Tarmillan. He took another swig on the strength of it. But his resentment was still surging. When Tarmillan went, and the three students were left by themselves, Gourlay continued to nag and bluster, for that blatant laugh of Armstrong's rankled in his mind.

"I saw Hepburn in the street today," said Gillespie, by way of a diversion.

"Who's Hepburn?" snapped Gourlay.

"Oh, don't you remember? He's the big Border chap who got into a row with auld Tam on the day you won your prize essay." (That should surely appease the fool, thought Gillespie.) "It was only for the fun of the thing Hepburn was at College, for he has lots of money; and, here, he never apologized to Tam! He said he would go down first."

"He was damned right," spluttered Gourlay. "Some of these Profs. think too much of themselves. They wouldn't bully *me!* There's good stuff in the Gourlays," he went on with a meaning look at Armstrong; "they're not to be scoffed at. I would stand insolence from no man."

"Aye, man," said Armstrong, "would you face up to a professor?"

"Wouldn't I?" said the tipsy youth, "and to you, too, if you went too far."

He became so quarrelsome as the night went on that his comrades filled him up with drink, in the hope of deadening his ruffled sensibilities. It was: "Yes, yes, Jack; but never mind about that! Have another drink, just to show there's no ill-feeling among friends."

When they left the Howff they went to Gillespie's and drank more, and, after that, they roamed about the town. At two in the morning the other two brought Gourlay to his door. He was assuring Armstrong he was not a gentleman.

When he went to bed the fancied insult he had suffered swelled to monstrous proportions in his fevered brain. Did Armstrong despise him? The thought was poison! He lay in brooding anger, and his mind was fluent in wrathful harangues in some imaginary encounter of the future, in which he was a glorious victor. He flowed in eloquent scorn of Armstrong and his ways. If I could talk like this always, he thought, what a fellow I would be! He seemed gifted with uncanny insight into Armstrong's character. He noted every weakness in the rushing whirl of his thoughts, set them in order one by one, saw himself laying bare the man with savage glee when next they should encounter. He would whiten the big brute's face by shewing he had probed him to the quick. Just let him laugh at me again, thought Gourlay, and I'll analyse each mean quirk of his dirty soul to him!

The drink was dying in him now, for the trio had walked for more than an hour through the open air when they left Gillespie's rooms. The stupefaction of alcohol was gone, leaving his brain morbidly alive. He was anxious to sleep, but drowsy dullness kept away. His mind began to visualize of its own accord, independent of his will; and, one after another, a crowd of pictures rose vivid in the darkness of his brain. He saw them as plainly as you see this page—but with a different clearness—for they seemed unnatural, belonging to a morbid world. Nor did one suggest the other; there was no connection between them; each came vivid of its own accord.

First it was an old pit-frame on a barren moor, gaunt against the yellow west. Gourlay saw bars of iron, left when the pit was abandoned, reddened by the rain; and the mounds of rubbish, and the scattered bricks, and the rusty clinkers from the furnace, and the melancholy shining pools. A four-wheeled old trolley had lost two of its wheels, and was tilted at a slant, one square end of it resting on the ground.

"Why do I think of an old pit?" he thought angrily; "curse it, why can't I sleep?"

Next moment he was gazing at a ruined castle, its mouldering walls mounded atop with decaying rubble; from a loose crumb of mortar, a long, thin film of the spider's weaving stretched bellying away, to a tall weed waving on the crazy brink—Gourlay saw its glisten in the wind. He saw each crack in the wall, each stain of lichen; a myriad details stamped themselves together on his raw mind. Then a constant procession of figures passed across the inner curtain of his closed eyes. Each figure was cowled; but when it came directly opposite, it turned and looked at him with a white face. "Stop, stop!" cried his mind, "I don't want to think of you, I don't want to think of you, I don't want to think of you! Go away!" But as they came of themselves, so they went of themselves. He could not banish them.

He turned on his side, but a hundred other pictures pursued him. From an inland hollow he saw the great dawn flooding up from the sea, over a sharp line of cliff, wave after wave of brilliance surging up the heavens. The landward slope of the cliff was gray with dew. The inland hollow was full of little fields, divided by stone walls, and he could not have recalled the fields round Barbie with half their distinctness. For a moment they possessed his brain. Then an autumn wood rose on his vision. He was gazing down a vista of yellow leaves; a long, deep slanting cleft, framed in lit foliage. Leaves, leaves; everywhere yellow leaves, luminous, burning. He saw them falling through the lucid air. The scene was as vivid as fire to his brain, though of magic stillness. Then the foliage changed suddenly to great serpents twined about the boughs. Their colours were of monstrous beauty. They glistened as they moved.

He leapt in his bed with a throb of horror. Could this be the delirium of drink? But no; he had often had an experience like this when he was sleepless; he had the learned description of it pat and ready; it was only automatic visualization.

Damn! Why couldn't he sleep! He flung out of bed, uncorked a bottle with his teeth, tilted it up, and gulped the gurgling fire in the darkness. Ha! that was better.

His room was already gray with the coming dawn. He went to the window and opened it. The town was stirring uneasily in its morning sleep. Somewhere in the distance a train was shunting; *clank, clank, clank* went the waggons. What an accursed sound! A dray went past the end of his street rumbling hollowly, and the rumble died drearily away. Then the footsteps of an early workman going to his toil were heard in the deserted thoroughfare. Gourlay looked down and saw him pass far beneath him on the glimmering pavement. He was whistling. Why did the fool

whistle? What had he got to whistle about? It was unnatural that one man should go whistling to his work,
when another had not been able to sleep the whole night
long.

He took another vast glut of whiskey, and the moment
after was dead to the world.

He was awakened at eight o'clock by a monstrous hammering on his door. By the excessive loudness of the first
knock he heard on returning to consciousness, he knew that
his landlady had lost her temper in trying to get him up. Ere
he could shout she had thumped again. He stared at the
ceiling in sullen misery. The middle of his tongue was as
dry as bark.

For his breakfast there were thick slabs of rancid bacon,
from the top of which two yellow eggs had spewed themselves away among the cold gravy. His gorge rose at them.
He nibbled a piece of dry bread and drained the teapot; then
shouldering into his great-coat he tramped off to the
University.

It was a wretched morning. The wind had veered once
more, and a cold drizzle of rain was falling through a yellow
fog. The reflections of the street lamps in the sloppy pavement went down through spiral gleams, to an infinite
depth of misery. Young Gourlay's brain was aching from
his last night's debauch, and his body was weakened with
the want both of sleep and food. The cold yellow mist
chilled him to the bone. What a fool I was to get drunk
last night, he thought. Why am I here? Why am I trudging
through mud and misery to the University? What has it all
got to do with me? Oh, what a fool I am, what a fool!

"Drown dull care," said the Devil in his ear.

He took a sixpence from his trouser pocket, and looked
down at the white bit of money in his hand, till it was wet
with the falling rain. Then he went into a flashy tavern, and,
standing by a sloppy bar, drank sixpennyworth of cheap
whiskey. It went to his head at once, owing to his want of
food, and with a dull warm feeling in his body, he lurched off
to his first lecture for the day. His outlook on the world had
changed. The fog was now a comfortable yellowness.

"Freedom and whiskey gang thegither, Tak aff your dram," he quoted to his own mind. "That stuff did me good. Whiskey's the boy to fettle you."

He was in his element the moment he entered the class-room. It was a bear garden. The most moral individual has his days of perversity when a malign fate compels him to show the worst he has in him. A Scotch[1] University class—which is many most moral individuals—has a similar eruptive tendency when it gets into the hands of a weak professor. It will behave well enough for a fortnight, then a morning comes when nothing can control it. This was a morning of the kind. The lecturer, who was an able man but a weakling, had begun by apologizing for the condition of his voice, on the ground that he had a bad cold. Instantly every man in the class was blowing his nose. One fellow, of a most portentous snout, who could trumpet like an elephant, with a last triumphant snort sent his handkerchief across the room. When called to account for his conduct, "Really, sir." he said, "er-er-oom—bad cold!" Up rose a universal sneeze. Then the "roughing" began to the tune of "John Brown's body lies a-mouldering in the grave"—which no man seemed to sing, but every man could hear. They were playing the tune with their feet.

The lecturer glared with white repugnance at his tormentors.

Young Gourlay flung himself heart and soul into the cruel baiting. It was partly from his usual love of showing off, partly from the drink still seething within him; but largely, also, as a reaction from his morning's misery. This was another way of drowning reflection. The morbidly gloomy one moment often shout madly on the next.

At last the lecturer plunged widly at the door and flung it open. "Go!" he shrieked, and pointed in superb dismissal.

A hundred and fifty barbarians sat where they were, and laughed at him; and he must needs come back to the platform, with a baffled and vindictive glower.

He was just turning, as it chanced, when young Gourlay put his hands to his mouth, and bellowed "*Cock-a-doodle-*

[1]The reading of earlier editions. Later editions prefer *Scottish*.

do!"

Ere the roar could swell, the lecturer had leapt to the front of the rostrum with flaming eyes. "Mr Gourlay," he screamed furiously, "you there, sir; you will apologize humbly to me for this outrage at the end of the hour."

There was a womanish shrillness in the scream, a kind of hysteria on the stretch, that (contrasted with his big threat) might have provoked them at other times to a roar of laughter. But there was a sincerity in his rage today that rose above its faults of manner, and an immediate silence took the room—the more impressive for the former noise. Every eye turned to Gourlay. He sat gaping at the lecturer.

If he had been swept to the anteroom there and then, he would have been cowed by the suddenness of his own change, from a loud tormentor in the company of others, to a silent culprit in a room alone. And apologies would have been ready to tumble out, while he was thus loosened by surprise and fear.

Unluckily he had time to think, and the longer he thought the more sullen he became. It was only an accident that led to his discovery, while the rest escaped, and that the others should escape, when they were just as much to blame as he was, was an injustice that made him furious. His anger was equally divided between the cursed mischance itself, the teacher who had "jumped" on him so suddenly, and the other rowdies who had escaped to laugh at his discomfiture; he had the same burning resentment to them all. When he thought of his chuckling fellow-students they seemed to engross his rage; when he thought of the mishap he damned it and nothing else; when he thought of the lecturer he felt he had no rage to fling away upon others—the Snuffler took it all. As his mind shot backwards and forwards in an angry gloom, it suddenly encountered the image of his father. Not a professor of the lot, he reflected, could stand the look of black Gourlay. And he wouldn't knuckle under, either, so he wouldn't. He came of a hardy stock. He would show them! He wasn't going to lick dirt for any man. Let him punish all or none, for they had all been kicking up a row—why, big Cunningham had been braying like an ass only a minute before.

He spied Armstrong and Gillespie glinting across at him with a curious look—they were wondering whether he had courage enough to stand to his guns with a professor. He knew the meaning of the look, and resented it. He was on his mettle before them, it seemed. The fellow who had swaggered at the Howff last night about "what *he* would do if a professor jumped on *him*," musn't prove wanting in the present trial, beneath the eyes of those on whom he had imposed his blatancy.

When we think of what Gourlay did that day, we must remember that he was soaked in alcohol; not merely with his morning's potation, but with the dregs of previous carousals. And the dregs of drink, a thorough toper will tell you, never leave him. He is drunk on Monday with his Saturday's debauch. As "Drucken Wabster" of Barbie put it once, "When a body's hard-up, his braith's a consolation." If that be so—and Wabster, remember, was an expert whose opinion on this matter is entitled to the highest credence—if that be so, it proves the strength and persistence of a thorough alcoholic impregnation, or as Wabster called it, of "a good soak." In young Gourlay's case, at any rate, the impregnation was enduring and complete. He was like a rag steeped in fusel oil.

As the end of the hour drew near, he sank deeper in his dogged sullenness. When the class streamed from the large door on the right, he turned aside to the little anteroom on the left, with an insolent swing of the shoulders. He knew the fellows were watching him curiously—he felt their eyes upon his back. And, therefore, as he went through the little door, he stood for a moment on his right foot, and waggled his left, on a level with his hip behind, in a vulgar derision of them, the professor, and the whole situation. That was a fine taunt flung back at them!

There is nothing on earth more vindictive than a weakling. When he gets a chance he takes revenge for everything his past cowardice forced him to endure. The timid lecturer, angry at the poor figure he had cut on the platform, was glad to take it out of young Gourlay for the wrong-doing of the class. Gourlay was their scapegoat. The lecturer had no longer over a hundred men to deal with, but one lout only, sullen yet shrinking in the room before him. Instead of coming to the point at once, he played with his victim. It was less from intentional cruelty than from an instinctive desire to recover his lost feeling of superiority. The class was his master, but here was one of them he could cowe at any rate.

"Well?" he asked, bringing his thin finger-tips together, and flinging one thigh across the other.

Gourlay shuffled his feet uneasily.

"Yes?" enquired the other, enjoying his discomfiture.

Gourlay lowered. "Whatna gate was this to gang on? Why couldn't he let a blatter out of his thin mouth, and ha' done wi't?"

"I'm waiting!" said the lecturer.

The words "I apologize" rose in Gourlay, but refused to pass his throat. No, he wouldn't, so he wouldn't! He would see the lecturer far enough, ere he gave an apology before it was expressly required.

"Oh, that's the line you go on, is it?" said the lecturer, nodding his head as if he had sized up a curious animal. "I see, I see! You add contumacy to insolence, do you? . . . Imphm."

Gourlay was not quite sure what contumacy meant, and the uncertainty added to his anger.

"There were others making a noise besides me," he blurted. "I don't see why *I* should be blamed for it all."

"Oh, you don't see why *you* should be had up, indeed? I think we'll bring you to a different conclusion. Yes, I think so."

Gourlay, being forced to stand always on the one spot, felt himself swaying in a drunken stupor. He blinked at the lecturer like an angry owl—the blinking regard of a sodden mind, yet fiery with a spiteful rage. His wrath was rising and falling like a quick tide. He would have liked one moment to give a rein to the Gourlay temper, and let the lecturer have it hot and strong—the next, he was quivering in a cowardly horror of the desperate attempt he had so nearly made. Curse his tormentor! Why did he keep him here, when his head was aching so badly? Another taunt was enough to spring his drunken rage.

"I wonder what you think you came to College for?" said the lecturer. "I have been looking at your records in the class. They're the worst I ever saw. And you're not content with that, it seems. You add misbehaviour to gross stupidity."

"To Hell wi' ye!" said Gourlay.

There was a feeling in the room as if the air was stunned. The silence throbbed.

The lecturer, who had risen, sat down suddenly as if going at the knees, and went white about the gills. Some men would have swept the ruffian with a burst of generous wrath, a few might have pitied in their anger—but this young Solomon was thin and acid, a vindictive rat. Unable to cowe the insolent in present and full-blooded rage, he fell to thinking of the great machine he might set in motion to destroy him. As he sat there in silence, his eyes grew ferrety, and a sleek revenge peeped from the corners of his mouth. "I'll show him what I'll do to him for this!" is a translation of his thought. He was thinking, with great satisfaction to himself, of how the Senatus would deal with young Gourlay.

Gourlay grew weak with fear the moment the words escaped him. They had been a thunderclap to his own ears. He had been thinking them, but—as he pleaded far within him now—had never meant to utter them; they had been mere spume off the surge of cowardly wrath seething up within him, longing to burst but afraid. It was the taunt of stupidity that fired his drunken vanity to blurt them forth.

The lecturer eyed him sideways where he shrank in fear. "You may go," he said at last. "I will report your conduct to the University."

Gourlay was sitting alone in his room when he heard that he had been expelled. For many days he had drunk to deaden fear, but he was sober now, being newly out of bed. A dreary ray of sunshine came through the window, and fell on a wisp of flame, blinking in the grate. As Gourlay sat, his eyes fixed dully on the faded ray, a flash of intuition laid his character bare to him. He read himself ruthlessly. It was not by conscious effort; insight was uncanny and apart from will. He saw that blatancy had joined with weakness, morbidity with want of brains; and that the results of these, converging to a point, had produced the present issue, his expulsion. His mind recognized how logical the issue was, assenting wearily as to a problem proved. Given those qualities, in those circumstances, what else could have happened? And such a weakling as he knew himself to be, could never—he thought—make effort sufficient to alter his qualities. A sense of fatalism came over him, as of one doomed. He bowed his head, and let his arms fall by the sides of his chair, dropping them like a spent swimmer ready to sink. The sudden revelation of himself to himself had taken the heart out of him. "I'm a waster!" he said aghast. And then, at the sound of his own voice, a fear came over him, a fear of his own nature, and he started to his feet and strode feverishly, as if by mere locomotion, to escape from his clinging and inherent ill. It was as if he were trying to run away from himself.

He faced round at the mirror on his mantel, and looked at his own image with staring and startled eyes, his mouth open, the breath coming hard through his nostrils. "You're a gey ill ane," he said: "You're a gey ill ane! My God, where have you landed yourself!"

He went out to escape from his thoughts. Instinctively he turned to the Howff for consolation.

With the panic despair of the weak, he abandoned hope of his character at its first collapse, and plunged into a wild debauch, to avoid reflecting where it would lead him in the end. But he had a more definite reason for prolonging his bout in Edinburgh. He was afraid to go home and meet his father. He shrank, in visioning fear, before the dour face, loaded with scorn, that would swing round to meet him as he entered through the door. Though he swore every night in his cups that he would "square up to the Governor the morn, so he would!" always, when the cold light came, fear of the interview drove him to his cups again. His courage zigzagged, as it always did; one moment he towered in imagination, the next he grovelled in fear.

Sometimes, when he was fired with whiskey, another element entered into his mood, no less big with destruction. It was all his father's fault for sending him to Edinburgh, and no matter what happened, it would serve the old fellow right! He had a kind of fierce satisfaction in his own ruin, because his ruin would show them at home what a mistake they had made in sending him to College. It was the old man's tyranny, in forcing him to College, that had brought all this on his miserable head. Well, he was damned glad, so he was, that they should be punished at home by their own foolish scheme—it had punished *him* enough, for one. And then he would set his mouth insolent and hard, and drink the more fiercely, finding a consolation in the thought that his tyrannical father would suffer through his degradation, too.

At last he must go home. He drifted to the station aimlessly; he had ceased to be self-determined. His compartment happened to be empty; so, free to behave as he liked, he yelled music-hall snatches in a tuneless voice, hammering with his feet on the wooden floor. The noise pleased his sodden mind which had narrowed to a comfortable stupor— outside of which his troubles seemed to lie, as if they belonged not to him but to somebody else. With the same sodden interest he was staring through the window, at one of the little stations on the line, when a boy, pointing, said, "*Flat white nose!*" and Gourlay laughed uproariously, adding at the end: "He's a clever child, that; my nose *would* look flat and white against the pane." But this outbreak of mirth seemed to break in on his comfortable vagueness; it roused him by a kind of reaction to think of home, and of what his father would say. A minute after he had been laughing so madly, he was staring sullenly in front of him. Well, it didn't matter; it was all the old fellow's fault, and he wasn't going to stand any of his jaw. "None of your jaw, John Gourlay!" he said, nodding his head viciously, and thrusting out his clenched fist. "None of your jaw, d'ye hear?"

He crept into Barbie through the dusk. It had been market

day and knots of people were still about the streets. Gourlay stole softly through the shadows, and turned his coat-collar high about his ears. He nearly ran into two men who were talking apart, and his heart stopped dead at their words.

"No, no, Mr Gourlay," said one of them, "it's quite impossible. I'm not unwilling to oblige ye, but I cannot take the risk."

John heard the mumble of his father's voice.

"Well," said the other reluctantly, "if ye get the baker and Tam Wylie for security? I'll be on the street for another half hour."

"Another half hour!" thought John with relief. He would not have to face his father the moment he went in. He would be able to get home before him. He crept on through the gloaming to the House with the Green Shutters.

CHAPTER 24

day, and knots of people were still about the streets. Gourlay stole softly through them, ... turned his coat-collar high about his ears. He nearly ran into two men who were talking apart, and his heart stopped dead at their words. "No, no, Mr Gourlay," said one of them, "it's quite impossible. I'm not unwilling to oblige ye, but I cannot

THERE had been fine cackling in Barbie, as Gourlay's men dropped away from him one by one; and now it was worse then ever. When Jimmy Bain and Sandy Cross were dismissed last winter, "He canna last long now," mused the bodies, and then when even Riney got the sack, "Lord!" they cried, "this maun be the end o't!" The downfall of Gourlay had an unholy fascination for his neighbours. And that not merely because of their dislike to the man. That was a whet to their curiosity, of course, but, over and above it, they seemed to be watching, with bated breath, for the final collapse of an edifice that was bound to fall. Simple expectation held them. It was a dramatic interest—of suspense, yet certainty—that had them in its grip. "He's *bound* to come down," said Certainty—"Yes, but *when*, though?" cried Curiosity, all the more eager because of its instinct for the coming crash. And so they waited for the great catastrophe which they felt to be so near. It was as if they were watching a tragedy near at hand, and noting with keen interest every step in it that must lead to inevitable ruin. That invariably happens when a family tragedy is played out in the midst of a small community. Each step in it is discussed with a prying interest, that is neither malevolent nor sympathetic, but simply curious. In this case it was chiefly malevolent, only because Gourlay had been such a brute to Barbie.

Though there were thus two reasons for public interest, the result was one and the same, constant tittle-tattling. Particular spite and a more general curiosity brought the grain merchant's name on to every tongue. Not even in the gawcey days of its prosperity had the House with Green Shutters been so much talked of.

"Pride *will* have a downcome," said some, with a gleg look and a smack of the lip, trying to veil their personal malevolence in a common proverb. "He's simply in debt in every corner," goldered the keener spirits; "he never had a brain for business. He's had money for stuff he's unable to deliver! Not a day gangs by but the big blue envelopes are coming. How do a ken? say ye! How do I ken, indeed? Oh-ooh, I ken perfectly. Perfectly! It was Postie himsell that telled me!"

Yet all this was merely guesswork. For Gourlay had hitherto gone away from Barbie for his monies and accommodations, so that the bodies could only surmise; they had nothing definite to go on. And through it all, the gurly old fellow kept a brave front to the world. He was thinking of retiring, he said, and gradually drawing in his business. This offhand and lordly, to hide the patent diminution of his trade.

"Hi-hi!" said the old Provost, with a cruel laugh, when he heard of Gourlay's remark, "drawing in his business, aye! It's like Lang Jean Lingleton's waist, I'm thinking. It's thin eneugh drawn a'readys!"

On the morning of the last market day he was ever to see in Barbie, old Gourlay was standing at the green gate, when the postman came up with a smirk, and put a letter in his hand. He betrayed a wish to hover in gossip, while Gourlay opened his letter, but "Less lip!" said surly John, and the fellow went away.

Ere he had reached the corner, a gowl of anger and grief struck his ear, and he wheeled eagerly.

Gourlay was standing with open mouth and outstretched arm, staring at the letter in his clenched fist with a look of horror, as if it had stung him.

"My God!" he cried, "had *I* not enough to thole?"

"Aha!" thought Postie, "yon letter Wilson got this morning was correct, then! His son had sent the true story. That letter o' Gourlay's had the Edinburgh postmark—somebody has sent him word about his son.—Lord! What a tit-bit for my rounds."

Mrs Gourlay, who was washing dishes, looked up to see her husband standing in the kitchen door. His face frightened her. She had often seen the blaze in his eye, and often the

199

dark scowl, but never this bloodless pallor in his cheek. Yet his eyes were flaming.

"Aye, aye," he birred, "a fine job you have made of him!"

"Oh, what is it?" she quavered, and the dish she was wiping clashed on the floor.

"That's it!" said he, "that's it! Breck the dishes next; breck the dishes! Everything seems gaun to smash. If ye keep on lang eneugh, ye'll put a bonny end till't or ye're bye wi't—the lot o' ye."

The taunt passed in the anxiety that stormed her.

"Tell me, see!" she cried, imperious in stress of appeal. "Oh, what is it, John?" She stretched out her thin, red hands, and clasped them tightly before her. "Is it from Embro? Is there ainything the matter with *my* boy? Is there ainything the matter with *my* boy?"

The hard eye surveyed her a while in grim contempt of her weakness. She was a fluttering thing in his grip.

"*Every* thing's the matter with *your* boy," he sneered slowly, "*every* thing's the matter with *your* boy. And it's your fault, too, damn you, for you always spoiled him!"

With sudden wrath he strode over to the famous range and threw the letter within the great fender.

"What is it?" he cried, wheeling round on his wife. "The son you were so wild about sending to College has been flung in disgrace from its door! That's what it is!" He swept from the house like a madman.

Mrs Gourlay sank into her old nursing chair and wailed, "Oh, my wean, my wean; my dear; my poor dear!" She drew the letter from the ashes, but could not read it for her tears. The words "drunkenness" and "expulsion" swam before her eyes. The manner of his disgrace she did not care to hear; she only knew her first-born was in sorrow.

"Oh, my son, my son," she cried; "my laddie; my wee laddie!" She was thinking of the time when he trotted at her petticoat.

It was market day, and Gourlay must face the town. There was interest due on a mortgage which he could not pay; he must swallow his pride and try to borrow it in

Barbie. He thought of trying Johnny Coe, for Johnny was of yielding nature, and had never been unfriendly.

He turned, twenty yards from his gate, and looked at the House with the Green Shutters. He had often turned to look back with pride at the gawcey building on its terrace; but never as he looked today. All that his life meant was bound up in that house, it had been the pride of the Gourlays; now it was no longer his, and the Gourlays' pride was in the dust—their name a byword. As Gourlay looked, a robin was perched on the quiet rooftree, its breast vivid in the sun. One of his metaphors flashed at the sight. "Shame is sitting there, too," he muttered—and added with a proud angry snarl, "on the riggin' o' *my* hoose!"

He had a triple wrath to his son. He had not only ruined his own life, he had destroyed his father's hope that by entering the ministry he might restore the Gourlay reputation. Above all he had disgraced the House with the Green Shutters. That was the crown of his offending. Gourlay felt for the house of his pride even more than for himself—rather the house was himself; there was no division between them. He had built it bluff to represent him to the world. It was his character in stone and lime. He clung to it, as the dull, fierce mind, unable to live in thought, clings to a material source of pride. And John had disgraced it. Even if fortune took a turn for the better, Green Shutters would be laughed at the country over, as the home of a prodigal.

As he went by the Cross, Wilson (Provost this long while) broke off a conversation with Templandmuir, to yell "It's gra-and weather, Mr Gourlay!" The men had not spoken for years. So to shout at poor Gourlay in his black hour, from the pinnacle of civic greatness, was a fine stroke; it was gloating, it was rubbing in the contrast. The words were innocent, but that was nothing; whatever the remark, for a declared enemy to address Gourlay in his shame, was an insult: that was why Wilson addressed him. There was something in the very loudness of his tones that cried plainly: "Aha, Gourlay! Your son has disgraced you, my man!" Gourlay glowered at the animal and plodded dourly. Ere he had gone ten yards a coarse laugh came bellowing behind him. They saw the colour surge up the back of his neck, to the roots of his hair.

He stopped. Was his son's disgrace known in Barbie already? He had hoped to get through the market day without anybody knowing. But Wilson had a son in Edinburgh; he had written, it was like. The salutation, therefore, and the laugh, had both been uttered in derision. He wheeled, his face black with the passionate blood. His mouth yawed with anger. His voice had a moan of intensity.

"What are 'ee laughing at?" he said, with a mastering quietness . . . . "Eh? . . . . Just tell me, please, what you're laughing at."

He was crouching for the grip, his hands out like a gorilla's. The quiet voice, from the yawing mouth, beneath the steady flaming eyes, was deadly. There is something inhuman in a rage so still.

"Eh?" he said slowly, and the moan seemed to come from the midst of a vast intensity rather than a human being. It was the question that must grind an answer.

Wilson was wishing to all his gods that he had not insulted this awful man. He remembered what had happened to Gibson. This, he had heard, was the very voice with which Gourlay moaned: "Take your hand off *my* shouther!" ere he hurled Gibson through the window of the Red Lion. Barbie might soon want a new Provost, if he ran in now.

But there is always one way of evading punishment for a veiled insult, and of adding to its sting by your evasion. Repudiate the remotest thought of the protester. Thus you enjoy your previous gibe, with the additional pleasure of making your victim seem a fool, for thinking you referred to him. You not only insult him on the first count, but send him off with an additional hint, that he isn't worth your notice. Wilson was an adept in the art.

"Man!" he lied blandly—but his voice was quivering— "Ma-a-an, I wasn't so much as giving ye a thoat! It's verra strange if I cannot pass a joke with my o-old friend, Templandmuir, without *you* calling me to book. It's a free country, I shuppose! Ye weren't in my mind at a-all.

I have more important matters to think of," he ventured to add, seeing he had baffled Gourlay.

For Gourlay was baffled. For a directer insult, an offensive gesture, one fierce word, he would have hammered the road with the Provost. But he was helpless before the bland quivering lie. Maybe they werena referring to him, maybe they knew nothing of John in Edinburgh, maybe he had been foolishly suspeecious. A subtle yet baffling check was put upon his anger. Madman as he was in wrath, he never struck without direct provocation; there was none in this pulpy gentleness. And he was too dull of wit to get round the common ruse and find a means of getting at them.

He let loose a great breath through his nostrils, as if releasing a deadly force which he had pent within him, ready should he need to spring. His mouth opened again, and he gaped at them with a great, round, unseeing stare. Then he swung on his heel.

But wrath clung round him like a garment. His anger fed on its uncertainties. For that is the beauty of the Wilson method of insult; you leave the poison in your victim's blood, and he torments himself. "Was Wilson referring to *me, after all?*" he pondered slowly; and his body surged at the thought. "If he was, I have let him get away unkilled"—and he clutched the hands whence Wilson had escaped. Suddenly a flashing thought stopped him dead in the middle of his walk, staring hornily before him. He had seen the point at last, that a quicker man would have seized on at the first. Why had Wilson thrust his damned voice on him on this particular morning of all days in the year, if he was not gloating over some news which he had just heard about the Gourlays? It was as plain as daylight; his son had sent word from Edinburgh. That was why he brayed and ho-ho-ho'ed when Gourlay went by. Gourlay felt a great flutter of pulses against his collar; there was a pain in his throat, an ache of madness in his breast. He turned once more. But Wilson and the Templar had withdrawn discreetly to the Black Bull; the street wasna canny. Gourlay resumed his way, his being a dumb gowl of rage. His angry thought swept to John. Each insult, and fancied insult, he endured that day, was another item in the long account of vengeance with his son. It was John who had brought all this flaming round his ears—John whose colleging he had lippened to so muckle. The staff on which he leaned had pierced him. By the eternal heavens he would tramp it into atoms. His legs felt John beneath them.

As the market grew busy, Gourlay was the aim of innumerable eyes. He would turn his head to find himself the object of a queer considering look—then the eyes of the starer would flutter abashed, as though detected spying the forbidden. The most innocent look at him was poison. "Do they know?" was his constant thought; "Have they heard the news? What's Loranogie looking at me like that for?"

Not a man ventured to address him about John—he had cowed them too long. One man, however, shewed a wish to try. A pretended sympathy, from behind the veil of which you probe a man's anguish at your ease, is a favourite weapon of human beasts anxious to wound. The Deacon longed to try it on Gourlay. But his courage failed him. It was the only time he was ever worsted in malignity. Never a man went forth, bowed down with a recent shame, wounded and wincing from the public gaze, but that old rogue hirpled up to him, and lisped with false smoothness: "Thirce me, neebour, I'm thorry for ye! Thith ith a *terrible* affair! It'th on everybody'th tongue. But ye have my thympathy, neebour—ye have tha-at. My warmetht thympathy"—and, all the while, the shifty eyes above the lying mouth would peer and probe, to see if the soul within the other was writhing at his words.

Now, though everybody was spying at Gourlay in the market, all were giving him a wide berth; for they knew that he was dangerous. He was no longer the man whom they had baited on the way to Skeighan; then he had some control, now three years' calamities had fretted his temper to a raw wound. To flick it was perilous. Great was the surprise of the starers, therefore, when the idle old Deacon was seen to detach himself and hail the grain merchant. Gourlay wheeled, and waited with a levelled eye. All were agog at the sight—something would be sure to come o' this—here would be an encounter worth the speaking o'. But the Deacon, having toddled forward a bittock on his thin shanks, stopped half-roads, took snuff, trumpeted into his big red handkerchief, and then, feebly waving, "I'll thee ye again, Dyohn!" clean turned tail and toddled back to his cronies.

A roar went up at his expense.

"God!" said Tam Wylie, "did ye see yon? Gourlay stopped him wi' a glower."

But the laugh was maddening to Gourlay. Its readiness, its volume, shewed him that scores of folk had him in their minds, were watching him, considering his position, cognisant of where he stood. "They ken," he thought. "They were a' waiting to see what would happen. They wanted to watch how Gourlay tholed the mention o' his son's disgrace. I'm a kind o' show to them."

Johnny Coe, idle and well-to-pass, though he had no business of his own to attend to, was always present where business men assembled. It was a gra-and way of getting news. Today, however, Gourlay could not find him. He went into the cattle mart to see if he was there. For two years now, Barbie had a market for cattle, on the first Tuesday of the month.

The auctioneer, a jovial dog, was in the middle of his roaring game. A big, red bullock, the coat of which made a rich colour in the ring, came bounding in, scared at its surroundings—staring one moment and the next careering.

"There's meat for you," said he of the hammer; "see how it runs! How much am I offered for *this* fine bullock?" He sing-songed, always saying "*this* fine bullock" in exactly the same tone of voice. "Thirteen pounds for *this* fine bullock, thirteen-five; thirteen-ten; thirteen-ten for *this* fine bullock; thirteen-ten; any further bids on thirteen-ten?—why it's worth that for the colour o't; thank ye sir—thirteen-fifteen; fourteen pounds; fourteen pounds for *this* fine bullock; see how the stot stots* about the ring; that joke should raise him another half sovereign; ah, I knew it would—fourteen-five; fourteen-five for *this* fine bullock; fourteen-ten; no

*Stot, a bullock; to stot, to bound.

more than fourteen-ten for *this* fine bullock; going at fourteen-ten; gone—Irrendavie."

Now that he was in the circle, however, the mad, big, handsome beast refused to go out again. When the cattlemen would drive him to the yard, he snorted and galloped round, till he had to be driven from the ring with blows. When at last he bounded through the door, he flung up his heels with a bellow, and sent the sand of his arena showering on the people round.

"I seh!" roared Brodie in his coarsest voice, from the side of the ring opposite to Gourlay. "I seh, owctioner! That maun be a College-bred stot, from the way he behaves. He flung dirt at his masters and had to be expelled."

"Put Brodie in the ring and rowp him!" cried Irrendavie. "He roars like a bull at ony rate."

There was a laugh at Brodie, true; but it was at Gourlay that a hundred big red faces turned to look. He did not look at them, though. He sent his eyes across the ring at Brodie.

"Lord!" said Irrendavie, "it's weel for Brodie that the ring's acqueesh them! Gourlay'll murder somebody yet. Red hell lap out o' his e'en when he looked at Brodie."

Gourlay's suspicion that his son's disgrace was a matter of common knowledge, had now become a certainty. Brodie's taunt shewed that everybody knew it. He walked out of the building very quietly, pale but resolute; no meanness in his carriage, no cowering. He was an arresting figure of a man as he stood for a moment in the door, and looked round for the man whom he was seeking. "Weel, weel," he was thinking, "I maun thole, I suppose. They were under *my* feet for many a day, and they're taking their advantage now."

But though he could thole, his anger against John was none the less. It was because they had been under his feet for many a day that John's conduct was the more heinous. It was his son's conduct that gave Gourlay's enemies their first opportunity against him, that enabled them to turn the tables. They might sneer at his trollop of a wife, they might sneer at his want of mere cleverness; still he held his head high amongst them. They might suspect his poverty; but so far, for anything they knew, he might have thousands behind him. He owed not a man in Barbie. The appointments of Green Shutters were as brave as ever. The selling of his horses, the dismissal of his men, might mean the completion of a furtune, not its loss, Hitherto, then, he was invulnerable —so he reasoned. It was his son's disgrace that gave the men he had trodden underfoot the first weapon they could use against him. That was why it was more damnable in Gourlay's eyes than the conduct of all the prodigals that ever lived. It had enabled his foes to get their knife into him at last—and they were turning the dagger in the wound. All owing to the boy on whom he had staked such hopes of keeping up the Gourlay name! His account with John was lengthening steadily.

Coe was nowhere to be seen. At last Gourlay made up his mind to go out and make enquiries at his house, out the Fleckie Road. It was a quiet big house, standing by itself, and Gourlay was glad there was nobody to see him.

It was Miss Coe herself who answered his knock at the door.

She was a withered old shrew, with fifty times the spunk of Johnny. On her thin wrists and long hands there was always a pair of bright red mittens, only her finger-tips showing. Her far-sunken and toothless mouth was always working, with a sucking motion of the lips; and her round little knob of a sticking out chin munched up and down when she spoke, a long stiff whitish hair slanting out its middle. However much you wished to avoid doing so, you could not keep your eyes from staring at that solitary hair while she was addressing you. It worked up and down so, keeping time to every word she spoke.

"Is your brother in?" said Gourlay. He was too near reality in this sad pass of his to think of "mistering." "Is your brother in?" said he.

"No-a!" she shrilled—for Miss Coe answered questions with an old-maidish scream, as if the news she was giving must be a great surprise, both to you and her. "No-a!" she skirled; "he's no-a in-a! Was it ainything particular?"

"No," said Gourlay heavily; "I—I just wanted to see him," and he trudged away.

Miss Coe looked after him for a moment ere she closed the door. "He's wanting to barrow money," she cried; "I'm nearly sure o't! I maun caution Johnny when he comes back frae Fleckie, afore he gangs east the toon. Gourlay could get him to do ocht! He always admired the brute— I'm sure I kenna why. Because he's siccan a silly body himsell, I suppose!"

It was after dark when Gourlay met Coe on the street. He drew him aside in the shadows, and asked for a loan of eighty pounds.

Johnny stammered a refusal. "Hauf the bawbees is mine," his sister had skirled, "and I daur ye to do ony siccan thing, John Coe!"

"It's only for a time," pleaded Gourlay—"and, by God," he flashed, "it's hell in *my* throat to ask from any man."

"No, no, Mr Gourlay," said Johnny, "it's quite impossible. I've always looked up to ye, and I'm not unwilling to oblige ye, but I cannot take the risk."

"Risk!" said Gourlay, and stared at the darkness. By hook or by crook he must raise the money to save the House with the Green Shutters. It was no use trying the bank; he had a letter from the banker in his desk, to tell him that his account was overdrawn. And yet if the interest were not paid at once, the lawyers in Glasgow would foreclose, and the Gourlays would be flung upon the street. His proud soul must eat dirt, if need be, for the sake of eighty pounds.

"If I get the baker, or Tam Wylie, to stand security," he asked, "would ye not oblige me? I think they would do it. I have always felt they respected me."

"Well," said Johnny slowly, fearing his sister's anger, "if ye get the baker and Tam Wylie for security. I'll be on the street for another half hour."

A figure, muffled in a great coat, was seen stealing off through the shadows.

"God's curse on whoever that is!" snarled Gourlay, "creeping up to listen to our talk."

"I don't think so," said Johnny, "it seemed a young chap trying to hide himself."

Gourlay failed to get his securities. The baker, though a

poor man, would have stood for him, if Tam Wylie would have joined; but Tam would not budge. He was as clean as gray granite, and as hard.

So Gourlay trudged home through the darkness, beaten at last, mad with shame and anger and foreboding.

The first thing he saw on entering the kitchen was his son —sitting muffled in his coat by the great fender.

209

CHAPTER 25

JANET and her mother saw a quiver run through Gourlay, as
he stood and glowered from the threshold. He seemed of
monstrous bulk and significance, filling the doorway in his
silence.

The quiver that went through him was a sign of his
contending angers, his will struggling with the tumult of
wrath that threatened to spoil his revenge. To fell that
huddled oaf with a blow would be a poor return for all he
had endured because of him. He meant to sweat punishment
out of him drop by drop, with slow and vicious enjoyment.
But the sudden sight of that living disgrace to the Gourlays
woke a wild desire to leap on him at once, and glut his rage,
a madness which only a will like his could control. He
quivered with the effort to keep it in.

To bring a beaten and degraded look into a man's face,
rend manhood out of him in fear, is a sight that makes decent
men wince in pain; for it is an outrage on the decency of life,
an offence to natural religion, a violation of the human
sanctities. Yet Gourlay had done it once and again. I saw
him "down" a man at the Cross once, a big man with a
viking beard, dark brown, from which you would have
looked for manliness. Gourlay, with stabbing eyes,
threatened, and birred, and "downed" him, till he crept
away with a face like chalk, and a hunted, furtive eye.
Curiously it was his manly beard that made the look such a
pain, for its contrasting colour shewed the white face of the
coward—and a coward had no right to such a beard. A
grim and cruel smile went after him as he slunk away.
"*Ha!*" barked Gourlay, in lordly and pursuing scorn, and
the fellow leapt where he walked, as the cry went through
him. To break a man's spirit so, take that from him which
he will never recover while he lives, send him slinking away
animo castrato—for that is what it comes to—is a sinister

outrage of the world. It is as bad as the rape of a woman, and ranks with the sin against the Holy Ghost—derives from it, indeed. Yet it was this outrage that Gourlay meant to work upon his son. He would work him down and down, this son of his, till he was less than a man, a frightened, furtive animal. Then, perhaps, he would give a loose to his other rage, unbuckle his belt, and thrash the grown man like a wriggling urchin on the floor.

As he stood glowering from the door Mrs Gourlay rose, with an appealing cry of "*John!*"—but Gourlay put his eye on her, and she sank into her chair, staring up at him in terror. The strings of the tawdry cap she wore seemed to choke her, and she unfastened them with nervous fingers, fumbling long beneath her lifted chin to get them loose. She did not remove the cap, but let the strings dangle by her jaw. The silly bits of cloth waggling and quivering, as she turned her head repeatedly from son to husband and from husband to son, added to her air of helplessness and inefficiency. Once she whispered with ghastly intensity, "*God have mercy!*"

For a length of time there was a loaded silence.

Gourlay went up to the hearth, and looked down on his son from near at hand. John shrank down in his greatcoat. A reek of alcohol rose from around him. Janet whimpered.

But when Gourlay spoke, it was with deadly quietude. The moan was in his voice. So great was his controlled wrath that he drew in great shivering breastfuls of air between the words, as if for strength to utter them; and they quavered forth on it again. He seemed weakened by his own rage.

"Aye man!" he breathed . . . "Ye've won hame, I observe! . . . Dee-ee-ar me! . . . Im-phm!"

The contrast between the lowness of his voice and his steady breathing anger that possessed the air (they felt it coming as on waves) was demoniac, appalling.

John could not speak; he was paralysed by fear. To have this vast hostile force touch him, yet be still, struck him dumb. Why did his father not break out on him at once? What did he mean? What was he going to do? The jamb of the fireplace cut his right shoulder as he cowered into it, to get away as far as he could.

"I'm saying . . . ye've won hame!" quivered Gourlay in a deadly slowness, and his eyes never left his son.

And still the son made no reply. In the silence, the ticking of the big clock seemed to fill their world. They were conscious of nothing else. It smote the ear.

"Aye," John gulped at last from a throat that felt closing. The answer seemed dragged out of him by the insistent silence.

"Just so-a!" breathed his father, and his eyes opened in wide flame. He heaved with the great breath he drew . . . "Im-phm!" he drawled.

He went through to the scullery at the back of the kitchen to wash his hands. Through the open door Janet and her mother—looking at each other with affrighted eyes—could hear him sneering at intervals, "Aye man!" . . . "Just that, now!" . . . "Im-phm!" And again, "Aye, aye! . . . Dee-ee-ar me!" in grim, falsetto irony.

When he came back to the kitchen, he turned to Janet, and left his son in a suspended agony.

"Aye woman, Jenny; ye're there!" he said, and nipped her ear as he passed over to his chair. "Were ye in Skeighan the day?"

"Aye, faither," she answered.

"And what did the Skeighan doctor say?"

She raised her large pale eyes to his with a strange look. Then her head sank low on her breast.

"Nothing!" she said at last.

"Nothing!" said he. "Nothing for nothing, then. I hope you didna pay him?"

"No, faither," she answered. "I hadna the bawbees."

"When did ye get back?" he asked.

"Just after—just after—" her eyes flickered over to John, as if she were afraid of mentioning his name.

"Oh, just after this gentleman! But there's noathing strange in tha-at; you were always after him! You were born after him; and considered after him; he aye had the best o't! —I howp *you* are in good health?" he sneered, turning to his son. "It would never do for a man to break down at the outset o' a great career! . . . For ye *are* at the outset o' a great career; are ye na?"

His speech was as soft as the foot of a tiger, and sheathed as rending a cruelty. There was no escaping the crouching stealth of it. If he had leapt with a roar, John's drunken fury might have lashed itself to rage. But the younger and weaker man was fascinated and helpless before the creeping approach of so monstrous a wrath.

"Eh?" asked Gourlay softly, when John made no reply, "I'm saying you're at the outset o' a great career, are ye not? Eh?"

Soft as his "Eh" was in utterance, it was insinuating, pursuing; it had to be answered.

"No," whimpered John.

"Well, well; you're maybe at the end o't! Have ye been studying hard?"

"Yes," lied John.

"That's right!" cried his father with great heartiness. "There's my brave fellow! Noathing like studying! . . . And no doubt—he leaned over suavely—"and no doubt ye've brought a wheen prizes home wi' ye as usual? Eh?"

There was no answer.

"Eh?"

"No," gulped the cowerer.

"*Nae* prizes!" cried Gourlay, and his eyebrows went up in a pretended surprise. "*Nae-ae* prizes! Aye, man! Fow's that, na?"

Young Gourlay was being reduced to the condition of a beaten child, who, when his mother asks if he has been a bad boy, is made to sob "Yes," at her knee. "Have you been a good boy?" she asks—"No," he pants; and "Are you sorry for being a bad boy?"—"Yes," he sobs; and "Will you be a good boy now, then?"—"Yes," he almost shrieks, in his desire to be at one with his mother. Young Gourlay was being equally beaten from his own nature, equally battered under by another personality. Only he was not asked to be a good boy. He might gang to hell for anything auld Gourlay cared—when once he had bye with him.

Even as he degraded his son to this state of unnatural

cowardice, Gourlay felt a vast disgust swell within him that a son of his should be such a coward. "Damn him!" he thought, glowering with big-eyed contempt at the huddled creature, "he hasna the pluck o' a pig! How can he stand talk like this without showing he's a man? When I was a child on the brisket, if a man had used me, as I'm using him, I would have flung mysell at him. He's a pretty-looking object to carry the name o' John Gourla! My God, what a ke-o of *my* life I've made—that auld trollop for my wife, that sumph for my son, and that dying lassie for my dochter! Was it I that bred him? *That!*"

He leapt to his feet in devilish merriment.

"Set out the spirits, Jenny!" he cried; "set out the spirits! My son and I must have a drink together—to celebrate the occeesion; ou aye," he sneered, drawling out the word with sharp, unfamiliar sound, "just to celebrate the occeesion!"

The wild humour that seized him was inevitable, born of a vicious effort to control a rage that was constantly increasing, fed by the sight of the offender. Every time he glanced across at the thing sitting there, he was swept with fresh surges of fury and disgust. But his vicious constraint curbed them under, and refused them a natural expression. They sought an unnatural. Some vent they must have, and they found it in a score of wild devilries he began to practise on his son. Wrath fed and checked, in one, brings the hell on which man is built, to the surface. Gourlay was transformed. He had a fluency of speech, a power of banter, a readiness of tongue, which he had never shewn before. He was beyond himself. Have you heard the snarl with which a wild beast arrests the escaping prey which it has just let go in enjoying cruelty? Gourlay was that animal. For a moment he would cease to torture his son, feed his disgust with a glower; then the sight of him huddled there would wake a desire to stamp on him; but his will would not allow that, for it would spoil the sport he had set his mind on; and so he played with the victim which he would not kill.

"Set out the speerits, Jenny," he birred, when she wavered in fear. "What are ye shaking for? Set out the speerits—just to shelebrate the joyful occeesion, ye know—aye, aye, just to shelebrate the joyful occeesion!"

Janet brought a tray, with glasses, from the pantry. As she walked, the rims of the glasses shivered and tinkled against each other, from her trembling. Then she set a bottle on the table.

Gourlay sent it crashing to the floor. "A bottle!" he roared. "A bottle for huz twa! To Hell wi' bottles! The jar, Jenny, the jar; set out the jar, lass, set out the jar. For we mean to make a night of it, this gentleman and me. Aye," he yawed with a vicious smile, "we'll make a night o't—we two. A night that Barbie'll remember loang!"

"Have ye skill o' drink?" he asked, turning to his son.

"No," wheezed John.

"No!" cried his father. "I thought ye learned everything at College! Your education's been neglected. But I'll teach ye a lesson, or *this* nicht's bye. Aye, by God," he growled, "I'll teach ye a lesson."

Curb his temper as he might, his own behaviour was lashing it to frenzy. Through the moaning intensity peculiar to his vicious rage, there leapt at times a wild-beast snarl. Every time they heard it, it cut the veins of his listeners with a start of fear—it leapt so suddenly.

"Ha'e, Sir!" he cried.

John raised his dull, white face and looked across at the bumper which his father poured him. But he felt the limbs too weak beneath him to go and take it.

"Bide where ye are!" sneered his father, "bide where ye are! I'll wait on ye; I'll wait on ye. Man, I waited on ye the day that ye were bo-orn! The heavens were hammering the world as John Gourla rode through the storm for a doctor to bring hame his heir. The world was feared, but *he* wasna feared," he roared in Titanic pride, "*he* wasna feared; no, by God, for he never met what scaured him! . . . . Aye, aye," he birred softly again, "aye, aye, ye were ushered loudly to the world, serr! Verra appropriate for a man who was destined to make such a name! . . . Eh? . . . Verra appropriate, serr; verra appropriate! And you'll be ushered just as loudly out o't. Oh, young Gourlay's death maun make a splurge, ye know—a splurge to attract folk's attention!"

John's shaking hand was wet with the spilled whiskey.

"Take it off," sneered his father, boring into him with a vicious eye; "take it off, serr; take off your dram!—Stop! Somebody wrote something about that—some poetry or other. Who was it?"

"I dinna ken," whimpered John.

"Don't tell lies now. You do ken. I heard you mention it to Loranogie. Come on now—who was it?"

"It was Burns," said John.

"Oh, it was Burns, was it? And what had Mr Burns to say on the subject? Eh?"

" 'Freedom and whiskey gang thegither, Tak aff your dram,' " stammered John.

"A verra wise remark," said Gourlay gravely. " 'Freedom and whiskey gang thegither,' " he turned the quotation on his tongue, as if he were savouring a tit-bit. "That's verra good," he approved. "You're a great admirer of Burns, I hear. Eh?"

"Yes," said John.

"Do what he bids ye, then. Take off your dram! It'll show what a fine free fellow you are!"

It was a big, old-fashioned Scotch drinking glass, containing more than half-a-gill of whiskey, and John drained it to the bottom. To him it had been a deadly thing at first, coming thus from his father's hand. He had taken it into his own, with a feeling of aversion, that was strangely blended of disgust and fear. But the moment it touched his lips, desire leapt in his throat to get at it.

"Good!" roared his father in mock admiration. "God, ye have the thrapple! When I was your age that would have choked me. I must have a look at that throat o' yours. Stand up! . . . *Stand up when I tall 'ee!*"

John rose swaying to his feet. Months of constant tippling, culminating in a wild debauch, had shattered him. He stood in a reeling world. And the fear weakening his limbs changed his drunken stupor to a heart-heaving sickness. He swayed to and fro, with a cold sweat oozing from his chalky face.

"What's ado with the fellow?" cried Gourlay. "Oom?

216

Chapter Twenty-Five

He's swinging like a saugh-wand. I must wa-alk round this, and have a look!"

John's drunken submissiveness encouraged his father to new devilries. The ease with which he tortured him provoked him to more torture; he went on more and more viciously, as if he were conducting an experiment, to see how much the creature would bear before he turned. Gourlay was enjoying the glutting of his own wrath.

He turned his son round with a finger and thumb on his shoulder, in insolent inspection, as you turn an urchin round to see him in his new suit of clothes. Then he crouched before him, his face thrust close to the other, and peered into his eyes, his mouth distent with an infernal smile. "My boy, Johnny," he said sweetly, "my boy, Johnny," and patted him gently on the cheek. John raised dull eyes and looked into his father's. Far within him a great wrath was gathering through his fear. Another voice, another self, seemed to whimper, with dull iteration, "I'll *kill* him; I'll *kill* him; by God, I'll *kill* him—if he doesna stop this—if he keeps on like this at me!" But his present and material self was paralyzed with fear.

"Open your mouth!" came the snarl—"*wider, damn ye! wider!*"

"Im-phm!" said Gourlay, with a critical drawl, pulling John's chin about to see into him the deeper. "Im-phm! God, it's like a furnace! What's the Latin for throat?"

"Guttur," said John.

"Gutter!" said his father. "A verra appropriate name! Yours stinks like a cess-pool! what have you been doing till't? I'm afraid ye aren't in very good health, after a-all . . . Eh? . . . Mrs Gourla, Mrs Gourla! He's in verra bad case, this son of yours, Mrs Gourla! Fine I ken what he needs, though. Set out the brandy, Jenny, set out the brandy," he roared; "whiskey's not worth a damn for him! Stop; it was you gaed the last time; it's *your* turn now, auld wife, it's *your* turn now! Gang for the brandy to your twa John Gourlas. We're a pair for a woman to be proud of!"

He gazed after his wife as she tottered to the pantry.

"Your skirt's on the gape, auld wife," he sang; "your

skirts on the gape; as use-u-al," he drawled; "as use-u-al. It was always like that; and it always scunnered me, for I aye liked things tidy—though I never got them. However, I maunna compleen when ye bore sic a braw son to my name. He's a great consolation! Imphm, he is that—a great consolation!"

The brandy-bottle slipped from the quivering fingers and was smashed to pieces on the floor.

"Hurrah!" yelled Gourlay.

He seemed rapt and carried by his own devilry. The wreck and ruin strewn about the floor consorted with the ruin of his fortunes; let all go smash—what was the use of caring? Now in his frenzy, he, ordinarily so careful, seemed to delight in the smashings and the breakings; they suited his despair.

He saw that his spirit of destruction frightened them, too, and that was another reason to indulge it.

"To Hell with everything," he yelled, like a mock-bacchanal. "*We're* the hearty fellows! We'll make a red night now we're at it!" And with that he took the heel of a bottle on his toe and sent it flying, among the dishes on the dresser. A great plate fell, split in two.

"Poor fellow!" he whined, turning to his son; "poo-oor fellow! I fear he has lost his pheesic. For that was the last bottle o' brandy in my aucht; the last John Gourlay had, the last he'll ever buy. What am I to do wi' ye, now?... Eh?... I must do something; it's coming to the bit, now, Sir."

As he stood in a heaving silence the sobbing of the two women was heard through the room. John was still swaying on the floor.

Sometimes Gourlay would run the full length of the kitchen, and stand there glowering on a stoop; then he would come crouching up to his son on a vicious little trot, pattering in rage, the broken glass crunching and grinding beneath his feet. At any moment he might spring.

"What do ye think I mean to do wi' ye now?" he moaned. ... "Eh?... What do ye think I mean to do wi' ye now?"

As he came grinning in rage his lips ran out to their full width, and the tense slit shewed his teeth to their roots. The gums were white. The stricture of the lips had squeezed them bloodless.

He went back to the dresser once more and bent low beside it, glancing at his son across his left shoulder, with his head flung back sideways, his right fist clenched low and ready from a curve of the elbow. It swung heavy as a mallet by his thigh. Janet got to her knees and came shuffling across the floor on them, though her dress was tripping her, clasping her outstretched hands, and sobbing in appeal, "Faither, faither; oh, faither; for God's sake, faither!" She clung to him. He unclenched his fist and lifted her away. Then he came crouching and quivering across the floor, slowly, a gleaming devilry in the eyes that devoured his son. His hands were like outstretched claws, and shivered with each shiver of the voice that moaned, through set teeth, "What do ye think I mean to do wi' ye now? . . . What do ye think I mean to do wi' ye now? . . . Ye damned sorrow and disgrace that ye are—what do ye think I mean to do wi' ye now?"

"Run, John!" screamed Mrs Gourlay, leaping to her feet. With a hunted cry young Gourlay sprang to the door. So great had been the fixity of Gourlay's wrath, so tense had he been in one direction, as he moved slowly on his prey, that he could not leap to prevent him. As John plunged into the cool, soft darkness, his mother's "Thank God!" rang past him on the night.

His immediate feeling was of coolness and width and spaciousness, in contrast with the hot grinding hostility, that had bored so closely in on him, for the last hour. He felt the benignness of the darkened heavens. A tag of some forgotten poem he had read came back to his mind, and, "Come kindly night and cover me," he muttered, with shaking lips; and felt how true it was. My God, what a relief to be free of his father's eyes! They had held him till his mother's voice broke the spell. They seemed to burn him now.

What a fool he had been to face his father when empty both of food and drink. Every man was downhearted when he was empty. If his mother had had time to get the tea, it would have been different,—but the fire had been out when he went in. "He wouldn't have downed me so easy, if I had

had anything in me," he muttered, and his anger grew, as he thought of all he had been made to suffer. For he was still the swaggerer. Now that the incubus of his father's tyranny no longer pressed on him directly, a great hate rose within him for the tyrant. He would go back and have it out when he was primed. "It's the only hame I have," he sobbed angrily to the darkness; "I have no other place to gang till! Yes, I'll go back and have it out with him when once I get something in me, so I will." It was no disgrace to suck courage from the bottle, for that encounter with his father, for nobody could stand up to black Gourlay; nobody. Young Gourlay was yielding to a peculiar fatalism of minds diseased: all that affects them seems different from all that affects everybody else; they are even proud of their separate and peculiar doom. Young Gourlay not thought, but felt it—he was different from everybody else. The heavens had cursed nobody else with such a terrible sire. It was no cowardice to fill yourself with drink before you faced him.

A drunkard will howl you an obscene chorus the moment after he has wept about his dead child. For a mind in the delirium of drink is no longer a coherent whole, but a heap of shattered bits, which it shows one after the other to the world. Hence the many transformations of that semi-madness, and their quick variety. Young Gourlay was shewing them now. His had always been a wandering mind, deficient in application and control, and as he neared his final collapse, it became more and more variable, the prey of each momentary thought. In a short five minutes of time, he had been alive to the beauty of the darkness, cowering before the memory of his father's eyes, sobbing in self-pity and angry resolve, shaking in terror—indeed he was shaking now. But his vanity came uppermost. As he neared the Red Lion, he stopped suddenly, and the darkness seemed on fire against his cheeks. He would have to face curious eyes, he reflected. It was from the Red Lion he and Aird had started so grandly in the autumn. It would never do to come slinking back like a whipped cur; he must carry it off bravely in case the usual busybodies should be gathered round the bar. So with his coat flapping lordly on either side of him, his hands deep in his trouser-pockets, and his hat on the back of his head, he drove at the swing-doors with an outshot chest, and entered with a "breenge." But for all his swagger he must have had a face like death, for there was a cry among the idlers. A man breathed, "My God! What's the matter?" With shaking knees Gourlay advanced to the bar, and, "For God's sake, Aggie," he whispered, "give me a Kinblythmont!"

It went at a gulp.

"Another!" he gasped, like a man dying of thirst, whom his first sip maddens for more. "Another! Another!"

He had tossed the other down his burning throat, when Deacon Allardyce came in.

He knew his man the moment he set eyes on him, but, standing at the door, he arched his hand above his brow, as you do in gazing at a dear unexpected friend, whom you pretend not to be quite sure of, so surprised and pleased are you to see him there.

"Ith it Dyohn?" he cried. "It *ith* Dyohn!" And he toddled forward with outstretched hand. "Man Dyohn!" he said again, as if he could scarce believe the good news, and he waggled the other's hand up and down, with both his own clasped over it. "I'm proud to thee you, thir; I am that. And tho you're won hame, aye! Im-phm! And how are ye tummin on?"

"Oh, *I'm* all right, Deacon," said Gourlay with a silly laugh. "Have a wet?" The whiskey had begun to warm him.

"A wha-at?" said the Deacon, blinking in a puzzled fashion with his bleary old eyes.

"A dram—a drink—a drop o' the Auld Kirk," said Gourlay, with a stertorous laugh down through his nostrils.

"Hi! Hi!" laughed the Deacon in his best falsetto. "Ith that what ye call it up in Embro? A wet, aye! Ah, well, maybe I will take a little drope—theeing you're tho ready wi' your offer."

They drank together.

"Aggie, fill me a mutchkin when you're at it," said Gourlay to the pretty barmaid with the curly hair. He had spent many an hour with her last summer in the bar. The

221

four large whiskies he had swallowed in the last half hour were singing in him now, and he blinked at her drunkenly.

There was a scarlet ribbon on her dark curls, coquettish, vivid, and Gourlay stared at it dreamily, partly in a drunken daze, and partly because a striking colour always brought a musing and self-forgetting look within his eyes. All his life he used to stare at things dreamily, and come to himself with a start when spoken to. He forgot himself now.

"Aggie," he said, and put his hand out to hers clumsily where it rested on the counter; "Aggie, that ribbon's infernal bonny on your dark hair!"

She tossed her head, and perked away from him on her little high heels. Him, indeed!—the drunkard! She wanted none of his compliments!

There were half a dozen in the place by this time, and they all stared with greedy eyes. "That's young Gourlay—him that was *expelled*," was heard, the last an emphatic whisper, with round eyes of awe at the offence that must have merited such punishment. "*Expelled,* mind ye!"—with a round shake of the head. "Watch Allardyce. We'll see fun."

"What's this 'expelled,' now?"[1] said John Toddle, with a very considering look and tone in his uplifted face— "properly speaking, that is," he added—implying that of course he knew the word in its ordinary sense, but was not sure of it "properly speaking."

"Flung oot," said Drucken Wabster, speaking from the fulness of his own experience.

"Whisht!" said a third. "Here's Tam Brodie. Watch what *he* does."

The entrance of Brodie spoiled sport for the Deacon. He had nothing of that malicious *finesse* that made Allardyce a genius at flicking men on the raw. He went straight to his work, stabbing like an awl.

"Hal-lo!" he cried, pausing with contempt in the middle of the word, when he saw young Gourlay. "Hal-lo! *You* here!— Brig o' the Mains, Miss, if *you* please.—Aye man! God, you've been making a name up in Embro. I hear you stood up till him gey weel"—and he winked openly to those

[1]All other editions read: "What's this 'expelled' is, now?"

around.

Young Gourlay's maddened nature broke at the insult. "Damn you," he screamed, "leave *me* alone, will you? I have done nothing to *you,* have I?"

Brodie stared at him across his suspended whiskey-glass, an easy and assured contempt curling his lip. "Don't greet owre't, my bairn," said he—and even as he spoke John's glass shivered on his grinning teeth. Brodie leapt on him, and sent him flying.

"That's a game of your father's, you damned dog," he roared. "But there's mair than him can play the game!"

"Canny, my freendth, canny!" piped Allardyce, who was vexed at a fine chance for his peculiar craft being spoiled by mere brutality of handling. All this was most inartistic. Brodie never had the fine stroke.

Gourlay picked himself bleeding from the floor, and holding a handkerchief to his mouth, plunged headlong from the room. He heard the derisive roar that came after him stop—strangled by the sharp swing-to of the door. But it seemed to echo in his burning ears as he strode madly on through the darkness. He uncorked his mutchkin and drank it like water. His swollen lip smarted at first, but he drank till it was a mere dead lump to his tongue, and he could not feel the whiskey on the wound.

His mind at first was a burning whirl through drink and rage; with nothing determined and nothing definite. But thought began to shape itself. In a vast vague circle of consciousness his mind seemed to sit in the centre and think with preternatural clearness. Though all around was whirling and confused, drink had endowed some inner eye of the brain with unnatural swift vividness. Far within the humming circle of his mind he saw an instant and terrible revenge on Brodie, acted it and lived it now. His desires were murderers, and he let them slip, gloating in the cruelties that hot fancy wreaked upon his enemy. Then he suddenly remembered his father. A rush of fiery blood seemed to drench all his body, as he thought of what had passed between them. "But, by Heaven," he swore, as he threw away his empty bottle, "he won't use me like that another time; I have blood in me now." His maddened fancy began building a new scene, with the same actors, the same conditions, as the other, but an issue gloriously diverse. With vicious delight he heard his father use the same sneers, the same gibes, the same brutalities—then he turned suddenly and had him under foot, kicking, bludgeoning, stamping the life out. He would do it, by Heaven, he would do it! The memory of what had happened came fierily back, and made the pressing darkness burn. His wrath was brimming on the edge, ready to burst, and he felt proudly that it would no longer ebb in fear. Whiskey had killed fear, and left a hysterical madman, all the more dangerous because he was so weak. Let his father try it on now! He was ready for him!

And his father was ready for him; for he knew what had happened at the inn. Mrs Webster, on her nightly hunt for the man she had sworn to honour and obey, having drawn several public houses blank, ran him to earth at last, in the bar-room of the Red Lion. "Yes, yes, Kirsty," he cried, eager to prevent her tongue, "I know I'm a blagyird—but, oh the terrible thing that has happened!" He so possessed her with his graphic tale that he was allowed to go chuckling back to his potations, while she ran hot-foot to the Green Shutters.

"Eh, poo-oor Mrs Gourlay; and oh, your poo-oor boy, too; and eh, that brute, Tam Brodie!—" even as she came through the door the voluble chatter was shrilling out the big tidings, before she was aware of Gourlay's presence. She faltered beneath his black glower.

"Go on!" he said, and ground it out of her.

"The damned sumph!" he growled, "to let Brodie hammer him!" For a moment, it is true, his anger was divided, stood in equipoise, even dipped "Brodie-ward." "I've an account to sattle wi' *him*!" he thought grimly. "When *I* get my claw on his neck, I'll teach him better than to hit a Gourlay! I wonder," he mused, with a pride in which was neither doubt nor wonder, "I wonder will he fling the father as he flang the son!" But that was the instinct of his blood, not enough to make him pardon John. On the contrary here was a new offence of his offspring. On the morrow Barbie would be burning with another affront which he had put upon the name of Gourlay. He would waste no time when he came back, be he drunk or be he sober; he would strip the flesh off him.

"Jenny," he said, "bring me the step-ladder."

He would pass the time till the prodigal came back—and he was almost certain to come back, for where could he go in Barbie?—he would pass the time, by trying to improve the appearance of the House. He had spent money on his house till the last, and even now, had the instinct to embellish it. Not that it mattered to him now, still he could carry out a small improvement he had planned before. The kitchen was ceiled in dark timber, and on the rich brown rafters there were wooden pegs and bars, for the hanging of Gourlay's sticks and fishing rods. His gun was up there, too, just above the hearth. It had occurred to him about a month ago, however, that a pair of curving steel rests, that would catch the glint from the fire, would look better beneath his gun than the dull pegs, where it now lay against a joist. He might as well pass the time by putting them up.

The bringing of the steps, light though they were, was too much for Janet's weak frame, and she stopped in a fit of coughing, clutching the ladder for support, while it shook her to spasms.

"Tuts, Jenny, this'll never do," said Gourlay, not unkindly. He took the ladder away from her and laid his hand on her shoulder. "Away to your bed, lass! You maunna sit up so late."

But Janet was anxious for her brother, and wanted to sit up till he came home. She answered, "Yes," to her father, but idled discreetly, to consume the time.

"Where's my hammer?" snarled Gourlay.

"Is it no by the clock?" said his wife wearily. "Oh, I remember, I remember! I gied it to Mrs Webster to break some brie-stone, to rub the front door-step wi'. It'll be lying in the porch!"

"Oh, aye, as usual," said Gourlay; "as usual!"

"John!" she cried in alarm, "you don't mean to take down the gun, do ye?"

"Huts, you auld fule, what are you skirling for? D'ye think I mean to shoot the dog? Set back on your creepie, and make less noise, will ye?"

Ere he had driven a nail in the rafter John came in, and sat down by the fire, taking up the great poker, as if to cover his nervousness. If Gourlay had been on the floor he would have grappled with him there and then. But the temptation to gloat over his victim from his present height was irresistible. He went up another step, and sat down on the very summit of the ladder, his feet resting on one of the lower rounds. The hammer he had been using was lying on his thigh, his hand clutched about its haft.

"Aye man, you've been taking a bit walk, I hear!"

John made no reply, but played with the poker. It was so huge, owing to Gourlay's whim, that when it slid through his fingers, it came down on the muffled hearthstone with a thud like a paviour's hammer.

"I'm told you saw the Deacon on your rounds? Did he compliment you on your return?"

At the quiet sneer a lightning-flash shewed John that Allardyce had quizzed him, too. For a moment he was conscious of a vast self-pity. "Damn them, they're all down on me," he thought. Then a vindictive rage against them all took hold of him, tense, quivering.

"Did you see Thomas Brodie when you were out?" came the sauve enquiry.

"I saw him," said John, raising fierce eyes to his father's. He was proud of the sudden firmness in his voice. There was no fear in it, no quivering. He was beyond caring what happened to the world or him.

"Oh, you saw him," roared Gourlay, as his anger leapt to meet the anger of his son. "And what did he say to you, may I speir? . . . Or may be I should speir what he did . . . Eh?" he grinned.

"By God, I'll kill ye," screamed John, springing to his feet, with the poker in his hand. The hammer went whizzing past his ear. Mrs Gourlay screamed and tried to rise from her chair, her eyes goggling in terror. As Gourlay leapt, John brought the huge poker with a crash on the descending brow.

The fiercest joy of his life was the dirl that went up his arm, as the steel thrilled to its own hard impact on the bone. Gourlay thudded on the fender, his brow crashing on the rim.

At the blow there had been a cry as of animals, from the two women. There followed an eternity of silence, it seemed, and a haze about the place, yet not a haze, for everything was intensely clear, only it belonged to another world. One terrible fact had changed the Universe. The air was different now; it was full of murder. Everything in the room had a new significance, a sinister meaning. The effect was that of an unholy spell.

As through a dream Mrs Gourlay's voice was heard crying on her God.

John stood there, suddenly weak in his limbs, and stared, as if petrified, at the red poker in his hand. A little wisp of grizzled hair stuck to the square of it, severed, as by scissors, between the sharp edge and the bone. It was the sight of that bit of hair that roused him from his stupor—it seemed so monstrous and horrible, sticking all by itself to the poker. "I didna strike him so hard," he pleaded, staring vaguely, "I didna strike him so hard". Now that the frenzy had left him, he failed to realize the force of his own blow. Then with a horrid fear on him, "Get up, faither," he entreated, "get up, faither; oh man, you micht get up!"

Janet, who had bent above the fallen man, raised an ashen face to her brother, and whispered hoarsely, "His heart has stopped, John; you have killed him!"

Steps were heard coming through the scullery. In the fear of discovery Mrs Gourlay shook off the apathy that held her paralyzed. She sprang up, snatched the poker from her son, and thrust it in the embers.

"Run, John; run for the doctor," she screamed. "Oh, Mrs Webster, Mrs Webster, I'm glad to see ye. Mr Gourlay fell from the top o' the ladder, and smashed his brow on the muckle fender."

CHAPTER 26

"MOTHER!" came the startled whisper, "Mother! Oh, woman, waken and speak to me!"

No comforting answer came from the darkness to tell of a human being close at hand: the girl, intently listening, was alone with her fear. All was silent in the room and the terror deepened. Then the far-off sound in the house was heard once more.

"Mother—mother, what's that?"

"What is it, Janet?" came a feebly complaining voice, "what's wrong wi' ye, lassie?"

Janet and her mother were sleeping in the big bedroom, Janet in the place that had been her father's. He had been buried through the day, the second day after his murder. Mrs Gourlay had shown a feverish anxiety to get the corpse out of the house as soon as possible. And there had been nothing to prevent it. "Oh," said Doctor Dandy to the gossips, "it would have killed any man to fall from such a height on to the sharp edge of yon fender.—No; he was not quite dead when I got to him. He opened his eyes on me, once—a terrible look—and then life went out of him with a great quiver."

Ere Janet could answer her mother, she was seized with a racking cough, and her hoarse bark sounded hollow in the silence. At last she sat up and gasped fearfully, "I thocht— I thocht I heard something moving!"

"It would be the wind," plained her mother; "it would just be the wind. John's asleep this strucken hour and mair. I sat by his bed for a lang while, and he prigged and prayed for a dose o' the whiskey ere he won away. He wouldna let go my hand till he slept, puir fallow. There's an unco fear on him—an unco fear. But try and fa' owre," she soothed her daughter. "That would just be the wind ye heard."

"There's nae wind!" said Janet.

The stair creaked. The two women clung to each other, gripping tight fingers, and their hearts throbbed like big separate beings in their breasts. There was a rustle, as of something coming, then the door opened, and John flitted to the bedside with a candle in his hand. Above his night shirt his bloodless face looked grey.

"Mother!" he panted, "there's something in my room!"

"What is it, John?" said his mother in surprise and fear.

"I—I thocht it was himsell! Oh, mother, I'm feared, I'm feared! Oh, mother, I'm *feared*!" He sang the words in a hysterical chant, his voice rising at the end.

The door of the bedroom clicked. It was not a slamming sound, only the door went to gently, as if someone closed it. John dropped the candle from his shaking hand, and was left standing in the living darkness.

"*Save me!*" he screamed, and leaped into the bed, burrowing down between the women till his head was covered by the bed clothes. He trembled so violently that the bed shook beneath them.

"Let me bide wi' ye!" he pleaded, with chattering jaws. "Oh, let me bide wi' ye! I daurna gang back to that room by mysell again."

His mother put her thin arms round him. "Yes, dear," she said; "you may bide wi' us. Janet and me wouldna let anything harm you." She placed her hand on his brow caressingly. His hair was damp with a cold sweat. He reeked of alcohol.

Someone went through the Square playing a concertina. That sound of the careless world came strangely in upon their lonely tragedy. By contrast the cheerful silly noise, out there, seemed to intensify their darkness and isolation here. Occasional far-off shouts were heard from roysterers going home.

Mrs Gourlay lay staring at the darkness with intent eyes. What horror might assail her she did not know, but she was ready to meet it for the sake of John. "Ye brought it on yoursell," she breathed once, as if defying an unseen accuser.

It was hours ere he slept, but at last a heavy sough told her he had found oblivion. "He's won owre," she murmured thankfully. At times he muttered in his sleep. And, at times, Janet coughed hoarsely at his ear.

"Janet, dinna hoast sae loud, woman! You'll waken your brother."

Janet was silent. Then she choked—trying to stifle another cough.

"Woman!" said her mother complainingly, "that's surely an unco hoast ye hae!"

"Aye," said Janet, "it's a gey hoast."

Next morning Postie came clattering through the paved yard in his tacketty boots, and handed in a blue envelope at the back door with a business-like air, his ferrety eyes searching Mrs Gourlay's face, as she took the letter from his hand. But she betrayed nothing to his curiosity since she knew nothing of her husband's affairs, and had no fear, therefore, of what the letter might portend. She received the missive with a vacant unconcern. It was addressed to "John Gourlay, Esquire." She turned it over in a silly puzzlement, and, "Janet!" she cried, "what am I to do wi' this?"

She shrank from opening a letter addressed to her dead tyrant, unless she had Janet by her side. It was so many years since he had allowed her to take an active interest in their common life (indeed he never had) that she was as helpless as a child.

"It's to faither," said Janet, "shall I waken John?"

"No, puir fellow, let him sleep," said his mother. "I stole in to look at him enow, and his face was unco wan lying down on the pillow. I'll open the letter mysell, though, as your faither used to tell me, I never had a heid for business."

She broke the seal, and Janet, looking over her shoulder, read aloud to her slower mind:

"Glasgow,

"Sir,   "March 12th 18—

"We desire once more to call your attention to the fact that the arrears of interest on the mortgage of your house have not been paid. Our client is unwilling to proceed to extremities, but unless you make some arrangement within a week, he will be forced to take the necessary steps to safeguard his interests.

"Yours faithfully,

"Brodie, Gurney & Yarrowby."

Mrs Gourlay sank into a chair, and the letter slipped from her upturned palm, lying slack upon her knee.

"Janet," she said appealingly; "what's this that has come on us? Does the house we live in, the House with the Green Shutters, not belong to us ainy more? Tell me, lassie. What does it mean?"

"I don't ken," whispered Janet with big eyes. "Did faither never tell ye of the bond?"

"He never told me about anything," cried Mrs Gourlay with a sudden passion. "I was aye the one to be keepit in the dark—to be keepit in the dark and sore hadden doon. Oh! are we left destitute, Janet—and us was aye sae muckle thocht o'! And me, too, that's come of decent folk, and brought him a gey pickle bawbees! Am I to be on the parish in my auld age?—Oh, *my* faither, *my* faither!"

Her mind flashed back to the jocose and well-to-do father who had been but a blurred thought to her for twenty years. That his daughter should come to a pass like this was enough to make him turn in his grave. Janet was astonished by her sudden passion in feebleness. Even the murder of her husband had been met by her weak mind with a dazed resignation. For her natural horror at the deed was swallowed by her anxiety to shield the murderer; and she experienced a vague relief—felt, but not considered—at being freed from the incubus of Gourlay's tyranny. It seemed, too, as if she was incapable of feeling anything poignantly, deadened now by these quick calamities. But that *she*, that Tenshillingland's daughter, should come to be an object of common charity, touched some hidden nerve of pride, and made her writhe in agony.

"It mayna be sae bad," Janet tried to comfort her.

"Waken John," said her mother feverishly, "waken John and we'll gang through his faither's dask. There may be something gude amang his papers. There may be something gude!" she gabbled nervously; "yes, there may be something gude! In the dask; in the dask; there may be something gude in the dask!"

John staggered into the kitchen five minutes later. Half way to the table where his mother sat, he reeled and fell over on a chair, where he lay with an ashen face, his eyes mere slits in his head, the upturned whites shewing through. They brought him whiskey, and he drank and was recovered. And then they went through to the parlour, and opened the great desk that stood in the corner. It was the first time they had ever dared to raise its lid. John took up a letter lying loosely on the top of the other papers, and, after a hasty glance, "This settles it!" said he. It was the note from Gourlay's banker, warning him that his account was overdrawn.

"God help us!" cried Mrs Gourlay, and Janet began to whimper. John slipped out of the room. He was still in his stocking-feet, and the women, dazed by this sudden and appalling news, were scarcely aware of his departure.

He passed through the kitchen, and stood on the step of the back door, looking out on the quiet little paved yard. Everything there was remarkably still and bright. It was an early spring that year, and the hot March sun beat down on him, paining his bleared and puffy eyes. The contrast between his own lump of a body, drink-dazed, dull-throbbing, and the warm bright day, came in on him with a sudden sinking of the heart, a sense of degradation and personal abasement. He realized, however obscurely, that he was an eyesore in nature, a blotch on the surface of the world, an offence to the sweet-breathing heavens. And that bright silence was so strange and still. He could have screamed to escape it.

The slow ticking of the kitchen clock seemed to beat upon his raw brain. Damn the thing, why didn't it stop—with its monotonous tick-tack; tick-tack; tick-tack?—he could feel it inside his head where it seemed to strike innumerable little blows, on a strained chord it was bent on snapping.

He tiptoed back to the kitchen on noiseless feet, and cocking his ear to listen, he heard the murmur of women's voices in the parlour. There was a look of slyness and cunning in his face; and his eyes glittered with desire. The whiskey was still on the table. He seized the bottle greedily, and, tilting it up, let the raw liquid gurgle into him like cooling water. It seemed to flood his parched being with a new vitality.

"Oh, I doubt we'll be gey ill-off!" he heard his mother's

whine, and, at that reminder of her nearness, he checked the great satisfied breath he had begun to blow. He set the bottle on the table, bringing the glass noiselessly down upon the wood, with a tense, unnatural precision possible only to drink-steadied nerves—a steadiness like the humming top's whirled to its fastest. Then he sped silently through the courtyard and locked himself into the stable, chuckling in drunken triumph as he turned the key. He pitched forward on a litter of dirty straw, and in a moment, sleep came over his mind in a huge wave of darkness.

An hour later he woke from a terrible dream, flinging his arms up, to ward off a face that had been pressing on his own. Were the eyes that had burned his brain still glaring above him? He looked about him in drunken wonder. From a sky-window a shaft of golden light came slanting into the loose-box, living with yellow motes in the dimness. The world seemed dead; he was alone in the silent building, and from without there was no sound. Then a panic terror flashed on his mind, that those eyes had actually been here—and were here with him still—where he was locked up with them alone. He strained his eyeballs in a horrified stare at vacancy. Then he shut them in terror, for why did he look? If he looked, the eyes might burn on him out of nothingness. The innocent air had become his enemy—pregnant with unseen terrors to glare at him. To breathe it stifled him; each draught of it was full of menace. With a shrill cry he dashed at the door, and felt in the clutch of his ghostly enemy when he failed to open it at once, breaking his nails on the baffling lock. He mowed and chattered and stamped, and tore at the lock, frustrate in fear. At last he was free! He broke into the kitchen where his mother sat weeping—she raised her eyes to see a dishevelled thing, with bits of straw scattered on his clothes and hair.

"Mother!" he screamed, "Mother!" and stopped suddenly, his startling eyes seeming to follow something in the room.

"What are ye glowering at, John?" she wailed.

"Thae damned e'en," he said slowly, "they're burning my soul! Look, look!" he cried, clutching her thin wrist, "see,

233

there, there!—coming round by the dresser! A-ah!" he screamed in hoarse execration. "Would ye, then?"—and he hurled a great jug from the table at the pursuing unseen.

The jug struck the yellow face of the clock, and the glass jangled on the floor.

Mrs Gourlay raised her arms, like a gaunt sibyl, and spoke to her Maker, quietly, as if He were a man before her in the room. "Ruin and murder," she said slowly; "and madness; and death at my nipple like a child! When will Ye be satisfied?"

Drucken Wabster's wife spread the news, of course, and that night it went humming through the town that young Gourlay had the horrors, and was throwing tumblers at his mother!

"Puir body!" said the baker, in the long–drawn tones of an infinite compassion; "puir body!"

"Aye," said Toddle drily, he'll be wanting to put an end to *her* next, after killing his faither."

"Killing his faither?" said the baker with a quick look, "what do you mean?"

"Mean? Ou, I just mean what the doctor says! Gourlay was that mad at the drucken young swine that he got the 'plexies, fell aff the ladder, and felled himsell deid! That's what I mean, no less!" said Toddle, nettled at the sharp question.

"Aye man! That accounts for't," said Tam Wylie. "It did seem queer Gourlay's dying the verra nicht the prodigal cam hame. He was a heavy man, too; he would come down with an infernal thud. It seems uncanny, though, it seems uncanny."

"Strange!" murmured another, and they looked at each other in silent wonder.

"But will this be true, think ye?" said Brodie. "About the horrors, I mean. *Did* he throw the tumbler at his mother?"

"Lord, it's true!" said Sandy Toddle. "I gaed into the kitchen, on purpose, to make sure o' the matter with my own eyes. I let on I wanted to borrow auld Gourlay's key-hole saw —I can tell ye he had a' his orders—his tool-chest's the finest I ever saw in my life! I mean to bid for some o' yon

234

when the rowp comes. Weel, as I was saying, I let on I wanted the wee saw, and went into the kitchen one end's errand. The tumbler (Johnny Coe says it was a bottle, however; but I'm no avised o' that—I speired Webster's wife, and I think my details are correct)—the tumbler went flying past his mother, and smashed the face o' the eight-day. It happened about the mid-hour o' the day. The clock had stoppit, I observed, at three and a half minutes to the twelve.".

"Hi!" cried the Deacon, "it'th a pity auld Gourlay wathna alive thith day!"

"Faith, aye," cried Wylie. "*He* would have sorted him! *He* would have trimmed the young ruffian!"

"No doubt," said the Deacon gravely; "no doubt. But it wath scarcely that I wath thinking of. Yah!" he grinned, "thith would have been a thlap in the face till him!"

Wylie looked at him for awhile with a white scunner in his face. He wore the musing and disgusted look of a man whose wounded mind retires within itself, to brood over a sight of unnatural cruelty. The Deacon grew uncomfortable beneath his sideward, estimating eye.

"Deacon Allardyce, your heart's black-rotten," he said at last.

The Deacon blinked and was silent. Tam had summed him up. There was no appeal.

"John, dear," said his mother that evening, "we'll take the big sofa into our bedroom, and make up a grand bed for ye, and then we'll be company to one another. Eh, dear?" she pleaded. "Winna that be a fine way? When you have Janet and me beside you, you winna be feared o' ainything coming near you. You should gang to bed early, dear. A sleep would restore your mind."

"I don't mean to go to bed," he said slowly. He spoke staringly, with the same fixity in his voice and gaze. There was neither rise nor fall in his voice, only a dull level of intensity.

"You don't mean to go to bed, John! What for, dear? Man, a sleep would calm your mind for ye."

"Na-a-a!" he smiled, and shook his head like a cunning madman, who had detected her trying to get round him.

"Na-a-a! No sleep for me—no sleep for me! I'm feared I would see the red e'en," he whispered, "the red e'en; coming at me out o' the darkness—the darkness!" he nodded, staring at her and breathing the word, "the darkness! the darkness! The darkness is the warst, mother," he added in his natural voice, leaning forward as if he explained some simple curious thing of every day. "The darkness is the warst, you know. I've seen them in the broad licht, but in the lobby," he whispered hoarsely; "in the lobby when it was dark; in the lobby they were terrible. Just twa e'en, and they aye keep thegither, though they're aye moving. That's why I canna pin them. And it's because I ken they're aye watching me, watching me, watching me, that I get so feared. They're red," he nodded and whispered, "they're red . . . they're red." His mouth gaped in horror, and he stared as if he saw them now.

He had boasted long ago of being able to see things inside his head; in his drunken hysteria he was to see them always. The vision he beheld against the darkness of his mind, projected itself, and glared at him. He was pursued by a spectre in his own brain, and for that reason there was no escape. Wherever he went it followed him.

"Oh man, John," wailed his mother, "what are ye feared for your faither's e'en for? He wouldna persecute his boy."

"Would he no?" he said slowly. "You ken yoursell that he never liked me! And naebody could stand his glower. Oh, he was a terrible man, *my* faither! You could feel the passion in him when he stood still. He could throw himsell at ye without moving. And he's throwing himsell at *me* frae beyond the grave."

Mrs Gourlay beat her desperate hands. Her feeble remonstrance was a snowflake on a hill, to the dull intensity of this conviction. So colossal was it that it gripped herself, and she glanced dreadfully across her shoulder. But, in spite of her fears, she must plead with him to save.

"Johnnie dear," she wept passionately, "there's no e'en! It's just the drink gars you think sae."

"No," he said dully; "the drink's my refuge. It's a kind thing, drink. It helps a body."

"But, John, nobody believes in these things nowadays.

236

Chapter Twenty-Six

It's just fancy in you. I wonder at a college-bred man like
you giving heed to a wheen nonsense!"

"Ye ken yoursell it was a by-word in the place that he
would haunt the House with the Green Shutters."

"God help me!" cried Mrs Gourlay; "what am I to do?"

She piled up a great fire in the parlour, and the three poor
creatures gathered round it for the night. (They were afraid
to sit in the kitchen of an evening, for even the silent furniture seemed to talk of the murder it had witnessed.) John was
on a carpet stool by his mother's feet, his head resting on her
knee.

They heard the rattle of Wilson's brake as it swung over
the town-head from Auchterwheeze, and the laughter of its
jovial crew. They heard the town clock chiming the lonesome
passage of the hours. A dog was barking in the street.

Gradually all other sounds died away.

"Mother," said John, "lay your hand alang my shouther,
touching my neck. I want to be sure that you're near me."

"I'll do that, my bairn," said his mother. And soon he was
asleep.

Janet was reading a novel. The children had their mother's
silly gift, a gift of the weak-minded, of forgetting their own
duties and their own sorrows, in a vacant interest which they
found in books. She had wrapped a piece of coarse red
flannel round her head to comfort a swollen jaw, and her
face appeared from within like a tallowy oval.

"I didna get that story finished," said Mrs Gourlay vacantly, staring at the fire open-mouthed, her mutchstrings
dangling. It was the remark of a stricken mind that speaks
vacantly of anything. "Does Herbert Montgomery marry
Sir James's niece?"

"No," said Janet, "he's killed at the war. It's a gey pity of
him, isn't it?—Oh, what's that?"

It was John talking in his sleep.

"I have killed my faither," he said slowly, pausing long
between every phrase: "I have killed my faither . . . I have
killed my faither. And he's foll-owing me, . . . he's foll-owing
me . . . he's foll-owing me." It was the voice of a thing, not
a man. It swelled and dwelt on the "follow," as if the horror

237

of the pursuit made it moan. "He's foll-owing me . . . he's foll-owing me . . . he's foll-owing me. A face like a dark mist—and e'en like hell. Oh, they're foll-owing me . . . they're foll-owing me . . . they're foll-owing me!" His voice seemed to come from an infinite distance. It was like a lost soul moaning in a solitude.

The dog was barking in the street. A cry of the night came from far away.

That voice was as if a corpse opened its lips, and told of horrors beyond the grave. It brought the other world into the homely room, and made it all demoniac. The women felt the presence of the unknown. It was their own flesh and blood that spoke the words, and by their own quiet hearth. But hell seemed with them in the room.

Mrs Gourlay drew back from John's head on her lap, as from something monstrous and unholy. But he moaned in deprivation, craving her support, and she edged nearer to supply his need. Possessed with a devil or no, he was her son.

"Mother!" gasped Janet suddenly, the white circles of her eyes staring from the red flannel, her voice hoarse with a new fear, "Mother, suppose—suppose he said that before anybody else!"

"Don't mention't," cried her mother with sudden passion; "how daur ye, how daur ye? My God!" she broke down and wept, "they would hang him, so they would; they would hang *my* boy; they would take and hang *my* boy!"

They stared at each other wildly. John slept, his head twisted over on his mother's knee, his eyes sunken, his mouth wide open.

"Mother," Janet whispered, "you must send him away."

"I have only three pounds in the world," said Mrs Gourlay—and she put her hand to her breast where it was, but winced as if a pain had bitten her.

"Send him away wi't," said Janet. "The furniture may bring something. And you and me can aye thole."

In the morning Mrs Gourlay brought two greasy notes to the table, and placed them in her son's slack hand. He was saner now; he had slept off his drunken madness through the night.

"John," she said in pitiful appeal, "you maunna stay here, laddie. Ye'll gie up the drink when you're away—will ye na? —and then thae e'en ye're sae feared of'll no trouble you ony mair. Gang to Glasgow and see the lawyer folk about the bond. And, John dear," she pleaded, "if there's nothing left for us, you'll try to work for Janet and me, will ye no? You've a grand education, and you'll surely get a place as a teacher or something; I'm sure you would make a grand teacher. Ye wouldna like to think of your mother trailing every week to the like of Wilson for an awmous, streeking out her auld hand for charity. The folk would stand in their doors to look at me, man—they would that—they would cry ben to each other to come oot and see Gourlay's wife gaun slinkin doon the brae. Doon the brae it would be," she repeated, "doon the brae it would be"—and her mind drifted away on the sorrowful future which her fear made so vivid and real. It was only John's going that roused her.

Thomas Brodie, glowering abroad from a shop door festooned in boots, his leather apron in front, and his thumbs in the armholes of his waistcoat, as befitted an important man, saw young Gourlay pass the Cross with his bag in his hand, and dwindle up the road to the station.

"Where's *he* off to now?" he muttered, "there's something at the boddom o' this, if a body could find it out!"

CHAPTER 27

WHEN John had gone his mother roused herself to a feverish industry. Even in the early days of her strength, she had never been so busy in her home. But her work was aimless and to no purpose. When tidying she would take a cup without its saucer from the table, and set off with it through the room, but stopping suddenly in the middle of the floor, would fall into a muse with the dish in her hand; coming to herself long afterwards to ask vaguely, "What's this cup for?... Janet, lassie, what was it I was doing?" Her energy, and its frustration, had the same reason. The burden on her mind constantly impelled her to do something to escape from it—and the same burden paralysed her mind in everything she did. So with another of her vacant whims. Every morning she rose at an unearthly hour, to fish out of old closets rag-bags bellied big with the odds and ends of thirty years' assemblage. "I'll make a patch-work quilt o' thir!" she explained with a foolish, eager smile—and she spent hours snatching up rags and vainly trying to match them. But the quilt made no progress. She would look at a patch for a while, with her head on one side, and pat it all over with restless hands; then she would turn it round, to see if it would look better that way, only to tear it off when it was half sewn, to try another and yet another. Often she would forget the work on her lap, and stare across the room, open-mouthed; her fingers plucking at her withered throat. Janet became afraid of her mother.

Once she saw her smiling to herself, when she thought nobody was watching her, an uncanny smile as of one who hugged a secret to her breast—a secret that, eluding others, would enable its holder to elude them too.

"What can *she* have to laugh at?" Janet wondered.

At times, the haze that seemed gathering round Mrs Gourlay's mind would be dispelled by sudden rushes of fear, when she would whimper lest her son be hanged, or herself come on the parish in her old age. But that was rarely. Her brain was mercifully dulled, and her days were passed in a restless vacancy.

She was sitting with the rags scattered round her when John walked in on the evening of the third day. There were rags everywhere; on the table, and all about the kitchen; she sat in their midst like a witch among the autumn leaves. When she looked towards his entrance the smell of drink was wafted from the door.

"John!" she panted in surprise, "John, did ye not go to Glasgow, boy?"

"Aye," he said slowly, "I gaed to Glasgow."

"And the bond, John?—did ye speir about the bond?"

"Aye," he said, "I speired about the bond. The whole house is sunk in't."

"Oh!" she gasped, and the whole world seemed to go from beneath her, so weak did she feel through her limbs.

"John," she said after a while, "did ye no try to get something to do, that you might help me and Janet now we're helpless?"

"No," he said, "for the e'en wouldna let me. Nicht and day they follow me a'where; nicht and day."

"Are they following ye yet, John?" she whispered, leaning forward seriously. She did not try to disabuse him now; she accepted what he said. Her mind was on a level with his own "Are they following ye yet?" she asked with large eyes of sympathy and awe.

"Aye, and waur than ever, too. They're getting redder and redder. It's not a dull red," he said, with a faint return of his old interest in the curious physical; "it's a gleaming red. They lowe. A' last nicht they woudna let me sleep. There was nae gas in my room, and when the candle went out I could see them everywhere. When I looked to one corner o' the room, they were there; and when I looked to another corner, they were there, too; glowering at me; glowering at me in the darkness; glowering at me. Ye mind what a glower he had! I hid from them ablow the claes, but they followed me—they were burning in my brain. So I gaed oot and stood by a lamp-post for company. But a constable moved me on; he said I was drunk because I muttered to mysell. But I wasna drunk then, mother; I wa-as *not*. So I walkit on, and on, and on, the whole nicht—but I aye keepit to the lamp-posts for company. And then when the public houses opened, I gaed in and drank and drank. I didna like the drink, for whiskey has no taste to me now. But it helps ye to forget.

"Mother?" he went on complainingly, "is it no queer that a pair of e'en should follow a man? Just a pair of e'en! It never happened to onybody but me," he said dully; "never to onybody but me."

His mother was panting open-mouthed, as if she choked for air, both hands clutching at her bosom. "Aye," she whispered, "it's queer," and kept on gasping at intervals with staring eyes, "it's gey queer; it's gey queer; it's gey queer."

She took up the needle once more and tried to sew, but her hand was trembling so violently that she pricked the left forefinger which upheld her work. She was content thereafter to make loose stabs at the cloth, with a result that she made great stitches which drew her seam together in a pucker. Vacantly she tried to smooth them out, stroking them over with her hand, constantly stroking and to no purpose. John watched the aimless work with dull and heavy eyes.

For a while there was silence in the kitchen. Janet was coughing in the room above.

"There's just ae thing'll end it!" said John. "Mother, give me three shillings."

It was not a request, and not a demand; it was the dull statement of a need. Yet the need appeared so relentless, uttered in the set fixity of his impassive voice, that she could not gainsay it. She felt that this was not merely her son making a demand; it was a compulsion on him greater than himself.

"There's the money!" she said, clinking it down on the table, and flashed a resentful smile at him, close upon the brink of tears.

She had a fleeting anger. It was scarcely at him, though; it was at the fate that drove him. Nor was it for herself, for her own mood was, "Well, well; let it gang." But she had a sense of unfairness, and a flicker of quite impersonal resentment, that fate should wring the last few shillings from a poor being. It wasna fair. She had the emotion of it; and it spoke in the strange look at her son, and in the smiling flush with the tears behind it. Then she sank into apathy.

John took up the money and went out, heedless of his mother where she sat by the table—he had a doom on him, and could see nothing that did not lie within his path. Nor did she take any note of his going; she was callous. The tie between them was being annulled by misery. She was ceasing to be his mother, he to be her son; they were not younger and older, they were the equal victims of necessity. Fate set each of them apart to dree a separate weird.

In a house of long years of misery, the weak become callous to their dearest's agony. The hard strong characters are kindest in the end; they will help while their hearts are breaking. But the weak fall asunder at the last. It was not that Mrs Gourlay was thinking of herself, rather than of him. She was stunned by fate—as was he—and could think of nothing.

Ten minutes later John came out of the Black Bull with a bottle of whiskey.

It was a mellow evening, one of those evenings when Barbie, the mean and dull, is transfigured to a gem-like purity, and catches a radiance. There was a dreaming sky above the town, and its light less came to the earth than was on it, shining in every path with a gracious immanence. John came on through the glow with his burden undisguised, wrapped in a tissue paper which shewed its outlines. He stared right before him like a man walking in his sleep, and never once looked to either side. At word of his coming the doors were filled with mutches and bald heads, keeking by the jambs to get a look. Many were indecent in their haste, not waiting till he passed ere they peeped—which was their usual way. Some even stood away out in front of their doors to glower at him advancing, turning slowly with him as he passed, and glowering behind him as he went. They saw they might do so with impunity; that he did not see them, but walked like a man in a dream. He passed up the street and through the Square, beneath a hundred eyes, the sun shining softly round him. Every eye followed till he disappeared through his own door.

He went through the kitchen, where his mother sat, carrying the bottle openly, and entered the parlour without speaking. He came back and asked her for the corkscrew, but when she said "Eh?" with a vague wildness in her manner, and did not seem to understand, he went and got it for himself. She continued making stabs at her cloth and smoothing out the puckers in her seam.

John was heard moving in the parlour. There was the sharp *plunk* of a cork being drawn, followed by a clink of glass. And then came a heavy thud like a fall.

To Mrs Gourlay the sounds meant nothing; she heard them with her ear, not her mind. The world around her had retreated to a hazy distance, so that it had no meaning. She would have gazed vaguely at a shell about to burst beside her.

In the evening, Janet, who had been in bed all the afternoon, came down and lit the lamp for her mother. It was a large lamp which Gourlay had bought, and it shed a rich light through the room.

"I heard John come in," she said, turning wearily round; "but I was too ill to come down and ask what had happened. Where is he?"

"John?" questioned her mother, "John?... Ou, aye!" she panted, vaguely recalling, "ou, aye! I think—I think ... he gaed ben the parlour."

"The parlour!" cried Janet, "but he must be in the dark! And he canna thole the darkness!"

"John!" she cried, going to the parlour door, "John!"

There was a silence of the grave.

She lit a candle, and went into the room. And then she gave a squeal like a rabbit in a dog's jaws.

Mrs Gourlay dragged her gaunt limbs wearily across the floor. By the wavering light, which shook in Janet's hand, she saw her son lying dead across the sofa. The whiskey-bottle on the table was half empty, and of a smaller bottle beside it he had drunk a third. He had taken all that whiskey that he might deaden his mind to the horror of swallowing the poison. His legs had slipped to the floor when he died, but his body was lying back across the couch, his mouth open, his eyes staring horridly up. They were not the eyes of the quiet dead, but bulged in frozen fear, as if his father's eyes had watched him from aloft while he died.

"There's twa thirds of the poison left," commented Mrs Gourlay.

"Mother!" Janet screamed, and shook her. "Mother, John's deid! John's deid. Don't ye see John's deid?"

"Aye, he's deid," said Mrs Gourlay, staring. "He winna be hanged now!"

"Mother!" cried Janet, desperate before this apathy, "what shall we do? What shall we do? Shall I run and bring the neebours?"

"The neebours!" said Mrs Gourlay, rousing herself wildly. "The neebours! What have *we* to do with the neebours? We are by ourselves—the Gourlays whom God has cursed; we can have no neebours. Come ben the house and I'll tell ye something," she whispered wildly. "Aye," she nodded, smiling with mad significance, "I'll tell ye something . . . I'll tell ye something," and she dragged Janet to the kitchen.

Janet's heart was rent for her brother, but the frenzy on her mother killed sorrow with a new fear.

"Janet!" smiled Mrs Gourlay, with insane soft interest, "Janet! D'ye mind yon nicht langsyne when your faither came in wi' a terrible look in his e'en, and struck me in the breist? Aye," she whispered hoarsely, staring at the fire, "he struck me in the breist. But I didna ken what it was for, Janet . . . No," she shook her head, "he never telled me what it was for."

"Aye, mother," whispered Janet, "I have mind o't."

"Weel, an abscess o' some kind formed—I kenna weel what it was—but it gathered and broke, and gathered and broke, till my breist's near eaten awa wi't. Look!" she cried, tearing open her bosom, and Janet's head flung back in horror and disgust.

"Oh, mother!" she panted, "was it that that the wee

245

clouts were for?"

"Aye, it was that," said her mother. "Mony a clout I had to wash, and mony a nicht I sat lonely by mysell, plaistering my withered breist. But I never let onybody ken," she added with pride; "na-a-a; I never let onybody ken. When your faither nipped me wi' his tongue, it nipped me wi' its pain, and, woman, it consoled me. 'Aye, aye,' I used to think; 'jibe awa, jibe awa; but I hae a freend in my breist that'll end it some day.' I likit to keep it to mysell. When it bit me it seemed to whisper I had a freend that nane o' them kenned o'—a freend that would deliver me! The mair he badgered me, the closer I hugged it; and when my he'rt was br'akin I enjoyed the pain o't."

"Oh, my poor, poor mother!" cried Janet with a bursting sob, her eyes raining hot tears. Her very body seemed to feel compassion; it quivered and crept near, as though it would brood over her mother and protect her. She raised the poor hand and kissed it, and fondled it between her own.

But her mother had forgotten the world in one of her wild lapses, and was staring fixedly.

"I'll no lang be a burden to onybody," she said to herself. "It should sune be wearing to a heid now. But I thought of something the day John gaed away. Aye, I thought of something," she said vaguely. "Janet, what was it I was thinking of?"

"I dinna ken," whispered Janet.

"I was thinking of something!" her mother mused. Her voice all through was a far-off voice, remote from understanding. "Yes, I remember. Ye're young, Jenny, and you learned the dressmaking—do ye think ye could sew, or something, to keep a bit garret owre my heid till I dee? Aye, it was that I was thinking of—though it doesna matter much now.—Eh, Jenny? I'll no bother you for verra lang. But I'll no gang on the parish," she said in a passionless voice, "I'll no gang on the parish.—I'm Miss Richmond o' Tenshilling-land."

She had no interest in her own suggestion. It was an idea that had flitted through her mind before, which came back to her now in feeble recollection. She seemed not to wait for an answer, to have forgotten what she said.

"Oh, mother," cried Janet, "there's a curse on us all! I would work my fingers raw for ye if I could, but I canna," she screamed, "I canna, I canna! My lungs are bye wi't. On Tuesday in Skeighan the doctor told me I would soon be deid—he didna say't, but fine I saw what he was hinting. He advised me to gang to Ventnor in the Isle o' Wight," she added wanly, "as if I could gang to the Isle o' Wight. I cam hame trembling and wanted to tell ye, but when I cam in ye were ta'en up wi' John, and, 'Oh, lassie,' said you, 'dinna bother me wi' your complaints enow.' I was hurt at that, and 'Well, well,' I thocht, 'if she doesna want to hear, I'll no tell her!' I was huffed at ye. And then my faither came in, and ye ken what happened. I hadna the heart to speak o't after that; I didna seem to care. I ken what it is to nurse daith in my breist wi' pride, too, mother," she went on. "Ye never cared verra much for me, it was John was your favourite. I used to be angry because you neglected my illness, and I never telled you how heavily I hoasted blood. 'She'll be sorry for this when I'm deid,' I used to think—and I hoped you would be. I had a kind of pride in saying nothing. But, oh, mother, I didna ken *you* were just the same, I didna ken *you* were just the same." She looked. Her mother was not listening.

Suddenly Mrs Gourlay screamed with wild laughter, and, laughing, eyed with mirthless merriment the look of horror with which Janet was regarding her. "Ha, ha, ha!" she screamed, "it's to be a clean sweep o' the Gourlays! Ha, ha, ha! it's to be a clean sweep o' the Gourlays!"

There is nothing uglier in life than a woman's cruel laugh, but Mrs Gourlay's laugh was more than cruel, it was demoniac; the skirl of a human being carried by misery beyond the confines of humanity. Janet stared at her in speechless fear.

"Mother," she whispered at last, "what are we to do?"

"There's twa thirds of the poison left," said Mrs Gourlay.

"Mother!" cried Janet.

"Gourlay's dochter may gang on the parish if she likes, but his wife never will. *You* may hoast yourself to death in a garret in the poorhouse, but *I'll* follow my boy."

The sudden picture of her own lonely death as a pauper among strangers, when her mother and brother should be gone, was so appalling to Janet, that to die with her mother seemed pleasanter. She could not bear to be left alone.

"Mother," she cried in a frenzy, "I'll keep ye company!"

"Let us read a Chapter," said Mrs Gourlay.

She took down the big Bible, and "the thirteent' Chapter o' first Corinthians," she announced in a loud voice, as if giving it out from the pulpit, "the thirteent'—o' the first Corinthians":

"'Though I speak with the tongues of men and of angels, and have not charity, I am become as sounding brass, or a tinkling cymbal.

"'And though I have the gift of prophecy, and understand all mysteries, and all knowledge; and though I have all faith, so that I could remove mountains, and have not charity, I am nothing.'"

Mrs Gourlay's manner had changed; she was in the high exaltation of madness. Callous she still appeared, so possessed by her general doom that she had no sense of its particular woes. But she was listless no more. Willing her death, she seemed to borrow its greatness and become one with the law that punished her. Arrogating the Almighty's function to expedite her doom, she was the equal of the Most High. It was her feebleness that made her great. Because in her feebleness she yielded entirely to the fate that swept her on, she was imbued with its demoniac power.

"'Charity suffereth long, and is kind; charity envieth not; charity vaunteth not itself, is not puffed up.

"'Doth not behave itself unseemly, seeketh not her own, is not easily provoked, thinketh no evil;

"'Rejoiceth not in iniquity, but rejoiceth in the truth;

"'Beareth all things, believeth all things, hopeth all things, endureth all things.

"'Charity never faileth: but whether there be prophecies, they shall fail; whether there be tongues, they shall cease; whether there be knowledge, it shall vanish away.

"'For we know in part, and we prophesy in part.

"'But when that which is perfect is come, then that which

is in part shall be done away.' "

Her voice rose high and shrill as she read the great verses. Her large blue eyes shone with ecstasy. Janet looked at her in fear. This was more than her mother speaking, it was more than human, it was a voice from beyond the world. Alone, the timid girl would have shrunk from death, but her mother's inspiration held her.

" *'And now abideth faith, hope, charity, these three: but the greatest of these is charity.' "*

Janet had been listening with such strained attention that the "Amen" rang out of her loud and involuntary, like an answer to a compelling Deity. She had clung to this reading as the one thing left to her before death, and out of her nature thus strained to listen the "Amen" came, as sped by an inner will. She scarcely knew that she said it.

They rose, and the scrunt of Janet's chair on the floor, when she pushed it behind her, sent a thrilling shiver through her body, so tense was her mood. They stood with their hands on their chair-backs, and looked at each other, in a curious palsy of the will. The first step to the parlour door would commit them to the deed; to take it was to take the poison, and they paused, feeling its significance. To move was to give themselves to the irrevocable. When they stirred at length they felt as if the ultimate crisis had been passed; there could be no return. Mrs Gourlay had Janet by the wrist.

She turned and looked at her daughter, and for one fleeting moment she ceased to be above humanity.

"Janet," she said wistfully, "*I* have had a heap to thole! Maybe the Lord Jesus Christ'll no' be owre sair on me."

"Oh, mother!" Janet screamed, yielding to her terror when her mother weakened. "Oh, mother, I'm feared! I'm feared! Oh, mother, I'm feared!"

"Come!" said her mother; "Come!" and drew her by the wrist. They went into the parlour.

The post was a square-built, bandy-legged little man, with a bristle of grizzled hair about his twisted mouth, perpetually cocking up an ill-bred face in the sight of Heaven. Physically

and morally he had in him something both of the Scotch
terrier and the London sparrow—the shagginess of the one,
the cocked eye of the other, the one's snarling temper, the
other's assured impudence. In Gourlay's day he had never
got by the gateway of the yard, much as he had wanted to
come farther. Gourlay had an eye for a thing like him.
"Damn the gurly brute!" Postie complained once; "when I
passed a pleasant remark about the weather the other
morning, he just looked at me and blew the reek of his pipe
in my face. And that was his only answer!"

Now that Gourlay was gone, however, Postie clattered
through the yard every morning, right up to the back door.

"A heap o' correspondence *thir* mornins!" he would
simper—his greedy little eye trying to glean revelations from
the women's faces, as they took the letters from his hand.

On the morning after young Gourlay came home for the
last time, Postie was pelting along with his quick thudding
step near the head of the Square, when whom should he meet
but Sandy Toddle, still unwashed and yawning from his bed.
It was early and the streets were empty, except where in the
distance the bent figure of an old man was seen hirpling off
to his work, first twisting round stiffly to cock his eye right
and left at the sky, to forecast the weather for the day.

From the chimneys the fair white spirlies of reek were
rising in the pure air. The Gourlays did not seem to be
stirring yet; there was no smoke above their rooftree to
show that there was life within.

Postie jerked his thumb across his shoulder at the House
with the Green Shutters.

"There'll be chynges there the day," he said, chirruping.

"Wha-at!" Toddle breathed in a hoarse whisper of
astonishment, "sequesteration?" and he stared, big-eyed,
with his brows arched.

"Something o' that kind," said the post carelessly. "I'm
no' weel acquaint wi' the law-wers' lingo."

"Will't be true, think ye?" said Sandy.

"God, it's true," said the post. "I had it frae Jock
Hutchison, the clerk in Skeighan Goudie's. He got fou
yestreen on the road to Barbie and blabbed it—he'll lose

his job, yon chap, if he doesna keep his mouth shut.—True, aye! It's true! There's damn the doubt o' that."

Toddle corrugated his mouth to whistle. He turned and stared at the House with the Green Shutters, gawcey and substantial on its terrace, beneath the tremulous beauty of the dawn. There was a glorious sunrise.

"God!" he said, "what a downcome for that hoose!"

"Is it no'?" chuckled Postie.

"Whose account is it on?" said Toddle.

"Oh, I don't ken," said Postie, carelessly. "He had creditors a' owre the country. I was aye bringing the big blue envelopes from different airts. Don't mention this, now," he added, his finger up, his eye significant. "It shouldn't be known at a-all." He was unwilling that Toddle should get an unfair start, and spoil his own market for the news.

"*Nut* me!" Toddle assured him grandly, shaking his head as one who should put conduct of that kind a thousand miles off.[1] "*Nut* me, post! I'll no breathe it to a living soul."

The post clattered in to Mrs Gourlay's back-door. He had a heavy under-stamped letter on which there was threepence to pay. He might pick up an item or two while she was getting him the bawbees.

He knocked, but there was no answer.

"The sluts!" said he, with a humph of disgust; "they're still on their backs, it seems."

He knocked again. The sound of his knuckles on the door rang out hollowly, as if there was nothing but emptiness within. While he waited he turned on the step, and looked idly at the courtyard. The enwalled little place was curiously still.

At last in his impatience he turned the handle, when to his surprise the door opened, and let him enter.

The leaves of a Bible fluttered in the fresh wind from the door. A large lamp was burning on the table. Its big yellow flame was unnatural in the sunshine.

[1] This is the reading of the Memorial edition of 1923. The other editions consulted print an obviously defective version – "as who should conduct of that kind a (or of) thousand miles off".

"H'mph!" said Postie, tossing his chin in disgust, "little wonder everything gaed to wreck and ruin in this house! The slovens have left the lamp burning the whole nicht lang. But less licht'll serve them now, I'm thinking!"

A few dead ashes were sticking from the lower bars of the range. Postie crossed to the fireplace and looked down at the fender. That bright spot would be the place, now, where auld Gourlay killed himself. The women must have rubbed it so bright in trying to get out the blood. It was an uncanny thing to keep in the house, that. He stared at the fatal spot till he grew eerie in the strange stillness.

"Guidwife!" he cried, "Jennet! Don't ye hear?"

They did not hear, it seemed.

"God!" said he, "they sleep sound after all their misfortunes!"

At last—partly in impatience, and partly from a wish to pry—he opened the door of the parlour. "*Oh, my God!*" he screamed, leaping back, and with his bulky bag got stuck in the kitchen door, in his desperate hurry to be gone.

He ran round to the Square in front, and down to Sandy Toddle, who was informing a bunch of unshaven bodies that the Gourlays were "sequestered".

"Oh, my God, post, what have you seen, to bring that look to your eyes? What have you seen, man? Speak for God's sake! What is it?"

The post gasped and stammered—then "Ooh!" he shivered in horror, and covered his eyes, at a sudden picture in his brain.

"Speak!" said a man solemnly.

"They have—they have—they have a' killed themselves," stammered the postman, pointing to the Gourlays'.

Their loins were loosened beneath them. The scrape of their feet on the road, as they turned to stare, sounded monstrous in the silence. No man dared to speak. They gazed with blanched faces at the House with the Green Shutters, sitting dark there and terrible, beneath the radiant arch of the dawn.

NOTES

1   **"Red Lion":** the hotels in Ochiltree are the Head and
the Commercial. From its position below "The
Square" and Gourlay's house, the "Red Lion"
might correspond to the Head Inn.

Barbie: this name for George Douglas Brown's
fictitious Ayrshire village may have been suggested
by Barbieston, the name of a hamlet situated six
miles from Ochiltree and one-and-a-half south of
Coylton.

2   **... everything ... was a delicate flattery to his pride ...
His sense of prosperity was soothing and pervasive:**
this opening strikes the high note of pride and
prosperity as at the opening of a classical tragedy.

5   **The Bend o' the Brae:** the road at the bottom of the
main street in Ochiltree turns sharply right between
a corner shop and the Head Inn.

6   **It had been ... "See what I have done to ye!":** an interesting final paragraph this, dramatically. We see
Gourlay at the height of his prosperity gloating over
his defeated rivals.

7   **In the days ... railways were only beginning ... quiet
hills:** the story is set in a period rather more than
thirty years earlier than the time of writing – a
period just after the middle of the nineteenth
century when railways were beginning to spread.

8   **Skeighan on the one side and Fleckie on the other:** if
we take Barbie to be Ochiltree, Skeighan would be
Cumnock and Fleckie Coylton.

8   **Miss Richmond of Tenshillingland:** seven or so miles
from Ochiltree and less than a mile from Barbieston
there is a farm called Tenshillingland just off the
secondary road that runs south from Coylton. This
name is characteristic of similar names found in
various parts of Scotland indicating the original
annual rent – Pennyland, Twelveshillingland,
Fifteenshillingland, Poundland, and so on.

8   **When the main line went north through Skeighan and
Poltandie:** the main railway line from Dumfries
and Sanquhar runs through Cumnock and near
Mauchline.

253

The House with the Green Shutters

Page

8	**Templandmuir's estate:** a mile west of Auchinleck stands a farm or estate called Temple. There is also a Templandshaw 655 feet up on Aird's Moss north of Cronberry and Cumnock.
14–5	**Both in appearance and position the house ... satisfied your eye as he did:** this third chapter eventually concentrates on the House – as dominating building, as symbol of pride, and as object of scorn or envy.
19	**She would fix her eyes ... there was something tragic in her pose ... helplessness, staring in sorrowful vacancy:** in this impression of Mrs Gourlay George Douglas Brown catches an attitude that has both pathos and potential tragedy.
19–20	**Stupidity and pride provoked the brute in him ... It struck life like a black frost:** a portrait of the Scot ignorant and malignant, harsh and almost inarticulate. Gourlay is a sharp contrast to the couthie Kailyard character.
26	**nows and nans:** now and again.
28	**Mossgiel:** i.e. Robert Burns. In 1784 Burns with his brother Gilbert leased Mossgiel, a farm one mile north of Mauchline (which is some five miles north of Ochiltree). The verse quoted ("The Muse nae poet ever fand her") is from the epistle "To William Simson, Ochiltree" and is dated May 1785. Simson was the son of an Ochiltree farmer and himself became schoolmaster there.
32–3	**For many reasons ... "nesty" Scotsman:** this famous passage presents the "malignant" aspect of the Scot's character – his envy and his need to cut down a successful neighbour to size. Lewis Grassic Gibbon, commenting on the adverse reception in Scotland of his book on Mungo Park, quoted a story told by George Blake that illustrates the same aspect. Two small-town Scots were discussing Blake and his books. "Him write a book?" said one of them contemptuously. "Him? Man, I kent his faither!"
36	**"... And yet I mind her a braw lass, too ... whisked her away:** this impression of the "braw lass" Miss

254

Richmond of Tenshillingland who became Mrs Gourlay is fleeting, but it is a light touch that contrasts with the dark psychological interior of the novel.

42 **. . . vivid presentment of Gourlay's manhood . . . the man's courage . . . admiring awe:** George Douglas Brown rouses admiration here for Gourlay in the same way as Stevenson rouses admiration for Weir. A passage like this may seem at first to contradict the over-all impression of the character, but on the other hand it rounds off the characterisation and gives it a living quality that, for example, Brodie in A. J. Cronin's *Hatter's Castle* seems to me to lack.

54-5 **The grain merchant . . . "You could murder a man wi't" . . . "You could kill a man with that" . . . "You'll be killing folk next":** an illustration of how the poker is used as an important 'prop' and a means of sustaining and concentrating tragic irony. The iterated motif – "killing a man" – is passed round the voices with a grim humour that anticipates the final act of murder.

58-61 **The stranger wore a light yellow overcoat . . . he would maybe be upsides with Gourlay yet, so he might:** this confrontation between Gourlay and Wilson sets off the action that is to lead to Gourlay's downfall. The technique of the narration is worth noting: the author begins as objective observer, changes to moralising narrator, then moves into the mind of Gourlay, and ends by giving us impressions out of the mind of Wilson.

62 **. . . or all's bye wi't:** before very long.

67 **Golconda:** a ruined city in India west of Hyderabad, at one time the capital of a powerful kingdom and famous for its diamonds.

69 **When you mounted two steps . . . went away, sadly:** a vivid and humorous impression of the shop 'wifie' of the old-time Scottish village that lightens the tone and fills out the social background.

70-1 **Mrs Wilson . . . trimmed for prosperity:** one of the best paced passages in the novel. It contains not only a brightly presented character sketch of Mrs Wilson

Page

72   **perfervidum ingenium:** "ardent temper" – part of a quotation from George Buchanan's *History of Scotland.* The original version is – *Scotorum praefervida ingenia:* the hot or impetuous character, the ardent spirits or temper of the Scots. (*Praefervida* was misread as *perfervida,* hence the adjective perfervid – ardent, enthusiastically patriotic.) Buchanan (1506-1582) was a Scottish classicist and historian who translated Euripides and himself wrote tragedies. He was tutor to Mary Stuart and James VI. As an enthusiastic Protestant he presented the Scottish lords' case against the queen in his *Detectio Mariae Reginae.*

78   **Wilson's yard . . . Gourlay's:** even the order and tidiness that Gourlay insists on is seen to be the result of *hubris* and therefore to contain within itself the seeds of destruction; whereas Mrs Wilson's cosy humanity is seen to have the potential of prosperity because of its energy and resilience.

80   **Then a strange thing happened . . . rotten twig:** this incident of Gourlay's suppressed fury is a foreshadowing of the culminating act of violence to come. The central tragedy itself is ironically anticipated in the deacon's remark about the possibility of Gourlay's "thwinging in a towe for his thplendid wrath yet".

80-1   **From that day . . . little town:** the final passage to Chapter 11 contains as clear and explicit an exposition of the function and rôle of the bodies as we need – as Greek chorus and as "villains of the piece". Even if George Douglas Brown becomes too openly the commenting author here, the commentary fits in well with the scheme and structure; and the final short sentence, by the power of its hell-brew imagery, marks the inexorable pace at which the evil is developing.

85   **their first libation:** the word libation is significant in the context of a novel that is consciously based on Greek dramatic method; and the libation here is

Page

ironical in being the forerunner of disharmony
rather than concord.

95   But Mrs Gourlay . . . ". . . geyan pity o' me": the
conclusion to this highly dramatic chapter is on a
note of peripheral but strong pathos. The movement has passed from Templandmuir's domestic
troubles to the drama of the public meeting and
Gourlay's undoing, and finally to Gourlay's brutal
attack on his wife. The chapter draws an excep-
tionally harsh picture of private and public life in
Barbie.

105   or a's bye: before everything is settled.

**108   his grin a rictus of wrath, his green teeth wolfish with
anger:** *rictus* has special reference to the gape of a
bird. The association of Gibson with a creature of
prey is continued in the adjective *wolfish*.

110   In those days it came to pass . . . House of Gourlay:
the mock biblical style suggests a lighter tone of
satire in the novel at this point where the process
of envious emulation – Gourlay keeping up with
Wilson – is outlined.

**120   The place of departure for the brake was the "Black
Bull", at the Cross, nearly opposite Wilson's:** the
Cross at Ochiltree is at the bottom of the brae; the
Head Inn is on the right; and there are shops and
houses centre and left.

**123   The brake swung on through merry cornfields . . . the
human pismires stung each other . . . petty rage:**
an illustration of George Douglas Brown's tendency to contrast the beauty of life with the petty
malice of people.
This incident is based on an experience the author
himself had. On a journey by brake, he heard himself discussed and referred to as "auld Broon's
bastard".

124   But the evil was done . . . of his life: it is worth noting
that this high climax of Gourlay's disastrous resolution is placed at the very centre of the novel.

126   Old Bleach-the-boys, the bitter dominie . . .: Grassic
Gibbon in *Sunset Song* and *Cloud Howe* was to
continue this tendency to satirise Scottish dominies.

257

Chris's teachers are satirised for their love of the gentry, and Murdoch in *Cloud Howe* is presented as an opportunist of little humanity. In *The House* Bleach-the-boys is very sketchily presented as a dry satirist with little in common even with James Hyslop, one of George Douglas Brown's less sympathetic teachers, and certainly completely different from John Smith of Coylton and William Maybin of Ayr Academy, both of whom encouraged George Douglas Brown.

129 **far-off Fechars, yea even to the groset-fair:** Fechars is clearly identifiable with Kilmarnock here. The groset-fair, an agricultural fair held at the time when gooseberries ('grosets') are in season (about the beginning of August), is associated particularly with Kilmarnock.

130 **Nith . . . and yonder's Corsoncon:** the Nith rises between Drumbrush Rig and Prickeny Hill east of Dalmellington, joins the Afton Water near New Cumnock, and flows past Sanquhar and Dumfries into the Solway Firth. Corsoncon or Corsencon Hill (1554 ft.) is on the north side of the Nith, about 3 miles east of New Cumnock.

131 **Milmannoch Hill:** the OS map shows the name Milmannoch one mile south-east of Coylton.

140 **"The thumb mark of his Maker was wet in the clay of him":** ". . . we are the clay, and thou our potter; and we are all the work of thy hand" – Isaiah 64.8. See also Job 33.6, and Jeremiah 18.4 and 6.
This sentence was quoted by Brown in notes on Ayrshire characters included in a letter to Meldrum in which he discusses the language and phrase-making of Scottish countryfolk of the S.W.

142 **"Metaphor comes from . . ." said the unconscious disciple of Aristotle:** Aristotle deals with metaphor in Chapters 21 and 22 in *The Art of Poetry*:" . . . a good metaphor implies an intuitive perception of the similarity in dissimilars" (translation by Bywater, Oxford, p. 78).

145 **Omar:** Edward Fitzgerald's *Rubáiyát of Omar Khayyam* (1859) has as dual theme the mystery of exis-

            tence and the solace of wine.

154-5   **He peeped through . . . made John cry her name:** this is unmistakably autobiographical. The story was told to me by people in Ochiltree that on one occasion when he was returning from Oxford Brown peeped through the window of their house and caught his mother applying bandages to her breast.

162   **The influence of a wealthy patron then presented him to Barbie:** during the eighteenth and early nineteenth centuries a growing minority in the Assembly of the Church of Scotland believed that the congregation and not a patron should appoint a minister to his kirk. The Disruption of the Scottish Church in May 1843 was brought about through the enforcement of patronage which had been restored by the Patronage Act of 1712. Over 400 ministers seceded to form the Free Church of Scotland. The Patronage Act was repealed in 1874.

162-3   **the Roman Curia:** the *Curia Romana* – the assemblage of departments and offices – judicial and administrative – by means of which the Pope organises the government of the Church.

167   **". . . dinna be hard on the ministers . . . but the feck o' them's frostit:** a critical view of the nature of ministers of the church affording a complete contrast to the Kailyard attitude of deference.

173   **"Dinna spae ill-fortune!":** don't foretell bad luck.

       ". . . . I would rather an ill deil sat fornenst me at the table, than parratch in a poke": I would rather an ill-natured but vigorous person sat opposite me at the table than an inert sour solemn character.

173-4   **" 'Yet mony a ragged cowte's been known . . . For monie a day' ":** stanza XI of "A Dream", a not very complimentary poem written by Burns in 1786 as a follow-up to the official Pindaric Ode by Thomas Warton, the poet laureate, to celebrate the forty-eighth bithday of George III. It comes after the stanza criticising the Prince of Wales's pleasure-loving ways. The analogy with Prince Hal, the dissolute son of Henry IV who reformed, is not entirely apposite, as the ex-Provost suggests.

176   **Theatre Royal**: this stood in Shakespeare Square at the top of Broughton Street on present-day Leith Walk, Edinburgh. In the nineteenth century it was celebrated for productions of plays based on Scott's novels.

184   **"Tam Glen"**: "Tam Glen" was one of the songs Burns sent to Johnson in November 1788, prescribing for it the tune "Merry Beggars". Johnson set it instead to the tune "The Muckin' o' Geordie's Byre".

        "Miss Drummond o' Perth" . . . "Gray Daylicht": these are tunes used for Scottish country dances – strathspeys.

185   **" 'Risu inepto res ineptior nulla est' "**: this is a quotation from Catullus – Ode 39, 1, 16: *Nam risu inepto res ineptior nullast* – for nothing is sillier than a silly laugh.

198   **There had been . . . inevitable ruin**: the author deliberately stresses, perhaps in too self-conscious a manner, the tragic structure and nature of the novel at this point, particularly by the vocabulary – "great catastrophe", "tragedy", "inevitable ruin", but also by the thematic symbolism – "collapse of an edifice".

204   **"Thirce me . . . "**: i.e. Sirce me – an exclamation of surprise. It is a corruption of Serve's – God preserve us! (Sometimes given as "Sircy" or "Sirs")

209   **The first thing . . . great fender**: another example of George Douglas Brown's fondness for a highly dramatic ending to a chapter and for a dramatic stressing of a symbol or prop.

210   **animo castrato**: his mind or soul unmanned or debilitated or weakened.

210–1   **To bring a beaten and degraded look . . . sin against the Holy Ghost**: of all the sins committed by Gourlay *pere* this is the one that George Douglas Brown singles out as the most outrageous.

213   **". . . Fow's that, na?"**: how is that now? The form *fow* or *foo* is insular (Shetland and Orkney) and northern Scots. It is odd to find it in Ayrshire.

215–6   **". . . Man, I waited on ye . . . to attract folk's attention"**: a powerful echo of the great scene depicted

earlier of the journey Gourlay made to fetch a
doctor to help to bring young Gourlay into the
world.

226–7 **The hammer . . . crashing on the rim:** this represents
the high point of the carefully built up tragedy:
poker and fender, originally symbols of pride, now
become the instruments of violent death.

233–4 **An hour later . . . pursuing unseen:** this recalls the
plight of Orestes pursued and tormented by the
Furies at the end of *The Choephori,* the second part
of Aeschylus' trilogy:

> . . . . More and more of them! Look there!
> And see – their dreadful eyes dripping with
> bloody pus!

(Penguin edition – translation by Philip Vellacott).

235 **one end's errand:** Anglicised form of "ane end's
errand" which is an erroneous form of "aince-
errand" – on the single errand or for the one
purpose mentioned. (Anglo-Saxon *anes errandes*
– on one errand).

247 **Suddenly Mrs Gourlay . . . clean sweep o' the Gourlays:**
Mrs Gourlay is more than a character here: she
becomes the mouthpiece of destiny – like Cassandra.

248–9 **She took down the big Bible . . . charity:** the theme of
the quotation – charity – is in ironical contrast to
the portrayal of society in the novel. It is *caritas*
that Barbie and Gourlay lack most of all.

252 **Their loins . . . radiant arch of the dawn:** over the final
scene of a bright dawn the House looms like an
evil influence.

SELECT BIBLIOGRAPHY

Texts of The House with the Green Shutters

First edition: John Macqueen, London, 1901.
    Do.   5th impression: John Macqueen, London, 1902.
Popular edition: Geo. A. Morton, Edinburgh, 1905.
Memorial edition: Andrew Melrose, London and New York, 1923.
Travellers' Library edition, with introduction by J. B. Priestley: Jonathan Cape, London, 1929.
World's Classics edition, with introduction by Somerset Maugham, OUP, London, 1938.
Undated edition (purchased 1960): Thomas Nelson & Sons, Edinburgh and London.
First Novel Library edition, with introduction by Herbert van Thal: Cassell, London, 1967.

Manuscripts

George Douglas Brown: Letters to Tom Smith.
George Douglas Brown: *The House with the Green Shutters* – opening of Chapter 15.

General

AESCHYLUS. *The Oresteian Trilogy,* translated by Philip Vellacott. Penguin, Harmondsworth, Middlesex, England, 1956.
ARISTOTLE. *On the Art of Poetry,* translated by Ingram Bywater with a preface by Gilbert Murray, Oxford, Clarendon Press, 1920.
BLAKE, GEORGE. *Barrie and the Kailyard School,* Arthur Barker, London, 1951.
BROWN, P. HUME. *A Short History of Scotland,* (new edition by Henry W. Meikle). Oliver & Boyd, Edinburgh, 1955.
BURNS, ROBERT. *The Poems and Songs of,* edited by James Kinsley Volumes I-III. Oxford, Clarendon Press, 1968.
CAIRD, JAMES B. "Neil Gunn and Scottish Fiction". essay in Scott, Alexander and Gifford, Douglas (eds.) *Neil M. Gunn: the Man and the Writer,* 1973, q.v.
CRAIG, DAVID. *Scottish Literature and the Scottish People* 1680–1830. Chatto & Windus, London, 1961.

CROCKETT, S. R. *The Raiders* and *The Lilac Sunbonnet,* with an introduction by George Blake. Collins, London and Glasgow, 1954.

CRONIN, A. J. *Hatter's Castle.* Gollancz, London, 1931.

GALT, JOHN. *Annals of the Parish,* edited by James Kinsley. O.U.P., London, 1967.

GALT, JOHN. *The Provost,* illustrated in colour by John M. Aiken. T. N. Foulis, London and Edinburgh, 1913.

GIBBON, LEWIS GRASSIC. *Sunset Song,* with commentary and notes by J. T. Low. Longman, London, 1971.

HOGG, JAMES. *The Private Memoirs and Confessions of a Justified Sinner,* edited with an introduction by John Carey, O.U.P., London, 1969.

LANG, ANDREW. Introduction to Lennox, Cuthbert: *George Douglas Brown* (q.v.)

LEAVIS, F. R. *The Great Tradition,* Chatto & Windus, London, 1948.

LENNOX, CUTHBERT. *George Douglas Brown*, Hodder & Stoughton, London, 1903.

LOW, J. T. "Three in One Tradition" and "Point and Counterpoint," articles on the Scottish Tradition in the Novel in *The Weekend Scotsman*, October 27 and November 3, 1973.

McCLURE, J. DERRICK. "Dialect in *The House with the Green Shutters*", article in *Studies in Scottish Literature*, Vol. IX, Nos. 2-3, October-January, 1971-2.

MACDIARMID, HUGH. "Neil Gunn and the Scottish Renaissance", essay in Scott, Alexander and Gifford, Douglas (eds.) *Neil M. Gunn: the Man and the Writer*, 1973, q.v.

MACDONALD, ANGUS. "Modern Scots Novelists", chapter in *Edinburgh Essays in Scots Literature*, preface by H. J. C. Grierson, Edinburgh, Oliver & Boyd, 1933.

MELROSE, ANDREW. "George Douglas Brown. A Biographical Sketch and an Appreciation", printed at the end of the Memorial edition, 1923, q.v.

MELROSE, ANDREW. "George Douglas Brown. Reminiscences of a Friendship and a Notable Novel", printed at the end of Lennox, Cuthbert: *George Douglas Brown*, 1903 q.v.

MUIR WILLA. *Mrs Ritchie*, Martin Secker, London, 1933,

MURISON, DAVID. editor, *The Scottish National Dictionary*. Edinburgh, 1929—

PARKER, W. M. *Modern Scottish Writers*, William Hodge & Co., Edinburgh and Glasgow, 1917.

SCOTT, ALEXANDER and GIFFORD, DOUGLAS (eds.) *Neil M. Gunn: the Man and the Writer*, William Blackwood, Edinburgh and London, 1973.

SCOTT, J. D. "Novelist-philosophers — ix R. L. Stevenson and G. D. Brown: the myth of Lord Braxfield", article in *Horizon*, vol. xiii, no. 77, May 1946.

SMITH, IAIN CRICHTON. "The House with the Green Shutters", article in *Studies in Scottish Literature*, vol. vii, Nos. 1&2, July-October, 1969.

SPEIRS, JOHN. *The Scots Literary Tradition*, Chatto and Windus, London, 1940.

STEVENSON, R. L. *Weir of Hermiston*, edited with introduction and notes by J. T. Low, Holmes McDougall, Edinburgh, 1973.

VEITCH, JAMES. *George Douglas Brown*, Herbert Jenkins, London, 1952.

WARRACK, ALEXANDER, editor, *Chambers's Scots Dictionary*, W. & R. Chambers, Edinburgh, 1911.

WITTIG, KURT. *The Scottish Tradition in Literature*, Oliver & Boyd, Edinburgh, 1958.

WITTIG, KURT. "Neil Gunn's Animistic Vision", essay in Scott Alexander, and Gifford, Douglas (eds.) *Neil M. Gunn: the Man and the Writer*, 1973, q.v.

GLOSSARY

A	
ablow	below
ae	one
acqueesh	between
a-hame	at home
ahint	behind
aicht	eight
aince	once
airt	direction, quarter; direct, put on to (**airt you the road of** – put you on to)
aiver	horse used for heavy work, a cart-horse
ane	one
a'readys	already
atweel	indeed, truly; surely, certainly (emphatic)
atweel aye	yes, indeed!
aucht	possession
auld	old
auld-farrant	old-fashioned, precocious, knowing, cunning
avised	informed, aware of
awmous	alms
ayont	beyond

baikie	square box, a small stool
bairn	child
bane	bone
barley-bree	whisky
bass	a door mat
batts (botts)	a disease in horses caused by the bob-fly or worms
bauld	bold
bawbees	money (bawbee = halfpenny)
ben (the hoose)	inside, further into, within (the house)
besom	wretch (term of contempt)
bide	stay
bien	comfortable, prosperous, well-doing
billies	young fellows
birkie	smart, lively
birl (the bottle)	pour our drink; spin, hurry along
birr	impetus, drive, passion
bittock	a little bit or distance
blagyird	blackguard
bleeze	blaze, sudden gust of wind
blether	prattle, foolish talk
bock (boke)	retch, vomit

bodie	human being, creature (term of mild contempt or sympathy)
bole	opening or recess in wall
book-lear	book-learning, (formal) education
brae	hillside, incline
branks	bridle
braw	fine, beautiful (**braw penny** = a lot of money)
braws	fine clothes
breck	break
breeks	trousers
breenge	rush, dash; impetuous or hasty movement
breist	breast
brie-stone	sandstone for rubbing on a doorstep (**brie** = crushed sandstone for floors)
brig	bridge
brisket	(*breaskit*) part of the breast next to the ribs
brose	lump, character
brose	porridge; (by extension – contents of stomach)
brosey	flabby, stout; coarse and clumsy in speech and manners
browdened	closely attached
brust	burst
bude	had (to), must
bummler	buzzing insect
burn	stream
bye	past
ca'	name
cadger	a carrier or hawker; a disagreeable character
canny	careful; safe, favourable, normal
canty	lively, cheerful, neat
certy	truth (**my certy** = in truth, upon my word)
chaw	vex, humiliate; bitter disappointment
cheatry	fraud, cheating
chirt	squeeze, grate, grind
clachan	hamlet, village
clarty	dirty, muddy, filthy
clishmaclaver	idle talk
clype	tell tales
cockit	set up, erect
cornkist	a chest or bin for storing corn
coulter	blade, cutter (of a plough)
counts	sums, arithmetic
couthie	pleasant
cowp	overturn, fall
cowte	colt

crack	chat, gossip
creepie	a low stool
creeshy	greasy, oily
cuddie	stupid person (a donkey)
cutty	short clay pipe
dander	saunter
darg	toil, work, day's work
dask	writing desk
daudin	hitting, striking, falling violently
daurna	dare not
dee	die
deil	devil
diddle	cheat
dirl	vibration, violent shake
dirt	a piece of excrement; a worthless person
div	do
dod	God!
dominie	schoolmaster
doos	doves, pigeons
douce	gentle, modest, kind
downcome (dooncome)	humiliation, fall in social position
dowp (doup)	behind, buttocks
dree	suffer, endure
drucken	drunken
dub	pool of water, puddle
duds	clothes (esp. shabby or dirty)
Embro	Edinburgh
e'en	eyes; evening
enow	just now
ettle	expect
extr'ornar	extraordinary
fa' owre	fall asleep
feck	bulk, amount
feckless	feeble, ineffectual
fliskie	frivolous person; lively gay lassie
flyte	scold, argue
forbye	in addition, besides
fornenst	opposite, in front of
fosie	soft
foy	farewell feast or party
frae	from
fu' (fou)	full; drunk
fuff	slight explosion, sputter, whiff or puff of wind

gae	gave
gaed	went
gang	go
gar	compel, force, make
gaun	going
gate	way
gawcey (gawsie, gawsy)	spacious, jolly, large, stately, imposing-looking
gerse	grass
geyan	(*gey an* or *and*) great, considerable, terrible
geyly	(too) much, greatly, considerably
gey pickle	quite a lot, a fair amount, a great deal (lit. quite a few)
gie	give
glaikit	silly, affected, senseless
gleg	sharp, keen, pert
glimmer	blink
glower	glare
gob	mass or lump
golder	shout, roar, bawl
gowan	daisy
gowk	fool (lit. cuckoo)
gowl	yell, growl
gowsterous	boisterous, vigorous, hearty
greet	weep
groset	gooseberry
gumption	common sense
gunk	trick, disappoint; cause chagrin or disappointment
gurly	surly, bitter, rough
hadden doon	held down (sore hadden doon = suppressed)
haet	atom, small quantity, "slightest thing"
hairst	harvest (-time)
half-roads	half-way
hanker	hesitate, linger, ponder
hantle	a great deal, much
hauds	holds
haver	(talk) nonsense
hawk	cough, bring up phlegm
hereaway	to this place
hirpled	limped, hobbled
hoast	cough
hotch	shake (with laughter); fidget
howff	haunt, tavern, place of resort
howk	dig
howp	hope

hunkers	hams, haunches
hunks	'character', miser, (properly – a lazy slut)
hurdies	buttocks
hut	hit (past tense)
jalouse	guess, suspect
jamb	post of a door
jaup	splash (of mud or dirty water); bespatter, sprinkle
jing-bang	the (whole) lot
jo	sweetheart
jocose	facetious, merry, jovial; friendly, intimate
jouk	duck, swerve, dodge
jouking	cunning
joukery-pawkery	deceit, trickery, roguery
juist	simply, merely, truly
kane (kain, cain)	a quantity of cheese (300 stones)
keek	peep, pry, look
keepit	kept
ken	know
ke-o	fiasco, shambles, footling mess
kimmers	gossips; women, wives
kirk	church
kist	chest, box
lang syne	long ago
lap	leapt
lauch	laugh
linn	waterfall
linty	linnet
lippen	rely, depend on
lowe	blaze, flame; glow
lug	ear
mart	market
maun	must
mavis	song thrush
micht	might
mim	prim, sedate
mowdie-man	mole catcher
muckle	great, big; a great deal; much
mutch	a woman's cap

271

nain	own
nebby	sharp, difficult, ill-natured
needcessity	necessity
nicher	neigh, whinny
novelles	novels
now: "the now"	at present
ochonee	O dear, alas!
ocht	anything
onnecessar	unnecessary
oom	eh?
or	before
orra	odd-job, doing occasional jobs
owre	(over) too
owre-bye	out there, over there
pack	friendly, intimate, familiar
packit	packed
paidling	paddling
peep	faint sound or glimpse
pelter (pelt)	downpour
pickle	a small quantity, a few (**a gey pickle bawbees** = quite an amount of money)
pith	substance, power, vital force or essence (**here's pith** = good health)
ploy	activity, occupation, entertainment
pow	head
powney	pony
pree	taste, take
preen	pin
prig	beg, plead
puddock stool	toadstool
puir	poor
quean	girl, young woman
rag-folk	tinks, disreputable people
redd	clear, tidy up, set in order; free
reek	smoke
rone	spout for carrying off rain water
rowp	auction, sell by auction
ruction	disturbance, trouble
rype	clear out

sairly	badly (sorely)
saugh-wand	willow wand
scrunt	grating sound
scunner	disgust, loathing
sederunt	a sitting of a court; a meeting
set	sit
shaw	cut off the tops (of turnips or other vegetables)
shilp	thin pinched-looking girl
shouther	shoulder
sic	such
siller	money
skelloch	shriek, scream
skelp	rush, drive, dash
skirl	scream
skreigh	scream, screech
slabber	a slovenly person
slaik	light wash or wipe
smeddum	spirit, liveliness, strength of character
smeowt	(*smout*) little creature, small insignificant person (lit. – small trout)
smiddyshed	blacksmith's shed
sneck-drawer (or sneck-draw)	sly, crafty or covetous person; petty thief
snirt	(suppressed) laugh
snoove	move or glide (gently away)
sonsy	comely, comfortable, handsome, buxom
spae	foretell
speir	ask
spirlies	(of reek) thin spirals of smoke
splash-brods	mud-guards
splore	let (a thing) be known
splorroch	noise made by man or beast on a wet or muddy road
spue (spew)	pour forth, vomit
spunk	spirit
spunkie	lively young man
stell	plant firmly, bring to a stop, brake
stick	stoppage, standstill
stour	dust
stravaig	wander, walk aimlessly
streek	stretch
stunt	stamp
sumph	fool, stupid person
swankie	smart, active
swatch	piece cut off as a sample or pattern
swure	swore

273

The House with the Green Shutters

tack	lease, tenure
tacketty	hobnailed
tallowy (tallowny)	sallow
tattie-walin	sorting out potatoes
tawse	belt, leather strap used by schoolmasters to punish pupils
thae	those
than	then
thegither	together
thereaway	down there, in that direction
thir	these
thole	stand, suffer, bear
thowless	spiritless, lacking energy
thrang	pressing, brisk
thrapple	throat
till	to
tousy	untidy, dishevelled
towe	rope, noose
trauchle	sloven, drudge
tryst	appointment, meeting, fixed cattle-market
trysted	booked, engaged
tweesht	between
unco	uncommon, great, unusual
upsides	level, on equal footing; revenged (on)
warrant	guarantee, be sure (Ise warrant = I'm sure)
warst	worst
warstle	wrestle
wat	wet
waur	worse
wean	child
weanly	childish
weird	fate, destiny, doom
well-to-pass	prosperous, well-to-do
whalp	whelp
whaur	where
wheen	a few, a lot (of), a number (of)
wheeple	whistle (softly)
whilie	short time
whigmaleerie	useless thing – ornament or toy; foolish notion
winna	will not
wintled	tumbled, rolled, reeled
wud	mad, silly
wudny-un	wouldn't have
wunst	once

274

yestreen	yesterday evening
yett	gate
yin	one
yill	ale
yon	that